Michael Wills, Mr, who writes under the name David McKeowen, has written two novels, both thrillers. His first, *Grip*, was shortlisted for the CWA John Creasey Memorial Dagger Award for best debut crime novel in 2005. His second novel, *Trapped*, was first published in hardback in February 2007. A former diplomat, TV producer and director, Michael Wills has been MP for Swindon North since 1997 and was appointed Minister of State in the Ministry of Justice in June 2007.

Also by David McKeowen

Grip

DAVID McKEOWEN

TRAPPED

HODDER

First published in Great Britain in 2007 by Hodder & Stoughton
An Hachette Livre UK company

First published in paperback in 2007

2

A CIP catalogue record for this title
is available from the British Library

ISBN 978 0 340 83598 2

Typeset in Plantin by Hewer Text UK Ltd, Edinburgh
Printed and bound by Clays Ltd, St Ives plc

Hodder & Stoughton policy is to use papers that are natural, renewable
and recyclable products and made from wood grown in sustainable
forests. The logging and manufacturing processes are expected to
conform to the environmental regulations of the country of origin.

Hodder & Stoughton Ltd
338 Euston Road
London NW1 3BH

www.hodder.co.uk

For Jill, Thomas, Joe, Sarah,
Nicholas and Katherine

one

The boat left a murky wake as it roared through the water. It was a crisp clear night and over to her right, Mara saw the moon laying a silver path over the sea. Behind them the lights of Vlore twinkled orange along the bay, stretched beneath the dark headlands of Albania. Millions of stars dotted the sky and, far overhead, a plane, red lights winking on its wings, flew towards Italy.

'Look, Silvana,' she whispered. 'It's going to Italy. I'm going there one day.'

In the bow of the boat, her brother's friend Florian laughed. 'Yeah,' he said, 'one day.' Beside him, Vasili was staring straight ahead as he opened the throttle and the powerboat throbbed as it picked up speed. Vasili was the one Mara liked. He was so tall and handsome with his long dark sideburns. He never said much. Florian did the talking.

'I'll take you for a ride in my boat,' he had said. 'For your birthday. And you can bring that friend of yours, Silvana.' The boat was now bouncing over the waves. Silvana also liked Vasili more than Florian. She thought he looked like Antony from Blue. Mara couldn't see it but Silvana thought he was just like him. Strong and silent but she just knew he was kind and sensitive, like Antony.

The wind brought the blood into Mara's face and her skin tingled. The boat was long and sleek, like a dart, and it had white leather seats and Mara had never seen anything so luxurious.

'Don't tell your parents,' Florian had said. 'We'll just go out for the evening. For your birthday.' Kostandin must have told him she was twelve on Sunday. It was not like her brother to be so nice. Perhaps it was his birthday present to her. 'And bring your friend Silvana,' he had said. That had been nice of him too. She squeezed Silvana's hand as happiness bubbled through her.

Silvana was looking at Vasili standing motionless at the wheel. He was so handsome. She brushed her dark hair away from her face. She could taste the salt on the breeze.

In the bow, Florian reached down below the wheel beside Vasili and took out a bottle and swigged from it. '*Salute,*' he said and Vasili smiled. Then Florian wiped his sleeve across the neck and handed it to Vasili who took a sip and then he smiled again.

'*Salute,*' he said.

'Kalaj should be pleased,' Florian said.

Vasili nodded ruminatively and then he half turned away from the wheel and looked back towards Mara and Silvana. 'Here,' he said, passing the bottle to them. 'You have some of this.'

'See,' Silvana whispered to Mara. 'Kind.'

'Have you ever met him?' Florian said.

'Who?' Vasili was watching the sea ahead.

'Kalaj.'

Vasili shook his head. 'None of us ever meet him,' he said. 'He lives in London now. Kalaj probably isn't his real name anyway.'

Mara took the bottle. Raki. She had seen Kostandin drink this. She swigged it back as Florian had done. The aniseed liquor hit the back of her throat and she spluttered. It was horrible. Florian was smiling at her. It was not a nice smile.

She glared at him and took another large swig at the bottle. That would show him. This time she felt the warmth of the alcohol flowing down her throat.

'You have some,' she said, passing the bottle to Silvana and staring at Florian. 'It's nice.'

Florian laughed. It was not a nice laugh. 'Yes, go on,' he said. 'You have some.'

'No thank you,' Silvana said. 'I don't like it.'

'I'll have some more,' Mara said, reaching for the bottle. She took another swig and then her stomach lurched. The raki and the motion of the boat were making her feel sick.

'You have some.' Florian wrenched the bottle away from Mara and thrust it at Silvana. 'Go on,' he said. 'You'll like it.'

'No thank you,' Silvana said.

'I said, have some.' And Florian put his hand behind her head and pushed the bottle into her mouth. 'Go on, drink.'

'I feel sick,' Mara said and then she vomited all over the white leather seats.

'You stupid bitch,' Florian yelled. 'Do you know how much this boat cost?'

Mara retched again. Florian hit her in the face with the back of his hand.

Silvana screamed. 'Leave her alone,' she said. 'I'll tell my parents.'

Florian laughed. 'When?' he said. And, as the powerboat surged through the sea, Silvana and Mara saw the lights of Italy getting closer and closer.

'Careful,' Vasili said. 'Don't damage the little bitches. Or you can explain it to Kalaj.'

two

The first time Martin heard Viktor's name was at one of Jenny's dinner parties. Striding up the path to the front door, late, he saw through the window that the other guests had already sat down and, from outside in the dark autumn night, the room glowed hospitably in soft light. He saw Jenny laughing while David handed a bottle of wine to a smiling bald man.

He rang the bell. 'Late again, Hughes,' David called from the table as Jenny opened the door.

'I'm so sorry, Jenny,' Martin said. 'I had to finish off something at work. I didn't think it would take so long.' As he came in from the cold, stooping to get through the eighteenth-century doorway, the blood flushed back into his cheeks and he heard conversation burbling round the room.

'Hush, David,' Jenny called back into the room over her shoulder. 'Come in, Martin.' She hugged him and kissed him on both cheeks. 'Throw your coat over there.' He felt her soft and comfortable underneath the cashmere.

'Hands off the wife,' David said, coming out into the narrow hall. 'How are you?' he asked, shaking Martin's hand firmly.

'Fine, fine,' Martin muttered. 'Sorry I'm late.'

'Don't worry,' Jenny said. The scent of autumn spices, cinnamon, nutmeg, wafted through from the kitchen. 'How have you been?' she asked, patting his arm.

'All right,' he said. 'Really. All right.'

Jenny looked at him. 'Really?' she asked.

'Really.' Martin made himself smile at her. 'Here,' he said, 'I've brought you something.' He held out the small oblong package to her.

'You shouldn't have,' Jenny said, smiling at him. He took off his coat and placed it over a chair as she tore off the wrapping paper. 'Oh,' she said. 'This looks interesting.' She turned the book over and looked at the back. '*A Natural History of the Lime.*'

'I'm sure it's better than it looks,' he said. 'It's the story of how it came from Indonesia along the trade routes and how all the different cultures along the way have used it in their cooking. And it shows you all the different varieties. And I thought you're such a good cook that you'd be interested in all that. And it's an interesting take on an apparently boring subject. And it probably still is boring. And I should have brought you flowers.'

Jenny laughed. 'It's the thought that counts,' she said.

'Exactly,' Martin said. 'That's what I meant. I should have brought you flowers.'

'It's lovely, thank you. Now, come on in,' Jenny said and then dropping her voice, 'I want you to sit beside Miranda. Don't look now but she's the one with the short hair. Be gentle with her. She's still getting over the divorce.'

'You don't need to go on doing this, Jenny,' he said. 'I'm fine.'

'Let's meet Miranda,' Jenny said, linking her arm through his and steering him to the table.

Miranda had dark hair, cut in layers and grave brown eyes. At the other end of the table, David talked loudly about co-financing in Estonia and, next to him, a man Martin did not know chuckled appreciatively at something his blonde neighbour had whispered to him. Jenny passed around another bottle of wine.

'Hello,' Martin said. 'I'm Martin. Shall I squeeze in here?' He twisted his long legs sideways to get them under the table.

'I'm Miranda,' she said, smiling at him.

Martin had been to so many dinner parties like this with Clare, where Jenny mixed old university friends with new ones from work, and David served cult wines to accompany Moroccan casseroles and interesting salads. Candles flickered around the centrepiece of moss and tortured twigs.

'What do you do?' Miranda said politely.

'I'm a lawyer,' he apologised.

'And I'm a Gemini,' she said. 'What kind of lawyer?'

'You don't want to know.'

'Yes I do,' and she said it as if she meant it.

Down the table, Martin heard brisk opinions on the prospects for the Baltic economies, flat tax here, timber products there, market opportunities everywhere.

'It's very boring,' he said to Miranda.

'I'll only find it boring if you do,' she said.

Beside David, a man with a shaven head and narrow rectangular spectacles explained how his consultancy had developed a strategy for privatising London Underground. 'About time too,' the blonde woman said enthusiastically.

'Do I find it boring?' Martin said reflectively. 'Well, it's what I do.'

Miranda laughed. 'Does that mean you find it boring or not?' she said.

Johnnie Knox, who had started reviewing for the *Daily Mail*, was explaining how a new novel had captured multicultural Britain and the table was buzzing with the energy and confidence of a generation coming into its own. 'All our social and commercial relationships would break down without trust law,' Martin said and he forked some couscous into his mouth. Miranda, cupping her face in her hands, nodded courteously.

This was kabuki, Martin thought, an exhibition of masks and symbols. Not real. When Clare had been here with him, he had felt part of this fellowship but now he felt he was simultaneously outside the circle observing the ceremony, while at the same time, he was still trapped inside it.

'Sounds worrying,' Miranda said. And then he felt a flick of desire as her aphrodisiac attentiveness began to work on him.

But how could he go through with it? Clare was still everywhere. These guests at the table had been her friends too. He could still see her sitting in that chair where now the shaven-headed man was expostulating about London Transport and he still felt for her in the dark of the night. What could he say – or do – that would not be mechanical mimicry of everything he had done and said with her?

'Would you like some more?' Miranda asked.

'I was brought up not to leave anything,' he said and, gratifyingly, she smiled. She seemed to like him.

'How are you two getting on?' Jenny was now leaning down between them. 'Don't you think he looks like an el Greco hidalgo, Miranda?' Jenny said. Miranda smiled but said nothing. 'Come on, both of you, eat up,' Jenny said. 'I don't want to face all this at breakfast.'

'We were just talking about that,' Miranda said.

'Good, good,' Jenny said. 'By the way,' she added, 'I've found someone to do the afternoon on Saturday.'

'Well done,' Miranda said.

'For the St Luke's fair,' Jenny explained to Martin.

'Who?' Miranda asked.

'Some new parent,' Jenny said. 'Victor something. Nice. And his daughter is sweet. Come on, Martin, have some more. You need feeding.'

'That's one thing I don't need,' he said. 'But thank you anyway.' He had little appetite these days.

'Which one's Victor?' Miranda asked.

'Tall, dark, beard. European. Something. You know. He's always picking up his daughter. I don't know if there's a Mrs Victor. And the little girl is really sweet. You know, the one who's in love with that pink coat she's always wearing.'

The book said that grief went through stages. Shock was followed by anger and sadness and silence and then rage and inconsolable yearning. And Martin was swinging through all those stages. And eventually, the book promised, would come letting go and moving on. But Martin knew he was nowhere near letting Clare go and moving on.

'Oh yes,' Miranda said. 'I've seen the little girl. But I'm not sure I'd recognise him.'

'You would,' Jenny said emphatically. 'Brooding. Attractive. Distinguished. Probably one of these Russian billionaires.'

'Not at St Luke's,' Miranda said. 'Surely?'

'You can scoff,' Jenny said. 'I'm certainly going to get to know him. And so should you, Martin. He'll have lots of work to hand out.'

'You're insatiable.' Martin smiled.

'Whatever,' Jenny said. 'I'm an impresario. I bring people together.' She waved her hands in the air. 'And electricity happens.'

She got up from the table. 'Come on Saturday, Martin,' she said, 'and spend all that money you're making. And meet people.'

He grimaced at her.

'And now,' Jenny said, 'I'm going to leave you two to it and radiate at the other end of the table.'

Into the patch of silence Jenny left behind her, Martin's mobile phone rang. He struggled to get it out of his jacket pocket. 'Sorry,' he said and he smiled apologetically at Miranda. 'I should have turned it off.'

'Hello,' he said. 'Oh, hello, Clare.' He saw Jenny turn back to look at him when she heard the name.

'Yes,' he said. 'Yes I could take her.' He had to work on the brief from Clements but he could do that on Saturday evening. He needed to do this. 'I'll pick her up at three.' He put the phone back in his pocket. 'I will be coming to the fair,' he said to Jenny. 'Clare's asked if I would take Megan.'

'That'll be nice,' Jenny said. 'You can come with Miranda and meet the mysterious Victor.'

three

'Kalaj should give us a bonus for this,' Florian said, 'coming after those two last week.'

Vasili grunted as he walked beside him. He never said much but he was reliable and Florian liked working with him. They had spent the evening drinking in the village bar with a friend of one of Vasili's cousins and Florian was flushed and warm from the raki, feeling good. There was a good prospect in the village and the contact seemed confident he could fix it. They had given him fifty dollars to come up with a plan and they were going to return next week to do the deal.

It was another beautiful night, and the cold, dark sky was spangled with stars. Florian heard the frost crunch under his feet as they walked back to the car, parked a kilometre away, out of sight of those bandits in the village. 'We could make five thousand dollars out of this,' Florian said.

'Maybe,' Vasili said. His voice was muffled and small in the vast silence.

'Sure we could,' Florian said. 'Kalaj would easily pay us five thousand for this one.' They walked past three small houses, dark against the night sky. A peep of light escaped from the curtains in one of them. Otherwise it was black. No streetlights and no moon.

A dog started barking. So something does live here, Florian thought. Then the barking grew louder. And louder. And suddenly a snarling missile hurled itself at Florian and knocked him off balance and the animal was tearing at his leather jacket trying to sink its teeth in far enough to get a grip. Florian cried out, flailing his arm as he tried to shake it off. He heard someone shouting in rage and pain and then realised that it was him. Lights came on in the houses. The dog let go of his arm and bit his leg. He fell over and the dog went for his neck. And then there was a shot and the dog dropped dead beside him.

'Are you OK?' Vasili said.

'Just as well you're a good shot,' Florian said, keeping his voice steady, but he wanted to cry. That mongrel had nearly killed him. He stood up carefully and his legs wobbled underneath him.

'We should get out of here,' Vasili said. Then there was a shout from one of the houses and then a burst of gunfire.

'Come on,' Vasili shouted. 'Run.' Florian started lurching down the road. And then the gun fired again and Vasili gave a little gasp and fell over. 'Help me,' he called. 'My leg.'

Florian stopped.

'Help me,' Vasili whimpered again. 'Come on. They're coming.'

Florian took out his gun as a man shouted down the road. They were coming. He could not leave Vasili here. These peasants were cruel bastards and he had killed their dog.

'Come on,' Vasili yelped, 'help me. They'll be here any second.'

The shouts came nearer. Florian released the safety catch. If they got hold of Vasili they would torture his name out of him and the law of kanun meant they would never forgive or forget. He could never come back to the neighbourhood. The dog's death would be avenged. That was kanun and that was a lot of business lost. And if he had to carry Vasili with his wounded leg it would slow them down so much that the peasants would catch them anyway.

Florian put the gun to Vasili's head and pulled the trigger and started to run. He heard one of the peasants fall over Vasili's body and curse. Good. That should give him a few more seconds. Florian was running faster now, as panic and fear drove his trembling legs zigzagging down the road. A bullet sighed past his face.

Where was the car? It must be somewhere near here. He stumbled over a stone on the road but kept running. The voices behind him seemed to be getting more distant as he ran. Perhaps they had stopped to see what they could steal from Vasili.

Florian pushed his legs to go faster. And then round a bend he saw the BMW. Thank you, God. Thank you. He crouched behind the car and fumbled in his pocket for the keys. He would have been dead if Vasili had been driving tonight, as he usually did. He would have been crouched behind the car waiting for them to find him. But for some reason Vasili had wanted

Florian to drive. And so he had the keys. Sometimes things just worked out like that.

Behind him, he could hear the voices getting louder again. He got himself into the car and started the engine. The men came round the corner and fired at the car. Florian put his foot on the accelerator and roared off down the road.

Florian was sorry about Vasili but killing the dog had done for him. It was bad luck that they must have been seen from one of those houses. But there was no way back from killing a dog in villages like this. Kanun prescribed it. Blood feud. It had been a bad night. They had wasted fifty dollars and lost five thousand more. But, as Florian raced down the twisting dark country road, with the headlights full on, he thought there must be some purpose behind this. Too many separate things had come together to save him. It was more than luck. The dog could have gone for Vasili and Florian would have had to shoot it and been shot. Vasili could have been driving. He could have fallen over while he was running away. He could so easily have been lying in a heap beside Vasili on the road back there. There must be some reason why he had been spared.

As the adrenalin kept surging and the BMW hurtled round the bends in the country road, tyres screeching, a strange calm crept over Florian. This must be the grace Father Severian used to talk about when his mother had dragged him to church.

But then, suddenly, a wriggling question ruptured his mood. How was he going to explain all this to

Kalaj? From what he had heard about him, he did not think Kalaj would like what had happened this evening. The more he thought about it, the less Florian looked forward to explaining himself to Kalaj.

four

Two days before he met Viktor for the first time, Martin was sitting at his desk and thinking about Clare and what she might have been doing last night.

'Do you want the work or not?' the voice barked down the phone at him.

Martin looked out at the lawns of Lincoln's Inn, dusted with frost, and wondered how he could find out about Clare. 'I'm happy to try to help,' he said professionally.

'Then get over here.' The voice wanted to tick Martin off its list. 'Now.'

Locke said the law existed to enlarge freedom but clients like Stephen Chalmers made it hard to believe that. Through the window, Martin saw a hunched figure scurrying between skeletal trees on its way to court. Had Clare started seeing someone else? Was she already seeing another man when she dumped him?

'Jenny gave me your name.' Stephen Chalmers was irritated by Martin's silence. 'Was she wrong?'

Jenny never stopped. If someone said their tax return was late, Jenny knew the accountant to fix it. When a roof was leaking, Jenny had the number for a roofer. And when anyone needed a lawyer she referred them to Martin. Which was nice of her. Except when it was someone like this.

'Usually, Mr Chalmers, clients come to chambers to consult a barrister,' Martin said. The last time Jenny had referred someone to him, the brief came in late on Friday afternoon so he'd had to work on it over the weekend and he had not been able to take Megan swimming. And Clare had dumped him.

'I don't give a fuck what people usually do,' Stephen Chalmers said. 'I don't have time to poodle across London to call on you in your chambers.'

'You choose,' Clare had said. 'But we're not going to be your second choice. I won't let it happen to Megan again. One commitment-phobic is enough for my lifetime.'

'It's only one weekend. I can't let these people down,' he had said.

'So you let Megan down instead,' Clare had said. 'And not for the first time.'

'OK,' Martin said to Stephen Chalmers. 'I'll be there in an hour.' It was a lovely crisp morning and he could walk along the river most of the way.

'Don't be late,' his new client said.

Six weeks after the cataclysm, as he thought of it, Martin still struggled to see himself as a man who let people down. How could Clare think love was measured out in ice-rinks and birthday parties? But apparently she did. 'You always have a choice,' she said. 'And you just chose.' Didn't she realise his hard work paid for the ice-rinks and birthday parties?

'Where are you going?' his clerk said as Martin put on his coat.

'Out,' Martin said.

'Yes, Mr Hughes,' his clerk said, 'but where? What if someone calls for you? With work to pay your mortgage? And mine?' Today Phil Matthews was wearing a black suit with a red stripe and matching scarlet tie.

'I'm going to see a client,' Martin said. The chambers now had a website, decorated with photographs of its dynamic barristers and every month Phil emailed each of them a list of the fees they had generated. Every month, month after month.

'Clients come here, Mr Hughes,' Phil said. 'You do not go to them.'

Martin wrapped his scarf round his neck. 'I could do with the walk,' he said. 'Don't worry, Phil, I'll come back with a big fat fee. For you and for me.'

'You won't be late with that opinion for Clements, will you, Mr Hughes?' Phil Matthews said. 'Fastest growing firm in the City. It would be sensible to keep in with them.'

'Stop worrying,' Martin said as he walked out the door. The river glittered in the pale sunshine and the cold made the blood sparkle in his cheeks as he walked. Why hadn't Clare understood that he worked to provide for all of them, for her and Megan and for their life together?

Mist was still drifting among the trees when he reached St James's Park. All the meetings and opinions, and impressing clients and judges, and the fees which flowed in as a result, had been for all of them.

Now it was the same work and the same fees but there was no all of them, no Clare and no Megan. As he waited for the traffic lights to change, Martin thought this was the first time in his life that things had not turned out as he had planned.

Stephen Chalmers worked in a terraced townhouse in a side street and when Martin was shown into his office on the first floor, he was standing, looking out of the window and barking into a phone. 'I told you ten thousand,' he said. 'Now do it.'

Martin waited in the doorway while Stephen Chalmers talked by the window which ran from floor to ceiling. Leafless branches outside were framed like expensive art and a computer purred on the desk. Where had Clare woken up this morning? Was his workload just an excuse for her to go off with someone else?

Eventually Stephen Chalmers paused and turned round. 'Yes?' he said.

'I'm Martin Hughes,' Martin said.

Stephen Chalmers gestured towards an armchair by the fireplace. 'Sit down,' he said. 'Do you want anything to drink?'

'I'm fine,' Martin said, sitting down.

'I'm not,' Stephen Chalmers said, starting to type, still standing up. 'I've got this wine, good stuff, and for ten years I've been paying storage. And now these fuckwits have gone bust and the liquidators say I can't have my own wine.' He punched out another number on his phone. 'Manfred,' he said, 'I've just seen the email from Guernsey. What are you doing on those T-Bills?'

Martin looked out of the window at the tree. Clare looked so soft when she was asleep.

He cleared his throat. 'You should talk to my clerk before I begin work on this,' he said.

'Whatever,' Stephen Chalmers said. 'Now do you want the job? Jenny said you were good at this sort of thing.'

'Well,' Martin said, 'it's true I do a lot of work with trusts.'

'So get on with it,' Stephen Chalmers said.

'There's a growing body of case law on just this sort of issue,' Martin said. 'In the case of London Wine Shippers, it was explored in some detail by Mr Justice Oliver.'

'Oh for fuck's sake, not now,' Stephen Chalmers said. 'I don't need a tutorial.'

Martin stood up. 'If you want me to take on this case,' he said, 'I'll need a brief. And if you're too busy, I'll get back to my chambers.' And call Clare. Perhaps she was trying to build bridges by asking him to take Megan to the fair on Saturday. Or perhaps she just needed a babysitter while she went shopping with her new man?

Chalmers looked up and smiled thinly. 'OK,' he said, 'OK,' and then looked back at the computer screen and dialled another number on his phone. 'Cliff,' he said into the speaker, still sifting through the papers, 'where the fuck are the Microsoft CFDs?'

'I'm going,' Martin said. 'Call my clerk if you want me to act for you.'

'Hold on, Cliff.' Stephen Chalmers picked up a file from the desk. 'It's all in there,' he said to Martin. 'Let me know when you've got my wine back. Bastards.'

'Hello, Daddy.' Martin turned round to see what this curious townhouse had produced now. And it was a little boy with a shaven head. And holding his hand was Miranda.

'What are you doing here?' she said.

'It's my office, Miranda. Remember?'

'Not you, Stephen. I was talking to Martin.'

'Who? Him?'

'I'm here to get Mr Chalmers's wine back from the fuckwits,' Martin said. 'What about you?'

'I'm bringing David to see his father,' she said.

And then Martin understood. Chalmers was Miranda's ex-husband and Jenny would have relished getting him to pay what she imagined were Martin's fat fees. And she would have loved picturing Martin's surprise when he discovered this rangy tyrant was Miranda's ex-husband. And she would have been plotting to use this to get Martin and Miranda together. Jenny never stopped.

'OK. OK,' Stephen Chalmers said. 'Fuck off. Hi, son. Ready?' He thrust the file into Martin's hands as he walked towards the door. 'It's all there,' he said. 'Come on, tiger.' He took David's hand and then they were gone.

'Don't worry,' Miranda said. 'He's like that with everyone.'

They stood awkwardly in the middle of the office. Her grave brown eyes were smiling at him. Thin sun streamed into the room and washed it with light. It was a still, perfect moment. A diamond. Martin felt Miranda waiting for something.

The phone rang on the desk and they both turned to look at it. A single low tone. And again. They looked at each other. And then it stopped. Someone must have picked it up elsewhere in the office but the moment had passed.

'I'd better go,' she said but she did not move.

'Yes,' he said. 'I've got to get back to work. I'll see you on Saturday.'

'That'll be nice,' she said, 'see you then,' and she turned and went.

As Martin stood in the street looking for a taxi, his mobile phone rang. 'Well?' Jenny said. 'What do you make of him?'

'Very amusing,' Martin said. 'And Miranda turned up. I suppose you arranged that too.'

Jenny chuckled. 'My powers are limitless, darling,' she said. 'However, in this case I didn't set it up. But now you see why Miranda is ready for some cherishing,' she said. 'You promise me you'll turn up on Saturday.'

'I've promised Clare,' he said.

'I'm not talking about Clare,' she said.

'But I am,' Martin said.

'Be careful,' she said. 'You need cherishing too.'

'I know what I'm doing,' he said.

Jenny laughed. 'Whatever,' she said. 'Just make sure you get on down to St Luke's on Saturday. Miranda may need your help, as I'm not sure about this Viktor,' she said. 'He could be unreliable. He may not be Russian. There's something Balkan about him.'

'What are you talking about, Jenny?' Martin said.

'Broody. I don't know. Moody. Not quite right,' she said. 'He said he'd do it but I don't know.'

'I'll be there,' he said. 'You don't need to worry about Balkan Viktor.'

five

Kalaj took the print-out from Boris and scanned through it. The figures were looking good. He had made ten thousand on the lorry-load of Bulgarians, there was a container of Chinese due next week and a consignment of Nigerians coming up through Spain, the house in Southgate was now working ten girls round the clock, the Romanian's operation had delivered thirty-seven thousand pounds gross last month, and the other businesses were all turning over juicy money as well.

'Not bad,' he said to Boris.

'Yes, Mr Kalaj,' Boris said.

Kalaj calculated the totals in his head. The business was getting ready to move on to the next stage. The cashflow was now strong enough for him to start investing in legitimate businesses and stashing the money away in comfortingly anonymous trusts. He thought he might start with a holding company in Jersey, an investment fund in the Cayman Islands and a closed-end trust in Zug. He was going to need some professional help.

'Do you know any corporate lawyers, Boris?' he asked.

'No, Mr Kalaj,' Boris said.

Kalaj laughed. 'Only joking,' he said. 'Don't look so worried, Boris. I know you don't mix with people like that.' But who did? He was going to need to ask around.

The phone rang. Kalaj picked it up and listened. He never spoke first because you never knew who it might be.

'I'm sorry, Mr Kalaj,' the voice said. 'I can't get you those two from Luginasi.'

'Who are you?' Kalaj said. 'What two?'

'I am Florian,' Florian said. 'Vasili's dead.'

And then Kalaj knew. 'Shut up,' he said. Anyone could be listening in. He did not know the two Albanians personally but they had been running a steady little profit centre. Unfortunately it now sounded as if they weren't any longer.

'They shot him,' Florian said.

'Shut up now,' Kalaj said. What had happened? 'You get over here and we'll discuss it then. Boris will call you to arrange it. Do you understand?'

'Yes, Mr Kalaj,' Florian said and Kalaj wondered who had stopped his cashflow from Vlore. One moment everything was fine, leks flowing out of Vlore like honey, and then, suddenly, Vasili was dead and Florian was panicking down the phone. What was going on? Someone must be moving in on him. He still needed to find a lawyer to take the business on to the next stage but first he needed to respond to this attack.

'I've got some things for you to do, Boris,' he said.

'Yes, Mr Kalaj,' Boris said. 'Of course, Mr Kalaj.'

six

Before Mihail went to war, there was something he had to do. He took the brush and carefully dipped it into the pot of Sunburst Yellow. This finishing touch was the tricky part. The Warhammer army was positioned on the table top, with the Knights of Chaos leading the charge. In his hand he held the Champion and now he had to apply the paint to his beard. Then he would be ready.

Music filled the house, drifting through the small rooms, with their low ceilings and wooden floors. Outside the sun warmed the fields but inside it was shady and cool. Through the open window, apples and plums ripened on the trees in the orchard and the stream gurgled through the meadow. This was the motherland, beset by enemies, jealous of her fertile land and beautiful women. Mihail was always watchful for the raised voice or the routine manoeuvre near the border that might signal invasion and pillage. He always knew the time would come when, like the Champion of Khorngor, he would need to take up his mighty sword and smite his enemies dead.

He steadied his elbow on the table and, with one deft movement, he painted the first line on the beard. And

then another. Mihail took off his glasses and peered
closely at the model. Righteous. The Sunburst Yellow
picked out every flowing line of the fine sculpted beard.
He was brilliant. This was the colour for the beard of a
legend. He realised that he had been pushing his
tongue out against his lips as he concentrated and,
self-consciously, he slid it back inside his mouth. But
now the Champion did look really good and ready for
the battle ahead.

Outside the house, a young calf lowed gently in the
barn and the hens were scuffling and clucking in the
yard. Inside all was still. Mihail placed the Knight of
Chaos, with his damp yellow beard on the table at the
head of his army. Spearmen and pistoliers flanked the
central squadrons of Knights. He pushed the hair off
his forehead and looked at the field spread out before
him. Something was wrong. He moved the pistoliers to
the other side of the Knights. That was it.

The staffwork might need improvement but the
front line was ready. The field was set and now blood
would flow as warriors laid into each other, churning
grass into red mud, and the country air was split by the
groans of dying men. The price would be paid. Mihail
pulled his shirt out of his trousers and polished his
glasses with the tail. Now he was ready to play. It was
war.

seven

'Am I being an idiot about Clare?' Martin said to Ben as he sat down. 'Tell me honestly.' There was no-one else in the restaurant and the waitress's heels clattered on the oak floorboards as she brought the menus.

'How have you been?' his friend said, ignoring the question. Since they graduated, they had met every month for lunch, twelve years of articles and pupillage and Ben's marriage and divorce, and Martin breaking up with Fiona and falling in love with Patsy, and Ben's diets and Martin's receding hairline and then Clare.

'I just told you,' Martin said. 'Moping around like a sack of acne.'

'Why change?' Ben said. 'What do you want to eat?'

'Fuck off,' Martin said. 'Egg and chips. How are you?'

'Trying to stop a nineteen-year-old heroin addict being evicted with her six-month-old daughter and suing the police for beating up a drunk Bengali teen-ager. I'm fine.'

'You're a hero,' Martin said. 'An inspiration to the rest of us.'

'Your choice,' Ben said.

'No,' Martin said. 'You had a choice. I didn't.'

'Please,' Ben said. 'Not your father again. What do you really want to eat? Haddock risotto? Isn't that what all the young judges are eating this year?'

'I need your help,' Martin said. 'Why did Clare dump me?'

'She told you.'

'It can't be that. What's the real reason?'

'Why can't that be the real reason? Choose your food.'

'I'm not hungry,' Martin said. 'She can't have left because I couldn't take Megan swimming on one Saturday.'

'Think, big boy. Just think about it.'

'What do you think I'm doing? Why can't she see that I love her and Megan? I'd do anything for them. That's what should matter to her.'

'Two haddock risottos,' Ben said to the waitress, his round face beaming behind the wire spectacles.

'And two glasses of house white,' Martin added.

'Don't you think you'd be sensitive,' Ben said patiently, 'if you were thirty-four years old with a small daughter, abandoned by a man who was in the office until ten o'clock every night or out shagging one of his partners. Who then kept forgetting to pay your maintenance. He used to tell her how much he loved her as well.'

'But I'm not like that,' Martin said. 'I want to provide for them. Why do you think I work so hard?'

Ben laughed. 'You're a sweetie-pop, Martin. You know that. I know that. But why should she believe it? Why wouldn't you turn out like Megan's dad? One little Saturday afternoon, that's all it takes. It's like an alcoholic with one little whisky. Slippery slope, my silky friend, one little whisky, one little Saturday. It's all the same.'

'But I'm really not like that,' Martin said. He knew how much Clare worried about making a secure home for Megan and how anxious it made her when Don forgot to send the cheque. And he tried so hard to contribute without making her feel dependent. How could she doubt him?

'You asked me,' Ben said.

'Do you think this could be a test of some sort?' Martin said. Could she be right about him using work to avoid an emotional commitment? He hadn't thought he was like that but could she be right? 'She asked me to look after Megan this Saturday. Perhaps she's testing me out.'

Ben stared at him and smiled.

'All right,' Martin said. 'Perhaps she really does just need a babysitter. Come on, Ben. What do you think?'

'You don't want to know what I think,' Ben said. 'I've told you and you're not listening. Maybe she means exactly what she says. Maybe she really was frightened you were going to end up dumping her and Megan just like Megan's dad.'

'So why did she ask me to look after Megan?'

'Does he look stupid to you?' Ben asked the waitress who had arrived at their table with two heaped plates of risotto.

She ignored him and put the plates on the table. 'I'll be back with the wine,' she said.

'I'm not sure you're in there,' Martin said. 'So why did Clare ask me to look after Megan?'

'You really don't get it, do you?' Ben said. 'Maybe she's just worried about Megan. Maybe she thinks that instead of you suddenly disappearing out of that little girl's life, you should still see her occasionally. After all, you've been her father for half her life.'

Martin shook his head. 'It didn't sound like that to me,' he said. Perhaps he hadn't tried hard enough to show Clare she was wrong. Instead of moping, he should be showing her she'd made a mistake.

'Obviously,' Ben said. 'But you asked me what I thought and that is what I think.'

'Do you think I could change her mind about me?' Martin said.

'Anything's possible,' Ben said, delicately positioning a flake of haddock on his fork.

'What do you think?' Martin said.

'I think you need to change your life,' Ben said. 'If you were doing something useful with it, you wouldn't be so neurotic about women.'

Martin laughed. 'Hello, pot,' he said. 'This is kettle.'

'Come on, Martin, why don't you come and join me? Use that great brain of yours to do something useful.'

'It's all right for you. You can afford to save the world.'

'And you can't? Why not? Your dad? Fuck him. It's your life, not his. Money? What do you need money for? You're single now. Clare's dumped you. Come on, Martin. Why don't you do something you really want to do, for once? Leave those smug, greedy, selfish gits, creeping their way to dusty death, and do something worthwhile. Honestly, do you know what a rush it is to feel you have helped someone, really helped them?'

'I do help people,' Martin said.

'That's not help, that's property management.'

'I could start on Saturday,' Martin said. 'At the fete.'

Concerts, skating, running in the park, Saturdays, Sundays: he would be there till Megan yawned herself to sleep.

'Suit yourself,' Ben said. 'Don't say you weren't warned when you wake up at fifty and ask yourself what was it all for.'

'You can ask me when you come to stay on my yacht,' Martin said. 'Do you think it would be pushing it if I asked Clare out when I take Megan back on Saturday?'

'You've been warned,' Ben said.

'I'll have to escape Jenny of course,' Martin ruminated. 'She's trying to fix me up with some friend of hers called Miranda.'

'Watch out,' Ben said.

'Why?' Martin said. 'Do you know Miranda?'

'No,' Ben said. 'But I know Jenny.'

'Yes,' Martin said gloomily. 'And she's right on form at the moment. She's got me doing something for Miranda's ex-husband. And I suspect she's now trying to get me work from some Balkan mystery man.'

eight

Kalaj scrolled down the spreadsheet, looking for the blips and dips that might wink to him that someone had been skimming off the top. Occasionally he turned a page in a large clip file beside the computer and ran his finger down a column of figures, checking, double-checking. He needed to find that corporate lawyer to set up a new structure. But first he needed to find out who was attacking him so he could deal with them.

Boris stood patiently beside the desk, waiting, knowing that eventually Kalaj would tell him what he wanted. Obsessive. That was the word for his boss and he was also a genius. No doubt about that at all. Like all great generals, nothing escaped him. He knew every little detail but, at the same time, he was always looking at the big picture. Boris had learned that there was no point trying to understand what Kalaj was doing. His job was to wait stoically until he was told what to do.

'Boris?'

'Yes, Mr Kalaj?'

'Open the left curtain a metre.'

Boris walked across the room and pulled the heavy brocade back. He remembered buying the curtains from a warehouse in East London. 'Do you want new or pre-loved?' the man had said. Pre-loved curtains were cheaper. Like women, Boris thought.

'More,' Kalaj said and Boris pulled the curtain open a little further. A shaft of pale winter sun fell across the clip file. 'That's it,' Kalaj said.

Boris waited by the window for new instructions. Kalaj tapped at the computer.

The sunlight caught little specks of dust dancing crazily in the air and Boris watched them, wondering if they ever stopped to rest. He had bought everything in the office for Kalaj from the warehouse, the traditional design desk in walnut veneer, the executive high-back swivel and tilt chair, carpets and cupboards, peeling off fifty-pound notes from the wad the boss had given him. He yawned.

'Bored, Boris?' Kalaj said. Once he finished with the spreadsheets, he would interrogate each of the different associates to work out which of them was trying to do him in. If he didn't stay ahead of the game and punish the attack on the Albanians' operation, he was dead. 'Are you finding it all tedious, Boris?' he said.

Boris knew he was not expected to answer. Kalaj reached the end of the last spreadsheet. Nothing unusual. Time to start on the associates.

'Bring the Romanian in', he said.

'Yes, Mr Kalaj.'

'Don't say anything about why.'

'No, Mr Kalaj.'

He had to be very careful. There was a lot going on at the moment and that always required extra vigilance, watching for those who saw his profits racking up and thought they deserved some of them before they got to him.

And there had also been some losses from the shipment through Tarifa that would get the Spanish police poking around for a few days. And that meant he would have to be careful how he dealt this new problem from Vlore. He needed to avoid anything that might attract further attention from the police.

All this was going to delay his move to the next stage. Still, these complications could be sorted out and then, as soon as that was done, he would find that lawyer and start siphoning the money into trusts. And punish whoever had attacked the Albanians. And if anyone else started poking around in his business in the meantime, they would get to meet Boris and Stepan as well.

nine

'I'm going for a run,' Charlotte said. She sat on the edge of the bed and bent down to lace up her trainers. Soft dawn light filtered through the blinds and outside she heard waves breaking on Spanish sand. She leant over and kissed Rob.

He turned and pulled the pillow under his head. 'What are you doing?' he mumbled, his voice thick with sleep. 'We're on holiday. You can't have a deadline.' He put his arms around her neck and drew her towards him.

'I'm just going for a run,' she whispered and put his hands gently back on the sheet.

'Couldn't you sleep?' he mumbled.

'I'm sorry I woke you up,' she said. 'I won't be long.'

'Are you OK?' he said. 'Can't you forget about the newspaper?' They had left the door of the bungalow ajar overnight and she could smell the salt on the early morning breeze.

'Go back to sleep,' she said.

Rob kissed her on the lips. 'I love you,' he said.

'Love you too.'

Outside it was chilly but the sun was already catching the white tips of the waves as they rolled in towards the shore. On top of the dunes, Charlotte raised her hands above her head and stretched. She was beginning to feel better. She had lain awake for an hour, trying not to disturb Rob but, finally, she had needed to get outside.

She picked her way down the slope. The sand was firm under her feet. Good. She looked up. The dull red tiles on the roofs of the bungalows were just visible above the scrubby clumps of grass. Rob's parents had agreed to look after Matthew and now they were having these rare, special days together on their own, just the two of them. Charlotte began to jog.

Ahead of her the white sand of the bay curved round to a rocky headland and the dawn sun picked out a gull on the wing. One. Two. Three. Four. She loved this windy corner of Spain. A few miles down the road in the Mediterranean, a polite sea lapped manicured beaches but, slip through the Straits of Gibraltar, and at Tarifa suddenly there was the vast swelling ocean on which the legendary Iberian navigators had once set off for the terrifying horizon.

Charlotte relaxed into a rhythm, pounding the thoughts of the night into the sand. Land soft, push hard. Concentrate on the core. That was it. Keep the rhythm going. Focus on the fundamental. One, two, three, four. Bastard, bastard. She ran closer to the water, splashing on the wet sand. One–two–three–four. Monkey-spanking muppet bastard.

Damian had elbowed her off the front page on three Sundays in the last two months. Through the noise of the waves, she heard the distant raucous cries of seagulls. He was a suck-up. There was no other explanation. No-one could seriously have thought that her Home Office story should have been pushed on to page two.

Her feet were springing off the sand. Splash, splash, splash. The rhythm was easy now. There was nothing wrong with my story, Maggie. All Damian did was cobble together a couple of conversations in the pub and you put him on the front page. Land soft, push hard. What sort of judgement was that?

Charlotte swerved to avoid a surging incoming wave. She could not clear her mind of work. 'Come back with some good stories,' George had warned her as she left and she knew he was trying to help. He must think she was already on Maggie Fairweather's list for the annual clear-out. She would run to the end of the bay and try to pound out this ill-temper before going back to wake up Rob for breakfast. She shouldn't inflict this mood on him.

Splash, splash, splash. Charlotte could feel her breath beginning to tighten in her chest. That was a good sign but how much longer could she go on at the paper? She ran around a tangled clump of dark seaweed. Maybe she was losing her edge and Damian was winning out because he was hungrier. Because he was better. Land soft, push hard. He was twenty-seven. She was thirty-eight. In good shape but still thirty-eight.

One, two, three, four. Would she care if she were cleared out? She could take the money and find a congenial berth somewhere else. One. Two. Three.

Four. Eleven. Thousand. Pounds a year. That's what the mortgage cost. What would they do if she lost her job and couldn't find another one? There was little equity in the house and Rob cleared, what, twenty-one thousand from Wandsworth. They'd be stuffed. And it wasn't just the money. It was the humiliation. Sacked.

She was alone on the beach. The wind kept the sunbathing tourists away from this end of the coast and the surfers did not get up until later. Her breathing was coming faster now. One, two, three, four. This was doing her good. Up ahead she could see another big dark clump of seaweed by the water's edge. There must have been a heavy sea during the night.

The waves crashed angrily on the shore. And that was something else. Matthew was angry so much of the time nowadays. Land soft, push hard. The water came swirling in exhausted round her feet and ebbed away. Last Monday, Mrs Warren had asked to see her because Matthew had been bullying Carmen. Picking on her, Mrs Warren had said. One of the youngest girls in the group.

On and on she ran. Her darling son. The class bully. The gulls shrieked above the waves and the fresh dawn air was cooling the sweat on her skin. Was everything all right at home? Mrs Warren had asked.

Splash, splash, splash. Charlotte smelt the salt on the breeze. She knew what Harriet Warren had meant. Spend more time with your son. She had not said that but Charlotte knew that was what she meant. He's going wrong. A gust of wind blew her hair across her eyes and she turned round and jogged on the spot while she pushed it back and twirled it up into a bun on top of her head.

Sometimes she looked at Matthew across the breakfast table, his tiny pink tongue peeping out between his lips as he slowly and carefully buttered his toast, and she wondered if there could be anything on earth more lovely and her eyes would fill. And now here was Harriet Warren telling her that he was bullying Carmen Davis. Charlotte jogged on the spot, on and on and on.

Why did Harriet Warren think it was her fault? Did it not occur to the teacher that perhaps she should keep better control of her classroom? Why was it always down to the parents? To the mother? Her breath was coming shorter and faster now. Charlotte had taken action as soon as she got into work, after that depressing session with Harriet Warren. She had turned to an old and trusted friend for help.

Google.

And her old friend let her down. The website of the American Psychiatric Association, with its thirty-six thousand physician members, suggested that Matthew was manifesting many of the symptoms that indicated mental illness. Anger at school. Difficulty in getting to sleep. Frequently asking for help. Crying. It said a combination of these symptoms could signal a need for professional intervention. Was she going to have to take her son to a psychiatrist? At five years old? What was she doing wrong?

Still jogging, she turned round into the breeze and then started off again, getting back into a rhythm. One, two, three, four. On the other hand, the American psychiatrists also said that having only one or two of the problems was not necessarily cause for alarm. Not necessarily. Charlotte felt her stride tightening and stiffening as she ran and worried.

She was sweating now and she wiped her brow with the back of her hand as she pounded over the sand. A trickle ran down her cheek and she licked the salty sweat. She should never have let Rob take charge of the child-care. He was not up to it. One, two, three, four. No. That was not fair. Land soft, push hard. It was her fault. She did not do her share. That was the problem. It was her fault. Splash, splash, splash. She should give up the paper. Go before she was pushed. And care for her son. And be the mother Harriet Warren expected her to be.

Damn. Water had got into her shoes and now as she ran she heard little wet belches beneath her feet. One, two, three, four. Squelch, squelch, squelch. She could not clear her head of the images and scraps of conversation. Maggie, Damian, Rob, Matthew, money, Matthew, they all went round and round in her mind. One, two, three, four.

She was coming up to the large dark clump of seaweed now. Except that it was not. As she got closer, she saw it was too big for that. Perhaps it was a rock. But there were no rocks on the bay. One, two, three, four, the breath was tight in her chest. And now she was there. And it was definitely not seaweed. And it was not a rock. It was a man.

Charlotte stopped. The man was dead. She stood, panting, her heart thudding in her chest as she recov-

ered her breath and the body lay sprawled on the shore
and the waves lapped around it. In they came and out
they went, swirling round the dark mass.

She knelt down. She should go back and get the
police. But she could not just turn away. She had not
seen a dead body since she had worked on the *Watford
Observer* and covered car crashes on the M1.

It was a young man, his head twisted awkwardly.
There was sand on his cheek and tiny bubbles of foam
around his mouth. A medallion on a long thin chain
trailed from his neck on to the beach, lifted and
dropped back again by the waves as they washed in
and out. The corpse looked as if it had been in the
water a long time. Thin jeans clung to his legs and a
stained white shirt was still wrapped around his torso
and the black skin was puffy and wrinkled.

He must have drowned. The currents round here
were treacherous and the wind made it dangerous even
for experienced sailors. He might have been a fisher-
man but she didn't suppose they would allow Africans
to fish in these waters. Whoever he was, it was a terrible
way to die.

As she looked at the young man, Charlotte felt her
breathing return to normal. There was nothing more
she could do here. She should get back and report it. As
she stood up, she noticed the medallion was an image
of St Christopher. That was a good bit of colour. She
must remember to write it down when she got back to
the bungalow.

She stood up and pushed the hair off her face. That
was a good sign, she thought. She couldn't be that

jaded if she still had this visceral instinct for a story. She stretched her hands above her head. She should run back to the villa and change and then go down to the police herself to report it and then rough something out for her return.

Another wave came swirling in around the body. The hopes of a continent washed on to the shores of the Mediterranean, Charlotte thought. And then she saw a lithe young man clambering up on to the back of a lorry, his pack slung over his shoulder, grinning and waving at his family as he left to start a new life and she flushed with shame. What sort of person had she become? How could she look at this drowned man and think only about what sort of story he would make?

ten

Great men are distinguished by their sense of destiny but Mihail knew that not everyone with a sense of destiny was great. What was the legacy of all those prime ministers and presidents, millionaires and billionaires, who had strutted their time, convinced of their place in the pantheon? Gone, forgotten, into the shadows, an evanescent breath upon the mirror of eternity, election triumphs fading into dusty history, laws mouldering obsolescent on statute books, trust funds squandered by wastrel progeny.

Mihail saw this clearly as he looked at his squadrons of Knights and Beastmen ranked on the table top. But for scholars, there was one man whose memory still glowed through the fickle centuries. His ravenous ego had devoured a continent but, in the wake of his armies, Napoleon had implanted the rule of law and ushered in a new age of rights and reason in Europe, a legacy that had withstood the obliterating floods of time.

Mihail recognised in the Emperor a great soul who would be remembered long after the deserts had covered over punier potentates. He picked up a Khorngor and pondered the fate of heroes and how he was going to take a place among them.

To honour his ancestors in the motherland, Mihail had placed a model cottage among the Knights of Chaos and the Beastmen. It did not come with the kit so he had had to buy it specially and it had taken him two days to assemble, painstakingly glueing together the hardboard panels and miniature real bricks. And now it stood on the battlefield as a memory of how music filled the wooden houses and sun warmed the fields and apples and plums ripened on the trees in the orchard and clear streams gurgled through the Balkan meadows.

The more Mihail studied the life of Napoleon, the more he learned from it. To initiative and mobility, the little corporal genius applied the concentration of force to sweep Europe before him. Of course, circumstances today were different. Mihail knew that. Today the concept of a Great Army marching across Europe, or indeed anywhere else, to fulfil a manifest destiny was, frankly, risible. Today, globalisation had located the wellsprings of power elsewhere. And Mihail knew that.

Today there were new worlds to conquer. Who cared about commanding territory when you could control the sinews of power itself? In the modern era, the might of the state had been founded on its ability to tax, which raised the banners of war and purchased the contentments of peace. But in these post-modern times, Mihail saw governments losing power as wealth escaped their clutches through every bit and byte of the Internet. This weightless world was the new battle-ground and the little corporal who found the way to control it would bestride the world as Napoleon had once done. Mihail knew that.

Napoleon had only been twenty-six when he marched into Italy and history. And now once again the world belonged to young men, armed as the young Bonaparte had been, with the vigour of genius. Mihail had no doubt about that. And he knew he had to learn the lessons from Napoleon's inspirational campaigns. Mobility. And the concentration of force and the application of maximum power.

Others had begun to blaze a path. The titans of personal computing had shown what might be possible but for all their achievements they had failed to realise their potential. In the end, Bill Gates and his cohorts had just been businessmen, avid for respectability and status. They had made so much and then given it all away. They had known their place. No-one could ever say that about Napoleon. Nothing had ever been beyond his reach.

Mihail replaced the Khorngor carefully on the table top, resplendent in red and gold. It was time for the battle to begin.

eleven

'People-trafficking is not a story any more, Charlotte,' Maggie said patiently. 'Have you got anything else?'

The twelfth-floor conference room smelt of stewed coffee and there was a platter of croissants and Danish pastries in the centre of the table. Everyone knew not to reach for it when the editor was speaking. Outside, rain drizzled down from a grey London sky and streaked the windows.

'It's a good idea,' Charlotte persisted. 'The misery trail across Africa, from the Sahara to Southwark.'

Maggie Fairweather swivelled her eyes to look out of the window. Charlotte knew that all the others sitting round the Wednesday conference table would have registered it. The exit sign. She saw Mark Wright reach for his coffee cup and take a long contemplative sip, trying to avoid getting caught in the crossfire.

'That's not old and boring,' her editor said. 'That's very old and boring. What else have you got?'

'Seriously, Maggie, this is a good story. Yards from where British tourists are sunning themselves, Africans are washing up dead. They come in search of a dream. They scrape the money together to pay for the ride in a decrepit lorry across the Sahara. They put themselves in hock to people-smugglers, hoping to earn enough over here to give their family a better life. And then they drown. Four thousand of them in the last five years.'

Charlotte saw Maggie's index finger tapping softly on the table as she looked out of the window. She was a slight pretty woman whose eyes sparkled and danced when she appeared on television but, in editorial meetings, they were distant and cold. Charlotte sensed the others round the table looking away, as Maggie's finger tapped on the table. Was she wrong? Perhaps there really was no story here and she was losing her touch.

'I saw it myself. And I've done some work on it. It's a hidden tragedy.' She spoke more quickly now, to try to get it all in before Maggie moved on. 'We hold the guilty to account. The smugglers. The Spanish police who let it happen. The politicians who've lost their grip on the situation.'

'I know your holiday must have been a shock for you, Charlotte,' Maggie said. 'And that good-looking boyfriend of yours. We sympathise. Not what you want on your holidays. But this is not "hidden". We know about it. And our readers do not need to worry about their holidays being ruined by dead Africans washing up by their sunbeds.'

Charlotte stared at her editor. How could there not be a story in that? 'But, Maggie,' she said, even though she knew you needed to be careful about persisting with Maggie. 'This is appointment journalism. A modern saga. Human tragedies thrown up by the tides of globalisation.'

'Charlotte,' Maggie said tolerantly, 'this is a newspaper, not a book.' She was gazing at her now, with a worrying little smile. 'Our readers don't read. They graze. It's a Chinese feast and every week I create a new one, every page a different course and every story refines the experience. Texture. Taste. Tanginess. There's a whole world in every edition and you're paid to make a contribution, a small contribution, to it. Not three thousands words, just your own little flavour. Our readers don't want three thousand words about anything. And certainly not from you.'

Charlotte glimpsed Damian smiling sycophantically. What a muppet. He hadn't washed his hair for days. Why was she spending her life with people like this? A Chinese meal? What was that about? But Maggie's careless authority worried her. Was this story really as stale and predictable as she said? Was she losing her touch? Journalism was like riding a bicycle. Once you started thinking about how to do it, you fell off. Perhaps Maggie was right and she didn't know what she was doing any more.

'Rhythm, pace, human interest, high politics,' Maggie was still going on, enjoying herself. 'Mix it up on every page. Make the reader smile and then make them spit with fury.'

Didn't Maggie realise what she sounded like? A caricature. A trivialising travesty of a journalist. She hadn't been on that beach in Tarifa and seen that young man. Charlotte pinched her earlobe until it hurt to prevent herself interrupting. She knew she had to wait till Maggie finished.

'So don't waste any more time on this,' Maggie said. 'Go and charm some middle-aged civil servant and find out who hates who in the Cabinet this week. Dress up as a dosser and beg outside some celebrity restaurants and see how many of those stuffing their faces give you sixpence. Go and do some proper work.'

Charlotte looked at Maggie and wondered how she could ever have thought she belonged with such people. Matthew had still been asleep when she left for the conference which Maggie scheduled to ensure her journalists had to choose between their families and their work. Tomorrow she would come in late so she could take Matthew to school herself and have another word with Harriet Warren.

'This would give you rhythm and pace,' Charlotte said. In colleges, they taught that journalism required dogged persistence. They never taught you about editors like Maggie. Boyfriend? She knew Rob was her partner and the father of her child. Boyfriend? What point was she trying to make?

'Not like that. Not on this paper,' Maggie said. 'If you want to go on a boring trek through misery, go and work for the *Guardian*. Here, we need to move on.'

Charlotte stared at her fingernails. Maybe Maggie was right about this story and she was losing it and it was time to go. Everyone round the table seemed to think so. And perhaps they were right. At least she'd have the redundancy money. But then how long would that last? The mortgage cost eleven thousand a year. Could they afford for her not to work?

'I think there might be something here, Maggie.' George Waddington was the Home Editor and he spoke with the lugubrious authority of a policeman discovering a dead body at the bottom of a quarry. He was her friend. 'I think Charlotte may be on to something.'

'I don't think she's on to anything,' Maggie said.

And then Charlotte got the message. There was something in the dismissive reference to her in the third person, not wasting any time on her name, that made her realise, in a moment of pitiless clarity, she wasn't being given any choices about her work–life balance. Maggie was going to sack her.

'Immigration usually works,' George said. 'And bodies on the beach is powerful. Charlotte just needs to crystallise the story.'

He made it sound easy but Charlotte knew Maggie had just called her number in. There she had been wondering whether they could afford to down-shift and what was the right thing for Matthew and Rob and whether she could still live with the ethical challenges of journalism, when suddenly along comes Maggie and makes the decision for her. Skanking rug-muncher.

'Just give me a week,' she said. She had thought her choice was between grinding on and down-shifting. Now Maggie had given her a different choice, one between giving in and fighting back.

And now, suddenly, unexpectedly, Charlotte felt a familiar surge of adrenalin. George's news sense was immaculate and if he thought there was something in it, she was not losing her touch and her instincts hadn't let her down after all. What had she been thinking? How could she give this up? And let Maggie trample all over her? This is who she was. She could do this as well as being Matthew's mummy. And make Maggie frightened to lose her.

'If you say so, George,' Maggie Fairweather said, ignoring Charlotte. 'You two talk about it and see if you can find a way to make something out of it. Not something for the *Guardian*. Something for us. And now we need to move on.'

Charlotte knew she didn't have more than a couple of weeks. Maggie had already raised the axe above her head. But a good story could make her put it away again just as quickly. And good stories is what Charlotte did.

'Fiona, what have you got?' Maggie was looking out of the window again. She had moved on but people-trafficking had survived.

twelve

'Where are the Africans now?'

'Lille, Mr Kalaj.'

'How many left?'

'Twenty-seven, Mr Kalaj.'

'How much did Nadia send in this week?'

'Three thousand, Mr Kalaj.'

'Pounds?'

'Euros.'

'Why so little?'

'I don't know. Do you want me to find out?'

'Let me think now. Yes, I am thinking. Now I am still thinking. And now I have thought. Of course I do, you donkey. Remind her I expect more and I expect more next week.'

'Yes, Mr Kalaj.'

'Have you found anyone poking around anywhere?'

'I haven't heard anything yet, Mr Kalaj.'

'Keep looking.'

'Of course, Mr Kalaj.'

'And get Stepan to help you.'

'Yes, Mr Kalaj.'

thirteen

'What's new?' Ben said, coming through the door holding two coffees.

'One eviction and two Incapacity Benefit appeals,' Anju said. 'And Mr Gill wants you to ring him.' She pushed her shiny black hair behind her ear and smiled at him.

'It's not funny,' Ben said, handing her a coffee. Three new cases and he was due in court all afternoon. He needed help. 'What do you think of Martin?' he said.

'Lovely.' Anju smiled at him again.

'I didn't mean like that. To work here.'

'No way.'

'Didn't you just say he was lovely?'

'Yes, but why would he come here?'

'Help humanity? Self-fulfilment? To see you every day? What else?'

'Give up, Ben,' she said. 'Who'd say goodbye to those fat fees? He's never going to come.'

Ben sat down and looked at the files on his desk. She was right but it wasn't the cash. Martin never spent all the money he earned. That was what made it so frustrating. Ben knew they would work well together.

Martin was a good man. 'It would give him a purpose,' he said.

Anju laughed. 'This?' she said.

'Yes. This,' Ben said. 'It'll make him realise some people have real things to worry about.' But Martin was imprisoned by expectations – his own and Clare's and his father's. Why did they matter so much to him? Martin saw them as his duty. But they weren't. They were a trap.

'Dream on,' Anju said.

Ben thought his friend was like a fly buzzing against a window to escape into the fresh air, furiously failing to understand why it couldn't get through the glass. Perhaps now Clare had dumped him he'd find a way out.

fourteen

'Am I being stupid about Martin?' Clare said, adjusting one of the photographs on the gallery wall.

'Top left a touch down, darling,' Marc said.

'Tell me honestly,' Clare pleaded. 'Am I being stupid?'

'You're being stupid,' Marc said, scrutinising the photographs of the ornately carved stones squatting on the Cornish clifftop. 'I'm really not sure if it wouldn't be better to set them out along the line of the petroglyph.'

'Please, Marc, this is important.' The gallery was closed while they set up the new exhibition and their voices echoed around the empty space.

'Why are you asking me?' Marc said. 'What do I know about boys?' Dull metal sky was framed by the Velux window in the roof. Clare had turned off the lighting to save electricity and the large square room with its cavernous ceiling was sunk in gloom.

'You're so clever, you know about everything,' she said. 'Please, Marc, what do you think? What should I do?'

'You should help me decide about these photographs,' he said. 'I just can't make up my mind.' He stepped back and squinted at the photographs set out neatly on the ochre walls of the gallery. 'If the essentiality of Aaron's work derives from not-ness, from not being confined in the space of the museum,' he murmured, debating with himself, 'then is it subverted by placing its representation within the mausoleum?'

'Please, Marc,' Clare said.

'Or does the fact that the photograph is just a representation, and not the thing itself, make its positioning ironic? Or subversive?'

'This is important, Marc,' Clare said.

'Don't tell me, babe,' Marc said, staring at the wall. 'We open in a fortnight.' He put his arm around her. 'But if it is ironic, then do we subvert the irony by replicating the petroglyph and enhance it by placing it within a grid which denies its essentiality? Or is it the other way round?' Marc screwed up his eyes. 'Oh my darling Clare, what should we do? Irony is so difficult.'

'I don't know if I've done the right thing,' Clare said. 'But I just can't take any more risks. He says he's working so hard for all of us. But he never stops to ask what we actually want. Everything's on his terms. It's so controlling. And how do I know when he'll want to control things differently?'

Marc removed his arm from her shoulders and turned to face her. 'Oh alright,' he sighed, 'I can see you're not going to focus. Five minutes then. I thought you said he really liked you?'

'That's not the point, Marc,' Clare said. 'I can't just wait and see what happens. It's Megan who's invested as well.'

'Will he still love you in the morning? I don't know, Clare. Please can we get back to Aaron?' He stared at the wall. 'I love you so much more when you boss me around and organise everything so brilliantly and don't waste your time on boys.'

'You said five minutes, Marc,' Clare said. 'Not thirty seconds. I know the signs. It's always fine at the beginning and then bit by bit they take it all for granted.' Clare tapped him on the shoulder. 'Stop looking at the photographs, Marc and listen to me. This is important. I can't take any more risks.'

'Do you love him?'

'I'm past that. But I do really like him.' And his bright eyes and his gentle kiss and the way he played so seriously with Megan. Was that enough?

'Like?' Marc looked up at her.

'Don't look at me like that,' Clare said. 'Yes. Like.' And he would provide for them. Clare never wanted to be dependent on any man again and it was no way to think of Martin but his income would make a difference. 'Help me decide, Marc. I'm ready to sort out my life.'

'Well, I'm not, I'm afraid,' Marc said. 'But if you must push me, keep him dumped. He's a man. He'll only bring you grief. Trust me.'

fifteen

In the middle of the room, Charlotte saw the editor of a national newspaper with a young woman. Good. At a large table by the door, a runner-up in the last series of *Pop Idol* held court with her entourage. Better. And there was a television chef in the corner by the kitchen and that was best of all. This was definitely the place to be.

She looked at her watch. He was late but then politicians usually were. It seemed that punctuality revealed an empty desk. She wasn't sure if this lunch was going to be any use. He was one of those bright, energetically loyal junior ministers who blurred into each other. Still, his department had an interest in the area and he might say something interesting. And anyway she had never eaten the royal Moroccan cuisine in which the restaurant specialised and she didn't know how much longer she would have an expense account.

'Hi,' Roger said. 'Charlotte? I'm sorry I'm late. I had a meeting at Number Ten which ran on a bit.'

Charlotte didn't get up but offered a hand. Effortless, she thought. In two sentences, an apology which conveyed simultaneously his own importance and her insignificance.

Waiters appeared bearing small, exquisitely orna-
mented menus. Charlotte saw the minister looking
round the room and registering the newspaper editor
and the *Pop Idol* runner-up and the television chef.

'So,' Charlotte said. 'Is there going to be a reshuffle
in January?' That should take the edge off his appetite.
He should have been on time.

'I wouldn't have thought so,' he said. She heard his
voice tighten. 'There's been no suggestion of anything
like that coming out of Number Ten.'

Charlotte smiled at him sympathetically. A nice long
sympathetic smile. That should do it. 'Who do you
reckon is in line for the Cabinet?' she said.

'Hard to say.' Roger wondered if they were going to
spend the entire lunch on this uncomfortable topic.

'How long have you been with the paper?' he said.
She was a good-looking woman and he liked the way
her dark blonde hair trailed down to her shoulders. She
breathed sly sophistication like an academic presenting
a television series on erotic woodcuts. He glanced
down surreptitiously to see if she was wearing a wedding ring.

'What about Francesca?' she said. 'She's doing well.
Or Colin?' He'd learn not to be late.

'That wouldn't be popular with the party,' he said.

'Who cares about the party?' she said. 'Oh good.
Here's the food.' That was enough punishment for the
little minister.

And she began to feel better as she ate her first
course of aubergines in honey with a hint of chilli.
Almost good enough to fill the hollow in her soul. She

was bored with the treadmill of these lunches and she hated the fear that Maggie made her feel and she needed to spend more time with Matthew, but walking away would be to admit failure. And what would they do for money? So where did all that leave her? Trapped.

'What's coming up?' she said.

'The Health Service,' he said and off he went about the latest round of reforms.

Charlotte gloomily poured herself another glass of wine and then refilled his glass. Yes, yes, she nodded. And drank some more. 'What about immigration?' she said finally as he took a sip of wine.

'That's always sensitive,' and he smiled the smile that had got him selected for one of the Midlands' safest seats. She had deep grey eyes.

'And what are you going to do about it?' she said, giving him the cue to go off again, word perfect, repeating the phrases and figures from the press briefing, demonstrating why they had made him a minister. He reminded her of William. Her brother had the same smug way with facts, trotting them out like prize poodles, performing for their master.

The main courses arrived. Had Roger not worked out that journalists read the briefings they were issued? And how tedious it was hearing them yet again trotted out in that sincere tone? She took a mouthful of apricot and lamb. It really was good here. And yet on and on the neat little minister went, Roger, that was his name, taking delicate little forkfuls of food to interrupt his conversation as little as possible. Perhaps these politicians thought that if they repeated the mantra enough times, some of it would sink in. Perhaps they thought that journalists were so lazy they would just print it all anyway. And they were probably right, Charlotte thought gloomily. Look at that muppet Damian. She carefully included a titbit of lamb in her next mouthful of couscous.

'But you're not all agreed on this, are you?' she said. 'Some departments have different agendas, don't they? What about the DTI?'

The minister made a dismissive face. Second division, it said. Everything about him was smug and neat. His suit fitted snugly round his shoulders, the knot of his expensive red silk tie sat firmly between his shirt-collar and his hair looked as if it had been cut yesterday, as it probably always had been. Charlotte wished he did not remind her so much of William. It made her want to give him a nipple-cripple.

'Look,' Roger said, 'immigration is a balancing act. That's the politics of it.' He smiled at her, that winning smile again, earning his lunch.

Oh God, she thought, he wasn't going to ruin the rice mousse by putting his hand on her knee, was he?

'Of course, there are bottlenecks in the labour market and we need to meet skills shortages,' he said. Every phrase was exact. Until she met politicians, Charlotte had never believed anyone actually talked like this. Any tendencies in that direction should have been bullied out of them at school. 'But equally you have to recognise the legitimate worries of voters,' Roger said.

William had been bullied at school and came home to take it out on her. Her parents thought it was nice the way they played Scrabble and Monopoly together in the evenings. 'Don't whinge, darling,' her mother said when William beat her yet again. 'Lottie the Clottie,' he jeered. 'It's only a game,' her father said. Mummy and Daddy didn't have William undermining them every single day of their lives.

'Isn't keeping that balance the problem?' Charlotte said. 'How you do that?'

'That's not a problem,' he said. 'It's a challenge. And that's where I come in.'

Of course, Charlotte thought. Pompous and self-satisfied, like William. 'You're not wearing that, are you,' he said when she was about to leave for her first teenage party. 'Don't try for Oxbridge,' he said. 'Spare yourself the humiliation.' Sometimes Charlotte thought that the only reason she kept going at the paper was to show him. She knew he had been sick when she got the job. How would he feel now if she were sacked? Or did she care any more?

'Politics is the art of definition,' Roger said and paused as if it was the clap-line in a speech.

Charlotte didn't understand what he meant.

'What I mean is you have to define the problem as something everyone can agree is a problem,' he said, seeming unnerved by her blank response. 'If you don't, someone is always going to disagree with you.' Again he paused, this time as if expecting dismay from his audience.

Charlotte smiled appreciatively and then realised he was serious.

'Making immigration the headline is a loser,' he said, 'you've got to have an enemy everyone can share.'

'And who's that?' Charlotte said.

'Gangs,' Roger said seriously. 'They bring in the illegals.' He locked eyes with her to show her that this was serious stuff. 'And when they smuggle in people, they're smuggling in other things as well. Drugs, cigarettes. And they link in to other crimes as well: prostitution is big, gambling, fraud. So we watch them, build up intelligence and then crack down. Hard. And that's how we reassure people. And that's what I do.'

That might be interesting, she thought, ignoring another winning smile. 'How serious a problem is this?' she said.

'Bad,' he said. 'And it's getting worse.'

'All of it?' she said, too quickly.

'No,' he said, finally sensing the trap, seeing the headline. 'We're making progress in some areas.'

'So where aren't you?'

Roger paused. 'Prostitution,' he said finally. 'It's modern-day slavery.'

Charlotte nodded. Change suggested a story. Deterioration into crisis was a story. She would look into that.

'Where else?' she said.

'Drugs. It's becoming increasingly violent. There have always been turf wars but now they're starting to spill over into the lives of decent people and that's why it's so important we crack down hard on it.'

'Isn't it very difficult,' she said, 'cracking down on these gangs?'

He leaned across the table towards her. She seemed absorbed by what he was saying and she was really quite good-looking. And he couldn't see a wedding ring.

Charlotte smiled at him. Just keep your hands on the table in front of you and tell me something interesting.

'It's a complex business,' he said importantly. 'Depends a lot on intelligence. And I can't say too much about that.'

Of course not. 'What about some pudding?' she said.

'Lovely,' he said. This was turning into rather a good lunch. 'I'll have the cardamom ice-cream,' he said, looking at her and smiling his bright eager smile at her. 'Let's be adventurous.'

'And I'll have the rose-petal semolina,' she said to the waiter. 'Thank you.'

'It's challenging,' he said. 'As soon as we plug one hole, they find another one to open up. But that's the challenge. That's what makes it interesting. That's why I do it.' And he smiled that smile at Charlotte again.

She spooned some semolina into her mouth. She could really taste the rose petals. Interesting.

'An opponent might say that sounds like an excuse,' she said. 'Shouldn't you stop the holes opening up in the first place? Shouldn't you be more proactive?' He would recognise that word. People like him and William used it all the time.

'Rubbish,' he said quickly. 'They don't understand the nature of the challenge we are facing here. Who said that to you?'

'It's nothing,' she said. It had worked better than she had hoped.

'No, go on, Charlotte,' he said. 'Who said that?'

'No, really. I can't say. It was just the sort of thing someone might say if they were an opponent.' She could see him wondering which of his ministerial colleagues she had lunched recently. What a life. 'So you're not ducking responsibility?' she said.

'Of course not,' he said. 'These people don't understand. Gangs feed off the most vulnerable people and that sort of crime is hard to stamp out. If you know where to look, on any given morning, you can find illegal immigrants waiting to be picked for work by gangmasters. It's nineteenth-century exploitation. But every time we stop it in one place, it moves somewhere else. People need to work.'

'That sounds interesting. Could I see it?'

'If I knew where it was, we'd stop it. It's illegal.' Roger smiled sympathetically. 'But large construction sites might be a good place to start looking.'

'Thank you,' Charlotte said, 'I'll have a look around.'

'Just don't tell me,' Roger said and smiled again, complicitly. 'The cardamom in this ice-cream is really delicious.'

'Anyway, so you're not having much success plugging those holes?' she said, putting out another probe.

'I didn't say that,' he said. 'I said it's difficult but we're making progress.'

'How are you doing that?' she said.

'This is off the record, isn't it?' he said.

Charlotte nodded. 'Of course,' she said.

'Look,' he said. 'These gangs are sophisticated. And technology is moving on all the time. Years ago, all we had to do was tap their phones and we got everything we needed to nail them. But nowadays the Internet makes it much more difficult. You've got to be much smarter to keep up.'

She nodded thoughtfully. Yes, yes, yes. These scraps were beginning to add up to the price of lunch.

'All these people who think it's so easy, they just don't know what they're talking about,' he said. She did seem to be sympathetic. You never knew with journalists but this one did seem nicer than most. And more attractive. Roger liked the way she smiled.

'I sometimes think,' he said, 'what we should do is hire gangs of teenage boys. They've got the real expertise in this sort of thing.' There, that should impress her. Imagination, intelligence, policy innovation. That should be worth a flattering personal adjective or two the next time she wrote about his department.

'That's interesting,' she said. And, interestingly enough, it was. This oleaginous muppet had just given her an idea. And one of those illegal job markets could provide colour.

'Waiter,' she called. 'The bill please.'

'Thank you very much,' Roger said.

'No,' she said. 'Thank you.'

'Let's keep in touch,' Roger said.

'Of course,' Charlotte said. 'I'll give you a ring.' Once she had followed up those leads. And she should also find out about those other activities he had mentioned, like the prostitutes.

sixteen

'*Zdrave*, Gavril.' Boris sat down beside the grey-faced man on the red plastic banquette beneath the mirror. 'Mr Kalaj is doing some spring-cleaning and I hear you've been naughty.' Stepan pulled out a chair and sat down opposite them. He looked at himself in the mirror and started to comb his hair back off his forehead. Back and back went the comb through his slick black hair.

'What do you mean?' Gavril said. The café was empty and a large stainless-steel catering urn grumbled gently on the counter. Behind it, the bald old man adjusted his glasses and turned a page in his newspaper. Stepan tapped one of the little pots on the table.

'You've been helping yourself to Mr Kalaj's money,' Boris said. When the boss was interrogating one of the Bulgarians about Vasili's shooting, he had asked in passing how much Gavril was getting for the cigarettes. And it turned out he was getting five per cent more than he was handing over to the boss. 'You never know what you'll find until you start looking,' Mr Kalaj had said. 'And when you find it, you need to stamp it out.'

'It's not true,' Gavril said. 'I swear. Who told you that?'

'Mr Kalaj knows,' Boris said and stared at Gavril.

Stepan put his thumb into his mouth and licked it and then ran it down his sculpted sideburns, slicking them down.

Gavril lit a cigarette. 'How?' he said. 'I've done nothing wrong.'

Boris and Stepan both stared at him. 'Gavril, Gavril,' Boris said sadly, shaking his head. Stepan tapped the glass pot.

'What does he want?' Gavril said.

'Ten thousand euros – what you stole – plus five thousand interest. By Friday,' Boris said.

Stepan took out his handkerchief and emptied the glass pot into it and then he put his thumb back in his mouth and then he placed it into the pepper and then he squelched it into Gavril's eye.

'Come on, Stepan,' Boris said, getting up. 'Leave the other eye. Kalaj has got other things for us to do.'

seventeen

That Saturday Martin met Viktor for the first time. 'Tuck your shirt in, Martin,' Polly said as he came bustling into the hall.

Martin looked down and saw, inexplicably, that it had escaped from his trousers. 'Hello, Polly,' he said, stuffing it back inside the waistband. 'Sorry.'

'Really, Martin,' she said, smiling affectionately at him. 'It's nice to see you again.' Polly's daughter, Rachel, was Megan's best friend and he had used to see a lot of Polly. Before the cataclysm. 'What are you doing here?' she said.

'Meeting Clare. I'm looking after Megan this afternoon.' As he spoke, he looked for her among the parents chatting amiably to each other and the children milling around in the hall but he couldn't see her anywhere. If Ben was right and she thought this was a way of easing him gently out of Megan's life, she was going to get a surprise. He not going to accept her decision. They were meant to be together and he would show her. Commitment. That was what he would show her.

'You are good,' Polly said and she gave him a quick sympathetic kiss on the cheek. She thought he was here to help Clare out. If only Polly knew. This was not the reflex action of a good heart but the beginning of a ruthless, relentless campaign to win Clare back.

'How are you, Polly?' he said, still looking around anxiously. He wanted Clare to see that he wasn't late. Where was she?

'Good,' Polly said. 'Good.'

Martin nodded and smiled and then his heart stumbled. Clare was standing at the far end of the hall, looking around. She was not wearing her glasses and she was letting her hair grow. He remembered the softness of her skin. She was exquisite. How could he have let himself lose her?

Polly said something about Rachel. Clare was a stationary figure, peering short-sightedly into the amiable chaos of weekend mothers swirling round her. Martin knew she was looking for him. 'I better go,' he said. 'There's Clare.' And he patted his hair into place.

Polly smiled at him. 'It's all right. It wasn't very interesting anyway.'

'Oh,' he said. 'I'm sorry, Polly.'

'I know,' she said. 'You mustn't keep Clare waiting.' She took pity on him. 'Go on,' she said. 'It's all right. Really.' She kissed him on the cheek again, a dry little peck.

He knew she thought Clare had treated him badly. If only she knew.

'Nice to see you again, Martin,' she said.

'Yes,' he said. 'You too. I'll catch up with you later once I've collected Megan. I do want to hear about Rachel. Really.'

'Go,' she said.

Martin edged his way through the throng. 'I'm sorry I'm late,' he said as he came up to Clare. It was easier than explaining he'd been here but couldn't find her. He knew that would make her think he was lying. Why was it so complicated?

'And?' she said. 'When aren't you?'

She was wearing a soft grey wool jacket he hadn't seen before. 'You look nice,' he said. 'I mean it's a lovely jacket.'

'Nicole Farhi,' she said.

'So Don sent the cheque this month then?' As soon as he spoke, Martin realised he shouldn't have done.

'I'll just get Megan,' Clare said curtly. 'She's been so looking forward to seeing you.' She peered around her. 'Where's she gone now?' she said. 'She was here a moment ago.' She did not seem awkward or embarrassed. Nothing to indicate she might be having second thoughts.

'Martin, Martin.' Suddenly Megan was beside him and pulling at his hand.

He glimpsed Clare smiling at her daughter as he bent down to her. 'Hello, Megan,' he said. 'How are you?'

'Give Martin a kiss,' Clare said. He was so good with her and Megan loved him. Was she being paranoid? Perhaps she should give him one last chance?

'Are you going to look after me this afternoon?' Megan asked Martin.

He could not have loved her more if she had been his own daughter. Why couldn't he convince Clare that he could do his job and look after them?

'I need to go to the gallery now, Martin.' Clare briskly buttoned up her tailored coat. 'I'll be back later.'

That should be fine. He could do the new brief for Clements in the evening. And this afternoon he would show Clare how he could devote himself to Megan.

'Let me know how much she spends,' she said, 'and I'll pay you back.'

'Please, Clare,' he said.

'Don't be ridiculous,' she said, glaring at him. Why did he have to confirm her worst fears about him, controlling everything? 'You're doing enough for us this afternoon. We don't need your money too. OK, I've got to go. Bye-bye, Megan. And Martin, thank you.' And she was gone.

'Come on, Martin.' Megan was tugging his hand. 'Let's go to the cakes.'

Miranda was standing behind a trestle table covered in plates of cupcakes. As Megan lugged him through the crowd, Martin watched Miranda brush the hair out of her face as she poured Coca-Cola into a plastic cup.

'You're working hard,' he said.

'What can I sell you?' she said. 'Everything must go. What do you want?'

'What would you like, Megan?' he asked.

'I was asking you,' Miranda said. 'You were the one brought up never to leave anything.' She smiled at him. She had remembered. And she was smiling. 'You don't know this Viktor, do you?' she said.

'Afraid not. Why?'

'Because he's meant to be here by now. And I have to go and reclaim my son from my ex-husband.'

Megan was tugging at his hand. 'I want to go to the toys now,' she said.

'Can I help out until Viktor turns up?' Martin asked.

'Would you mind?' Miranda said quickly. 'I'm due to get David in fifteen minutes and I really, really, do not want to give Stephen one single thing he can hold against me. You've seen what he's like. Are you sure you don't mind?'

'I'll be fine,' he said. 'Megan, sit here.'

'I want to go to the toys now,' Megan said.

'You are nice,' Miranda said.

'Why can't I go to the toys?' Megan muttered but she sat down obediently on the fold-up chair as Martin gave her a cake. When he turned back, Miranda had gone. He wondered if she was going to return or if he would have to stay on the stall if this Viktor didn't turn up. He wanted to show Clare how he could spend time, quality time, with Megan, and he did not want to waste it selling cakes. This Viktor better turn up.

'Sorry,' he said to Megan. 'You'll have to sit here with me. But you can eat lots of cake. I've got to work.'

'You always say that,' Megan said and the matter-of-fact way she said it made Martin feel sick. What a blunder. Megan was right. He shouldn't have said it. If Clare had heard him, that would have been it. End of all hope of ever getting her back. He hadn't got to work. He'd got to play.

'You're right,' he said to Megan. 'Don't tell Mummy I said that.'

'Toys, toys, toys, toys,' Megan chanted. 'I want to go to the toys.'

And then his first customer arrived: a woman in a blue quilted bodywarmer, harassed by three small boys. As he turned round to pour their Coca-Colas, he heard Megan calling, 'Suzana, Suzana.'

Martin turned back and saw a tall heavy-set man in a battered black leather jacket and jeans arriving at the table beside the woman in the bodywarmer. Waves of black and grey hair swept back off his forehead and his beard was full but carefully barbered and a little girl with fine blonde hair stood meekly holding his hand.

'Martin, Martin, it's Suzana.' Megan had got down from the chair and was jumping up and down. 'Suzana. Suzana.' Then before Martin could stop her she'd dived underneath the table and surfaced beside the little girl in the pink raincoat. 'Hi, Suzana,' Megan said. The man in the leather jacket stared at Martin.

'Where is Jenny?' he said.

Martin couldn't place the accent. German? Somewhere in Central Europe? 'I don't know,' Martin said. 'I'm just helping out here.'

'I must meet Jenny here to look after the cakes.' The man continued to stare at Martin as he spoke.

Martin felt uncomfortably as if he was being held responsible for Jenny's failure to appear. 'Is there anything I can do to help?' he asked.

'Where's Jenny?' the man said again.

'He doesn't know, Viktor.' The quiet voice came from a slight, dark woman who had appeared by the man's side. 'We'll go and look for her.'

'No,' said Martin. 'It's all right. You can take over.

Miranda was expecting you. She had to go and I was just standing in for her.'

'Who is Miranda?'

Martin wasn't sure how to respond to this implacable interrogation. 'Megan,' he called suddenly. 'Get back here.' Megan and Suzana had darted away from the table and disappeared into the crowd.

Viktor wheeled around to look and then bellowed, 'Suzana.' And then they all saw that Suzana had tripped over and, as they watched, a plump woman wearing glasses on a cord turned round. Martin recognised her. She was the mother of one of the boys in Megan's class. Liz. That was her name. Liz hadn't noticed the little child in the pink raincoat on the ground beside her. And she trod on her foot.

Suzana's scream pierced through the hubbub.

'Suzana,' Viktor yelled and ran to her. He grabbed hold of plump, surprised Liz and shook her. 'Stupid,' he shouted. 'Stupid. Stupid.' He looked as if he was about to punch her in the face.

Martin watched as the slight dark woman rushed after Viktor and started pulling him away from Liz. 'Sorry. Sorry,' Liz stammered. 'I am so sorry. I didn't see her there. Please. I am so sorry.'

'Viktor. Viktor,' the slight dark woman was saying in a soft calm voice. 'Viktor. Stop.'

Martin saw him tense and then let go of Liz. There was a shocked silence around them. Viktor knelt down beside Suzana. Parents and children stood and watched. Martin took hold of Megan's hand and they watched as Viktor spoke gently to Suzana in a language Martin did not recognise.

'I'm so sorry,' Liz said. 'Can I do anything?'

'It's OK,' the dark woman said soothingly. 'Please go.' There was quiet authority in her voice and the crowd began to stir again. Within seconds, they had all moved away, leaving Martin, Megan and the slight dark woman standing over Viktor and Suzana.

Viktor moved his hands gently over Suzana's foot, murmuring to her quietly as he did so. As Martin watched, he realised that this total commitment must be what Clare felt he lacked. She must feel that if it had been Megan who had fallen over and got trodden on, he would just pick her up and dust her down and give her a sherbet lemon and get back to his computer. 'We're not something you do in your coffee break,' she had said.

Viktor stood up, holding Suzana's hands, and pulled her up.

'Is she all right?' Martin said.

'Yes,' Viktor said. 'Mila, please look after Suzana. I promised to sell cakes.'

And then Jenny arrived. 'Hello, my darlings,' she said. 'Everything well?'

'Hello, Jenny,' Martin said.

'Hello,' Viktor said.

'Oh good,' Jenny said. 'You two have met. I'm sure you're going to get on. Now, Viktor, if you ever need a trusts lawyer, Martin is your man. He's the best at the Bar.'

'Please, Jenny,' Martin said.

Viktor looked at him quizzically.

'Well if I don't say it, you never will,' Jenny said. 'And you need to say it.'

'Come on, Suzana,' Megan said.

'Oh good,' Jenny said. 'You two girls are playing together. That's good. Martin, you should take Megan over to play with Suzana at home as well.' She smiled, satisfied with her dexterity – getting Martin back with Clare through looking after Megan and getting him work from Viktor. She was incorrigible.

'That's a good idea,' Martin said. It would be another afternoon with Megan. He was going to show Clare. 'What do you think, Viktor?'

'Yes,' he said.

'See,' Jenny said, 'sorted.'

'What about if we come over next Saturday?' Martin said. 'Would you like that, Megan?'

'Good, good,' Jenny said. 'That'll be lovely, won't it, Viktor?'

'OK,' Viktor said. He looked uncomfortable. 'We'll come to you,' he said.

'That will be lovely,' Mila said.

Martin glanced at her and suddenly noticed she had dark green eyes, looking intently at him as she spoke. And then he realised she was beautiful. 'Great,' he said. 'See you then.'

'And now I must give these prizes to the raffle-meister,' Jenny said. And then Clare arrived.

'Jenny told me you were looking after the cake stall, Martin,' she said. 'There's a queue of people and no-one serving them. Hello, Viktor, Mila.'

'Do you know each other?' Martin said.

'Yes, Martin,' Clare said patiently. 'We do. I try to know the parents of Megan's friends.'

'You can sell the cakes now,' Viktor said to Martin. 'I will care for Suzana.'

'What's happened?' Clare said.

'We must go now,' Mila said. And Viktor picked up Suzana and carried her in his arms out of the hall, with Mila walking beside them. And that was how Martin met Viktor and Suzana. And Mila.

eighteen

The Romanian looked out at the dank suburban lawn and tapped her fingers gently on the desk. What did Kalaj want? He was a murderous little bastard and he never did anything without first working out how he was going to make some treacherous profit out of it. In the garden of Kalaj, there was a scorpion under every stone.

Through the window, the Romanian heard distant shouts and laughter of children playing. There was a playground in the little park at the end of the street. Whatever Kalaj was after, it meant trouble. Perhaps this was a signal to move on? This had been a good business, better than anyone could have expected three years ago, but even the brightest sun had to set some time and perhaps, for this operation, that time had come.

The Romanian stood up. It was not prudent to keep Kalaj waiting. What was this summons about? As usual, Boris had not given any clues. 'Mr Kalaj wants to see you for a little talk.' That was all he had said. What did it mean?

She put on her coat. Better get this over. Once she had met him, she could work out what he was doing and then how she could get away from him. After this little talk, she could devise the next move, but now it was time to go. She had other things to do this morning and the longer she delayed seeing Kalaj, the later she was going to be.

nineteen

'You stay here,' Megan said when she heard the door-bell. 'You stay here with me.'

'I need to answer it, Megan,' Martin said to the little girl, busily heaping up leaves for a bonfire. 'You carry on.' Her auburn hair, so like her mother's, caught the light. 'I'll be back in a minute.'

He hurried back into the flat and down the narrow hallway to open the door. And there was Viktor filling the frame, cutting out the day from the gloomy base-ment stairwell while Suzana stood obediently by his side in her pink raincoat, holding his hand.

'Hello, hello,' Martin said. Viktor did not say any-thing but he stretched out his arm and his paw, dark and hairy, enveloped Martin's hand. 'Hello, Suzana,' Martin said. He was going to show Clare how good a parent he could be to Megan. If she wanted to play with Suzana, then play with her she would.

'Hello,' the little girl said.

'Come in, come in,' Martin said. 'Megan is in the garden.' Look, Clare, here I am having Megan's friends round to play. And when I should be working.

The small flat was suddenly full of Viktor. His leather jacket smelt of dank autumnal woods as he brushed past Martin. 'We will be here until two o'clock,' he said.

'Oh,' Martin said. 'OK.' That was longer than he had expected. Late on Friday, Phil Matthews had brought in another brief from Clements, wanting an opinion by Monday morning. That was a weekend's work but he had promised Clare he would see Megan again this Saturday and he had set aside the morning. He had not anticipated Viktor and Suzana wanting to stay so long.

The two men sat on the bench in Martin's forlorn little garden, mugs of coffee steaming in their hands, while Megan and Suzana diligently piled up the leaves. 'She loves that pink raincoat, doesn't she,' Martin said, conversationally. Viktor said nothing.

'Costa Rica, Costa Rica. Her, she and me, and Costa Rica coffee,' Megan chanted. 'Costa Rica, Costa Rica,' Suzana joined in.

'What is that?' Viktor asked, incredulously.

'Some television commercial,' Martin said. 'Silly, isn't it?'

Viktor said nothing and watched the little girls playing.

'So,' Martin said, trying again. 'What do you do?'

'Business,' Viktor said, curtly. Suzana ran and threw some leaves in his lap. Martin clenched, waiting for Viktor to start shouting, 'Stupid, stupid, stupid,' as he had done at the fair. But Viktor just smiled and brushed the leaves off his lap. 'Go play, my darling,' he said. Martin had not seen him smile before and he noticed the creases around his eyes.

'What kind of business?' Martin was determined to get this conversation going. Parents sitting together, watching their children play, chatted. That is what they did and Martin was not going to let Viktor sit in silence. It diminished his parenthood.

'Yes,' Viktor said.

Martin looked at Megan and Suzana playing. Perhaps he worked for one of those billionaire Russians. That would explain why he was so uncommunicative. And the leather jacket.

'They are pretty together,' Viktor said.

'Megan really likes Suzana,' Martin said, moving into the unexpected opening. 'She keeps asking: When's Suzana coming? When's she coming?' Parents chatted while their children played and Martin was going to be the father to Megan that Clare wanted him to be. He looked at his watch. He would just have to work into the night on the Clements brief. He had to show Clare he could do it all.

Martin glanced at Viktor who was staring at the two little girls, uninterested in conversation. With his neatly barbered beard and his hair swept down to his collar, he looked like a boyar surveying his estate as it stretched out endlessly over the steppes to the east. He was hard work but no-one could doubt this taciturn man loved his daughter the way a father should, the way Clare wanted him to love Megan. 'Will your wife be coming later?' Martin tried once more.

'She's not my wife.'

'I'm sorry?'

'My wife is dead.'

'Oh,' Martin said, 'I'm sorry.' Viktor's smile had vanished. Megan and Suzana were chattering cheerfully as they piled up the leaves, Suzana's blonde hair shining against the pink coat in the sullen morning. Martin saw Viktor watching them, his eyes far away. Martin saw him remembering his wife, Suzana's mother.

'How often do you see your daughter?' Viktor said.

'She's not my daughter,' Martin said.

'Oh?'

'I don't have a daughter. Clare was my girlfriend, my partner.' My love.

'Oh,' Viktor said. 'I'm sorry.'

'It's OK,' Martin said. 'We're having a trial separation.' He said it again to himself, in his head, trying out this new, more acceptable interpretation of what had happened. 'A trial separation.' Yes, that is what it was. Just a trial. He looked at his watch. Another hour and a half and he would see Clare again. Perhaps she would ask him in when he dropped off Megan.

'It's important to ensure you don't lose touch,' Martin explained, extemporising. 'In a trial separation.'

Viktor nodded. 'What happened?' he said. His voice was low and gentle and Martin looked at him to check this was the same boyar who had been sitting inscrutably in his garden a moment ago, pondering an underworld hit in Kiev or laundering drug dollars in the Cayman Islands.

'You know,' Martin said. 'The usual stuff.'

Suzana came running up. 'Look, Papa,' she said. 'Look at this.' She opened her hands and there was a glistening slug.

'Aha,' Viktor said. 'A gastropod. And what is the function of a gastropod, my darling?'

Suzana ran off, calling, 'Look, Megan, look.'

'Gastropods are scavengers,' Viktor muttered to himself. 'They eat leaves.'

'She thought I wasn't spending enough time with her,' Martin said. 'And Megan.'

Viktor turned to look at him, with an unexpectedly sympathetic expression in his eyes. 'You think she's wrong, don't you,' he said. 'Clare. About you not spending enough time with her and Megan. Don't you?'

'Why should you think that?' Martin said, irritated by the man's presumption. 'But as it so happens I do think she misunderstood. I spent lots of time with her and Megan.'

'Gastropod, gastropod,' Suzana and Megan were chanting as they danced round the garden. 'Gastropod, gastropod.'

Viktor gave a little shrug, a Balkan sigh. 'OK,' he said.

'Do you want some more coffee?' Martin said, unsettled by Viktor's siding with Clare who he hardly knew.

Viktor shook his head. 'Thank you,' he said. 'No.'

'Are you sure?' Martin said, worried now he had been too brusque. After all, Viktor had meant well. 'I'd be happy to make a fresh pot.'

'Be careful, Suzana,' Viktor called and then there was an awkward silence on the little bench as the girls ran around, chasing each other and shrieking happily.

And then the bell rang. Martin looked at his watch. Twelve thirty. Perhaps his efforts were paying off and it was Clare and she was coming round to talk. And now he could show her how good a father he was being to Megan. Him and Viktor, fathers together. 'Excuse me,' he said.

It was Mila. She stood, pale and slight in a fitted grey coat, with those large smudged green eyes smiling at him, on his doorstep. 'Hello, Martin,' she said. She remembered his name. 'I've come to see Viktor.'

'Of course, of course. Come in.' She slipped past him in the narrow hallway and went into the garden. She seemed to sense where she needed to go.

'Can I get you some coffee?' Martin called after her, but she did not reply.

'Hello, Viktor,' Mila said, sitting down beside him on the bench. Martin watched them from the doorway. They were oblivious of him as Mila put her arm round Viktor's shoulder. Why did they speak English? Her faint accent suggested she might also come from somewhere in Central Europe.

Viktor said something low and soft that Martin could not hear and Mila chuckled, a deep sound from her throat. Sex prickled in the air between them and Martin was jabbed by envy. They were a handsome couple. That could have been him and Clare sitting there, arms around each other.

While Mila snuggled up to Viktor, Martin watched Megan and Suzana chasing each other round the garden, shrieking in delight. And their happy energy began to infect him. Soon he and Clare would be sitting on his bench in a lovers' tableau just like Viktor and Mila. Martin glanced across at them. Mila seemed happy but Viktor looked distracted. At one point, Suzana stumbled and fell over but Viktor did not move. It was not like the St Luke's fair when he had leapt across the room to help her. Now he just called across to her, abstractedly, 'Be careful, my darling.' That was all. It looked to Martin as if Viktor was brooding about something.

twenty

'Vasili's dead.' Kalaj watched the Romanian intently as he spoke to gauge the reaction.

'Who?' she said.

'Shot.' He needed to find out whether the Romanian had anything to do with it.

'I'm sorry,' she said. 'But should I care?' Whatever Kalaj was after, it meant trouble.

'Somewhere outside Vlore,' he said. The Romanian was in a different line of business but Kalaj knew he could not be too careful. He needed to find out what had happened.

'I don't know Vlore. I didn't know Vasili. I'm sorry,' the Romanian said, looking bored. 'What's it got to do with me?'

'That depends,' Kalaj said, 'on what it's got to do with you.'

The Romanian laughed. 'Nothing. Why should it have anything to do with me?'

Kalaj pushed his hair off his face. He did not trust her.

'We'll see,' he said. 'Florian is coming over. He was there. I'll talk to him when he gets here and then we'll see.'

She laughed again. 'Why do you talk like it was something to do with me? I don't know these people. Why should this have anything to do with me?'

Kalaj had a bad feeling about this. He didn't know what was going on and that made him uneasy. Maybe the Romanian was involved. Maybe not. But he knew he had to watch out.

'This is a valuable business,' he said and stared at the Romanian. 'I don't want anyone thinking they can move in on it.'

'This is nothing to do with me. Nothing.'

'Maybe. Maybe not. We'll see when I have talked to Florian.'

'Yes, you'll see.' Maybe she was telling the truth but, if she was, she might become the next target. He could not be too careful.

'You better move the operation somewhere new. Safe. Just in case.'

'Why? This is nothing to do with me. We aren't ready for the next move.'

'Get ready. This may be the start of something. I want to be prepared. I'll get you new papers and get them sent round to you. I don't want you involved. I care about you too much.'

The Romanian laughed again, a throaty, chortling sound. 'Don't worry. The money machine will keep going round and round.'

'I hope so,' Kalaj said, 'I very much hope so.'

'I'll talk to you in a couple of days about whether we really need to move. When you have talked to Florian. You'll see. This is nothing to do with me.' She couldn't work out what Kalaj wanted but she knew it was going to be dangerous for her.

'I hope so,' Kalaj said, 'I very much hope so.' He cracked his knuckles. He didn't trust the Romanian any more now than he had at the beginning of the conversation and he still didn't know what was going on. But perhaps it was nothing to do with the Romanian. Perhaps it had something to do with the women.

twenty-one

'It's unlikely any of these women will want to talk to you.' As she spoke, Helen Borthwick looked away from Charlotte and her long fingers arranged the salt cellar neatly alongside the sugar bowl.

Charlotte noticed Helen Borthwick would not look her in the eye. Perhaps she was embarrassed about refusing to help? Perhaps a little gentle pressure might persuade her to be more helpful. But first Charlotte needed nicotine. She was trying to give up but her talk with Harriet Warren an hour ago had not resolved anything and she needed comfort. 'Do you mind if I smoke?' she said as she felt in her bag for a cigarette.

'I would prefer it if you did not.'

Charlotte took her hand out of the bag. What had she expected, asking a community social worker? 'Matthew is looking for attention,' Harriet had said. 'He needs to learn how to adapt his behaviour.'

'I understand what they must have been through,' Charlotte said to Helen Borthwick. 'But it would be strictly off the record.' She needed to talk to Rob. It was so unfair for Harriet Warren to blame her when it was the teacher's job to teach them. But Rob had been out of the office when she called.

'I doubt whether you do understand,' Helen Borth-wick said. 'These are young women who have been beaten up and raped. And they know that if they escape, their families at home will be punished. Beaten up. Killed. How can you possibly understand? They are terrified every second of every day. It takes me months to get them to say anything to me. Why should they talk to you?'

'Because you would persuade them. And they trust you.'

'And why should I trust you?'

'Look, I know you may not think much of me but this could actually help your clients. I can reveal the truth about what is going on. Get people behind what you are doing. Millions read my paper. Politicians listen to what we say.'

'Your paper?' Helen laughed. It was a dry, humour-less noise. 'Why should you help us? You'll make it a story about asylum seekers sponging off penniless British pensioners.'

'It's not like that.' Charlotte was used to mistrust and she knew how to deal with it. 'The paper has got its policy and I've got mine and I'll make sure this story is done properly. Really.' She told Helen how she had found the body on the beach at Tarifa but she did not explain how she was going to deal with Maggie Fair-weather.

As she spoke, the community social worker looked down at the chipped Formica table. The café was full and noisy and smelt of frying oil and the rain drizzled on the High Street outside. And now Charlotte recog-

nised Helen's expression. She had last seen it on
Maggie's face at the Wednesday conference.

'I'm sorry,' Helen said. 'It must have been terrible
for you.' She emphasised the pronoun. Charlotte was
not quite sure whether she was being sarcastic.

'It was worse for him.' Charlotte took no chances. 'I
want to tell the stories of victims and expose the
traffickers. People don't know what's going on. Right
here. And they should. It's slavery. In the twenty-first
century.' She was going to nail this story and then she
would decide what to do about the job and Matthew.
But she needed to get the story done first.

'If you really want to help,' Helen Borthwick said,
'why don't you write a story about the men who use
these women? The quickest way of stopping these
crimes is to criminalise the men who purchase sex.
That should shrink the market.'

'I'm not sure my editor would go for that,' Charlotte
said cautiously.

'Lose too many of your readers?' Helen said and
then she laughed, a short bark, and looked at Charlotte.
'I'm sorry,' she said, 'I'm sure you're just doing your
job. It's just that it looks different from this side of the
table.'

'All I want to do is to talk to them,' Charlotte said,
looking earnestly into Helen's eyes. 'You could be
there all the time. I just want to hear what they have
to say.'

'Who?' Helen Borthwick said. 'Who do you want to
talk to?'

'These women,' Charlotte said.

'Yes, but which women? Do you want to talk to the eleven-year-olds who have been kidnapped and sold to men who pay a lot of money for a young virgin? Or the nineteen-year-olds who thought they were coming to work as waitresses and found that waiting on tables means something different here than it does at home? Or the thirty-year-olds who thought they would come to clean offices and send the money back to their family but found they owed so much to the men who smuggled them here they had to prostitute themselves to pay it back. There's a market for every sort of woman. There's always a man who will pay for a woman, any woman. So which woman did you want to talk to? They're all beaten up and terrified. Which one do you want to speak to?'

'Anyone you suggest,' Charlotte said humbly. Helen Borthwick made her feel embarrassed, just as she had been by her response to the drowned man on the beach at Tarifa.

'And what do you think will happen to them if anyone finds out they've been talking to you?'

Charlotte waited to be told.

'Guess,' Helen Borthwick said. 'Do you know how many I can persuade to get out?'

Charlotte shook her head.

'One in the last nine months. One. They know what will happen to them if they get caught.'

Charlotte said nothing.

'And even if they get away,' Helen said, 'they know their relatives won't. That's often the worst for them. Knowing their families back home are hostages.' She looked at Charlotte and then sighed. 'Alright,' she said. 'I'll ask them and I'll ring you if any of them agree.'

Charlotte knew Helen Borthwick would never call her. But there must be something she could get out of this. She felt that hollow feeling again, looking through a telescope from a safe distance at other people living lives of trouble and pain, the dehumanising isolation of the voyeur. But this was what journalists did. This was her job.

'OK,' she said. 'Forget traffickers. What about people-smugglers? Do you know anyone brought in to pick strawberries or wash dishes? Paying their life-savings to a smuggler? How's it working out? You know the sort of thing. Anyone killed or injured through illegal health and safety practices? The shattered dream. Anything like that?'

Helen stared at her.

'Do you know anyone?' Charlotte asked. This was her job. And she liked it less and less.

'Be careful,' Helen Borthwick said. 'These are dangerous men.'

twenty-two

Women were vulnerable. And expensive. They required constant vigilance and discipline and that meant money, continuing investment in men to watch them and punish them and fend off predators offering an easier life. They earned well before they wore out but the high maintenance costs made the business precarious. Kalaj could not afford any disruptions and he would have to act now if someone was moving in on the women.

'So who shot this Vasili, Boris?' Kalaj said. 'We haven't found him yet. So who was it?' Boris stood by the desk, waiting to be told what to do. 'Well?' Kalaj said. He obviously expected an answer.

'I don't know, Mr Kalaj,' Boris said. How was he expected to know?

'Any guesses?'

'No, I'm sorry, Mr Kalaj.' The boss sounded as if he expected Boris to know the answer and it made him nervous. That wasn't his job. Kalaj was tapping his fingers lightly on the table and looking out of the window.

'It must be something to do with the women. I've tried everything else. Go round all the houses,' Kalaj said. 'Find out if there's been any trouble. Anyone complaining, any sign of anyone planning to leave.'

'Yes, Mr Kalaj,' Boris said. This was more like it. 'What do you want me to do if I find anything? Re-educate them? Get someone to look up their relatives back home?'

'Just tell me what you find,' Kalaj said. 'For now.' And they both laughed into the pause.

'And one other thing,' Kalaj said. 'Find out if anyone has been talking to the women. I don't want them getting wrong ideas.'

'Sure, Mr Kalaj.'

The boss stood up and patted him on the shoulder. 'Good, Boris,' he said. 'We don't want anything to interfere with the women.'

twenty-three

Mila sat on the park bench and watched Suzana playing on the carousel. What did they call it here? Roundabout. That was it. A roundabout. And round and around Suzana went on it in the overcast afternoon as the drizzle settled in a film on the pink raincoat.

'Look, Mila,' Suzana called. 'Mila, Mila, look.' She sounded English now. It was a miracle how quickly children adapted. No-one would guess this small child playing on her own in this damp municipal park in North London had spent almost all her life in a small Balkan town on the banks of the River Vrbas.

'I am looking,' she called. Suzana was an enchanting child and Mila took her out whenever she could. It made her feel that she was normal. When she was with Suzana, she could forget what she had to do every day and she could pretend that her life had turned out as she had always thought it would when she was a girl. With a man she loved and their child. Humdrum, normal, wonderful.

A small dog came sniffing round the bench followed by an old lady who bent down to fix a lead on to the dog's collar. 'Sit,' she said, patting it affectionately on the head.

'He's so naughty,' she said to Mila. 'He won't ever stay still.'

Mila smiled at her.

'Your daughter is lovely,' the old lady said. 'I was watching her playing. Enjoy it while it lasts.'

'Yes,' Mila said.

'Sit,' the old lady pleaded with her dog. 'They grow up so quickly. They're gone before you know it,' she said to Mila. 'Believe me.'

'Yes,' Mila said.

'What's her name?'

'Suzana.'

'Lovely.'

Mila could see the old lady settling in for a chat. 'Come on, Suzana,' she called. 'I'm sorry,' she said to the old lady, 'we have to go now.'

Suzana went on spinning round on the carousel. 'Suzana,' Mila called. 'Come now.'

Why did it have to be like this? Why couldn't she just chat with the old lady? Why couldn't she just be honest with Viktor? And go somewhere else with him and Suzana and get right away from all this? But how could she?

'She's lovely,' the old lady said.

'Yes,' Mila said. This was not her life but could it be? Too much had happened that she could never have expected and never have wanted. Her life had never been meant to be like this but could she go back now and start again? And if she could start again, what would it be like if she and Viktor lived together? They knew so little about each other, meeting by chance in this damp, grey country.

'Mila, Mila.' Suzana jumped off the carousel and ran over to her.

'Mila?' the old lady said. 'Is that your name? It's lovely. Is it English?'

'Say hello to this nice lady, Suzana,' Mila said.

'Hello, Suzana,' the old lady said and beamed at her. 'That's a lovely name.'

Was this really impossible? Why couldn't it be like this all the time? Chatting to old ladies in the park while Suzana frolicked in the rain? What really was stopping her changing her life?

twenty-four

'Are you unhappy?'

The woman sat in the chair, with her knees pressed together, looking at the floor, and said nothing.

'Well?' Kalaj paced up and down, staring at the slight pretty woman in the chair. 'Why would you want to leave us? That's what I don't understand. Do you, Boris?' He stopped and stroked his chin. He found the smoothness comforting. He had once grown a beard but it had taken three months to get to a reasonable thickness and then he hadn't liked it so he had shaved it off again.

The burly man leaning against the wall in the corner of the room laughed. 'No, Mr Kalaj.'

'So what am I going to do with you? How can I understand why you want to leave my employment?' Kalaj stopped in front of the woman and put his hand under her chin and gently tilted it up so she had to look at him. 'Eh?' he said. 'Can you help me understand?'

'No, Mr Kalaj,' she said. Her eyes did not look away from his. He could see her trying to make them dead but she could not hide the loathing.

'Are you getting bored?' he said.

'What do you think?' she hissed.

In the corner, Boris laughed. 'She's a cat,' he said.

Kalaj turned to look at him. 'Enough,' he said.

'Sorry, Mr Kalaj.'

Still looking at Boris, Kalaj put his hand on top of the woman's head and slowly tapped his fingers up and down. Once. Twice. He knew something was going on here and he wanted to know what it was. First Vasili and now this. It was too much of a coincidence. 'How much did they pay you?' he said. He stepped in front of her and bent his head down so it was close to her.

'You should know that,' the woman said.

'I didn't mean that,' he said. She sounded too bitter to have understood what he meant. 'What did they pay you to leave me?'

'Why do you think I needed to be paid to leave you?' She was smart and that made it more difficult to decide whether she was telling the truth.

'I know what's going on,' he said. 'It'll be better for you if you tell me yourself.'

She stared at him, her large eyes brimming with hatred.

'Do you know what happened to Vasili?' he said.

'Why should I?' she said. 'I don't know who Vasili is.'

He could see nothing in her eyes except contempt. Perhaps she was telling the truth. But then again it seemed too much of a coincidence. Kalaj came to a decision.

'I am afraid I have to leave you now,' he said. 'I've got work to do but Boris will look after you.'

As Kalaj reached the door his eyes met Boris's and he nodded, almost imperceptibly.

twenty-five

'What have you been doing?' The old man did not look up from the newspaper as he spoke. 'Anything interesting?'

Martin placed the cup of tea carefully on the table beside his father. 'Not really,' he said. 'The usual.' He knew what his father meant. Had he been doing the sort of cases that would get him made a judge. 'How have you been?' Martin said.

'The usual.' His father put down the paper and sipped his tea. 'Thank you, Martin,' he said. His face had shrunk in the last year. The eyes were pebbles and his lips had retreated into a thin line. 'Are there still any of those Rich Tea biscuits?' Every day, his father dressed himself in a heavy grey suit and sat in his chair and read the *Daily Mail* and listened to Radio 4 and read the law reports and longed for the day his clever son would be made a judge.

'I'll go and see,' Martin said as he went into the kitchen. 'How many do you want?' he called.

'I think I'll have three today,' the old man said. When Martin's father had left school, getting an office job had been a respectable achievement, especially if you didn't want to go on the tools like Martin's grandfather.

For thirty years his father had been the departmental administrator for the team of company lawyers, ensuring secretaries were prompt and tidy and stationery never ran out. But he had always wanted more for his only son, who had, so surprisingly and wonderfully, turned out clever.

'There's only two left,' Martin said. 'Do you want me to go out and get some?' Ever since he could remember, Martin had known that his father wanted him to become a lawyer, a member of that select tribe for whom he had worked so long. And, as Martin sailed through exam after exam, his father's ambition took wings. His son would become not a company lawyer, like those for whom he had given his working life, but one who strode steadily upwards to the summit of the profession. Martin's father dreamed of his son becoming a judge.

'That will be sufficient,' his father said. 'Perhaps you could bring some more next Saturday?'

Martin had always known that, for his doting father, every exam he passed and every prize he won was another step towards that shining destination of the Bench. And every time he visited his father he felt the pressure of his expectations crushing him. The meaning of the old man's life was anchored in his son.

'Did you see Tom's judgement on Donovan last week?'

Martin shook his head. As far as he knew, his father had never even met a judge but the easy use of the first name reassured him that he was still part of this world which he shared with his brilliant son.

'You should look at it,' his father said. 'Tom's always taken an adventurous view of the application of cyprès.'

Martin's father was a good man. Every Sunday he laid roses on the grave of the wife to whom he had been happily married for thirty-three years. Never, as child or man, had Martin heard them raise their voice to each other. Good job, happy marriage, successful son, what more could anyone reasonably hope for from their time on earth?

'Here you are,' Martin said, as he carried the biscuits, set out, side by side, on the Royal Worcester plate, back to his father.

'Thank you, Martin.' His father took a neat, dry bite at the biscuit. A powdery white crumb was left at the corner of his mouth. The old man's tongue emerged, delicate and reptilian, and precisely ferried it back into his mouth.

'How is Clare?' his father said.

'Fine,' Martin said. How could he explain without worrying his father that he was getting distracted from his work? Martin knew his father worried about him. His mother had said so, shortly before she died, when she must have known she was dying.

'Martin,' she said as they stood in the kitchen and he dried the dishes as she washed them. 'Don't worry about your father.'

He stopped drying the plate and looked at her. 'No,' he said, 'I won't. Why should I?'

'If he worries about you, it's only because he loves you.'

'I didn't know he was worried about me.'

'He's not really. Forget I said anything.'

'Why should he worry about me?'

'It's just him, darling. Forget it.'

'What is it?'

'There's no need to raise your voice, darling. It's just that sometimes he worries about your commitment to your work. He feels your heart may not be in it.'

'What? Doesn't he know how hard I work?' But Martin knew his father still fretted about Clare distracting him. While Clare worried about his commitment to her.

'When are you going to marry that poor woman?' his father said. Martin knew what he meant. If you are not going to settle down with her, find someone else you can marry, stop the searching and focus on your career.

'I'll wash up,' Martin said. Clare thought he worked too hard and his father thought she was a distraction from his career. How could he win?

'Sorry,' he called as he slammed the cutlery drawer shut harder than he had intended. 'I'll see you next week,' he said, returning from the kitchen. He bent over his father where he sat in the chair and kissed his parchment brow.

twenty-six

Viktor looked at his watch. Where was she? Mila was never late. Behind the curtain, he heard his daughter gently snoring.

He had put the curtain up himself, partitioning the room to provide privacy for Suzana. For this, and for the hotplate and kettle and the shared bathroom on the floor below, the landlord charged him eighty pounds a week. And that morose man, with grey hair straggling over his collar, waddled and wheezed his way up the stairs every Sunday evening to collect it. Nearly half of what Viktor was able to scrape together each week. And then he had to put up his own curtain. But the fat man never asked questions or wanted to see any papers, all he wanted was cash, in advance, every Sunday night. And the curtain gave Suzana her own space. And on the nights Mila came over it meant they could lie together on the sofa-bed and silently, urgently, be together.

He gently pulled the curtain aside and watched Suzana, sleeping, curled up with her tiny hand under the pillow. She was not sucking her thumb tonight. Awake she looked nothing like Jelena but sometimes when she was asleep, he glimpsed his wife.

Once on a Saturday afternoon, walking the streets aimlessly with Suzana, to keep out of their room, they had come upon a street market where one of the stalls was piled high with mushrooms and it reminded him of how he used to forage in the misty woods above Banja Luka on autumn mornings. He remembered bringing the mushrooms home to the flat and washing the earth off them and chopping them and sautéeing them in butter before folding them into light, creamy omelettes and serving breakfast to his family. And then he had hurried Suzana past the stall before she noticed the tears welling up in his eyes.

Now he bent down and stroked a wisp of hair away from her mouth. If Mila did not get back soon, they would have no time together before he had to leave for work. Three days a week he cleaned offices in the City of London between midnight and six o'clock in the morning, the only time these buzzing hives of capitalism were empty. Six pounds an hour, less two for the Croat who got him the job. It was a hefty commission but Viktor knew he was lucky to get a job where no papers were required and he could get back in time to give Suzana breakfast and take her to school.

The one problem with the job was that he had to leave Suzana alone in the middle of the night but it was only for a few hours and she was safe enough and he had explained to her where he went so she should not worry if she woke up.

Where was Mila? It was now half past nine and she was always so punctual. Where was she? He realised he was walking up and down the little room in his agitation. When Jelena had died, he had thought he could never love anyone again but then he found Mila and sometimes, waiting for the bus or cooking breakfast, he found himself thinking of her calm green eyes. What would he do if she left? This was not like her. What would he do if anything happened to her? How long should he leave it before he went out to look for her? But where would he look?

At home, he would have known what to do. There he had spent a lot of time searching for people who disappeared. The Bosniak landlord who refused to sell out to a Serb property developer and the Croat priest who had given the wrong sermon and one of the caretakers at the mosque who had seen something he should not have seen. Every few days, there had been another anxious family waiting outside his office door when he arrived in the morning. In Banja Luka, he knew who to call and how to talk to them. But here it was different. What would he do if she did not come?

Viktor paced around the room. Perhaps she had not noticed how late it was? But that was not like Mila. Was the bus late? What could have happened to her?

He knew very little about her life here. She said that she came from Bucharest three years ago where she worked in computers. He never asked her anything more about herself. What good would it do to know? Why should he embarrass her? She told him only what she wanted to tell him and he recognised the evasions. Avoiding personal details was routine for the illegal immigrant and he assumed she was illegal. He had met her in the Clarendon and almost everyone who drank there was illegal. Viktor was always surprised the police never came round as they would have got a rich haul. He assumed Goran must be paying someone.

He had noticed Mila immediately he walked in. She was the only woman in the bar, talking earnestly, near the door, to Felix, an Ivoirian computer engineer. She looked up as he came in and something happened. A flick of interest in her eyes and then she turned her gaze back to Felix. Viktor felt it. Perhaps it was because she was the only woman there but for the first time for a long time, desire stirred, living flesh beneath the scar tissue.

Married to Jelena, he had felt it all the time, whenever he glimpsed the swish of a skirt, or a slender neck inclined over a newspaper in a café, or laughing eyes on a bus, or slim fingers feeling material in a shop. Then he had lived in a stew of casual desire but then he had never done anything about it because he was a married man. And when Jelena died, desire died with her. After that, Viktor could only ever see the skull beneath the skin.

But, walking into the Clarendon, that wet spring afternoon, suddenly, unexpectedly, the hormones began to jangle in his blood again. And he went over to talk to Felix. And talk to Mila. And bought her a drink. And another. And took her to school to collect Suzana. And walking in the park on Saturday. And then home to his room three nights a week. And over and over again he thought about the mysteries of love and luck. Women never went to the Clarendon. Mila only ever went once. And how likely was it that he would turn up in just the twenty minutes she was there? But he did. And he met her. And oh how he loved her.

Over the months, they had settled into a rhythm. The nights in his room would be for them alone and on the weekends, they would play in the park with Suzana, Mila's green eyes dancing as she pushed the little girl on the swings and ran, holding her hand, chasing the ducks. But all this time, Viktor never asked her about herself. He did not want to enter the queasy territory of the past and talk about Jelena or explain how he came to London. And he did not want to open the door for her to ask about these things by enquiring into her own background. She would tell him if she wanted. And he did not need to know. He just wanted to be with her, holding her hand in the street, watching her playing with Suzana in the park, lying with her in his narrow, sagging bed.

But was it her past that had caught up with her now? Did she owe money to a gang who were demanding payment? Viktor had never been involved with smugglers or money-lenders but he had lived long enough in this world to know the consequences for those who crossed them. That could not have happened to Mila, could it? It did not seem likely as she was always so careful about everything. But was that why she was so late? It was quarter to ten. Where was she? How could he find out?

He thought of ringing Miroslav who knew everyone but Viktor worried about sharing anything with Miroslav. You could never be sure when he would use it against you. Viktor stopped pacing for a moment. Was that fair? After all, Miroslav had given him a job in his rackety language school, teaching English to the poorer Arabs and Venezuelan girls who if they ever wondered why they were being taught English in London by someone from the former Yugoslavia would justify it to themselves by the extraordinarily cheap fees that Miroslav charged. And he was able to do that because he paid Viktor so little. And he got away with that because Viktor had no papers. But he was easy-going enough and he allowed Viktor to turn up after he had dropped Suzana off at school and leave in time to collect her again. The arrangement suited them both.

But sometimes there were men in black suits and loud ties in Miroslav's office, arguing in Russian and Albanian and Viktor decided he did not want to risk getting Mila tangled up in whatever went on, in Russian and Albanian, in the back office of the Balmoral School of English. He could not ask Miroslav for help.

Where was Mila? It was now ten o'clock. Something must have happened. What should he do now? What about that lawyer he had met at Suzana's school? They had been to his flat, that expensively decorated flat. He was obviously doing well and he seemed like a nice man who would know his way around. Viktor felt his chest tighten. Something was wrong. He could feel it. If he was going to do anything before he went to work, he would have to get moving now. But he did not want to leave Suzana alone for so long.

He bent down and whispered in Suzana's ear. 'Wake up, my darling. Wake up. We have to go somewhere.'

twenty-seven

Pounding, pounding, pounding, Charlotte was on the treadmill, John Hiatt rocking through the iPod, 'Slow Turning,' on and on, five miles down, three to go, pounding on, the track springing beneath her feet.

What was she going to do? The story was going nowhere that would prevent Maggie knotting the noose. And it was not making her feel any better about what she did for a living. She had knelt on the sand by that drowned young man and watched the waves from Africa swirl around his swollen body and Maggie saw it as just another story that did not make the cut.

John Hiatt was hitting it and Charlotte was still pounding on. The gym was now empty, apart from a blonde woman with cellulite, doing weights on the other side of the room. She should go home. It was a long time to leave Rob alone with Matthew. But she needed to run until she was so exhausted that she no longer cared about today. Her conversation with Helen Borthwick still made her blush. She had only been doing her job but she hated how Helen Borthwick had been unable to hide her contempt. For Helen there were jobs worth doing and jobs that weren't. And Charlotte was not even doing her worthless job well.

Usually John Hiatt made her feel better. Those old rockers knew how to turn it out. Keeping on keeping on and, until recently, she had thought that was her. An old rocker who could always find a way to make a story work. But what if she couldn't do it any more? What if she had lost it? Then what would she and Rob do? They could sell the house, trade down and cut back on the eleven thousand a year for a start. And then what? They still couldn't live on what Rob brought in.

The prostitutes hadn't worked out but there were still the other leads from lunch with that little minister who reminded her of William. But there was no guarantee they would produce anything. She couldn't bear to think of her brother's patronising sympathy if she chucked it in. Or, even worse, if she was sacked. She wouldn't be able to stomach his offers to introduce her to contacts who might be able to open up something in PR for her.

Why had it seemed different in Tarifa? That forlorn corpse sprawled on the sand with the gulls screeching overhead while, in the pastel hotels, surfers yawned and stretched and swigged avocado smoothies for breakfast and down the road on the Costa del Sol a million sun-starved tourists from the grey cities of northern Europe slept off hangovers. The faces of globalisation. In Tarifa, it had seemed like a real story.

She picked up the towel from the handlebars, still running, and wiped the sweat from her brow. Three miles to go. Even in Tarifa the doubts had started to creep in. The policeman had politely written down her account of what she had discovered, as she stumbled through it in her GCSE Spanish, and then he said in English that there were so many of these people every year that he wondered why they had not learned to stop coming. He obviously thought it was a stale story as well.

The door into the gym opened but Charlotte did not notice. She took a swig from the water bottle and kept running. Two miles to go. A slight man with red curly hair, holding the hand of a small boy, stood watching her.

Charlotte kept running. Just over a mile and a half to go. She felt the perspiration coating her skin in a fine film.

Rob loved watching her like this. He loved her lithe determination. Matthew tugged at his hand and Rob bent down and whispered in his ear. 'Just another minute,' he breathed. 'And then we'll give Mummy her surprise.'

The music shuffled again and now it was the Queen of Soul belting through the iPod. 'Respect' Aretha Franklin sang. Charlotte ran to the beat. She had to keep going. Perhaps she should look at this as a test. If she could make this story work, it would show her instincts were still good and she was still a journalist and she would stay her execution by Maggie and keep going. But if Maggie turned out to be right about the story, then it would be a sign that she had come to the end of this part of her life. She should leave, whatever Maggie did, and they should down-shift, as the Living Section would put it. Charlotte thought she could probably learn to live with William's pity.

And as Charlotte ran, down-shifting did not seem too bad an option. Those final two days in Tarifa had been good. Rob taught her to windsurf, the weather had been perfect and when she looked in the mirror on their last night she saw the sun had given her an attractive dusting of freckles. And then they had a whole bream baked in salt and a bottle of Albarino and great last night of the holiday sex. Why didn't they just go away somewhere and live like that all the time? Her and Rob and Matthew. She didn't need to do this. Why didn't they just go away?

A mile to go. Charlotte mopped her brow again as she pounded away on the treadmill, feeling better now. The familiar cocktail of exhaustion and satisfaction that came at the end of a run was soothing her. 'R-E-S-P-E-C-T.' She had always hated giving up and now as she came to the end of the final mile, her mood began to swing back. Why did she have to choose? Choose or lose. That was the sort of thing William would say to her. Conceive, achieve. Prat, twat. Why couldn't she do it all?

Rob and Matthew had been second-best too long and she knew she had to commit more to them but that didn't mean she had to leave the paper. She noticed that every time she thought about giving up her job, some reason swam up and told her why she shouldn't. Money, self-respect, cowardice, laziness, William. There was always something that made her baulk at leaving and overwhelmed the guilt and doubts. This is what she did. This is who she was and she would find a way to get through all the problems.

That was it. Eight miles. Time to go home. She turned off the treadmill and stood on it, still, staring vacantly ahead, while the sweat trickled down her cheeks. There had to be some way to make this story work.

'Hello, Mummy.' Charlotte turned and looked across the room as the little voice cut through the iPod and she saw Rob and Matthew watching her and she smiled and then she ran across the room. 'Oh my darling,' she said and took Matthew into her arms and kissed his downy cheek. Suddenly the decision had complicated itself all over again.

twenty-eight

The banging on the door started again. Martin rolled over and searched for the alarm clock on the bedside table. Eleven o'clock. Who could it be at this time of night? Clare? Martin sat up. Perhaps she had finally realised how much she needed him. The banging stopped and Martin settled back down in the bed. It must have been a minicab for one of the other flats. They were always ringing the wrong bell. Then it started again. Bang, bang, bang. And someone was calling his name. 'Martin.' Bang, bang, bang. 'Martin Hughes.'

He stumbled out of bed and pulled on his dressing gown. Clare had always teased him about his dressing gown when she stayed at the flat. 'I'm coming,' he called as the banging seemed to be getting louder. 'Who is it?'

'Viktor.' The voice growled through the door.

Suzana's father. The businessman in the leather jacket. What did he want at this time of night? And then it hit him. He really did work for the Russian Mafia and he was in trouble. Martin hesitated and then squinted through the spyhole. There stood Viktor and in his arms, in her pink raincoat, was Suzana. Martin opened the door. 'What's happened?' he said. 'Is she OK?' And then he felt foolish as she obviously wasn't.

'She's asleep,' Viktor said and stepped into the flat, trailing those scents of dark autumn woods as he brushed past. 'Where can she lie down?' The man was as relentless as the ocean.

'In here,' Martin said. 'You can put her on the sofa.' He watched from the doorway as Viktor laid Suzana gently down, his large hands delicately removing the pink raincoat and placing it over her as she slept.

'Can I get you something to drink?' Martin said. What could this man want?

'She has not come back,' Viktor said. 'You must help.'

'Who? Mila?' Martin guessed.

'She has not come back,' Viktor said. 'You must help.'

'But what can I do?' Martin said.

'You're a lawyer. You can help.' Viktor did not look at Martin as he spoke. On the sofa, the little girl stirred in her sleep under the pink raincoat.

'But how can I help?' Martin said. 'What's happened?'

'She went to see friends. She said she'd be back by nine o'clock. There's more than one bus in two hours, even in London. Something's wrong.'

Martin stared at the large man clenching his hands together as he sat beside the little girl on the sofa. He wondered if he had misunderstood something. Why was Viktor so agitated when Mila was only two hours late? And anyway what could he do about it? 'Have you rung the police?' he said. 'What did they say?'

'The police?' Viktor snorted. 'I haven't rung the police. How can I ring the police?'

'It doesn't have to be an emergency,' Martin explained. 'Like someone being murdered. That's a 999 call. You can also ring them if you're worried someone is missing. It's a different number but I'm sure we can find it. I've got a directory somewhere here.' He had been looking at the Yellow Pages just the other day to find a present for Megan's birthday. Where had he put it?

'I can't ring the police. You must help.'

Viktor's tone made Martin look round. 'But the police can help you,' he said.

Viktor sighed. 'Sit down,' he said. 'Martin, please. I'll explain. I can't go to the police. I came here without permission. They'll send me and Suzana back to Bosnia.'

'But I thought you said you were a businessman.'

'I didn't say I was a businessman. You asked what I did and I said "business". That's true. I'm in the business of cleaning offices and teaching English. I came here without permission. They will send me back. I cannot go back. I cannot go to the police. You must help. You must tell the police.'

Martin saw Viktor watching him intently. He was not an international businessman and he was not running a London office for the Russian Mafia. He was an illegal immigrant. 'I am sure they won't send you back,' he said. 'This is a missing person we're talking about. They'll be concerned about that, not your immigration status.'

'Martin,' Viktor said, his dark eyes burning, 'I can't go back to Bosnia. I can't go to the police.'

Martin felt the pressure surging towards him. 'It's not like that in this country,' he said. 'The police aren't like that.'

'It's like that everywhere. They're the same everywhere. I can't go back to Bosnia.'

Martin had liked Viktor as an international businessman, and a good father and as providing a way to win Clare back, but now, in this new role of illegal immigrant, he was alarming.

'You must help me,' Viktor said and Martin knew Viktor was appealing to his better nature.

This was a nightmare. There was paragraph 301 of the Bar Code of Conduct prohibiting conduct prejudicial to the administration of justice. And there was Section C of the Application Form for Queen's Counsel requiring him to demonstrate conduct, in his personal as well as his professional life, that would maintain public confidence in the award of Queen's Counsel. And then there was helping an illegal immigrant and condoning breaches of immigration law which directly contradicted these requirements. In fact, however he looked at it, helping Viktor was incompatible with paragraph 301 and Section C, and, legally speaking, he was stuffed.

'You really don't need me,' Martin said. 'If you report a missing person they'll ask you questions about that,' he said, hopefully. 'Not about your immigration status. It's not a police state.'

Viktor snorted again. 'How do you know?' he said. 'You're English. You must help. You must go to them. You're a lawyer.'

'But I'm not that kind of lawyer.' How could he explain to this man who didn't want to listen? 'I'm a chancery barrister. I do trusts and wills, that sort of thing. Not this.'

It was as if he had been strolling home down a country lane in June, high hedgerows casting shadows in the late afternoon, and, back at the rectory, Clare was laying out tea, as crickets chirped in the golden fields and in the distance church bells pealed, and then he walked round a bend in the road suddenly to find himself on a bleak moor in a moonless January night, unable to see a foot in front of him, lost. Suddenly, everything was different.

'You are a lawyer. You are English. You can help,' Viktor said. 'But if you don't want to help, I understand. A woman is missing. In danger. You can help. But if you don't want to help, OK.'

Martin knew he was being squeezed and he didn't know what to do. He liked Viktor who was obviously wound up but it was nearly midnight and he was contravening paragraph 301. And Section C. What was he expected to do?

'Of course I'd help if she really was in danger,' he said. 'But you don't know that. Don't you think you should wait till morning? She might have just missed the bus and couldn't find a phone box to tell you.' Viktor got up, ignoring Martin, and adjusted the raincoat over Suzana. 'There's probably an explanation for this,' Martin said. 'I'm sure she's OK.'

'You?' Viktor said, sitting down again. 'How can you be sure? I'm not sure. I'm not sure at all. How can you be sure?'

'What do you suggest I do?' Martin said uncomfortably. 'In the middle of the night?'

The pink raincoat slipped back down on to the floor and Viktor picked it up and carefully rearranged it over Suzana. 'Go to the police,' he said.

'Me?' Martin said.

'You are English,' Viktor said. 'It's no problem for you.' And Martin saw that was true. Compared to the problems an illegal immigrant would face, it would be easy enough for Martin to do.

'Of course, you can choose not to help. You always have a choice,' Viktor said.

That was what Clare had said. And now Viktor too was suggesting that Martin was the type of person who ran away from a commitment that any decent human being would make without thinking.

'I know I've got a choice,' he said, irritably, feeling trapped, uneasily aware that both Viktor and Clare were demanding that he choose between his career and them. Why did they both think that he should be the one to make the sacrifices? What should he do now? Would it really make much difference if he contacted the police for Viktor?

'Please, Martin,' Viktor said, apparently sensing from his hesitation that he might be softening. 'It'll only take a few minutes.'

Martin sighed. This was not really a commitment. More a courtesy. 'All right,' he said heavily. 'I'll ring them and report it but that will be that and you'll have to go then.' It would only be a phone call and then he could go back to bed. Mila was bound to turn up in the morning and then he could deal with paragraph 301 and Section C by finding new friends for Megan and avoiding Viktor. 'What's her full name?' he said.

'Mila Hubchev,' Viktor said and as Martin wrote it down, he remembered how she looked at the St Luke's fair. 'Like that?' he asked. Viktor grunted. And as Martin filled the page of his pad with the answers to his questions about Mila, he felt her dark green eyes, with the smudged shadows underneath, calmly watching him.

'OK,' Martin said when he had finished, 'I'll call them now.' The number in the book rang and rang but no-one answered. Viktor sat in the chair, pressing the tips of his fingers together, watching his reluctant host holding on.

'There's no-one there,' Martin said eventually. 'It's late. Why don't you go home and see if she gets the first bus in the morning. It's only six hours to wait.'

'No. You must tell the police now. They must start looking now.'

'Look, Viktor, I know you're anxious but the police aren't going to do anything tonight. They're bound to wait at least twenty-four hours before they start looking. They'll want to wait to see if she turns up. There really are all sorts of possible reasons why she hasn't got home yet. I'm sure everything's all right.'

'I'm not sure. Please keep on the phone. They must answer.'

Then Martin was inspired. 'But how do you know,' he said, 'that she hasn't got home while you've been here looking for her?'

Viktor looked at him for a moment before replying. 'Because Mila is not like that,' he said. 'Mila is never late. There is a problem. I know it.'

'They're not going to answer,' Martin said. He was never going to get back to bed at this rate. But how could he throw Viktor and Suzana out? The man was clearly in a wretched state. And, one way or another, he had to put an end to this. Martin sighed. There appeared to be no alternative. 'We'd better go to the station,' he said. 'Come on, I'll drive us. But first let's check she hasn't got back.' She was bound to be back by now.

But he had only to wait three minutes with Suzana outside Viktor's flat before Viktor came back to the car. 'No,' he said, 'she's not here.'

And then, when Viktor rang the bell at Mila's house, no-one answered. So he rang it again and eventually an old man called through the closed door. 'Go away,' he said. 'Or we'll call the police.'

'I should have remembered,' Viktor said when he went back to the car. 'Mila said they never let anyone in after eleven. She can't be here. I told you something bad has happened.' He tugged down his seatbelt and clicked it into place. 'You must go to the police. I told you.'

In the police station, the policeman at reception sat behind a thick glass barrier and his head was bent over a computer screen. He did not look up as Martin came through the heavy swing doors, followed by Viktor and Suzana, into the room sterilised by fluorescent light.

'Why don't you sit there,' Martin said, indicating a row of plastic seats to Viktor. Suzana clung on to Viktor's hand, eyes bleary with sleep.

'Can I help you, sir?' the policeman said, his eyes still fixed on his computer screen, as Martin approached the glass barrier.

'I'd like to report a missing person,' Martin said.

The policeman looked up as he heard Martin speak. 'Of course, sir,' he said. 'Take a seat.'

'It's urgent,' Martin said. 'We think something may have happened to her.' And I want to go back to bed.

'I understand, sir,' the policeman said. 'If you take a seat someone will be with you shortly.'

Suzana was asleep in Viktor's arms. He stared ahead, unmoving, silent, as Martin sat down beside him. A car passed outside. The fluorescent light buzzed overhead. They were alone in the waiting area. 'Where did you learn to speak such good English?' Martin said to break the silence. 'Did you study here?'

Viktor glared at him and then glanced at the police-man behind the screen. Martin flushed. Why had he said that, drawing attention to Viktor like that? He was a tongue unable to keep away from a sore tooth. What was wrong with him? 'I'm sorry,' he said.

Viktor grunted. Then he looked again at the police-man still hunched behind his computer terminal, ap-parently oblivious. 'It's OK,' Viktor said. 'My wife taught me. She studied here – at the London School of Economics. And she taught me.'

'You were a good student,' Martin said.

'I loved her,' Viktor said. 'I wanted to learn for her. We wanted to work in America. And raise Suzana there. Free. Jelena thought I should learn before we went. We never thought I would need to use it like this.'

Then another policeman was standing in front of them. 'Mr Hughes?' he said. 'I'm Sergeant Palmer. Please come this way.' In the windowless interview room, Viktor sat cradling Suzana while Martin explained about Mila's disappearance. Sergeant Palmer wrote it all down, filling in a printed form. 'Thank you, sir,' he said finally. 'I think I've got everything I need. I'll forward the details to the Missing Persons Bureau.'

'How long will that take?' Martin could feel Viktor watching him as he spoke and he knew he wanted him to say this and he saw Mila's dark green eyes gazing at him. 'She could be in danger.'

'Yes, she might be.' Sergeant Palmer got up. 'But then again she might not be. Two hundred and fifty thousand people go missing every year and almost all of them return safely.'

'But some don't,' Martin persisted.

'Yes, sir. A very few do not.' Sergeant Palmer opened the door of the interview room. 'And we take every case seriously. But what would you like us to do here? It's difficult enough tracing someone who has some form of identity. But by your own account you're not sure what passport Ms Hubchev has. Indeed, from what you say, it appears she may be here illegally, probably with forged papers.' Martin sensed Viktor sitting tensely behind him. 'How do you suggest we start looking for someone like that?' Sergeant Palmer said. 'It's like trying to pin down air.'

'Martin,' Viktor said, 'we must go.'

Sergeant Palmer had paused by the doorway and turned to look at Viktor. 'With respect, sir, you're assuming something that may not be justified,' he said to Martin. 'You don't know she's in danger. People like this often have many good reasons to disappear. It doesn't mean she's in danger.'

'What do you mean "people like this"?' Martin felt himself bristling at the policeman's airy dismissal of Mila.

'Martin, we must go now.' Viktor had now stood up and was holding Suzana in his arms. 'We must go.'

'I suggest, sir,' Sergeant Palmer said, standing aside to let Martin and Viktor go through the door, 'you try to get some sleep. There's nothing more we can do tonight. I am sure the Missing Persons Bureau will get on to it as soon as possible.'

'We must go now, Martin,' Viktor said again. He had not spoken directly to Sergeant Palmer throughout the conversation. 'Now.'

'I'm sure the little girl is tired,' Sergeant Palmer said, looking at Viktor. 'Where is it you are from, sir?'

'Bosnia,' Viktor said. 'We are from Bosnia.'

'Thank you, Sergeant Palmer,' Martin said quickly.

'Good luck,' the policeman said. Then as Viktor and Suzana walked outside, he laid his hand on Martin's arm. 'Just a word, sir,' he said. 'I know the gentleman is upset but I wouldn't get too wound up about it if I were you.'

'What do you mean?' Martin said.

'Ninety-nine point nine per cent of the time with this sort of thing it's a domestic. They've had a row. Or she's got another man. They sort it out themselves, eventually.'

Another man? Martin remembered the way she had put her arm around Viktor's shoulders on Saturday. Not Mila.

'Look, it's not for me to say, sir. I don't want to upset anyone. It's just that most of the time there's a perfectly ordinary explanation why people don't turn up when they say. That's all. Give it a couple of days before you start worrying. That's what the Missing Persons Bureau will do.'

That seemed reasonable enough and now Martin felt embarrassed by how easily he had been infected by Viktor's hysteria. 'Thank you, Sergeant,' he said.

Viktor and Suzana were waiting outside in the freezing night air. 'What did he want?' Viktor said.

'Nothing much,' Martin said and they walked to the car in silence. Martin unlocked the doors and Viktor laid Suzana gently on the back seat. She had not woken at all.

'You better sit her up and put her seatbelt on,' Martin said. Perhaps Mila did have another man. Was Viktor so upset because he suspected that? When he thought of Mila with Viktor in his flat he found it hard to believe. But you never knew with women. He would never have thought Clare would leave him.

Women were a mystery. Whatever had happened, he had done all he could and now he would have to extricate himself from Viktor.

Viktor got into the front seat beside Martin. 'I told you we must be careful,' he said. 'If they ask for my papers, I will be arrested. And then Suzana and I will be sent back to Bosnia. And I must not go back. I promised. Suzana must not go back.'

'It's OK, Viktor,' Martin said and started the engine. 'He was only trying to help. I'll drive you home.' And say goodnight. And goodbye.

'We must look for her,' Viktor was muttering almost to himself. 'I will take Suzana to school tomorrow morning and then I will start.'

'I don't think there's any need for that,' Martin said. 'The police will get on with finding her now. You heard what the sergeant said. Hundreds of thousands of people go missing like this every year and they nearly always turn up.'

'Can you help me?' Viktor said.

'I'm not really that kind of lawyer,' Martin said. 'And I'm sure Mila will turn up tomorrow. Just try to get some sleep tonight.'

Viktor turned in his seat to look at him but he did not say anything.

'It's really best to leave it to the police now,' Martin said. 'They know what they're doing.' He yawned. He had an early start tomorrow and he had done what he could for Viktor. He had discharged his duty and now he needed to sleep. Tomorrow he would think up some new pretexts to get closer to Clare by spending time with Megan. Viktor had not worked out. So he would have to find some other way. He was going to show Clare they were meant to be together.

'OK, Martin,' Viktor said. 'You do what you think is right. It's your choice. You always have a choice.'

twenty-nine

Clare put Megan's shirt into the drying machine and closed the door and turned the dial to start the programme. Through the kitchen window, a streetlamp glowed and hummed. There were no other sounds. In this last hour before dawn, nothing moved. Including the tumble-dryer. Clare gave it a kick and it started.

She yawned and laid the table. Packet of cornflakes, bowl, spoon, special Princess Bride spoon, butter, jam and a napkin. Megan had recently encountered napkins at a friend's house and now she wanted one at every meal. Clare placed two pieces of bread by the toaster and took the eggs out of the fridge. Megan would start to wake up soon and everything needed to be ready so she could focus all her attention on her daughter. She took two bowls out of the cupboard and put them on the table. Martin might want some cereal today. Then she remembered and put one of the bowls back in the cupboard. Even now, once or twice a week, half-asleep in the early morning, as she plodded through the chores, Clare forgot and laid a place for Martin.

Did that mean she missed him? Clare made herself a cup of coffee and turned on the radio. That was one

good thing about him going. She could listen to Radio
4 in the morning. Martin hated it and he always wanted
to play his music. Now *Farming Today* was taking her
away to an alien world where people worried about
wheat yields and the Rural Payments Agency and older
cattle disposal schemes instead of getting Megan's shirt
dry in time for school and what to do about Martin
Hughes.

She made herself another cup of coffee. When
Megan woke up, the rush and tumult of her day would
begin. The thirty-eighth since Martin left. Since she
asked him to leave. Had she been rash? But she knew
the signs. Donald had been so attentive until Megan
was born and then month by month he had slipped
away until he disappeared altogether. Men were pro-
grammed to be restless.

The drying machine hummed in the corner. She was
going to have to buy a new one soon. It was always the
same. Just as she felt she was balancing the books there
was some sudden unexpected expense. And usually
when Donald had forgotten to send the cheque. How
was she going to find the money for a new drying
machine? And Megan needed new shoes. Still, Mila
was coming round, with Suzana, after school. And
after that, she could buy the shoes.

A door banged as Megan stumbled into the bathroom. And, on cue, the *Today* programme started.
Clare put her coffee cup into the dishwasher. She had
tried so hard to believe that Martin was different. He
was loving and kind and he adored Megan. But men
changed. Donald had. And Martin always wanted to

care for them his way. Not the way she and Megan may have wanted but the way he thought they should be cared for. This need to have everything his way, no matter how well-meaning it might be, worried her. What if he wanted something she really didn't?

If she had been on her own, Clare would have taken the risk but she wasn't and she couldn't let Megan's heart get broken too. She had been too young to be affected when her father left but Martin was different. She had to be sure the relationship would work on equal terms, not just the way Martin said it should be.

'Good morning, my darling,' she said as Megan appeared in the doorway. 'Would you like some break-fast?'

The little girl sat down at the table without a word and reached for the packet of cereal.

'Don't you want to say good morning?' Clare said.

Megan stared blearily at the cereal as she poured it into her bowl. 'Good morning, Mummy,' she said.

Clare leaned over the table and kissed her on the cheek. 'Good morning, my darling,' she said.

Martin belonged round this table with them. But Clare knew she must not blind herself to the warning signs. It would have been easy to ignore all those evenings hunched over the computer and the increasing number of briefs which meant he had to duck out of taking Megan somewhere. Much easier to overlook than confront them, but heartbreak lay at the end of that path.

'Can I have some toast, Mummy?' Megan said and pushed the empty bowl away from her. Clare picked it up and put it in the dishwasher and turned it on. It was developing an alarming rattle. It had been so easy when Martin had been here, with him taking care of everything like that.

How could she be certain that she was right about him? Yes, he was bound to his desk but couldn't that be him being conscientious and not selfish? Wasn't his sense of duty his essentiality, as Marc might say? Shouldn't she see whether he could make that essentiality work for her and Megan, as he said he wanted to do?

'Of course, my darling,' she said to Megan. Perhaps she should give him one last chance?

thirty

She was good-looking with short dark hair and a delicate mole by her nose and she must have been around thirty. She was wearing a short skirt and flat mauve pumps. Clive Walton thought she looked graceful. There were filigree lines round her mouth and her eyes were staring through the window and there was a fine red line round her neck where her throat had been cut.

'What should I do now, sir?'

He heard the police constable trying to keep his voice steady as they stood by the open doors of the carriage looking at the dead woman propped on the seat. 'Did you find her?'

'No, sir. The reporter called it in and we were nearest.'

Clive Walton could feel the cold nipping his fingertips through the gloves. The station had been closed off and soon the first disgruntled commuters would be gathering at the gates, demanding to speak to the manager. 'The reporter?'

'Over there, sir.'

Clive Walton turned and saw a stalky girl with long straight brown hair sitting at the far end of the carriage, balancing her notebook on her knees and writing rapidly. It was still dark and the pallid carriage lights glowed in the gloom.

'Her paper got a call telling her to meet this train with a photographer and when she saw this, she called it in.'

'What's your name?'

'Mike Reynolds, sir.'

'Thank you, Mike,' Clive Walton said. 'Good work.'

Even this early in the morning, barely awake, with the taste of coffee still coating his mouth, the elements were beginning to form a shape. The press alerted to meet the first Tube train of the morning into High Barnet. No-one around this early so there was little risk of getting caught. No blood on the seats so the killing had been done somewhere else and the body deliberately placed in its position at any one of the stations on the Northern Line. Someone could have stayed with the body until the carriage was empty. And murder on the Tube would guarantee press coverage.

It was a professional piece of work and whoever did it wanted it to be found and written about. They wanted to send a message. But what about? And to whom?

'Excuse me.' The tall girl had got up and walked over to him with her notebook. 'Are you in charge here?'

Every tragedy was attended by these young media graduates with their notebooks and digital tape-recorders eagerly recording the facts to entertain their readers. Clive Walton was suffering from early onset world-weariness. 'And who are you?' he said.

'What happened?' she said. 'It's awful. That poor woman.'

'And you are?' he said again.

'Karen Bates, *Hendon Gazette*. Here's my card. If you're in charge, I need to ask you a few questions about the victim.'

'Actually, Ms Bates, it's the other way round. At the moment, I need to ask you some questions.' But he knew there was no point. Someone else would have answered the phone. Someone else would have got her out of bed to get down here and she would not be able to tell him anything he needed to know.

It was still dark and another constable stood outside, peering in through the carriage windows, his breath misting the glass.

'As you can see, a young woman's been murdered here,' he said, softening at the sight of Karen Bates dutifully poised over her pad, ready to deploy her newly acquired shorthand. 'But I'm afraid I can't say much more than that at the moment. We'll release more details as they become known.'

'What's her name?'

'I really don't know any more at the moment,' Clive Walton said. 'My advice to you, Ms Bates, is to go back to your office and write up what you've got. And get someone else to drive you there. You may not realise it but you've just had a shock. It's stressful seeing a dead body, especially when they've had their throat cut.'

'I'm OK,' she said. 'I think.'

'Trust me, Ms Bates,' he said. 'There's nothing more for you here for now. Here's my card. Call me later today if you want but right now go and have a stiff drink. Believe me, you'll need it.' He looked around the carriage. Forensics would go over it later but he would be astonished if they found anything useful. This was professional.

'Thank you, Inspector Walton,' she said, looking at the card.

'Goodbye, Ms Bates,' he said. 'Anything else?' he asked Mike Reynolds.

'How many other women have been murdered like this on the Tube in the last month?' Karen Bates said.

'Are you still here?' he said. Clearly one murder was not enough for the *Hendon Gazette*. They wanted a serial killer.

'More than five?' Karen Bates said. 'Three?'

'Go home, Ms Bates, and let us get on with our job. Please.'

'So you're not denying that this is the latest in a series of murders.'

'Ms Bates, a young woman has been murdered and we need to find out who did it. One young woman. That's all and that should be enough for you to write about and right now you are obstructing the investigation.' He wasn't aware of any other murders and this didn't look like the work of a psychopath. It was all too careful and deliberate and the phone message had given no hint of self-aggrandisement. The caller had wanted the murder reported, not the murderer. It looked professional. But he did not want any of this to appear in the *Hendon Gazette*. Or anywhere else.

'Are you going to get a psychological profile of the killer?'

'You can write whatever you like,' Clive Walton said, 'but if you get it wrong you'll end up looking stupid so, if you want my advice, I would leave, now, and write what you know for a fact to be true and don't make it up. That way you won't end up looking stupid.'

'You do your job, Inspector,' Karen Bates said bravely, 'and I'll do mine,' but Clive Walton saw she had given up. She was still too young to hide the disappointment in her face.

'Don't worry,' he said, taking pity now he had won, 'there's more than enough to write about for now and you can ring me this afternoon to see how we're getting along.'

'I'll call you later,' she said as she stepped out of the carriage on to the platform.

Clive Walton and Mike Robinson glanced at each other, professionals enduring the clumsiness of outsiders.

'What else have you got, Mike?' Clive Walton said to the constable.

'There was some sort of identity card on the seat beside her,' Mike Reynolds said. 'I've bagged it up.'

'Was it hers?'

'The photo looked like her.'

So whoever had done this wanted her identity to be known. 'Did she have a name?'

'Looked like it, sir, but I couldn't understand the card. It's in some foreign language. Nothing I recognise.'

He'd look at it later but Clive Walton assumed it wouldn't help much. Whoever had done this had left it there as a statement, not a clue. 'Looks like gangs, Mike,' he said. But knowing that didn't make Clive Walton feel any better. The more he thought about it, the worse it became.

'What do you think, Mike?' he said. 'What are the options?' Clive Walton liked to take the uniformed officers along with him on his journeys of investigation. It was good for morale and it motivated them and made them keener and sharper.

'A domestic?' Mike Reynolds suggested.

'Yes, yes.' Clive Walton nodded thoughtfully. 'It could be, it could be, but probably not. Not on this occasion. Someone meant her to be found.'

'A prostitute?' Mike Reynolds said.

'More likely. But why do it like this?'

'Maybe as an example to others? Perhaps the pimp wants to teach his other girls a lesson?'

'Could be, could be.' Clive Walton nodded. If that was right, sooner or later they would nail whoever did it. There was always someone who talked in cases like that. But he had an uncomfortable feeling that Mike Reynolds was not right. The woman didn't look like a street-girl who would end up with her throat cut. Too good-looking, somehow too elegant.

'Any other possibilities?' he said.

Mike Reynolds shook his head. 'Can't think of anything obvious,' he said. 'If it's not a psychopath.'

'What if she was the girlfriend of a boss?' Clive Walton said. 'And this is the start of a vendetta? That could be a real problem, Mike. Let's hope it isn't.' But if it was, and Clive Walton had a bad feeling about this, then he knew this would not be the last glum, frosty dawn that he would have to come out to examine a corpse.

thirty-one

Adriana Popescu unlocked the door of her office. Her head hurt and she sat down heavily in her chair and rummaged in the drawer of her desk for aspirin. All gone. She turned on the computer and sat massaging her temples with her fingers while it booted up. She had better get used to it. It was never going to go away. Living with pain, the doctor called it.

Through the window, she could see a group of students walking across the little plaza in front of the computer block, hunched against the cold drizzling rain. There was Felicia, in her long dark coat, maroon scarf wound round her neck and tangled blonde hair falling over the collar, hugging her books to her, so bright and happy, so much before her, just waiting for life to open up. All those years ago, Mila had walked across the same plaza, her quiet beauty radiant in the grey air, oblivious to the Ceaucescu goons who sauntered menacingly among the students.

There was a knock on the door. 'Yes,' she said.

'Sorry to bother you, Professor.' Radu Lupescu poked his head round the door. 'I just wondered if you had had a chance to look at my thesis.'

'I haven't finished it yet.'

'Oh. Sorry to bother you.'

Adriana kept looking out of the window. Professor? It just made it worse. She was still an Associate Professor after twenty years.

'Do you know when you might be able to finish it?' Radu Lupescu said.

'No.'

'Can I ask what you think of it so far, Professor?'

He looked like a dejected frog. She shouldn't be so hard on him. She would have been anxious at his age. 'Don't worry,' she said. 'It's passable.' Her head was throbbing and it was never going to get better. 'I'm making notes showing where you need to re-write.'

'Thank you, Professor,' the boy said but he did not move.

He really was dense. No spark. Not like her darling Mila. Why hadn't she called? This was not like her. Adriana hoped she was all right. 'Yes?' she said. 'Anything else?'

'Is it really just passable?' he said, looking at the floor.

'That's what I said and that's what I meant,' she said and then felt abashed. It wasn't fair to take it out on this earnest young man. 'Passable means it is capable of being passed. You just need to do a bit more work on it, that's all.' What if Mila had lost her job and was too ashamed to tell her? What would she do then? Adriana needed the money for the treatment. How would she live without it?

Radu Lupescu smiled and a moment of grace passed

across his plain face. 'Thank you, Professor,' he said. 'Thank you. I'll get on with it.'

Where was she? Mila was usually so good about keeping in touch with her old mother. Adriana smiled at the thought of her calm and beautiful daughter and, briefly, the room was warmed as the professor and her student separately and privately found light in the grey day.

'Goodbye, Radu.' Five thousand lei a month. That was all she took home after twenty years at the university. One thousand English pounds. Mila was sending home twice that every month. She was doing well. She had always been going to do well, her darling Mila.

'Thank you, Professor.' He shut the door punctiliously carefully behind him.

Her head was still throbbing. Cancer. At her age she had come to realise that her time was not unlimited but knowing how it was going to end made it no easier. And nor did knowing that there were all these options to prolong it and make her feel better in the meantime and that she could not afford any of them unless Mila kept sending her the money.

The phone rang. Perhaps this was Mila. She had not rung for two weeks now. 'Professor Popescu, where are you?'

'Hello, Georghe.'

'The committee has been waiting for you for fifteen minutes now. Are you going to honour us with your presence today or not?'

'I'm sorry. I'll be right there.' How could she have forgotten the Strategy Committee? She had set it up five years ago. Everything was changing in her profession and they had needed a committee to manage their response to the permanent revolution. But in her life, everything was narrowing down to this disease, day by day destroying her.

What could have happened to Mila? She was usually so good about ringing, so good about sending money to her old mother especially since she had been told about the tumour. Mila must be doing well in that IT consultancy in London, the amounts she was sending home, but she never said anything about it. She was so private. Like her father. Adriana smiled to herself again. Nicolae had been a good man. And a good husband to her. And he had loved Mila. Her life had been good really, despite everything.

Perhaps soon Mila would feel settled enough to invite her over. Adriana did not like to ask but wouldn't that be wonderful? To stay with her daughter. In London. She could have the treatment there. But why had Mila not rung?

thirty-two

'Are you ready to move yet?' Kalaj took off his glasses and polished them on a corner of the tablecloth. He was keeping a very careful eye on this Romanian.

'Have you spoken to Florian yet?' she said. These Albanians were so suspicious. It came from still being a tribal society. Although it was said this one had been educated in the United States. Boston. Tufts University.

'I know what I know. Are you ready to move?'

'I'm working on it,' she said.

'Don't work on it too long,' he said. 'I'm getting you everything you need, new identities, passports, new location. You get ready to move.'

'I'll let you know,' she said. Kalaj could save her time and trouble but not yet.

'How much did you make last week?' he said.

'Fifty-three thousand. It was a good week,' she said. If you gave an Albanian five brass bani, they would take a silver leu. You had to watch them like a hawk.

'Was that from all the operations?' Kalaj put his glasses back on. You could never relax around these Romanians.

'Thirty thousand from phishing,' she said. 'And the eleven new identities you gave us averaged two thousand each.' He didn't need to know about the casino scam. They had done all of that themselves so why should they give anything to the Albanian?

'Two thousand?' he said. 'Couldn't you do better than that? Do you know how much it cost me to get those identities?' He sensed something was going on here and he had learned to trust his instincts.

'I know, but you've got to be careful how you do it,' she said.

Right. Now Kalaj knew that something was definitely going on here. But he would give her one more chance. 'Three new passports – good as new anyway – three thousand each. Nine thousand English pounds. I expect a return on that,' he said. 'And I had to pay the thieves a thousand pounds each for the rest. That's seventeen thousand pounds. Plus the set-up costs. Plus the risk. I expect a return on that.'

The Romanian nodded seriously. 'I understand,' she said.

'Do you? Really? I'm not sure. If you did understand, you wouldn't be offering me two thousand each. You'd be giving me a proper return.'

'More will come next week. Be patient. It will come.'

Kalaj hoped so. He didn't want trouble with the Romanian as she ran a good operation. Even after all the set-up costs and operating expenses, this could bring in over a million a year and he could see no reason why they should ever get caught. As long as they kept moving. And as long as he could keep the pirates away.

'These documents are only good for two weeks,' he

said. 'You know it's not safe to use them longer than that.'

'You'll be a happy man, next week,' she said, twinkling at him. She knew the effect of those dark green eyes on men, once they had noticed them. 'You'll see your return then, I promise you.'

'I hope so.'

The Romanian smiled. It was well known what the Albanian did when he was not happy. 'You worry too much,' she said.

'You'll owe me thirty-five thousand pounds.'

'You'll get it next week,' she said.

'There is no misunderstanding here, is there?'

'You will get it.' She smiled again, her eyes sparkling and dancing, charming. She didn't want to do anything to encourage him to poke around. The online casino scam was proving very lucrative, forty thousand dollars a month, and they could still get a few more weeks out of that. And then they could use the same little team on something else below the Albanian's radar. It was only Ilie and Gabriel after all. No-one would notice them taking a few hours out every week to work on a special project. As long as they didn't do anything to get the Albanian poking around. The casino operation was hers.

thirty-three

Bernie Newman stared out, unseeing, at Santa Monica Bay which glittered in the sunshine far away below him. There was something wrong. He couldn't quite put his finger on it but there was something in the figures from the online casino that kept snagging on him. Something was wrong. He looked again at the spreadsheet that Marlene had printed out for him. The numbers jerked and skipped in a graceless dance. His phone buzzed.

'Yes.'

'Just to remind you, Disney are here in fifteen minutes. And then Carl Romney is coming in at twelve.'

'Who's he?'

'That new vice-president.'

'Rearrange them.'

'Are you sure, Bernie?'

'Marlene, if I was not sure, I would not have said it. Rearrange them.' The phone gave a muted click of disapproval as she hung up.

He remembered sitting on the grass at Berkeley one May afternoon as David Unsworth talked about neo-platonism in twentieth-century mathematics. 'Beauty is the first test,' he had said, quoting the great G.H. Hardy, 'there is no permanent place in the world for ugly mathematics.' How true that had seemed, sprawling on the spreading lawns, smelling the cut grass, watching Lisa Jones as she sat opposite him in the circle of students, her chestnut hair catching the late sun. Mathematics are discovered not invented, Hardy had argued, and Bernie knew there was a pattern to discover here in this spreadsheet from the casino. He just knew it. There was no place in the world for ugly mathematics. So what the fuck was wrong with these figures?

The intense blue sky peeped through the blinds, mirroring the vivid ultramarine of the little Dufy oil on the wall opposite his desk. There was no place for the ugly and there was something wrong in this spreadsheet. But what was it?

The phone buzzed again.

'Yes?'

'Carl Romney is not happy.'

'He will be when he sees how I have re-engineered his finances.' He heard Marlene breathing at the other end of the phone. 'What?'

'Nothing.'

'I'll see him tomorrow.'

'I'll tell him that.'

Bernie was a virtuoso among accountants. No humdrum tax returns or cases of litigation support crossed his desk, no financial forecasts and projections nor cashflow and budgeting analyses nor any representations to the IRS or retirement planning. If that was what you wanted, you could choose from hundreds of good CPAs in Los Angeles County. But if you wanted Bauhaus finance or fiscal kathakali or minimalist twelve-tone book-keeping and you could afford it, then you came to Bernie Newman.

He got up from his desk and paced up and down his office, staring at the spreadsheet in his hand. Under his feet he felt the Mughal millefleurs rug, its reds and pinks glowing comfortingly up at him from across the centuries but there was something wrong. What the fuck was it?

He looked out of the window. He looked down at the spreadsheet. He stroked his earlobe between his finger and his thumb. And he paced up and down his large, immaculate office.

He knew there was a pattern in these figures and he could feel it but he could not see it. And yet Bernie was confident he would get it eventually. You just had to keep looking. He had learned that. You had to clear your head and let the meaning come in as it wanted. You couldn't force it. He knew that you just had to leave the door open and wait but it was still making him mad.

Out in the sparkling bay, a corpulent cruise ship was dragging itself north from San Pedro. The sun winked off its windows as West Coast burghers were lugged off to the frozen north to see the whales. Nice day for it, Bernie thought. He looked back at the spreadsheet and then, suddenly, the numbers danced into position. There was rhythm and shape and the ballet suddenly assumed meaning. And he saw it. Clever. Very clever.

He had not been intended to see it but he did. Now he had got it. He did not know yet how it was being done but he could see what was being done. And it was wrong. Very wrong. He strode over to the door and opened it.

'Yes?' Marlene looked up as he came out, and crossed her legs under the desk.

'Can you convene the Executive Committee? Please. At three o'clock. And I'll be leaving now. I'm taking the scenic route.' Her silent sigh followed him back out through the door.

He felt better once he was on the Interstate. Steppenwolf was on the CD player and the bass went thundering through him. It took him back. It was a perfect California day, the sun beating on the highway and, over to his right, the deep blue ocean. The buzz was still there. He felt the freedom of the road spreading before him as he opened up the throttle on the BMW. What a motor. Worth every cent. Sunlight danced and sparkled on the surf, setting him up for what he was going to have to do at the committee meeting. Someone was ripping off the casino and someone was going to have to pay for it.

thirty-four

It was now fourteen hours since Mila had not come home and something terrible had happened to her. As he watched, fearfully, relentlessly, the hands edge round the clock, Viktor could no longer find comfort in alternative explanations. There could be no benign reasons for Mila's disappearance. Something bad had happened to her.

At the school gate he kissed goodbye to Suzana. 'Have a lovely day, my darling,' he said. 'Be good. Be careful.'

'I love you, Papa,' she said, skipping into the playground. He had woven her hair the way Jelena used to do it and the blonde plait bounced over her pink raincoat as she ran. He was on his own now. The way that English lawyer had shrugged him off so casually had made him realise he could depend on no-one. The bonds he thought the children were forging between them had disintegrated under the first pressure.

He watched Suzana disappear into the classroom. What now? Mila's flat was clearly where he should start looking. Perhaps she had got in last night without the landlord noticing, and she had not been feeling well and now she was sleeping it off and that was why she had not contacted him. She had no phone there, so perhaps that was it.

From the bus stop, he walked through a dilapidated estate. A gang of young children, who should have been in school, swooped by him on bicycles, yelling something as they passed. Otherwise, the streets were empty apart from the cigarette butts and crumpled beer cans on the pavements and the dog turds everywhere. It was a dull morning and a gritty breeze sent litter scurrying over the neglected pavements.

He walked past a bedraggled little park and turned into a narrow street of Edwardian terraced houses, past a rusting Ford Escort without wheels sitting outside a house with a buggy in the front garden. And then walking round another corner took him into a wider street of larger, semi-detached houses. Many had fresh paint around the windows and flowers in the front gardens. The salaried middle classes were moving back in. And it was here that Mila lived, in a house in the middle of the street.

On the advice of their younger son, an entrepreneurial civil servant, the elderly Irish owners had converted the top two floors into four flats while they continued to live on the ground floor. Viktor rang the bell. No answer. He rang again and heard someone move and then the door opened.

'Good morning, Mrs Flynn,' he said. 'I'm a friend of Mila Hubchev. Viktor Markov.'

The old lady peered benignly at him. 'I can't say I remember you,' she said. 'But you look nice enough. What can I do for you?'

'I'm looking for Mila,' he said. 'Have you seen her today?'

'Today?' The old lady thought. 'No. I can't say I have.'

'When did you last see her?'

'So many questions. You had better come in and have a cup of tea.' She noticed Viktor hesitate. 'Come on,' she said. 'We won't kill you.' And she reached across and patted him on the hand. 'Gerald,' she called back into the house, 'put the kettle on. We've got a visitor.'

The living room was newly painted in turquoise. The curtains were drawn against the day but a dull light filtered in through the cracks. Viktor was at the bottom of the ocean, where passing ships had dropped silver-framed photographs on to the mantelpiece. Messages from Earth.

'Sit here,' Mrs Flynn said, indicating a large arm-chair with antimacassars on the arms.

Viktor sat down carefully. 'When did you last see Mila?' he said again.

'You sound worried, my dear.' Mrs Flynn was small and round with short grey hair, wearing a green cardigan that blended with the walls, concealing her from marine predators. She smiled at Viktor. 'But I'm sorry, dear, I can't remember,' she said. 'Was it yester-day? We certainly haven't seen her today. But then we wouldn't expect to. She is always so busy, dear Mila. She never has time for a cup of tea.'

He would have to be patient. Old people could not be hurried but Viktor felt his fingers going numb as he pressed them together. He needed to see Mila's room.

Gerald came in, carefully bearing before him a tray on which sat a large brown teapot, three cups, a jug of milk and a bowl of sugar lumps. He placed it on the low table by the sofa where he now sat beside his wife. He was a tall angular man, cheeks hollowed by age and watery eyes that looked warily at the tray as if he had forgotten something.

'Here you are, dear,' Mrs Flynn said, handing him a cup of tea to which she had added milk without asking him. 'I hope that's how you like it. Gerald, here's yours.'

Gerald brought the cup up to his lips and blew over it carefully and lengthily, as if reminding himself that he must not burn his lips on the hot drink.

'This is nice,' Mrs Flynn said. 'We get so few visitors nowadays. All our guests are always so busy. They never have time for a cup of tea. It's a nice change to meet a young man who has got time for a chat.'

Perhaps Mila was upstairs right now, asleep, and these two had not even noticed her come in.

'Where are you from, dear? Not around here, are you?'

'Bosnia,' he said.

'Bosnia?' she tried. 'And where might that be? I have never heard of that. Have you, Gerald?'

He was still holding his cup, apparently trying to decide whether it had cooled enough for him to risk drinking it. 'No, dear,' he said.

'The former Yugoslavia,' Viktor said.

'The former Yugoslavia?' Mrs Flynn said, raising her eyebrows. 'Is that right? That's a long way to come. And how do you like it here?'

'Very nice,' Viktor said. Mrs Flynn looked at him, obviously expecting him to expand on this. 'Can you remember the last time you saw Mila?' he said.

'You are worried about her, aren't you?' she said. 'Has something happened?'

'She was meant to meet me last night and she never came.'

'Oh dear.' Mrs Flynn shook her head and pursed her lips in a delicate gesture of concern. 'Have you seen her, Gerald?'

'No, dear.'

'I am sorry, my dear,' she said. 'We just don't see our guests that often. They keep themselves to themselves. They know they are always welcome to a cup of tea whenever they want. But young people are all so busy nowadays.'

'But can you remember the last time you saw her?'

'Thinking about it,' she said, 'now you ask, no, I can't.' She must have heard Viktor sigh because she continued. 'I am sorry, my dear. At our age, the days just fold into each other. It's so hard to remember things. We're not what we were. I am sorry.' She reached across and patted his hand.

She was a kind old lady. Motherly. She seemed to feel for him. 'Do you think I could look in her room?' he said.

'I'm not sure that would be right,' she said. 'What do you think, Gerald?'

'No, dear.' Gerald shook his head.

'It's her room,' she said. 'We can't allow anyone to go in there. It wouldn't be right.'

'Could you at least see if she is there?' Viktor said.

'Gerald,' Mrs Flynn said. 'Go and knock on the door.'

The old man got up slowly without a word and walked out of the room. Viktor could hear him shuffling up the stairs in the small house.

Mrs Flynn placidly sipped her tea. 'I'm sure she's all right, dear,' she said.

Gerald came back into the room. 'No answer,' he said.

'She's not there, I'm afraid,' Mrs Flynn said.

'But perhaps she is sleeping,' Viktor said. 'And she didn't hear.' The senile old fool had probably forgotten to knock on the door, standing staring at it, trying to remember why he had gone up there.

'Oh, Gerald has got a good strong knock.' Mrs Flynn chuckled. 'Haven't you, dear?'

'Yes, dear,' he said.

'If she had been there, she would have heard him.'

Viktor wanted to throw the hot, sweet milky tea at her. He needed to see Mila's room. What was wrong with this stubborn old woman?

'Please,' he said. 'Please could I not look in her room? Just a quick look. You can come with me. She would not mind. I promise you. Please. I need to see it.' Mrs Flynn was looking at him curiously. 'Please,' he said, 'I am so worried.'

'A big strong man like you,' she said. 'You shouldn't be worried. I am sure she's fine.'

He could just get up and go upstairs before these two old people could stop him. But they might call the police. Old people got worried very easily. And the police must not come looking for him.

'But all right,' she said. 'I don't suppose it will do any harm. Gerald, go with him.'

But when Gerald opened the door for him, Mila was not asleep there. The room was empty. The bed was neatly made with the sheet folded tidily back over the blanket. No duvets in the Flynn household. The little table by the window was bare and there was no sign that anyone lived there at all.

'She's gone,' Viktor said. 'She's gone.' Gerald's expression did not change. Viktor went over to the wardrobe. It was empty. What had happened to her?

'She's gone,' Gerald said to Mrs Flynn when they went back downstairs.

'Are you sure, dear?' she said.

'Our man here is sure,' he said. 'There's no clothes there or anything.'

'Has she paid the rent?' she asked.

'Yes, dear. She paid this week on Sunday,' he said.

'I will miss her,' she said, 'she was a nice young girl. Not that we saw very much of her. She was always too busy for a cup of tea.'

She looked at Viktor. 'I am sorry, my dear,' she said. 'It looks like she's walked out on you. The path of true love is hard and cruel.' She patted his hand again. 'Gerald and I were lucky. Weren't we, dear?'

'Yes, dear,' he said.

Viktor was sure she had not walked out on him. He took nothing for granted any more but she had told him she loved him. And when they were together, he knew it was true. He could tell. You could always tell when it was real.

What had he not known about? She must have been trying to escape from something. What danger was she in? Why had she not told him? Perhaps she had been trying to protect him and Suzana from whatever it was? That would have been typical of her.

She needed help. Viktor knew he had to find her and help her. 'Thank you,' he said. 'Thank you for the tea. I must go and find her.'

'If you want my advice, my dear,' Mrs Flynn said, 'learn to let go. There will be plenty more young women for a good-looking man like you. It's hard but you have to let go. Gerald, show our guest to the door.'

In the narrow hallway outside the living room, the Flynns had squeezed a table and Viktor could see the mail piled up for the tenants. And on the top in an oblong manila envelope he could see Mila's name. No stamp but her name.

He didn't stop to think. As Gerald opened the front door, he picked it up and put it inside his jacket. He didn't know why. It was just something of hers. 'Goodbye,' he said.

'Goodbye,' Gerald said and shut the door.

As Viktor walked back through the grey damp streets to the bus stop, he could feel the envelope inside his jacket. There was something hard inside it. It was comforting, continuing contact with Mila.

What could have happened to make her disappear like this? She must be in danger. Perhaps she owed money to smugglers. Or to money-lenders for her passage here. Viktor knew how brutal these gangs could be. He must find her. After Jelena, he could not lose Mila too.

Perhaps the envelope was a clue. He looked at it. It was addressed to her and he had no right to open it. She was always careful to protect her privacy and he respected that. Worry should not overcome duty. He should not open it. He should keep it for her. When he found her, he could give it to her. That was an important thought to grasp, for the future. He would find her and give it to her. But first he had to find her.

thirty-five

'Someone is robbing us.' Bernie Newman looked round the cherrywood table at his committee. He still felt good from the ride down on the BMW, the music playing and the wind in his hair, but now he had to deal with this problem threatening their online casino.

'Someone is robbing us, gentlemen.' He tapped the print-out insistently with his index finger. 'There's no doubt. It's a pattern. Every two or three days some punter wins every other play. For two to three hours. And then it stops. And two days later someone else wins every other time for a few hours and then stops.'

Outside, the Pacific Ocean broke in long rollers on the sandy beach that stretched away from the cabana. 'It's not a lot each time but it is adding up,' he said. 'They are taking us, gentlemen. Six months ago, we were making fifty thousand a month. Every month. Without fail. Now it's down to ten thousand. Someone is skimming us.'

He looked round the table. Eight prosperous professionals, hair thinning, paunches gently swelling, eyes hard, looked back at him. The Outlaw Poets. Bikers. Through the blinds he saw the sun glinting off the handlebars of Richie's Ducati parked in the lot by the window. There was a time when there would have been nothing but Harleys out there. But times had changed and he was happy enough with his K1200.

'Compadres,' he said. 'We need to do something about this.'

'What do you suggest, Bernie?' Lee Hewitt said. He was a graphic designer from Pasadena who approached decisions as cautiously as a crab. Bernie knew he would have parked his Goldwing carefully in the shade of the largest palm in the car park.

'Find out who's doing this and stop them.'

'Sounds good to me,' Lee Hewitt said and trailed the tips of his fingers under his nose, as if shielding it from the alien odours of his compadres.

'How do you propose to do that, Bernie?' Charlie Maxwell bought a new Harley every year and a different set of leathers to demonstrate how much money he was making as dentist to the stars.

'First let's find out who's doing it and then we can decide how to deal with it.' Bernie did not yet know how they were going to react. They were assessing the situation, taking in the information and analysing it, each in their own way, careful, successful professionals who, each in their own way, always did the right thing. And they would all have to deal with this problem. Half a million dollars a year was a big problem.

'We could go to the police,' he said. 'But they won't have a clue how to deal with this. They do guns and sirens, not this. And while they get round to looking at this, we're losing 40k a month. So, anyone want to hand this over to the cops?'

He looked round the table. No-one moved. 'Wise choice, gentlemen, in my view,' he said. 'I concur. So I've looked into hiring a teenage genius to track down who's hacking into our system. It'll cost three thousand a week.'

'Was that the genius who set the system up?' Ken Singer was ostentatiously taking notes as he spoke. Another dentist. San Diego. Kawasaki. Committee Secretary. Prick. 'What makes you think he can sort this out?'

'This is a different one,' Bernie said. 'Different problem, different genius.'

'How many weeks will it take?' Ken Singer said.

'How do I know? Two? Three? Maybe more.'

'And what guarantee do we have this teenage genius will find them?'

'No guarantee, Ken. None. But a good chance. I am proposing to use only the best. And what choice do we have? We're being robbed. Every month, someone is helping themselves to forty thousand of our dollars. What choice do we have?'

'Actually, to be precise, there are three choices,' Ken Singer said. 'One, we can do what you suggest. Two, we can shut the site down. Or, three, we can just take the loss. We're still making 10k a month. It's just a game. We never expected it to go so well. Anything we make is a bonus.'

Bernie could see a couple of the others were nodding. He might have known. Weekenders.

'Do you really want to shut the site down, Ken?' he said. 'This is something we do together, as a crew. Do you want to bring us down to just doing a run on Labor Day? This casino is our Tao. That is why we do it. And the money is our karma. We agreed this as a committee. You minuted it.'

'What about the other option? Just live with it?' Lee said, still creeping round towards a decision. Bernie saw the others sitting still and watching to see how it was going to work out.

'Live with it?' he said. 'Is that what we do? This is the Outlaw Poets here. Not some band of weekend amateurs. We do not ever just live with it. With this or with anything. The Outlaw Poets do it properly or don't do it at all. Hell is reserved for people who don't make clear and passionate choices. Dante said that. And who here wants to quarrel with the immortal Dante?' Bernie glared round the table but he could tell it was not working.

'It's not that, Bernie,' Charlie Maxwell muttered. 'It's just we don't know what we're getting into.'

'Someone is robbing us,' Bernie said.

'Yes, but what are we getting into here?'

'Too much thinking,' Bernie said. 'Remember *Zen and the Art of Motorcycle Maintenance*? Engage. Identify. And then wait for the outcome. Quality. That's the outcome. Quality. That was the great and possibly late Robert Pirsig. Remember? The Zen of Action. Identify with whatever you do and out of that act of engagement comes quality. We decided to do this and we should do it right.'

And that was when Ken Singer piled in, his bony forehead gleaming in the afternoon sun that filtered through the blinds. 'This is why I said we should have set it up in Curaçao. They have the best regime in the world for online casinos. I said so. I minuted it. Multiple layers of advanced prevention technologies to protect online products from malicious attack. If we had set it up in Curaçao instead of trying to save money, as our president argued, then we might not have this problem now.'

'Yes, Ken,' Bernie said. 'You are right. Of course. I am the president but you are a genius. The cleverest dentist in California. You can minute that. Now, what do you, as a dentist genius, suggest we do about this? You really want some teenage pimple, or whoever it is, to go on taking us for forty thousand of our dollars a month?'

'Shut it down. Start again in Curaçao.'

'OK. Anyone else?'

'How much would it cost to shut down?' Lee Hewitt asked.

'Nothing. We just shut it down. That's it. Great Adventure Over. We just give it up. It never costs anything to give up. It just costs everything.' Bernie knew he was playing this wrong. Bitterness was never persuasive but he couldn't stop himself. What did they think they were here for?

'Look,' he said. 'You've heard Ken's suggestion but this is not a business, it's a ride. We all make money every day in the office. This is different. This is something we do together for the hit. To see if we can. And we can. But some acned cracker is getting in the way. He's a roadblock. Now do we just stop when we see a roadblock? Or go over it? Keep on riding?'

'Or go round it,' Bernie thought he heard someone mutter but it was submerged by the noise of Otto Nielsen joining the discussion.

'Why not?' he boomed. He was the only one of them who looked like a biker, towering and fat, forearms like hams and red-golden hair curling below his ears. He was a freelance production accountant and Lee Hewitt's tennis partner.

'You're the president, Bernie,' he said. 'Let's try it for three weeks as you say. And then if it doesn't work by then, we can try it Ken's way.'

Bernie looked round the table. It was as good as he was going to get. 'OK,' he said. 'We'll meet back here in three weeks and I'll report back. I'll get this kid on to it. If he cracks it, am I authorised to take all the necessary steps to sort it out or do you want to meet again first?'

'I'm busy the next two weeks,' Otto said. 'You do it.'

'I've already had to blow out two patients this afternoon,' Charlie Maxwell said. 'I can't keep on doing that.'

'I'm away for the next ten days,' Lee Hewitt said. 'Go for it, Bernie.'

'Is that then the will of this committee?' Bernie said.

Heads nodded round the table.

'Minute that please, Mr Secretary,' Bernie said.

'Minuted,' Ken Singer said.

'That's it, gentlemen,' Bernie said. 'See you in three weeks. Ride free.'

'Ride free,' Lee Hewitt and Otto chimed.

'Yeah,' Charlie Maxwell said. 'Ride free.'

'Ride free,' Ken Singer said.

And then as the others filed out, Bernie stayed sitting and pretended to make notes. And as he sat and looked out of the window, he heard the bikes starting up in the car park. Ken Singer was such a prick. Then the bikes roared off into the distance and all he could hear was the waves on the shore. There was never such a thing as the perfect ride. You only ever got a shadow of it. There was always something. There was always a bug on the visor.

The online casino had been a good ride. They had designed it together as a team project, surfing new technology, cool games, foxy front page. And it was making money until that pimpled cracker, whoever he was, got in the way. Well, he would just have to get out of the way. He, Bernie, would just have to sort it out. And now he had been given the authority, he knew what he was going to do. It was time for the Outlaw Poets to become desperadoes.

Bernie took his helmet off the side table. He didn't feel like wearing it on the ride home. He wanted to feel the wind in his face. He would take a chance on the Highway Patrol. He could afford the fine. He needed to ride free.

thirty-six

The gallery flooded with light as Clare flicked the switch and the monochrome photographs round the wall were picked out by the staring halogen. 'What do you think, Marc?' she said.

'Good,' he said. 'Very good. The essentiality is there. Without sacrificing the irony. Very good.'

'About Martin,' Clare said.

Marc sighed. 'How do I know?' he said. 'I've got a show to open.'

'I'm just asking for advice,' Clare said. 'You're always so clever about boys.'

In Martin's room in Lincoln's Inn, Gavin Wilcox described why the 1953 corporate trust had outlived its usefulness. He was a loose-framed man, with sandy hair and a greengrocer's grasp of small numbers, sitting with his legs apart, and poking the air with his finger as he explained why the trust had to be dissolved. Beside him, his solicitor leafed though a fat file containing the plans of the Manchester block that was the trust's main asset. Martin nodded as Gavin Wilcox jabbed out the position of the trustees. Milroy v Lord might be relevant, Martin thought. Through the gloomy morning, lights glowed in the rooms on the other side of Lincoln's Inn. The trust sounded straight-forward enough but, now he could no longer take Megan to play with Suzana, what should he do with her that would convince Clare of his commitment?

In the gallery, Marc said, 'Haven't you got anything better to worry about?' He looked out of the window. 'It's raining – what about the homeless?'

'Don't be facetious,' Clare said. 'It's so nineties. Come on, Marc, help me. One moment, I think I've been strong and the next I think I've been an idiot. What should I do? How do I know whether I am being controlled or cared for?'

'Which is the bad one?' Marc said.

As the rain started to freckle Martin's windows, Gavin Wilcox said, 'You'll need to meet the trustees. In Manchester.'

Martin nodded. 'Fine,' he said.

The solicitor passed him a folder. 'The accounts,' he said.

'Thank you,' Martin said. If he took Megan skating or to the park, it would look too obviously as if he was trying to make good where he had failed before. It had to seem natural, as if it was something he really wanted to do, as if it came from the heart. Jenny had been astute the way she had orchestrated the date with Suzana. Perhaps he should ask her advice?

Gavin Wilcox and his solicitor got up. 'Thank you, Mr Hughes,' the solicitor said. They shook hands and Martin walked them to the door.

Why did he find it so difficult to think of ways to convince Clare? She could be such hard work. Perhaps that was a warning? Perhaps they were not meant to be together. Although he had thought they were happy, she had dumped him, just like that. No matter what Ben might say about her insecurity, there had to be a coldness in her heart to be able to do that.

Clare turned off the lights and the gallery reverted to gloom. 'Maybe I should give him just one last chance?' she said. 'One final chance.'

'Whatever,' Marc said.

thirty-seven

There were thick curtains across the windows and 'The Clarendon' was written in faded blue letters over the door. Viktor stood outside the door and listened to the hubbub inside, as he waited to recover his breath. It had taken him an hour's brisk walking to get from Mila's room to the corner of this short, sad street near Lisson Grove. He had no money to waste on another bus. Going to the police station had cost him a night's work and he might even have lost the job if the Croat reacted badly to him not turning up.

A man came out into the cold lunchtime air and Viktor smelt the alcohol and smoke on his breath as he brushed past him. He would have to find Mila on his own. That English lawyer had made it clear he didn't want anything more to do with this. Why would he? He was not that kind of lawyer.

As Viktor pulled the door open, noise spilled into the street along with the warm, companionable smells of beer and cigarettes. Inside, young men, with long, greasy hair and haunted faces, drank beer, and older men wearing drab anoraks and dull expressions gestured with their hands as they talked and stood by the bar, tossing back shots of liquor. All men, no women.

The air was fuddled with tobacco and dialect. Different languages surfaced and sank in the babble, none of them English.

What had Mila done last night? She had said she was going to meet her friend Josephine and Viktor knew Josephine occasionally worked in this smoky refuge. He shouldered his way through the throng to the bar and called something to an older man, wearing a red jacket and a yellow polo-neck jumper, behind the bar. The man put down two small glasses and filled them with a clear liquor and then he and Viktor clicked their glasses together and emptied them in one swallow. The two men spoke for a few minutes and then the older one gestured to the back of the room.

Before Viktor met Mila, he sometimes came here during the day when Suzana was at school and Miroslav had no work for him. It was full of men who English lawyers like Martin Hughes never saw, who worked in the kitchens of hotels where English lawyers ate expensive lunches, who cleaned the hospitals where they went when they got sick and built the offices where they worked to make their money and decorated the houses they bought with their bonuses. These were the foreigners with whom expensive English lawyers did not deal, because they did not do the kind of law that commanded these sorts of men. They did wills and trusts, not that kind of law.

Viktor felt comfortable here because these were men like him, not like the way he used to be but like the way he was now. They were not the kind of men with whom he would have drunk in Banja Luka. There he would have gone to dinner with men like that English lawyer. But here it was different. Here, he and all the men in the bar shared the same experiences of living on the outside and the same wary sense of how careful they had to be, everywhere they went, to do the right thing because if they did the wrong thing they could lose what little they had been squirrelling away, because everywhere they went, they could be mugged for cash or hurt for pleasure or deported because it was the law. But here, in this island of aliens, they could relax.

At the end of the bar, the long thin room opened to a larger square space with more tables. It was a restaurant but no-one was eating in it. Four men in suits sat at one of the tables, playing cards and laughing boisterously. There was no-one else.

Viktor pulled out a chair from the table at the far side of the room and sat down. The man in the red jacket came and sat down beside him and put another two shot glasses of clear liquor in front of them. 'Cheers, Goran,' Viktor said and raised his glass and smiled.

'*Salud*, Englishman,' Goran said, and his eyes smiled as he raised his glass. And together, they swallowed the liquor and the taste of plum and the rush of alcohol hit the back of Viktor's throat. 'Josephine isn't working here any more,' Goran said, 'but I've sent Pavel out to find someone who knows her. Don't worry,' he said, 'I didn't say anything about Mila.'

They sat in silence while the noise of the bar flowed back towards them from the front. There was a shout from the table where the men were playing cards. Viktor heard one of them laughing, a raucous gurgling chortle. Then a tall good-looking man in a battered tweed overcoat, with a long purple scarf wound round his neck, stood beside their table, his skin the colour of roasted coffee. 'Are you David Buchanan?' Goran said in English.

The man inclined his head.

'Good luck,' Goran said to Viktor and walked back towards the bar.

'Are you looking for Josephine?' David said.

'Yes,' Viktor said. 'Please, sit down. Would you like something to drink?'

'Of course.' David smiled.

'Two more, Goran,' Viktor called as Goran walked away.

The man in the red jacket made an elaborate bow.

'Do you know Josephine?' Viktor said.

'Of course.' David smiled again, this time as if he was remembering something particularly pleasurable.

'Where is she?'

'I don't know.'

Goran returned with two shot glasses on a tray. 'Call me if you need more,' he said to Viktor.

'Cheers,' Viktor said.

'L'chaim,' David said and laughed.

'When did you last see her?' Viktor said.

'Weeks ago. Is it serious?'

'Do you know her friend Mila?'

'What does she look like?' David smiled again as he had done when he was remembering Josephine.

'Do you know the name Mila?' Viktor said.

'Oh man, sometimes I don't remember their names.'

Viktor reached across the table and put his hand on David's arm and stared at him. 'This is important,' he said. 'Do you know Mila?'

'I don't think so.' The smile faded from David's face as he felt Viktor pressing his arm.

'Do you know where Josephine is now?'

'No, but her friend Simon might know. They are both Urhobos from Ibadan. He will know where she is.'

'Where do I find him?'

'I don't know where he lives but you will probably find him at Job Alley in the morning. He is usually there. Do you know Job Alley?'

'Everyone knows Job Alley. I'll find him there. What's his other name?'

'Ofasa. Simon Ofasa,' David said. He got up. He was not comfortable here with this large bearded man in a leather jacket. 'OK?' he said. 'I hope you find her.'

'Thank you,' Viktor said. 'If you see Josephine, please tell her to contact Goran here.'

'Sure,' David said and he was gone.

Viktor tilted his glass back and gloomily licked up the last lingering drops of slivovitz.

'Hey man, I just thought of something.'

Viktor looked up to see that David had returned to the table.

'I just thought if you can't find Simon, try Kalaj,' he said. 'Kalaj knows everything.'

'Who is he?' Viktor said.

David shrugged. He looked disgruntled that Viktor was not more grateful for his contribution. 'He knows a lot of women,' he said. 'Lots and lots of them.'

Viktor stared at him. 'What do you mean? Lots and lots?' he asked. 'Who is this man?'

David shrugged again. The beaming smile had vanished altogether and his handsome face was serious. 'Look,' he said, 'I'm just trying to be helpful.'

'Where do I find him?'

'I don't know.'

Viktor stood up. He was no taller than David but he was bulkier and David stepped back as he got up.

'You must know. You must tell me,' Viktor said. 'This is important.'

'Look, I'm just trying to be helpful. I don't want to get involved in this. But everyone knows Kalaj. Just ask someone else.'

'Is everything all right?' Goran had returned to the table. He had obviously seen Viktor standing up to David. 'Are you all right, Viktor?'

'Yes. I'm fine. This man says someone called Kalaj may know where Mila is.'

'I hope not,' Goran said.

'Why? Who is this man?'

'Viktor, please,' Goran said. 'Keep away from this. Kalaj will not have anything to do with Mila. I am sure she had nothing to do with him.'

'But David said he might know where she is.'

'I was only trying to be helpful,' David said. 'I also told him Simon Ofasa might know where Josephine is.'

'Viktor, Viktor, please listen to me.' Goran put his hands on Viktor's shoulders. 'You must listen to me. If Kalaj knows anything about Mila, you must let her go. You must keep away from this. I am sure he does not know anything. But if he does, believe me, you must keep away from it, let it go.'

'That's right, man,' David said. 'I don't know anything.'

'Goran, you must help me. I need to find her. Do you know this Kalaj? Do you know where I can find him?'

'Viktor, I am not going to tell you. You must keep away from this. For your sake. For Suzana's sake. Keep away from Kalaj.'

'He's right,' David said. 'I'm sorry. It was just a thought. I'm sure he won't know anything about your friend.' And he took two steps back and then turned and disappeared into the crowd in the front room.

'Don't worry, Viktor,' Goran said. 'I'm sure Ofasa will help you find Josephine and she'll know where Mila is.'

The noise in the front room suddenly seemed to get louder and then it was silent.

'What's that?' Viktor said.

Goran got up from the table. 'Wait here, I'll find out,' he said. 'And don't worry. I'll come back with a bottle.'

Viktor watched Goran as he went back into the front room, struggling to keep his panic under control. Both Goran and David thought this man Kalaj could help find Mila and they both thought this was bad news. Who was he? Pimp? Smuggler? Both? Viktor got up from the table and started to pace around the room. Something bad had happened. He had to find this Kalaj. He could not lose her.

'Viktor, sit down.' Goran came back carrying a bottle. 'Stop pacing around and sit down now. Just relax.'

'Easy for you to say. You'd be worried if it was you.'

'Viktor, please. Do as I say. There's a policeman in the front. Don't make yourself so obvious.'

Viktor stood by the table. 'What's a policeman doing here?' he said.

'Please, Viktor,' Goran said. 'Sit down now.'

'What is a policeman doing here?' Viktor said again.

'Nothing. Routine,' Goran said. 'Here. Drink.' And he poured out two more glasses of the clear liquor. 'Go on. Drink it. Relax. You can't go out the front till he's gone.'

Viktor knocked back the drink.

Goran watched him carefully. 'It'll be OK,' he said. 'There'll be an explanation. You'll find her,' he said.

'How do you know?' Viktor said and then he looked at the older man. 'But thank you, Goran,' he said. 'Really, thank you.' And then they sat in silence and waited.

'Do you think he's gone yet?' Viktor said eventually.

'Relax,' Goran said. 'I've told Pavel to come and get us when he's gone. And here he is.'

A slight, acned young man, with hair buzz-cut like a 1960s astronaut, approached the table, his eyes wild. 'He's gone,' he said. 'It sounds really bad.'

'It's OK, Pavel,' Goran said.

'No, it really does sound bad,' Pavel said. 'Some woman's been murdered. Her throat was slit. With a razor. Blood everywhere.'

'Pavel, it's OK,' Goran said, glancing at Viktor.

Pavel ignored him. 'No, really,' he said. 'The policeman was asking all these questions – they think it's some gang killing. They still don't know who she was. They think she might have been Romanian but the ID card might have been forged.'

'What ID card?' Viktor said.

'They found it with the body. He had this photo and he was asking if anyone recognised her.'

'What did she look like?' Viktor said.

'Pavel,' Goran said sternly but the youth had already started to answer.

'Pretty. A bit old for my taste. But good-looking. Dark hair. There was something familiar about her. But I don't know women like that.'

'Pavel,' Goran interrupted, 'go and look after the bar. Now.'

'I must see it,' Viktor said, getting up.

'Sit down, Viktor,' Goran said. 'You can't get involved. What do you think the police will do if they start talking to you? I'll find out for you.'

'I'm going,' Viktor said.

'Sit down,' Goran said, putting his hands on Viktor's shoulders and pushing him back into the chair. 'I will find out, I promise.'

'Yeah,' Pavel said. 'Leave it to Goran. It sounds really bad.'

'Pavel,' Goran said. 'Go and look after the bar. Now. I mean it.'

'OK,' Pavel said. 'But we're in for a hard time, Goran. The police will be all over us now. This is murder. Gangs. They're not going to leave us alone.'

'Now, young man.' The two men watched Pavel slouch back to the front room. 'It doesn't mean it's Mila,' Goran said gently.

Viktor said nothing.

'Viktor,' Goran said, 'it could be anyone. Pretty. Dark-haired. How many women are there like that?'

'Romanians?' Viktor said.

'Yes. How many pretty dark-haired Romanian women do you think there are in London? Thousands. And thousands. And they don't even know this one is Romanian. That's why the policeman was here. To try to find out. It doesn't mean anything, Viktor.'

'I told them.' Viktor was talking to himself now.

'What do you mean?' Goran said.

'I told the police she was missing last night. I told them last night she was in danger.'

Goran shook his head. 'Be careful, Viktor,' he said. 'They'll be looking for you now. They'll want to talk to you and this is serious. They can't ignore illegal immigrants involved in something like this. And you are involved. If you're just cleaning hospitals or working on a building site, OK, they aren't going to bother too much. But this is murder. Be very careful, Viktor. And remember we don't know this is Mila.'

'You think I don't realise all that?' Viktor said. 'But what can I do? She's disappeared. Of course, it may not be her. But there must be a reason why she's disappeared.' He filled the little shot glass from the bottle and knocked it back. 'I have got to find her,' he said.

'Be careful, Viktor,' Goran said again.

'I know, I know. You're right,' Viktor said. 'But there's a problem. I didn't give the police my name but I went with an English lawyer and he gave his name. And it won't be long before they remember we went to see them about a missing woman. And they contact him and then they catch up with me. And send me back to Bosnia. And I can't go back.'

'An English lawyer?'

'Someone I met at Suzana's school. He's not important. I can't wait for them to catch up with me. I must find out what's happened to Mila. If I know, I can get the Englishman to tell the police we've found her and that will be that. They won't come looking for us. But until then, they've got to keep looking for her as well.'

Viktor stopped and looked at Goran. He saw that they had realised at the same time that Viktor's plan depended on the assumption that the dead woman was not Mila. Goran said nothing.

'I must find this man Kalaj,' Viktor said.

'Be careful, Viktor,' Goran said. 'Be very careful.'

thirty-eight

'What's the matter, sunshine?' Martin said, standing in the doorway. 'Aren't you pleased to see me?'

Marc held up his left hand without speaking, a warden halting traffic, and continued his inspection of the photographs.

'Is she in?' Martin said. All the way over here, he had been conducting an extended fantasy about how he was going to take Megan home after an outing to the zoo. 'Here she is,' he was saying as Clare opened the door. He was carrying Megan on his shoulders and she was happily drumming on his head with her hands. And Clare was melting at the sight of warm, sympathetic, boyish Martin, doing what a father should. How could she not?

'Isn't she rather big to be doing this?' Clare was saying. And Martin realised he was not wholly in control of this fantasy.

'Have we had a good time, Megan?' he was saying.

'Martin wouldn't buy me an ice-cream, Mummy,' was Megan's response and 'Let me down,' and then, as the fantasy escaped out of control, 'Mummy, I want to get down.'

'Do you want to come in for a coffee?' Clare was back on cue.

'That would be nice.' Smoothly done.

'It can only be for ten minutes,' Clare was saying next. 'Megan's going to a party this afternoon.'

'I could take her.' He was in there quickly and Clare was smiling.

'I'm not looking for a taxi, Martin.' Where did that come from? 'But thanks anyway. Come in.'

In the real world, Marc still hadn't turned round. 'Is she here?' Martin said.

'This is a gallery,' Marc said, without taking his eyes away from the photographs. 'An art gallery. Not a singles bar.'

'Fuck off, Marc,' Martin said cheerily. 'Is she here?' He stepped into the room and, as he did so, he saw Clare coming out of the office at the far end. They stopped moving at the same time, frozen.

'Hello,' he said.

'How are you, Martin,' she said.

'Fine, fine,' he said. 'You?'

'Fine, fine.'

'Where's Megan?' he said. 'Shouldn't you have picked her up from school?'

'She's at a sleepover,' she said. 'We need to get the exhibition ready. Why are you here?'

'I was just passing. I thought I'd drop in to say hello. To Marc.'

'Oh, for God's sake,' Marc said. 'How old are you two?' Martin and Clare turned to look at him. 'I need an espresso,' he said. 'I'll be back in ten minutes.'

Martin and Clare both watched him as he put on his coat and left.

'Sorry,' Martin said. 'I just wanted to say hello.'

'Oh Martin,' she said, 'I'm glad you did. We can still be friends.'

'That's cruel,' he said.

'Don't be pathetic,' she said. He looked so forlorn, trying not to catch her eye, those hands with their long sensitive fingers stuffed in his pockets. 'Of course, we can be. We're not twenty-one any more.'

They stood, Clare looking at Martin as he looked at the floor.

'By the way,' she said, 'have you seen Mila recently?'

He looked up at her. 'No,' he said. 'Why?'

'She was meant to come over and she never turned up.'

'I think she and Viktor must have had a row,' he said, 'and she walked out. He asked me to go to the police with him to report her missing.'

'Do you think she's OK?'

'The police didn't seem very worried,' he said. 'I'm sure they had a row. Viktor doesn't seem like an easy person to live with. I can well imagine why someone might want to disappear out of his life.'

'Oh,' she said.

'Why?' he said.

'Nothing,' she said.

'Do you want to come for a drink?' he said.

'Not now,' she said. 'We really have got to get the exhibition ready. Marc's just being nice. Some other time perhaps.'

Martin looked at her. She sounded as if she might

mean it. Was this the moment he must not let pass? 'I don't want to push my luck,' he said.

'But I'm sure you're just about to,' she interrupted.

'Would you like to come over for dinner one evening,' he said, 'and we can just chat. Just a chat. Nothing more. We've never really talked about it all.' There, he had got it out.

This is where she would say, 'What a lovely idea but I'm not sure we're ready for that yet,' or 'What is there to talk about?'

'OK,' she said and there was a wry smile on her face. He could have this one last chance. 'But just a chat. It's still a long way back, Martin.'

'I know,' he said but inside he was grinning. Yes. Just a chat but there was a way back. A long one but still. Result. It had been a difficult few weeks but it was over. Clare was talking to him again. And he had emerged safely from the entanglement with Viktor and all the problems of him being an illegal immigrant and now he would not have to see him again. And soon he would be back together with Clare and Megan again, with his old life happily back on track.

thirty-nine

Viktor held Suzana's hand as he walked towards the men standing in little groups, muffled against the cold and shifting their feet to keep warm. The streetlamps along the treeless avenue of semi-detached houses glowed soft and orange in the grey dawn.

A battered BMW came crawling past the groups of men and then stopped. The driver wound down his window and called something and two of the men went over to the car and bent down to the window. After a brief conversation, the men opened the back door and got in and the car drove off.

Across the street, Charlotte watched. This is what she did, she thought. She spectated. She observed the men who offered themselves for work and the contractor who drove up and inspected them and took those he chose for a day on the shovel for fifty pounds, no questions asked, no papers required. She breathed on her hands to warm them up. She had left Rob and Matthew asleep and she had forgotten her gloves. Once she would have been making notes, making sure she didn't forget any of the details for background colour. Now she felt like a voyeur, watching uneasily the hangdog eagerness of the men as they approached the car.

Lights began to appear behind the curtains in upstairs rooms. The permanent residents of Job Alley
were getting ready to go to work, their steady, regular
work. Three houses down from where she stood, the
front door opened and a man, in a short, brown
anorak, emerged and hurried down the street, careful
to avoid looking at the rootless gypsies who waited to
see if they would work today.

Across the road, a tall good-looking man in a leather
jacket, holding the hand of a small girl, approached a
small group of men. They were talking in English and
she heard wisps of conversation.

'Are you sure you've never heard of him?'

'We are sure,' one of the men said, thin and bearded
and with a face like an Orthodox martyr. 'Please leave
us now.'

Who was this man with the girl in the pink raincoat?

Viktor turned and saw the blonde woman in a beige
suede coat crossing the road towards him. He held
Suzana's hand. She was such a good child. She never
complained even though she must be freezing and tired
from having been woken up so early.

'Can I talk to you?'

The woman spoke clearly and slowly. Close up,
Viktor could see she was in her thirties, good-
looking.

'Are you looking for work?' Charlotte said. He was a
handsome man holding on to that sweet little girl in her
pink raincoat. She thought of Matthew angelically
asleep at home and suddenly wished she was there
gently waking him and cooking his breakfast. What

kind of work did this man think he was going to find, carrying a little girl around with him?

'No,' Viktor said, 'I'm looking for a friend.' He needed to be careful with this woman asking such professional questions. Who was she?

'It's cold, isn't it?' she said. He spoke good English. Educated. What was he doing here?

'Freezing,' he said. She seemed nice enough. Perhaps she lived nearby and she was just being friendly on her way to work. Although she did not seem in a hurry to move on.

'Have you been here long?' Charlotte said. If he wasn't looking for work, perhaps he was ferreting around for a story. He didn't look like a journalist. But then neither did Damian. Why couldn't he be a journalist? Foreign journalists needed stories too. And this could play well in Munich or Warsaw. Poles and Germans would want to read about London's underbelly. But if he was after the same story, why had he brought along the little girl? Cover? Perhaps he was a single parent and couldn't find anywhere to leave her at this time of the morning?

'How old is your daughter?' Charlotte said. She did not want anyone blundering around, muddying the waters, taking over her leads and confusing contacts. This could be a gateway to the gangs and she did not want anyone getting in the way.

'Six,' Viktor said. The woman seemed to want to stay around and chat. Her grey eyes were keen and intelligent. He needed to be careful.

'I'm Charlotte,' she said, putting out her hand. 'Charlotte Cornforth.'

'I'm Martin,' Viktor said. 'Martin Hughes.' He handed over one of Martin's visiting cards. He had taken a stack from his hall as he had thought they might be useful. Camouflage.

'My name is Suzana,' Suzana said, looking at Charlotte.

'Hello, Suzana,' Charlotte said. 'So what are you doing here, Martin?' It was an English name but he definitely had an accent. Somewhere Central European, she thought. Something was not right here.

'We're looking for someone,' he said.

Charlotte glanced again at the card in her hand. Barrister. Perhaps he was an immigration lawyer. It would explain the accent – although not the name. And it could be useful. Immigration lawyers would know their way around. And the gangs and their bosses. He might even act for them. But Lincoln's Inn? Wouldn't an immigration lawyer be a solicitor with an address in Hounslow or Stoke Newington? But a Lincoln's Inn barrister? There was definitely something odd here. 'Here's my card,' she said.

Suzana nestled into her father, clinging to his arm as he reached across to take the card. It was the instinctive movement of a fledgling in search of shelter.

Viktor looked at the card. 'A journalist?' he said. That would explain the questions but what was she doing here? Perhaps she could be useful? Journalists investigated things. 'We're looking for a friend,' he said. 'If you hear anything about a woman called Mila Hubchev, please could you call me.' Even if he wouldn't help them, that English lawyer would surely pass on any messages.

'Mila Hubchev? Sure,' Charlotte said. 'What's happened to her?'

'We don't know. She just disappeared. That's why we're here.'

'Where is she from?'

'Romania,' Viktor said.

'Do you think gangs might be involved?' she said.

'Gangs? What gangs? Why would they be involved?'

'I don't know,' she said. 'If an illegal immigrant disappears, then gangs are often involved in it.'

'What do you mean an illegal immigrant? Why do you think Mila was an illegal immigrant?'

'You'd hardly be looking for her here if she wasn't, would you?' Charlotte said. 'Look, I'm only trying to help. I want to tell the stories of the victims.' Was she moving too fast for this man with fierce eyes? 'If you can tell me anything about the gangs,' she said, 'it will help me get this story up and that might help you find Mila.'

'Why do you think there are gangs here?' Viktor said. 'Look at them. Do they look like gangsters to you? They're just men, looking for work. That's it. No story.'

'Why were you speaking English to them?' Charlotte said. 'Wouldn't they trust you more if you spoke in their own language?'

'Because they're all pretending to be Greek. And they don't speak Greek.' Viktor laughed drily. 'And neither do I.'

'Why?'

'Because I never learned Greek.'

'No, I meant why are they pretending?'

Viktor looked at her, as if he was uncertain whether she was teasing him. 'Because Greece is in Europe and Europeans don't need papers to work,' he said patiently.

Of course.

'And the blacks pretend to be French,' Viktor said. 'It's all pointless. If the police come, they'll know in five seconds these people are not Greeks or French. But it makes them feel better.'

Business did not seem to be good because no more cars came by and Charlotte could see most of the men were still waiting around. She needed to leave soon to take Matthew to the nursery. 'You've got my card,' she said, 'if you do come across anything.' It was really freezing. She needed a cup of coffee and she should talk to some of these other men before they all drifted away.

'Yes, yes,' Viktor said. 'And please ring me if you hear anything about Mila Hubchev.'

Charlotte turned to walk back towards the men.

'Or a man called Kalaj,' he called after her. 'Please call me.'

She stopped and looked back at him. 'Kalaj,' she said. 'Mila Hubchev. Sure.' She shouldn't spend more than ten more minutes here or Matthew would be late again.

He watched her as she walked back to the men standing underneath the nearest streetlight. Simon

Ofasa had not come today. How much longer should he wait? No-one would come after seven o'clock as all the work would have gone by then. He crouched down in front of Suzana and kissed her. The little girl solemnly kissed him back on the cheek, carefully avoiding his beard. And then, as he got up, he saw a short, fat man ambling along the street from the far end. That could be him.

'Are you Simon?' he said as the man came nearer. 'Simon Ofasa?'

'Who wants to know?' the man said. He smiled but his eyes were watchful.

'David Buchanan said you might be able to help me,' Viktor said.

'David.' Simon Ofasa shook his head and smiled again. 'Don't believe a word he says.'

'I'm looking for Josephine,' Viktor said. 'Do you know where she is? My friend Mila went to see her last night.'

Simon looked at him for a moment before he replied. 'Josephine isn't here,' he said. 'She went to Frankfurt a week ago. I'm sorry.'

'Are you sure?' Viktor said. 'Are you sure? Mila said she was going to see Josephine.'

'I'm sorry,' Simon said. 'I am sure. Josephine went to Frankfurt a week ago. I'm sorry.'

What was going on? He was sure Mila had said she was going to visit Josephine. Why had she said that? 'Thank you,' he said. 'Thank you.' Suzana gave a little whimper and he realised he had begun squeezing her hand tightly. 'I'm sorry, my darling,' he said and bent down to kiss her. 'I'm sorry.'

He got up. 'Do you know a man called Kalaj?' he said to Simon Ofasa.

'Everyone knows about Kalaj.'

'Where do I find him?' Viktor said.

'I don't know,' Simon said. 'I've never met him. But everyone says he's the man. But are you sure you want to meet him?' He bent down and patted Suzana on the head. 'She's beautiful,' he said, 'your daughter.'

'Don't you have any idea where I might find him?'

'I'm sorry. I've got to go. No-one's going to give me a job when I'm talking to you.'

'Please,' Viktor said.

'Look, I really don't know,' Simon said. 'But you might try the Madonna Club.'

'What's that?' Viktor said.

'I've heard it's his club,' Simon said. 'In Soho. You could try that.'

Viktor carefully wrote down the name. 'Thank you,' he said. 'Thank you.' He had to get Suzana to school now but tonight he would go to find this Kalaj.

'Be careful,' Simon said.

Viktor nodded. He had got the idea about Kalaj. In their own ways, David and Goran and now Simon Ofasa had all said the same thing about him. Kalaj was a vicious thug. But what choice did he have? Kalaj was the only lead he had to Mila. All the same, Simon's sombre tone suggested that he should take some protection to the Madonna Club.

forty

'Do you want a game of chess?' Kalaj said.

'I can't play, Mr Kalaj,' Boris said. It was one of the boss's little jokes.

'Don't be modest, Boris, I'm sure you're a grand-master.'

Boris sprawled in the chair and said nothing. It didn't usually take long for the boss to get bored with these little games. He waited patiently to be told what to do.

Kalaj raised his hands above his head and stretched. Perhaps he had overreacted. Perhaps it was just bad luck that Vasili had got shot. Perhaps it was just restlessness that had made the woman want to leave. After all, no-one had come after him and there had been no further incidents and, as far as he could see, the businesses were all doing as well as usual. The Romanian was tricky but he was keeping a close eye on her and she would have to be a lot smarter than she was to put one over him. It looked as if everything may be back on an even keel.

Of course, Kalaj thought, there were one or two loose ends to tie up. He still needed to interrogate the surviving peasant from Vlore to find out what had really happened to Vasili. And, as always, he needed to keep his eyes open. But still, it did look as if everything was back on an even keel.

forty-one

Bernie was going to nail the fucker. And he knew how to do it. The solution lived in Temecula. Ron McClellan had won the Southern California Computing Sciences Bowl three years in a row between 1999 and 2002 and he was still only in tenth grade. Even at this age, he had rare skills that had already proved useful to one of Bernie's associates and it was time Bernie had a chat with him, face to face.

So while Marlene pursed her lips and rearranged his diary again, Bernie got on his bike and cruised down Highway 15 to Riverside County. He parked the BMW outside Ron's home on Stanford Drive and dismounted. And found no-one in. Even though he had called ahead himself and arranged with Ron to meet him at three o'clock.

Bernie walked down to the pavement and looked down the wide street, warm in the afternoon sun. Nothing moved. What a place. He drove down to the mall and walked around until finally, passing the Amerikhan Mongolian Grill and the Marble Slab Creamery, he had sat down and drunk a latte in Kelly's Coffee & Fudge Factory and then looked at his watch again. The little geek had better be back soon. He would have to learn that for three grand a week you turned up on time for your appointments. Especially when your employer travelled eighty-five miles to see you.

He cruised gently back through the deserted streets. What a place. How could anyone live here? Bernie had little sympathy for young families struggling to build the American dream for themselves in this balmy new town. He had Googled it and found Riverside County had five per cent of the population of California and only one per cent of the state's high-risk sex offenders. But it logged fourteen per cent of calls made under Megan's Law to discover where these perverts lived. In Bernie's view, that told you everything you needed to know about Riverside County. Disproportionately low risk. Disproportionately high worry about it. For the good life, the way the ancients lived it, you should only worry about what you needed to worry about. Otherwise you should live in Temecula.

As he rode back from the mall and turned into Stanford Drive, it looked as if the McClellans had returned from their family outing because a new Lincoln Navigator was now parked on the car-stand. Fifty thousand dollars even after the discount. Outside a house that was worth four hundred thousand dollars, tops. What sort of people would spend twelve and a half per cent of the value of their house on a car? And on a car like that? Sometimes Bernie was baffled by his own country.

He parked the BMW off the road behind the Lincoln and rang the bell. Something that sounded like zen wind chimes rang inside the house. And then a blonde woman with a fresh sweet expression opened the door.

'Hi,' she said and smiled, an open welcoming smile, as if Bernie was an old friend. That was the sort of person who lived in places like this. They were always trying to pretend the world was better than it was. They should live in LA. Or become a Certified Public Accountant.

'Hi, Mrs McClellan,' he said. 'I am Bernie Newman. I have come to see Ron.'

'Come in,' she said, still smiling.

'Thank you,' he said, following her into the light hallway. He caught a glimpse of a granite counter in the kitchen.

'Ron,' she called. 'Someone to see you.'

On the table in the hallway, there was a copy of *Advice for a Happy Marriage*. That was the sort of person who lived in places like this. How had Mr and Mrs McClellan managed to breed Ron? Because Ron was seriously smart and he certainly did not belong in a place like Temecula. He could make himself very useful in Los Angeles.

They sat on the flagstone patio as the shadows began to creep round the small kidney-shaped pool and Mrs McClellan brought them out iced tea she had made herself. And Ron explained how he was going to identify whoever was hacking into the casino. Checking and cross-checking, monitoring the site and everyone logging on to it, identifying the skimmer, tracing the route the hacker was taking, calculating the transmission times between the network components connecting the attacker and his target.

'How can you be sure?' Bernie said.

Ron was a slight fair-haired boy in a blue and yellow striped polo shirt and chinos who looked at the floor when he spoke. His face was pocked with acne but when it cleared up he would have his mother's friendly good looks.

'That is why you are paying me three thousand dollars a week, Mr Newman. To be sure.'

He was an awkward, unprepossessing young man but Bernie believed him. He knew what it meant to be professional. And this kid was a professional.

'How long will it take you?'

'It shouldn't take long. Two days. Three days.'

Bernie looked at the boy scuffling his feet as he spoke and he smiled. The boy was good.

Together, he and Ron were going to nail this fucker.

forty-two

Clive Walton was going to nail the killer, but now the vein had started fluttering in his left temple and he knew it was time for him to go home for the night. He swivelled on his chair and looked out at the car park, empty, apart from a blue Mondeo. Yesterday, the facts had been marshalling themselves towards an explanation, the first step towards a solution, but this evening they were scurrying anarchically all over the place and it made him uneasy. He didn't like cases where the more he learned the more difficult it was to make sense of it. But he was going to get a grip on it.

There was a muffled conversation in the corridor outside his office and then he heard a man laugh and a door slam and it was silent again. The security lights in the car park washed the room in a sodium glow. On his desk was the report on the ID card that had been placed on the seat by the dead woman in the Tube carriage. Forged. What was the point of that? And it meant they still had no idea who the victim was.

He looked at his watch. He should have called Stephanie and told her he was going to be late. He would do it in a moment when he had thought this through a little longer. He wrote down the key facts on a sheet of paper and drew a neat square box round each of them. 'Throat cut', 'Tube', 'Woman', 'Forged ID card'. He carefully circled the word 'Prostitute?' That was just a guess, not a fact.

The door opened. 'OK, Clive?' Dave Harmsworth leaned into the room, keeping his hand on the door-knob. 'Fancy a pint?' he said.

Clive shook his head. 'No thanks,' he said, 'I'm just off home.' He didn't want Dave Harmsworth thinking he was worried about this case.

'Don't stay too late,' Dave Harmsworth said. 'It'll still be here in the morning,' and he closed the door behind him. Clive heard him whistling as he walked down the corridor to the lift. He knew what Dave Harmsworth said about him behind his back, over a pint in the Red Lion. Dave was one of those inspectors who believed that building your base with other officers was important if you were to go on up through senior management.

What was the point of leaving a forged ID card beside the body? What message was that supposed to send? Clive Walton rubbed his eyes wearily. Sometimes there was no point. Sometimes it was just a mistake. Sometimes all the time spent truffling for significance was wasted. There was none. It was just one of those things.

He heard the lift in the distance, clanking and whirring downstairs, ferrying Dave Harmsworth towards the Red Lion and backbiting about him to their colleagues. Clive Walton didn't care much. When he had been promoted, the chief superintendent had warned him that getting on so young would provoke jealousy and he would have to live with it and justify the faith that had been placed in him. And that was fine by Clive Walton. As long as he could go on justifying it.

The problem was knowing when something, such as an ID card being forged, was significant and when it was irrelevant. Did the fact that it was forged mean nothing more than the fact that these people always used forged documents? Or was it part of the message in some way? Clive Walton could not see how it could be unless the message was so intricate and convoluted that only the intended recipient could decipher it.

He yawned. He picked up the file again and flicked through it. He needed to ring Stephanie. Anyway, he might as well go home now as he didn't think he was going to get much further tonight. The report suggested the card was the work of a forger whose work had been appearing all over southern England for the last six months. So the perpetrators were plugged in but why would he have thought anything else? On the last page, there was a paragraph, apparently tacked on as an afterthought, that they had picked up someone in Slough with one of these forged passports who had also been involved in an electronic scam. That was quite interesting, Clive Walton thought. A traditional craft linked with modern electronic counterfeiting. Similar skills in many ways. But they were not identical ones, so where did that thought lead?

That was it for the evening. He stretched and got up and picked up the phone to ring Stephanie. It was inevitable really, he thought, that the cunning and skills and ingenuity of the traditional forger would find some way to exploit the new opportunities of the Internet. One way or the other, he would nail this killer.

forty-three

Charlotte was going to nail this story. 'A thousand pounds, George,' she said. 'That's all I want.' Please, George. Come on, don't be a muppet. Make your mind up now. I need to get home and see Matthew before he goes to bed.

'That's a lot of money,' the Home Editor said carefully. 'How am I going to justify it?'

'It's a week's world-class consultancy,' she said. And another thousand pounds a week, until we get a result, she thought.

'I know that,' George Waddington said patiently. 'But how can I justify that?' He gently stroked the side of his nose as he looked at Charlotte. 'How do we know you are going to get something out of it?'

It was mesmerising, that gentle stroking. Is that why he did it? 'I know this is a good story, George,' she said. 'But I need help to get into the gangs and this guy is good. Really good, I'm told.'

It was just as well George had not asked to meet Giles. He was a beanpole with staring eyes, who, twenty-three years after starting nursery school, was still not effectively socialised. 'Inappropriately dressed for the weather, I see,' Giles had said when he first met

Charlotte. Not even 'hello'. And even though it was cold and raining outside she had thought her beige suit was a spirit-lifting outfit for a dull day. Giles made it clear that he disagreed. But she was told he was very good at what he did.

'A thousand pounds a week,' George said. 'It's not nothing.'

'It will be worth it, George,' she said, 'trust me.' Just make the decision now and let me get home. She couldn't bear the way Rob looked at her with those steady eyes when once again she got home too late to say goodnight to Matthew.

'I do trust you,' George said. 'But it's still a lot of money. Are you sure this will work?'

That wasn't the problem, she wanted to say. It would work. She'd been assured Giles was one of the best at what he did. The problem was George wouldn't pay up if he knew what Giles did.

'I wouldn't be asking if I wasn't sure,' she said. 'I know what Maggie feels about this. And me. I wouldn't be asking if I wasn't sure it would work. I wouldn't do it to you.'

George looked at her.

'I'll make this work,' she said. 'Please.' It had to work. Come on, George, I know you're not a muppet. Just give me the money and let me go home.

She was reliably informed that Giles could hack into anything. His competence was not in question. The problem was that what she wanted him to do was breaking the law and even this newspaper could not actively aid and abet an illegal act by funding it.

'And what exactly would we be buying with all this money?'

George Waddington was not stupid. Unfortunately. But he could not have guessed what she really wanted the money for, could he? He couldn't have. 'Research,' she said. That should cover it.

'Yes, Charlotte,' he said patiently. 'But what research? Into what?'

'Into the gangs. I need someone to help me understand them better. How they operate.' Daintily lubricious Roger, the neat little minister, would have been appalled if he had known that the suggestion to break the law had come from him, however inadvertently. But he had been too intent at sneaking a look at her breasts to notice her sudden spark of interest when he mentioned how traffickers used the Internet.

'And who is this extremely expensive consultant?' George said.

'He's well-connected, George, believe me.' If she could hack into their emails, she could see how they operated and out would flow award-winning journalism. Of course, it was illegal but no risk, no reward. Who would care when she had exposed these electronic Napoleons?

'Does this extremely expensive well-connected consultant have a name?'

'Giles,' she said.

'Giles? Just Giles?' George said.

'I'm sorry, George. I can't tell you anything more for now. It's confidential. He is so connected.' Saying anything more could open up unwelcome questioning about what exactly he was going to be consulted about. His full name would have to be on the invoice but by then she should have got the story and everyone would be happy. And no-one would be able to prove anything about what she had done to get it.

'There will be an invoice, won't there, Charlotte?'

'Of course, George. Everything will be straight for the books.' Giles would never say anything. He would be even more in the frame than her. Who else could know?

'This isn't anything dodgy, is it, Charlotte?'

'Would I do anything like that, George?' It had to be worth the risk. And anyway she had nothing else. This was her last resort. But it could turn out to be inspired. And then when she had delivered the story and proved she could still do it, she could walk out to Tarifa with her head held high. Come on, George. Please.

'OK. Don't push it, Charlotte. If I trust you, are you going to let me down?'

'Of course not, George. You know me. I always do my best.' Just say yes. Now. Have pity on me, George. I have got to get home.

'That's what worries me.'

Charlotte smiled at him reassuringly. 'You don't need to worry, George,' she said. Why had no-one done this before? It was so obvious. But it was the hallmark of genius that it seemed so obvious afterwards that everyone wondered why it had not been done before. But even geniuses had to get home sometimes.

'All right, I'm sure I'll regret this but you can have the money,' George said.

'Thank you, George. Thank you. I won't let you down.' She did not have much to give Giles to start with but that name she had got from that man at Job Alley could be a beginning. Mila Hubchev. That was it. And then one thing could lead to another. And Kalaj. That was another name.

'Make sure you don't,' George said. 'Let me know how you're getting on by Friday.'

'Of course. It's a deal.'

'No, it's not. It's a problem. Your problem. And my problem.'

But Charlotte didn't care. She was going to nail this story.

forty-four

Martin was going to nail Clare. As soon as he got back from work he showered and put James Brown on repeat and started to prepare the living room for her arrival. 'I Feel Good' sang the Godfather of Soul as Martin lit the fire and plumped up the cushions on the armchairs. And then he stopped, mortified. This was no way to think of Clare. He was not a shagger and she was not a target to be nailed. She was the woman he loved and wanted to make his wife. And this was not a date. It was just a chat. Between friends. If anything developed, so be it but he was not going to plan anything. It was a long way back, Clare had said, and tonight was just the beginning.

He drew back the curtains and turned on the lighting in the garden. Through the windows, the bare trees cast intricate shadows on the little lawn. But would it be better with the curtains closed? Martin tried it and the room turned from modern urban living into a warm comfortable home. Better. He turned off the overhead light. The fire cast shadows which flickered on the walls and the standard lamp glowed gentle and mellow in the corner. Yes. 'I Feel Good'. And then the doorbell rang.

Martin looked at his watch. She was nearly an hour early. That must be a good sign. He turned off James Brown and patted his hair into place. Ready. 'Coming,' he called and went to open the door. And there was Viktor.

'Where's Suzana?' Martin said. It was all he could think. He had never seen Viktor without his little daughter in the pink raincoat. It was as if one of the Orthodox Jews down the road had gone out into the street without his hat.

'She has gone for a sleepover with a friend,' Viktor said. 'You must help me.'

Martin knew he had to stay in the doorway and not move. If he gave the slightest signal of encouragement, he knew he would be lost. 'I'm really sorry, Viktor,' he said, 'I'm busy.'

'Please, Martin,' Viktor said. 'I need your help.' He sounded more formal and circumspect than he had done two nights ago but there was nothing submissive in his tone. It was still insistent but Martin did not move. Clare could arrive at any moment.

'I'm sorry, Viktor. I'm sure Mila will call you soon.'

'How can she call me if she is dead?'

Martin felt the blood leave his face. How could he have been such a clod?

'I am so sorry,' he said. 'Please come in.' He followed Viktor down the dark narrow hallway. 'Can I get you a drink?' he said.

'No,' Viktor said, 'I do not have time to drink. We must find her.'

Martin turned to look at him. 'I thought you said she was dead?' he said.

'No,' Viktor said. 'You said she'll call me and I said how can she call me if she's dead. I don't know if she's dead. But she may be and that's why she doesn't call. But I must know. If she's not dead she may be in danger and that is why she doesn't call. I must find out.' He started to pace up and down again. 'I must be able to help her.'

Martin wondered where he had left the whisky. What was he going to do? Now he had let him in and Clare would be here soon. As the policeman had said it was probably just a lovers' tiff and that was why Viktor was really so agitated. Guilt. Perhaps he hit her? Anger and violence hung in clouds around him.

'I'm sorry but I'm not that kind of lawyer,' he said. 'I'm sure the police are doing all they can. I know it's difficult but you must be patient.' Clare would be here soon and he couldn't afford to get it wrong this time. And this man was an illegal immigrant. He mustn't get involved with him.

'You know the police won't try,' Viktor said. 'You heard them. They don't try for "people like this".'

'You don't know that.'

'What do you think?'

'Actually I think the sergeant has done what he said and the Missing Persons Bureau are looking for her. And I'm sure they'll find her. And I don't know what you think you can do they cannot do better. And now I'm afraid I really do have to get ready.'

Viktor picked up the cushion Martin had positioned on the armchair and carefully placed it on the sofa and then sat down. 'I will explain,' he said.

'I'm sorry, Viktor. I'm sure this is worrying for you. But I'm also sure she's all right and I'm busy tonight. I'm sorry.'

'Sorry? What can you know about sorrow?' Viktor said. 'Let me tell you about sorrow. Until my wife died, we lived in Banja Luka. One of the largest cities in Bosnia. In the former Yugoslavia as you call it.' His hands were clasped together in his lap. 'Until the war it was a good place to live. Serbs and Croats and Bosniaks together. We've lost all that. Today it is the capital of Republika Srpska.'

He was a train crossing the endless steppe at the same steady relentless speed, with no possibility of stopping until it reached its destination. Martin felt Viktor tightening the pressure sentence by sentence. What should he do when Clare rang the bell?

'I came here so Suzana should be safe,' Viktor said. 'Because I promised my wife. I came with nothing. You think Suzana wears her coat all the time because she loves it. Because little girls are like that. But she wears it all the time because she has nothing else to wear. She doesn't like pink.' He unclasped his hands and pinched the top of his nose between his finger and thumb. 'And every day I miss my wife.'

Viktor paused and Martin knew what he was trying to do to him. He knew how easily he could be made to feel guilty. Clare had done it to him. So had his mother. Martin knew when he was being manipulated but still the images sprang into his mind. The pretty woman in a headscarf trying to dodge the sniper fire. The mortar bomb in the market-place. The mother putting her children into the back of a lorry. And the strutting young men with bandanas and Kalashnikovs. He imagined Viktor carrying his wounded wife from the sunlit street into the shelter of a doorway and cradling her, while an infant Suzana screamed uncomprehendingly.

'Then one day I met Mila,' Viktor said and Martin remembered the way she had looked at St Luke's. 'I cannot lose anyone else,' Viktor said. 'I cannot lose her.' He stopped and looked at the floor. For a moment, it seemed as if he had forgotten Martin and was thinking of something else, infinitely painful. His wife? Mila? And Martin felt the cruel history of the Balkans bleeding into his flat.

'It must have been terrible,' he said.

Viktor showed no sign of hearing him and stayed looking at the floor.

'I can only imagine how important it must be for you to find Mila. But don't you think we should leave it to the police?'

Viktor gave a dry laugh and looked up at Martin.

'Especially as there are question marks over your immigration status and the more you get involved the more difficult it might become.'

Viktor stood up again. 'I can't wait around to find out,' he said. 'I can't lose her too. I will not.'

'I know how difficult it must be. But what can you do? What can I do?' Martin said.

'I will tell you,' Viktor said.

Martin ran his hands through his hair. Wrong expression. He should have guessed Viktor would interpret it literally.

'I've been told about a man who could help. Kalaj. Tonight I am going to find him,' Viktor said. 'He's not a man I should see alone. Will you come?'

He stared at Martin. There was silence. Viktor had left him no space to think. Martin rehearsed to himself how he might explain about Clare but what would that sound like after what Viktor had just told him? What if something terrible really had happened to Mila? There was an insistent importance about Viktor's life that Martin could not ignore. Everything mattered to Viktor in a way nothing mattered to Martin. His daughter. His love. Life. Death. How could he walk away from all that?

And yet paragraph 301 kept clattering across his mind. What else was Viktor but prejudicial to the administration of justice? Everyone had problems and what, realistically, could he do about them? This was not his business. The police were there precisely to solve these sorts of problem. They should handle it.

'What's your problem?' Viktor said, seeing his hesitation. 'What are you worried about? That it will interrupt your busy schedule?'

Martin felt himself beginning to blush. Viktor was right.

'I used to be like that,' Viktor said. 'I had a routine, everything in its place. Before the war, Serbs and Croats and Bosniaks, we all lived together in the same town. A good life. No problems. We all swam in the same river, walked in the same woods. Living here, you can't know how it feels to see your world change. Die.'

Martin shook his head. Viktor was right. He didn't know. 'I'm sorry,' he said.

'How can you living here understand what it was like there?' Viktor said. 'Every day you go to the same bar and drink with the same people and watch the football on television together. Support the same team. You buy them a drink. They buy you a drink. They tell you about work and their family and their girlfriends. And you tell them about yours. And then one day it's different. You can smell it. The first time it's just a . . .' He paused, searching for the word. 'Whiff. It's just a whiff. At first, it's little things. They look at you differently when you walk in. And they don't talk about their family any more. Only the football. A few days later, they don't want to talk at all. And then you don't want to go to that bar any more. And then they are knocking at your door with guns and chains. That's how it works. The poison spreads quickly.'

'It must have been terrible,' Martin said. He thought of the river running through Banja Luka, clear and sparkling in the spring sunshine, old men fishing on the banks and young men competing to impress girlfriends with carelessly athletic dives. 'You should go back to the police,' he said 'Tell them what you have found out. Tell them about this Kalaj and let them handle it. It's their job.'

'I've lost that life. I can't lose Mila too,' Viktor said. 'But I can't go to the police.'

'But this is their job,' Martin said. 'What you've discovered about this man Kalaj might help them find Mila quicker. They aren't going to persecute you. Their job is to find Mila.'

Viktor said nothing. Martin glanced at his watch. Clare was going to be here soon and this man was sitting in his flat making him feel guilty. He was sorry but what had it got to do with him? And there was something bothering him about Viktor's story.

'Look,' he said, 'I'm sorry about Mila but actually I don't understand why it's so difficult for you to go to the police. Why can't you go back to Bosnia? The war's over. It's a democracy now, isn't it? Why can't you just go back?'

Viktor sat silently, looking at the floor.

'Don't you think it's time to think about going back with Suzana?' Martin said. 'Where you could feel at home. What kind of life is it here for you when you are too frightened even to go to the police when something like this happens?'

Martin wondered if Viktor had heard him or understood what he said. Or maybe the silence meant he was just trying to stop himself from hitting Martin for being such an insensitive clod. How could he understand what Viktor had been through?

'Martin,' Viktor said, 'I am grateful to you. But there are some things you do not understand. You cannot understand.'

'Tell me then,' Martin said. 'How can I understand when you don't tell me anything? Why can't you go back now? Hasn't the fighting stopped? You'd be safe.

You can't be here for money. You're a lawyer. You must be able to do better there.'

'Because I promised my wife,' Viktor said, but Martin still couldn't fit the pieces together.

Viktor's wife had been killed. There had been a civil war. Now there was not. What promise was there still to keep? Why should he not go back now it was safe? Was this Balkan pride, a tribute to his dead wife, a promise he made on her grave? 'She wouldn't have wanted you to be unhappy here,' he said.

'But she did,' Viktor said. 'She made me promise to come here with Suzana. Whatever happened, she said.'

The bullet must not have killed her outright and she had taken a long time to die, as Viktor cradled her head in his arms, kneeling in the dusty street as she made him promise to escape with Suzana.

'Promises made like that shouldn't bind you,' he said. These were precatory words, Martin thought. And, as the case of 'Adams and the Kensington Vestry Re.' made clear, these did not impose a trust.

'What do you mean, "promises made like that"?'

'The trauma,' Martin said. 'The shock of being shot. People can say things in extreme circumstances like that they might have said differently if they had time to reflect.'

'What do you mean "shot"? My wife was not shot.'

'You said she was killed.'

'Yes, she was. Killed by cancer. She was not shot. She was killed by cancer.'

How could he have been such an oaf? Why had he

thought she had been shot? How could he have made Viktor go over it again like this. 'I am so sorry,' he said.

'You have a busy imagination, Martin,' Viktor said.

'I didn't know,' Martin said.

'It's OK,' Viktor said. 'How could you know? I'll tell you how it was. I was a human rights lawyer. Never easy but it became more and more dangerous. I tried to use the law to protect Croats and Bosniaks. I could do nothing when the killing started but before that there was beating up and threats and cheating on business deals, all pushing, pushing to get them out. And the system connived. That's the word. Connived. I tried to stop it conniving.' As he talked, he saw again his little office in the centre of Banja Luka with his law certificate framed on the wall and the photos of Jelena and Suzana on his desk.

'I couldn't do much but I did what I could. I thought I was helping keep civilisation alive. Does that sound too grand? I thought I was tending a tiny flame that one day could burn brightly again. Whatever I did, it was a promise to the future that order would return and the law would mean something again. But this wasn't popular. And I'm a Serb so I was a special kind of traitor. And then the threats started to come. The phone calls in the middle of the night. At first, Jelena was OK with it. She believed in me and what I did. We were a team.'

Martin could imagine what Jelena had been like.

'And then she got cancer. I kept believing there was a chance but she knew. And everything changed. She wanted to put everything in order and know everyone she cared for was going to be OK after she'd gone. She was a strong woman. When she was living, she felt she could make sure Suzana and I would be OK, whatever the thugs did. But now she wanted to be sure that we would be OK when she had gone. So she made me promise to come here and make sure Suzana grew up safe, away from the psychopaths.'

'But you've honoured your promise,' Martin said. 'Now things are better in Banja Luka, you could go back, couldn't you?'

'Don't you think I want to?' Viktor said. 'You think I like it here? I dream of going back there with Suzana. And Mila. I dream of it. Here I am nothing. There I had my work. I knew who I was. What am I here?'

'So why don't you? Just go. You've kept your word.'

'It's not so easy,' Viktor said. 'You may be right. A hundred times a day I say to myself what you're saying to me. But then I think it isn't so safe. If I go back, there are those who still remember me. And don't like me.'

'But they're not going to kill you,' Martin said. 'Are they?'

'Martin, you're like the politicians who fly in and go on their tours of reconciliation and they see what they're meant to see, what they want to see,' Viktor said, 'and then they fly out again and then the Serbs go on just as they did before, keeping the Croats and the Bosniaks in their place. Down. They just don't kill so many of them nowadays. My sister lives in Sarajevo and she tells me. So how can I go back? They remember everything, these people. What do you think would happen to me? I promised Jelena to take no more risks. Yes, things are much better. But is there no risk? Can I honestly say there is no risk to me? No, I cannot. Less risk, yes. Little risk, perhaps. But no risk? And until I can honestly say there is no risk then how can I go back and keep my promise to Jelena? What would happen to Suzana if anything happened to me now? Our daughter an orphan?'

'But you could get run over by a bus here,' Martin said. 'You can't remove all risk from life.' And Clare must be almost here.

'It's not the same thing,' Viktor said and Martin knew he must do something to end the conversation now. He could not lose this chance with Clare. He steeled himself. 'I'm really sorry, Viktor,' he said, 'but there's nothing I can do. I hope it works out for you. But I'm afraid I've got to get ready now and you've got to go.' He felt himself bracing. He knew Viktor was going to shout at him or, worse, make him feel even more guilty. But he had made his choice. Clare came first. This was his life.

But Viktor surprised him. He did not shout or try to make him feel guilty. 'I'm sorry, Martin,' he said. 'I don't like doing this but you've given me no choice. I can't let you not help me. This is too important. I need your help and you must give it to me. I have no-one else.'

'I'm sorry, Viktor. I can't help you. And this is my flat and you must leave it now. I'm sorry.'

'You don't understand. You have no choice.'

'What do you mean?'

'You are already involved. You came with me to the police to report Mila missing. You gave them your name and now a young woman has been murdered.'

'What do you mean?' Martin said.

'The police are asking questions about her. They don't know who she was and I don't know either but it may be Mila. They are looking for people who may be able to give them a lead. You're a respectable lawyer.' Viktor looked around the flat. 'Do you want to help them with their enquiries into this murder?'

Martin snorted. 'If you're trying to blackmail me,' he said, 'you'll have to do better than that. Why should they think I had anything to do with this? Now get out.'

Viktor did not move. 'I will telephone the police and tell them that you were having an affair with Mila and that you had an argument.'

'Why should anyone believe you?' Martin said and then he remembered what the policeman had said about domestic arguments. 'It's not true and there's nothing to suggest it is.'

'True, but it is going to take you a long time to prove that. And it won't look good for a respectable lawyer having to explain himself in a murder case.'

'This is blackmail based on nothing,' Martin said. And yet he could see how this could hurt him. His father would be convinced this would ruin his chances of becoming a judge and he could be right. Even if the police dismissed any allegations that he had killed Mila in a jealous rage, the mere fact of Viktor making the allegation, no matter how bogus, would expose his conniving at illegal immigration and bring paragraph 301 and Section C into play. He hadn't reported Viktor to the police. It would break his father's heart.

'Yes, it's blackmail,' Viktor said, 'but I'm desperate. I wouldn't do this if I wasn't and I'm not asking much. Just come with me to see Kalaj. That's all and that will be it. I just need your help tonight. It's too risky for me to go on my own. They will be much more careful about doing anything to me if I go with an English lawyer. I need you to come with me and so if you don't, I will make trouble for you. I hope you understand.'

Martin understood. 'This is disgusting,' he said. 'You should be ashamed of yourself. You're only able to threaten me like this because I tried to help you in the first place. And this is what I get in return.'

'I'm desperate, Martin. Please help me.'

Martin imagined his father's reaction. It would confirm his worst worries about his son. He should never have got involved in the first place. He must already be in breach of paragraph 301 of the Code of Conduct. But what choice did he have? He supposed he could see Clare another time. 'I must make a phone call,' he said and he rang her number.

'Hello, Martin,' she said cheerily. 'Don't worry, I'm just leaving.'

'Well actually,' he said, 'something's just come up. Remember Viktor from school, well, I need to help him with something. I'm really sorry but it's literally just come up.'

'That's OK,' Clare said.

'I'm really sorry,' Martin said. 'I hope I'm not letting you down.'

'It's all right,' Clare said. She did not seem to mind. Her cool, distant tone suggested she did not care at all.

'I'm really sorry,' Martin said. 'Please can we re-arrange? I'll ring you.'

'Martin,' she said, 'it's all right. I'm sure that'll be fine. I've got to go now. Goodbye.'

As she rang off, Martin saw Viktor's eyes on him, burning impatiently. This evening was not turning out as he had intended.

forty-five

'It's not good for Matthew,' Rob said, holding her hand and looking into her eyes.

'Do you think I don't know that?' Charlotte said, pulling her hand away. They were sitting in the kitchen, with a half-empty bottle of Rioja and the remains of a pizza between them.

'I'm not criticising,' Rob said, 'I'm just saying we need to make some choices.'

'We?' Charlotte said. 'You don't have to make any choices. I do.' That afternoon she had spent too long trying to get hold of someone she had been told might be useful for the story, and when she arrived at the nursery Matthew was sitting in a chair, his cheeks wet with tears, while Harriet Warren kneeled beside him, stroking his hair. As Charlotte rushed into the room, the teacher looked up at her, cold and accusing.

'I'm so sorry,' Charlotte had said. 'The traffic was unbelievable.'

Harriet Warren had not replied. 'Here's your mummy, Matthew,' she had said as she got up. 'At last.'

Charlotte knew what she meant. No wonder the poor boy is going wrong with a mother like that.

'Why can't it be like Tarifa, Rob?' she said, pouring herself another glass of wine. 'Why don't we just move there, you, me and Matthew?'

'We could do,' Rob said. 'If that's really what you want,' and he took her hand back in his and started stroking her fingers. 'Is that what you really want?'

'I don't know,' Charlotte wailed. 'I'm conflicted.'

'Conflicted?' Rob said, smiling at her. 'Really?'

'Whatever,' Charlotte said. 'I don't know what to do. Help me.'

'I can't choose for you,' he said. 'It's your call. I'll fit in, I promise.'

'Why is it you always get the easy choice?' Charlotte said.

forty-six

'Have you got any money?' Viktor said to Martin on the bus.

Martin took out his wallet. 'About forty-five pounds,' he said. 'Why?'

'I will need to borrow some.'

'Anything else you need?' Viktor had bundled him on to treacherous terrain and now every step he took, the scree gave way and sent him slithering into more trouble.

'That's all.' Viktor seemed oblivious to sarcasm. 'We may need to buy drinks while we wait for him. I will repay you.' They got off the bus halfway down Shaftesbury Avenue. It was a cold evening but the streets were full of rubbish and tourists.

'It must be near here,' Viktor said, picking his way round a black plastic bag, spilling its contents out on to the pavement. Warm, rich smells came from the Chinese restaurants. Here was the Pearl where Martin used to come with Clare. And there were two drunk German businessmen lurching down the street, laughing happily.

'And here we are,' Viktor said.

Martin stopped watching where he was treading and looked up from the pavement and saw 'The Madonna

Club. Live girls'. He never understood what that meant. He used to laugh about it with Clare. What other kind of girls were there?

There was a very large man, with a shaven head, standing outside the entrance in a grey suit that he clearly could not button across his massive chest. He was staring impassively in front of him. 'We need to meet someone inside,' Viktor said. 'Mr Kalaj.'

'Twenty pounds,' the man said. 'Each.'

'We only need to talk to him. We don't want anything else.'

'Twenty pounds,' the man repeated, without any change in his dead tone. 'Each.'

'Martin,' Viktor said.

'Do you take credit cards?' Martin said.

'Inside,' the man said. 'There.' Just by the door there was a tiny window behind which sat a sallow youth with an angry red spot on his lip. 'Two,' the doorman called to him.

'Card,' the youth said.

Martin pushed his credit card through the little window.

'Wait,' the youth said. Through a maroon curtain, they heard loud rock music and felt the heavy warm air as it flowed past them to escape into the night. 'Sign,' the youth said and Martin signed the voucher poked through the window. 'Here,' the youth said and pushed two blue tickets back through the window. 'You get a free drink. Any more you pay for. It goes on your card. When you leave you get your card back.'

'What do you mean?' Martin said. 'Where's my card?'

'You get it back at the end. When you have paid.'

'Of course I'll pay but you can't just keep my card.'

'Tony,' the youth called, in a bored voice. 'The man wants his card back.'

The doorman turned round and leaned into the alcove. It was so small that Martin could smell the mint and cigarettes on his breath. His face was blank. 'You want to go in, he keeps the card.' He sounded bored too. 'You want your card, you don't go in.'

'Martin,' Viktor said, 'I will pay you back. I promise.'

Martin sighed. It got worse by the minute. 'OK,' he said, 'I assume I'll see the receipts before I sign them.'

'Whatever,' the youth said.

'Martin,' Viktor said. 'Please. We won't be long.' The room was like a long coffin, dark and lined in dark plush. At the end of it a spotlight illuminated a girl gyrating round a pole. Not a bad way to spend purgatory, Martin thought. She had no clothes on.

As they came in, a small, dark-haired woman, in a short black skirt and a white blouse unbuttoned to reveal the top of her bra, met them and indicated they should sit at a table at the side of the room. 'Welcome to the Madonna Club,' she said in an accent Martin could not place. 'My name is Maria. Please sit here.'

At the end of the room, Martin now saw the naked woman was not actually completely naked. She was wearing a thong and she twirled first this way round the pole and then that way, while all the time the rock music went on thumping out. Maria returned with a tray and put two drinks on the table. 'Enjoy,' she said.

'We want to see Mr Kalaj,' Viktor said.

Maria looked at him blankly.

'We are here to see Mr Kalaj,' Viktor said.

'I don't know,' she said. 'I will ask.'

Martin sipped his drink. It was fizzy and sweet. He was not sure whether it was alcoholic. A blonde girl now joined the dark-haired one dancing round the pole. Maria returned to their table with two more glasses. 'Is Mr Kalaj here?' Viktor said.

'Champagne,' Maria said. 'Enjoy.'

'We didn't ask for more drinks,' Martin said. Assuming they cost the same as the free drinks, that was now eighty pounds on his credit card. Helping Viktor was proving expensive in every way. 'Please take them away.' Maria ignored him.

'Martin please,' Viktor said. 'Is Mr Kalaj here?' he asked Maria. 'We want to see him.'

Maria turned away.

Viktor took hold of her hand. 'Please,' he said. 'It's important. Please can we see Mr Kalaj.'

'Let go,' she said. 'You must let go. I do not know. I will ask.' Viktor was leaning forward, still holding on to her hand, and staring at her.

'You better let her go,' Martin said. 'Don't cause a fuss.'

Viktor sat back, released Maria and raised his hand. 'OK,' he said. 'OK.'

Martin sipped his new drink, as he supposed he had now paid for it. It was not champagne. It was the same sweet fizzy drink as the free one that cost twenty pounds. Did they make it specially for clubs like this?

At the end of the room, the girls were still dancing. The dark one was prettier, with delicate small breasts and hair that curled down to her shoulders and bounced when she shook it in time to the music. How had such a pretty girl ended up doing that, somewhere like this?

'I hope Maria has told Mr Kalaj,' Martin said.

Viktor said nothing. He moved his glass a centimetre back and forth. Maria returned with two more glasses of the drink.

'Champagne,' she said.

'We don't want any more,' Martin said. Another forty pounds. One hundred and twenty pounds altogether.

'Please, Martin,' Viktor said, 'If we don't keep drinking, they'll throw us out.'

'I am not made of money,' Martin said. 'How much do these cost?'

'Enjoy,' Maria said. So possibly even more than twenty pounds each.

'Please, Martin,' Viktor said.

'Enjoy,' Maria said again, as she left the table. The two girls were now pretending to kiss each other.

'Are you sure he's going to meet us here?' Martin said. 'This is going to be a huge bill if we wait here much longer.'

'Don't worry,' Viktor said. 'I will repay you.'

'With what?' Martin said.

Viktor ignored him. They watched the girls. Coloured lights had started flashing, flickering red, green and blue on the lithe naked bodies. The music was beginning to hurt Martin's head and the room was full of smoke and foreigners.

Then two men were standing beside their table. One was tall and thin, in a silver suit and a grey shirt with a silver tie to match the suit. He looked like there was a razor-thin knife tucked into his boot and his face was full of sharp angles as if it had been planed from wood, with long dark sideburns, tapered into a point. The other man was shorter, burly, in a brown suit and yellow shirt and a red tie. He did not look as if he needed a knife tucked into his boot. He pulled a chair away from a neighbouring table and sat down with them.

Maria arrived with four more drinks on a tray which she carefully set down on the table. Another eighty pounds. Two hundred pounds altogether. Two hundred pounds. He hoped Clements liked the opinion he had done for them. He was going to need a lot more of them. 'Enjoy,' Maria said.

'Yes?' the man in the brown suit said. And then he swallowed the glass of sweet fizzy liquid in one gulp. '*Prost*,' he said. Martin now knew Maria would return shortly with more. 'You are looking for someone?' His accent was clotted with gutturals and sibilants.

'We are looking for Mr Kalaj,' Viktor said. He was either more used to dealing with this stewing physical menace than Martin had realised or he was so wound up that he had not noticed it.

'Mr Kalaj?' The man in the brown suit looked up at his comrade and smiled. He smiled too. It was not a nice smile. 'There's no Mr Kalaj here,' the man in the brown suit said. 'But I'm here. My name's Boris. How can I help you?'

'We're looking for Mr Kalaj. We were told we'd find him here,' Viktor said, ignoring the theatrical threat in Boris's voice.

'There is no Mr Kalaj here. What word do you not understand?' The music changed to a power ballad that Martin remembered coming out when he was still at school but the girls did not change their dance, sinuously gyrating round and round the pole, ignoring the surging rhythm of the new song.

'Where can we find him?' Viktor said.

'Why do you want to find Mr Kalaj?' The question seemed to amuse the man in the silver suit as he smiled again. A plump young man got up from the next-door table, belching discreetly. As he swayed past them, he bumped into Boris who turned to glare at him but the young man was too drunk to notice.

'We were told he could help us.'

'Why would Mr Kalaj want to help you?'

Viktor stared at the man in the brown suit. The question did not seem to have occurred to him. He needed help. Martin watched Maria coming back to the table with another four drinks. Two hundred and eighty pounds. Even Clements wouldn't be able to rescue him if this went on much longer.

'Because we have heard Mr Kalaj is a father to his community,' Martin said rapidly.

The man in the brown suit switched his gaze to him. 'Yes?' he said.

'And because we will make it worth his while,' Martin said.

'How?' Boris said.

'We will discuss that with Mr Kalaj,' Martin said. That was good. Out of the corner of his eye he could see that Viktor was impressed. And so he should be.

'Who is this Mr Kalaj?' Boris said.

The man in the silver suit laughed, a short harsh bark.

'We do not know Mr Kalaj, do we, Stepan?' They seemed to like this sally, because they smiled at each other again. And then Boris laughed suddenly and clapped Martin on the shoulder. It hurt. 'I am making a joke,' he said. 'Laugh. Everyone knows Mr Kalaj. But not everyone can see Mr Kalaj. He is a very important man. He cannot see everyone who wants to see him.'

'Please,' Viktor said. 'It's important.'

'Important to you, yes,' Boris said. 'But is it important to Mr Kalaj? I think possibly it is not.'

'We will make it worth his while,' Martin started to say but Viktor cut in.

'Someone important to me is missing,' he said. 'We're told he can help find her. We're told he is a father to his community. It is the act of a father to help with problems like this.'

'Mr Kalaj is a very busy and important man,' Boris said. 'He can't help everyone with problems.' Then he laughed. 'But don't worry,' he said. 'I like you. I will ask him.' He got up from the table.

'Telephone number?' he said.

Viktor looked at Martin pleadingly. Martin sighed. What could he do? He could not abandon Viktor now. He took out his wallet and gave Boris a card.

'Barrister?' Boris said, emphasising the last syllable. 'Is that important?'

'Very important,' Martin said.

Maria reappeared at the table with another four glasses on the tray.

'No thank you. We are leaving now,' Martin said, getting up rapidly. But he saw that Boris and Stepan had both already taken a glass from the tray and were swilling it back. Three hundred and sixty pounds.

'Enjoy,' Maria said.

Three hundred and sixty pounds but that was it. He had given in to Viktor and gone to the Madonna Club and he had ended up paying for the evening. Enough. He had done his duty and now it was over. The blackmail nullified any further obligation. This was the end of him and Viktor Markov. Now he had to find a way to make it up to Clare. Martin pushed his chair back from the table and stood up. 'Goodbye, Viktor,' he said.

forty-seven

The battle was at its height. The Knights of Chaos had withstood the onslaught of Beastmen and now they were counter-attacking. Leading the charge was their Champion, WhipMaul, his Sunburst Yellow beard catching the sun and acting as a beacon for the squadrons of spearmen and pistoliers who had followed him so valiantly into battle. This was leadership of Napoleonic quality.

It was quiet in the house and Mihail wiped the sweat off his brow with the back of his hand. He was concentrating on the task in front of him on the table top.

It was time for WhipMaul to dismount from his steed to confront the Beastlord Gorthor. He threw down his shield. Retreat was not an option. This was the final struggle. There could only be one warrior left standing at the end of this. WhipMaul raised his mighty sword and confronted the Beastlord, his giant axe dripping with the blood of the dead. Mihail could feel the music pounding and boiling in his head. Around the two great warriors swirled the noise of battle, the clash of pike and club on chainmail and the hideous shrieks of the wounded and dying.

The Beastlord struck first, his massive arms whirling his axe around his head before bringing it down on the Champion. But WhipMaul was too quick for him. Encumbered though he was with heavy armour, he managed to twist out of the way of the terrible blow and turned back to face his adversary. From somewhere, Mihail could hear knocking but he ignored it. The noise of the battlefield and its wailing and crying filled his ears.

Now was the moment. The warrior took his sword and smote the Beastlord. And it was a fearsome blow. And there was a terrible crack as the armour split and the ground trembled as the Beastlord crashed to the earth. And then the Champion took the helm of his sword and began to batter the Beastlord. And there was an awful groaning. And the Champion kept on battering and battering with the mighty weapon. And Mihail could hear the groaning growing louder and louder. And then the knocking started again.

He looked up from the board. 'Yes?' he called. 'What is it?'

The door opened and Boris came in. 'I am sorry to disturb you, Mr Kalaj,' he said, 'but you had better come next door.'

Now the door was open, Mihail heard the groans more clearly. He looked reluctantly back at the board. Among the Knights of Chaos and the Beastmen, the model cottage still conjured up the music of accordions and violins filling wooden houses as the sun warmed the fields and apples and plums ripened on the trees in the orchard and clear streams gurgled through the meadows. This was the holy motherland and, one day, he would go home there. Mihail Kalaj leaned back in his chair and stretched.

'OK,' he said. Orange light from a streetlamp filtered through the curtains in the room. Mihail Kalaj walked over and pulled them closer together, shutting out the night. And then he walked down a short hallway and into a room with no windows and where plastic sheets covered the walls. There was a naked man tied to the bed, with his eyes closed, making those groaning noises and the plastic sheets were spattered with his blood. Beside him Stepan stood in a boiler suit covered in more blood, holding a hammer. Mihail looked at the man on the bed. 'What's his name?' he said.

'Kreshnik,' Boris said.

'What's he done?' Kalaj said.

'He took a girl first. We brought her all the way here. She had been ordered. A thirteen-year-old virgin. And then this peasant helps himself.' Kreshnik was still softly moaning on the bed, mumbling prayers to himself.

'Five thousand English pounds we would have got for her.' Boris glared at Kreshnik. 'Now we will be lucky if we get a thousand.'

'So why did you need to get me in here?'

'What do you want us to do with him now, Mr Kalaj?'

Mihail pulled his shirt out from his trousers and polished his glasses with the tail. His pale eyes stared short-sightedly at Boris while he cleaned them. They really were stupid. Incapable of independent thought.

'Get rid of him,' he said. He needed to get back to the board and think about his problems.

'Yes, Mr Kalaj,' Boris said.

Then at the doorway, something occurred to Mihail and he turned back to Boris who was already bending over the body on the bed. 'What did Kreshnik do for us?'

'He handled the girls when they arrived,' Boris said. 'And other things.'

'Get someone to replace him,' Mihail said.

'Yes, Mr Kalaj,' Boris said.

'Make sure we know the family. I don't want any more misunderstandings. You've just lost four thousand pounds. Get someone in who can make that up. Quickly.'

'Yes, Mr Kalaj.'

Kreshnik groaned on the bed.

Irritated, Mihail turned to look at him. 'Shut him up,' he said. He needed to concentrate. He slammed the door irascibly behind him and walked back down the corridor to the gaming room. The battle remained on the board, frozen at the denouement. He stared at the pieces. Everything seemed to have calmed down and he had taken the necessary precautions, moving the other women on and the flat had been cleaned up so even if the police got to it, they wouldn't find anything useful. Everything seemed to be OK but Mihail Kalaj never stopped worrying. That was how he stayed ahead. What could go wrong?

He picked up WhipMaul and admired the paintwork. The police would still be blundering about, worrying about the woman. He needed to head them off, just in case they stumbled on something. What could he do? What would the greatest general have done? Napoleon's genius had revealed itself in his mastery of manoeuvre warfare and the adroit use of diversionary tactics. Look at the Italian campaign that created the legend.

Yes, that was it. Once again, the little corporal was his inspiration and Mihail Kalaj had an idea. This could be his crossing of the River Po at Valenza. He placed the Champion back on the table and took out his wallet. He thought he remembered putting it in there when Boris had given it to him this morning. 'Here you are, Mr Kalaj,' Boris had said. 'This might be useful.' And there it was. He took out the small white card and looked at it and nodded. The River Po was about to be crossed at Valenza.

forty-eight

Clive Walton stared at the flame flickering on the candle that Joanne had left behind when they had broken up. What was the message conveyed by the dead woman? Who sent it? And why?

Joanne had explained how the candle was an ancient tool for meditation and that there was an inner chatterer inside him, who clouded wisdom with comparisons and judgements but that watching the flame dance would quieten the chattering and burn up the destructive and the angry and the impatient and the painful. And then the healing energy would start and spread. And then the answers would come. That was what she had said and one evening after she left, he had tried it. And he was surprised. It did help. Watching the flame dance emptied his mind and helped him focus. Joanne had been right about that.

This was the stage of the investigation when he felt like a bird perched in a tree, talons clasping the branch as it swayed in the wind, peering anxiously down at the ground so far below and wondering if he was about to fall, waiting anxiously for the moment when, out of nowhere, the rush of confidence would come, and the belief that he could fly would free him to take off and soar above the earth.

The phone rang. Once. Twice. Three times. He dragged his eyes away from the flame and got up to answer it.

'Walton.'

'Clive, it's me.' Stephanie. He should have rung her.

'Hi.'

'How are you?'

'Fine. How are you?'

'I was just thinking about you. Nice things. Do you want to come over tonight?'

He looked at the flame on the table. 'I can't,' he said. 'I'm working.'

'Oh,' she said. 'OK. Soon?'

'I'm sorry,' he said. 'Stephanie, I am sorry. It's just that I need to get my head round this case. It's a murder. I'll call you tomorrow. I promise. Love you.'

'Love you too.'

He put down the phone and turned off the light. The flame danced alone in the gloom. He sat down and looked at it.

It was a professional hit. No doubt about that. The slit throat was an execution but how much further did that take it? It was probably just a grubby squabble between gangs about money.

The phone rang again. Once, twice. He dragged his eyes away from the candle and stared at it. Three times. Four times. He snatched it off the cradle. 'Walton,' he said.

'We've had a phone call, sir,' the voice said. 'You'll be interested in this.'

forty-nine

This was a lucky break, no doubt about it. Sitting in an armchair in the living room, waiting for Mr Kalaj to arrive, Florian felt good about it. When he had been told that Kalaj wanted to see him, he had not hesitated. London was bound to offer exciting opportunities. Sometimes Florian thought he had been born lucky.

'You the new one?'

Florian leapt to his feet. The boss was dressed in a dark green suit and a green shirt and a bright blue and yellow patterned tie. He looked as if he could handle himself in a fight. There was a lanky boy with fair hair standing beside him, who must be a book-keeper or something like that. He looked as if he just handled himself.

'Yes, Mr Kalaj.'

'I'm Boris,' Nice guy.

'Yes, Boris. I'm Florian.'

'Sit down,' the runt said.

Florian looked at him. The pale blue eyes stared at him from behind round glasses. Florian could not make out any expression in them.

'Go on,' Boris said. 'You heard what Mr Kalaj said. Sit down.'

Florian worked it out. That was not Mr Kalaj. The other one was. The tough-looking man was called Boris. So the other one must be Mr Kalaj. He sat down.

'A bit slow, this country cousin,' Boris said to Mihail Kalaj who ignored him.

'Thank you for this opportunity, Mr Kalaj,' Florian said.

'What opportunity?' Kalaj said.

'To come and work for you.'

'What were you told?' Kalaj said, still standing while Florian looked up at him.

'You wanted some help. I can do most things.'

'You were misinformed,' Mihail Kalaj said. 'I don't need that sort of help. I want to know what happened to Vasili.'

Florian could not speak while he adjusted to the fact that he was not being offered a job. He was being interrogated and Kalaj's tone was giving him an un-settling sense of what might happen to him if he gave the wrong answers.

'Did you hear Mr Kalaj?' Boris said. 'What happened to Vasili?'

'He was shot,' Florian said.

Mihail stared at him, trying to work out if he was stupid or just pretending to be stupid to cover up what had happened. 'How?'

'A dog attacked us. I shot it. Then the owners came after us and shot Vasili.'

The story was too bizarre for this clod to have invented it. 'A dog?' Kalaj said.

Florian nodded. This was not what he had expected.

'Where?' And, as Florian explained about the village and what they had been doing there, Mihail analysed the consequences if Florian was telling the truth. It would suggest that no-one was trying to muscle in on the business and that everything remained on an even keel. So had he made any mistakes as a result of misunderstanding the situation? Whatever the reason, the woman had been trying to leave, so she would have had to have been punished anyway, even if it had nothing to do with Vasili's death. So no harm done there. And he still needed to shield himself against any fall-out from that. So what he had done to do that was also OK.

'So I found the car and got out.' Florian finished his account of that awful night.

Mihail Kalaj looked at him and nodded and tried to decide if he was telling the truth.

'And you just left Vasili there with those peasants?' Boris said and he cracked his knuckles as if preparing to use them on Florian's face.

'What choice did I have?' Florian knew he had done the right thing. They wouldn't have done it any differently if they had been there. But he didn't think they needed to know exactly who had shot Vasili.

'Quiet,' Mihail said. 'I need to think.' The story was ridiculous but that didn't mean it was necessarily untrue. He needed to find out one way or the other, just to be certain and clear this up finally, and Florian's delusion that he had been coming to work for him could turn out to be useful.

'OK,' he said, 'sort him out, Boris. I will give him a try. He can help you and Stepan.' This way he could keep an eye on him and the man looked mean enough to be handy.

Boris clapped Florian on the shoulder. 'Come on, country boy,' he said. 'Didn't you hear Mr Kalaj?'

As Florian stood up, his legs were trembling. He realised it had been a close decision.

Mihail waited a few moments to be sure that they had disappeared before returning down the hallway to his room. He stared pensively at the table. All still there, looking good. He moved a Chaos Lord a centimetre to the left. Cool. Mihail Kalaj could not decide whether Florian was telling the truth but if his adversaries were closing in on him, it would be like in 1805 when the Third Coalition formed against Napoleon. Britain, Austria, Russia and Sweden all thought that together they could overwhelm him. But it was the battles of Ulm and Austerlitz that were now engraved in history. And Kalaj, like Napoleon, was always one step ahead of his enemies.

fifty

The first thing Clive Walton noticed when he went into the room were the curtains. Heavy, maroon, brocaded, and trailing opulently across the floor, they looked as if they had been borrowed from an Imperial Habsburg hotel. And then there was a double bed, with a cover made from the same maroon material as the curtains and a large wardrobe with mirrored doors and, on the wall, there was a large print of a blue yacht on an even bluer sea.

'Not much here, sir,' the constable said. 'There's more next door.'

'What happened?'

'Someone, foreign accent, rang and gave this address.'

'Did they say anything else?'

'Apparently not, sir.'

Clive Walton looked around the room. He saw what was going on. Someone was sending a message and whoever it was seemed to think it was smart to use the police as their messengers. They were going to find out that once they started playing this game, it was hard to stop it. In the end, he would get all of them. Those being set up and those setting them up.

He pulled on a pair of gloves and opened the wardrobe. There was a black velvet dress on a wire hanger and nothing else. He turned back the cover on the bed and there was a duvet in crisp white cotton. Inside the drawer on the bedside table, there was a packet of eighteen condoms, still in the cellophane, unopened, and a Bible.

'What do you think, Constable?' he said. 'Who do you think lived here?'

'I'm not sure anybody lived here, sir. It looks more like a hotel.'

'I don't expect many stayed the night,' Clive Walton said. It all fitted together as he supposed it was meant to. To solve the murder of an upmarket prostitute they'd been sent to an upmarket brothel to find a clue that he assumed had been carefully left somewhere. But it wasn't in this room.

'Get forensics in,' he said. 'See if they can match anything here to the victim.' Opposite the bedroom was a bathroom, clinical white tiles and gleaming chrome taps. Expensive. Beside it was the kitchen, a large square room with a dining table and two chairs and a coffee machine on the counter. Another constable stood beside the table and stared ahead.

'Thank you,' Clive Walton said. 'What have we got?'

'It's all there, sir.' On the table there was a paperback book, a plastic bag with packets of pills inside it, some papers and a plastic bottle of mineral water.

'Where did you find this?' he said.

'In the cupboards, sir.'

Clive Walton picked up the book and turned it over. John Grisham. Bought by millions. The pills were over-the-counter painkillers and indigestion tablets. Nothing helpful there either. He picked up the papers and leafed through them. Tables of figures. Meaningless. An article about Buckingham Palace, apparently printed out from the Internet. And a bus timetable. Again, calculated to be anonymous. No messages here. And then he saw it, caught between the timetable and the article on Buckingham Place, a rectangular white card. It was as if all the other things in the flat had been placed there to be as inconsequential as possible in order to point up the significance of this one small card. This was the message here.

Clive Walton picked up the card and looked at it and wondered how a barrister, a member of Lincoln's Inn, had got himself involved in something like this.

fifty-one

'Are you ready?' Martin said.

'Don't you ever knock?' Ben said, swivelling in his chair to look at Martin.

'Your receptionist let me in,' Martin said. 'Come on.'

Ben shook his head. 'I'm sorry,' he said, 'I've got to finish this report.'

'It's six o'clock,' Martin said. 'That's what we agreed.'

'Half past,' Ben said. 'That's what we agreed.'

'Fuck off,' Martin said. 'I need to talk now.'

'If you shut up, I'll get finished quicker,' Ben said.

Martin sat down beside Ben. 'I've rung three times in the last week,' he said. 'But she's not returning my calls.'

Ben grunted.

'What does that mean?' Martin said.

'Nothing,' Ben said. 'I've got to finish this report now, Martin.'

'You know I had to cancel our date,' Martin said. 'Well, it wasn't exactly a date but I couldn't make it.'

Ben grunted again.

'Come on,' Martin said. 'What should I do now? Send her flowers? Write? Go round to hers?'

'Look,' Ben said. 'This is nothing to do with me. You sort it out.'

'How?'

'Not my problem, big boy,' Ben said. 'The more you talk, the longer I'm going to be.'

'Come on,' Martin said. 'I want to make this right. Help me.'

'You're on your own,' Ben said, continuing to pick away at the keyboard. 'It wasn't very clever to stand her up.'

'It wasn't my fault. I had no choice.'

'You always have a choice,' Ben said quickly before Martin could start on the story of his evening with Viktor. 'Now let me finish this report and we can go and get a drink.'

'This is important,' Martin said.

'So is this,' Ben said. He stopped typing and looked up at Martin. 'If I don't finish this tonight, a woman with chronic diabetes will be evicted and her children taken into care.'

'Sorry,' Martin muttered. Ben always made him feel inadequate. He felt he did his duty to his father. And Clare. But Ben's whole life was duty, to the needy and vulnerable, whoever asked for help.

'Oh all right, suffering Jesus,' Ben said. 'Let's go for a drink. I'll come back and finish this later.'

'I just don't know what's going on,' Martin said as he came back from the bar with two pints of beer. 'Is she playing hard to get or does she really not want to see me?'

'Who knows? That's your problem,' Ben said. 'You waste your life fretting about women. What's going on? What's not going on? Is this the one? Or not? Does she mean it? Or not? Is she screwing someone on the side? Does she love me? Relax. Let it happen.'

'Easy for you to say,' Martin said. The pub had been remodelled recently as a Victorian tavern, brass gleaming among unfinished timber. At the table beside them, a group of Swedish businessmen toasted each other with pewter tankards of beer. 'We're not coming here again,' Martin said.

'Why don't you stop fretting about things that pass? Worry about important things,' Ben said. 'Come and work with me and then you'll see what matters. You'd be helping people who really need help. And you'd feel a lot better about yourself.'

'You might but it's not that easy for me,' Martin said.

'Why not? You can do anything you want. Remember. You always have a choice.'

'It doesn't seem like that,' Martin said.

'You're not happy,' Ben said. 'You think you are. But you're not. If you're happy in your work everything else falls into place.'

'Yes,' Martin said. 'Look at you.' There was a loud cheer as one of the businessmen drained his tankard in one Scandinavian swallow.

'We're not talking about me,' Ben said. 'We're talking about you. And you need to stop fussing about women and becoming a judge and do something worthwhile with your life. Work for me.'

'With you,' Martin said.

'Whatever,' Ben said. 'Don't brood. If she's not returning your calls, maybe it's because she doesn't want to see you again. Maybe that's because you've let her down once too often. Maybe it's not meant to be. Too bad. Move on. What about that Miranda woman who Jenny was trying to fix up for you?'

Martin sipped his beer. Maybe Ben was right and it was not meant to be. He could see why Clare felt he had let her down. He had. But equally she had failed to give him the benefit of the doubt. Yet again. She might have returned just one of his calls to see if he had an excuse. It was typical of her to assume it was his fault and he didn't care. How could she think he didn't care? Perhaps she didn't want to believe he cared? If something didn't fit exactly her view of it, she rejected it. When he thought about it, she was very controlling. Everything had to be her way. However you looked at it, Ben was probably right and this relationship was doomed.

fifty-two

'Hey, Fat Boy, give us a beer.' Stevie Farr was concentrating on rolling a joint, carefully tamping down the tobacco. In the corner, a huge plasma television was showing endlessly looping silent pictures of motocross. From the hefty Avant speakers, Joni Mitchell's pure voice soared and swooped through 'Cactus Tree'.

'Fuck off.' All Stevie could see of his sergeant-at-arms was a massive black leather jacket stooped over the fridge in the kitchen.

'I'm the fucking president. Get me a beer.'

'I'm not your bitch. Get it yourself.' And Joni Mitchell's sweet clear voice filled the room. 'And turn this shit off. Put on that new Metallica CD.'

'Fuck off. Joni goes with dope. Your trouble, Fat Boy, is you don't do mellow.'

Gary Wilson lumbered back into the club room, and tossed a can of beer across to his president and then slumped into one of the battered black leather armchairs. At the far end of the room, Big Jim and John-Paul were playing snooker. The curtains were drawn against the daylight but they did not keep out the constant roar of the traffic on the overpass above them.

'Where the fuck is Dean?' Stevie opened the can and took a swig.

'What's this?' Gary wheezed. 'I thought you were mellow. Joni Mitchell and all.'

'Fuck off. We've got business to do.' He lit the joint and passed it across to Gary. 'We've got to sort out the money and he's the fucking treasurer, so where the fuck is he?'

He got up and walked over to the windows and peered out through the curtains. The forecourt of the little industrial estate was almost deserted and the tarmac was damp from the intermittent drizzle. There was a large van parked by the builder's merchants and then directly outside were the Harley Davidsons belonging to the clubhouse. The tiger stripes painted on John-Paul's Sportster glowed in the grey afternoon light. Ahead, the cars streamed by on the overpass.

'Chill, Mr President,' Gary called to him from the armchair.

'Fuck off, Fat Boy,' Stevie muttered out of the window. Then, as he watched, Dean roared into the forecourt on his Dyna Glide, did a wheelie in front of the window and stopped with a flourish in front of the clubhouse. It was as if he knew Stevie was standing by the window, anxiously watching out for him. Pisspot.

'Where the fuck have you been?' Stevie said as Dean walked in.

'Fuck off,' Dean said amiably as he went over to the fridge and took out a beer. 'What's up?'

'Business is what's up, you fuck,' Stevie said. 'And you are late for it.'

'Fat Boy,' Dean said, sprawling on the leather sofa. 'All right?'

'Yeah. You?'

'Fucking duchesses,' Stevie said.

'What?' Dean said.

'Chat chat chat. Like a pair of fucking duchesses. You all right? Yeah. You? Would you be so very kind and oblige me by having some of these fucking cucumber sandwiches. For fuck's sake we've got work to do. This club is losing a grand a month and we need to sort it out. That's why we're having this meeting.'

'OK,' Dean said. 'OK.'

'We're ready,' Fat Boy said.

'Right, this finance subcommittee meeting is now in session,' Stevie said. 'Item One. Treasurer's Report.'

'We're three grand overdrawn and the bank's pushing,' Dean said. 'In the last three months, club night takings are down seven per cent on last year. The tiger is costing another grand a year. And we're going to replace some of the CCTV cameras. Probably another grand all in.'

'So what do you suggest we do about it?'

'Get rid of the tiger for a start.'

'What the fuck do you mean?'

'It's only going to cost more and more as it gets bigger and bigger. We're spending hundreds of pounds on raw meat.'

'What are you talking about? Copperknob's a symbol. Power and freedom. You can't put a price on that. Anyone looks at that cat and they know what they're going to get.'

'It's a fucking money-muncher, Stevie. Give it to a zoo. Get a German shepherd. It will tear out your throat just as well as that fucking cat and it will cost a grand a year less.'

'I like Copperknob,' Fat Boy said.

'And it smells,' Dean said.

'What else?' Stevie said. He took another swig at the can of beer.

'Put up membership fees ten per cent this year. That's another grand or so. And they can afford it.'

'And?'

'That's about it,' Dean said.

'Fat Boy?'

'That's about it, Stevie.'

'You are a pair of useless fucking duchesses.' Stevie threw the empty can at the wastepaper basket. They all turned to watch it bounce off the wall. 'It's just as well I'm here,' Stevie said. 'You'd all be fucking lost without me.'

'That's why you are president,' Dean said, 'Mr President.'

'Fuck off,' Stevie said. 'I've got a job for us that will bring in five grand. How will that do, Dean?'

'Good. Yeah. Good.'

'What is it?' Fat Boy said.

'Something for this gang of rich urban bikers. In California. They want something doing for them over here.'

'Who are they?' Fat Boy said.

'I don't know. I met one of them at that Tattoo Festival in Amsterdam. We exchanged cards. That's what you do, Fat Boy, when you're in business. You exchange cards. I gave him my card. And he gave me his. Bernie something. The Outlaw Poets. What kind of name is that? Fucking Yanks.'

There was a shout from the snooker table and Big Jim threw his cue on the floor.

'Outlaw Poets?' Dean said. 'What are they? Accountants?'

'Yeah. Exactly.'

'What the fuck are we doing with accountants?' Gary Wilson said. 'Not exactly outlaws, are they?' And he laughed, a gurgling self-satisfied chortle.

'Money, Fat Boy, that's what. We need it, they got it.'

'What's the job?' Dean said.

'Someone's skimming them on some gig they're running and they want it dealt with. Some computer scam. Someone's hacking into their system. Using false identities. They've found out it's being done over here. And they want it taken care of.'

'We could do that,' Gary Wilson said.

'Yes we could, Fat Boy,' Stevie said. 'That's why I'm telling you about it. It's five easy grand.'

'When?' Dean said.

'I don't know yet. They know the area – it's somewhere in London, north, west, that sort of area, but they don't know the address yet. They're still working on that. As soon as they know, they'll tell us. And then we nail whoever we find there.'

'Again, Mr President, when is that likely to be?' Dean said. 'The bank's hassling about the overdraft.'

'How the fuck do I know? But soon. The guy sounded really pissed. He didn't sound as if he wanted to hang around.'

'And we get paid up front?'

'We get paid when we do the job.'

'Are you crazy?' Dean said. 'How do you know some American you met at some Tattoo Festival is going to pay up?'

'That's above your pay grade, Dean. You're just the fucking treasurer. Just keep the fucking books.'

'Yeah, I am just the fucking treasurer. And it's just because I am the fucking treasurer that I fucking worry about getting fucking paid.'

'Well don't.'

'Why not?'

'Because the Yank's a fucking accountant.'

'And they always pay their bills?'

'And he knows I will fucking kill him if he doesn't. He knows I will go out to California and eat his throat.'

Fat Boy nodded ruminatively. 'Yeah,' he said. 'That should do it.'

'And how do we know when we've done the job?' Dean said.

'When we've found this prick and stopped him doing whatever he's doing, whoever he is, whoever he's pretending to be.'

fifty-three

It had been raining most of the morning and now the park was damp and glistening. Viktor watched the reflections on the path as a young woman pushed a pram past him with the dog-tired diligence of a new mother and he wondered what he should do about the envelope in his hand.

He was out of ideas. He had invested so much hope in the visit to the Madonna Club but then nothing had come of it. Kalaj had not contacted him and Viktor did not know where to look for Mila now. Those elderly landlords had nothing more to say and the only friend he had ever heard her talk about had vanished. And that was it. She had gone as if she had never existed and all he had left was a memory of how she looked laughing with Suzana and dozing in his narrow bed. And the envelope in his hand.

Viktor sat on the bench and stared at the deserted roundabout where Suzana loved to play. He felt the hard rectangular shape inside the envelope and looked at her name written on the outside. Mila Hubchev. Mila, Mila. Where are you?

A teenage boy came wheeling by on a bicycle, the tyres hissing on the wet path. Why wasn't he in school?

This envelope was now the only contact he had with Mila. Should he open it? It might just give him something he could pursue. He had nothing else. But what right did he have to look into her private correspondence? They had always respected each other's privacy, how could he invade it now? If he did, it would be an admission that something so terrible had happened that it justified breaching that pact.

A gentle drizzle started to tattoo the envelope and Viktor tucked it inside his coat. Why was he still pretending to himself that something terrible had not happened? Clearly it had. And this envelope was all he possessed that might help him find Mila. He took it out again and slid his finger under the flap and ripped it open and pulled out a British passport.

The photograph looked as if it could have been Mila but the name on the passport was Marian Hart. Perhaps it was just someone who looked like Mila? But why would she have someone else's passport? Or one in someone else's name? What had Mila got mixed up in?

fifty-four

Kalaj had told him to find the fucking passport and so Boris stood in the porch and rang the bell again. Inside he heard sirens and screeching brakes from the television but no-one answered the door. He stood and watched the rain falling in thin streaks across the street of terraced houses. The new man stood beside him, hunched against the cold in a brown leather coat.

Boris put his hand inside his jacket and felt the Colt Cobra snug in its holster. 'Ready?' he said to the new man.

Florian nodded. This was better than being interrogated by Mr Kalaj. He knew about this sort of thing.

Boris put his hand on the bell again and kept it there. They heard the noise from the television inside but nothing else. Boris kept his hand on the bell and then suddenly the television was turned off. Boris kept on ringing the bell into the abrupt silence. And then they heard someone move inside and a voice called through the door in English.

'Yes?'

'I've come from Mr Kalaj,' Boris said.

'Yes?'

'Open the door.' And Boris put his left hand back on the bell and his right hand inside his jacket resting on the handle of the Cobra. The man inside sighed so heavily they heard it through the door and a chain was undone and the door opened. A small, wiry man, in jeans and an orange T-shirt was walking away from them back down the hallway. Boris and Florian followed him inside and Florian kicked the door shut behind them. The man had gone into a room at the back of the small house and they heard him turn the television back on.

Boris kept his hand on the gun and followed him into the room. Thick felt curtains were drawn against the day and the only light came from a standard lamp in the corner. The wiry little man had slumped down on to a sofa and was playing a computer game on the television. On the screen, cars were racing through an urban landscape and they recognised the noises they had heard from outside the door.

'Are you Giraud?'

The man grunted.

Boris saw a stain on the front of his T-shirt. Boris bent down and put his mouth close to the man's ear. 'I said: are you Giraud?' he shouted.

The man did not move but kept his eyes fixed on the screen as he continued to manipulate the controls with his hands.

Florian gave him a swift hard kick to the shin. 'Didn't you hear Mr Boris?' he said.

The wiry little man yelped but kept watching the screen, his fingers flicking over the buttons on the console.

Boris cuffed Florian round the head. 'Shut up, you peasant,' he said. 'I'll handle this.' Mr Kalaj had told them to be disciplined with the little Frenchman. Florian rubbed his head resentfully and glared at the man on the sofa.

'Are you Giraud?' Boris said again.

'Yes,' the man on the sofa grumbled.

Boris gently took the console out of his hands and turned off the screen and then sat down beside Giraud. The boss had told him to be careful as this man had precious skills.

'You have lost a passport,' he said. 'And Mr Kalaj is worried about it.'

The man stared forlornly at the blank screen. 'Which one?' he said.

'The woman's,' Boris said. 'Where is it?' Kalaj had gone on and on at him about it.

'How should I know?' Giraud was still staring at the screen. 'I delivered it to her house myself.'

Boris leaned in towards him so his shoulder was pressing against the little Frenchman. The contact seemed to release a faint scent of sour sweat or perhaps Boris was now close enough to smell it. 'Are you sure you haven't sold it to someone else?' he said.

'How do I know what she did with it?' Giraud said. 'It's not my business. I was paid to make and deliver the passport. I made it and I delivered it. What happened after that is none of my business.' He picked up the console and turned on the screen again.

Boris watched the game load and then took the console away from Giraud and turned it off again.

'You can play your game again when we've finished talking about this,' he said. 'The sooner you tell me what Mr Kalaj wants to know, the sooner you can start playing with yourself again.' Mihail Kalaj never stopped worrying. He told Boris he needed the passport back. He said it was dangerous to leave it out here. It could be traced back. He said Boris was accountable for getting it back. Boris knew that Kalaj was always working to cover all the angles. Boris never understood how he managed to think it all through but he did and Boris knew that was why Kalaj was the boss.

Giraud said nothing.

Boris took the Cobra out of its holster and looked at the barrel. 'You are important, Frenchman,' he said. 'But no-one is that important. Remember that. Mr Kalaj wants to know something. Tell me what he wants to know.'

'Yeah,' Florian said, glaring at Giraud.

'Shut up, peasant,' Boris said. He rested the gun gently against Giraud's temple. 'What did you do with the passport?' he said.

Giraud did not move. 'Please put the gun away from my head,' he said. He sounded bored. 'I can't think if you blow out my brains.'

Boris did not move the gun. 'You're not thinking now,' he said. 'What did you do with the passport?'

Giraud said nothing and stayed staring at the blank screen.

Boris sighed and lowered the gun. 'OK,' he said. 'Now what did you do with the passport? Exactly?'

'I made it as Kalaj asked. Exactly as he asked. Outstanding quality. The best. As always.'

'You are a genius,' Boris said and clicked the safety catch on the gun on and off. 'And then what did you do with it?'

'I took it to to the house.'

'And?'

'What do you mean? I delivered it to the house. And what?'

'Did you give it to her?'

'No. She was not there.' David Giraud picked up the console and started playing with it. Boris sighed and took the console out of his hands and threw it against the wall. They both watched it crash to the floor and a tiny chip of plastic flew into the air.

'So what did you do with it?' Boris said patiently. 'Please do not make me shoot the television.'

'What did you do that for?' David Giraud whined. 'You will have to pay for that. What am I supposed to do now? You will have to pay for it. And you can bring me the new one. Why should I have to go to the shops to buy it? Why did you do that?'

'To get your attention,' Boris said. 'Which you were not giving to me. And now I've answered your question, please will you answer mine. What exactly did you do with the passport?'

'I gave it to some old man.'

'You gave it to some old man?' Boris said. 'Just gave it? Are you mad? Which old man?'

'The old man who lived there. What's the problem?' David Giraud leaned over and stretched out his hand to turn the television on. Trisha was interrogating a young woman about whether her marriage could survive her husband sleeping with her sister.

'The problem is that the passport did not get to where it was meant to be and you have just caused me a lot of unnecessary extra work.' Boris got up and pointed his gun at the screen and shot it. They watched it explode in a white flash and a shower of glass.

'Now I am going to have to go and look for it,' Boris said. On top of all the other things he had to do for the boss. But Boris knew he had to find the passport and deal with whoever had stolen it. Mr Kalaj expected nothing less.

fifty-five

Click click click. So many problems. Click click click. Mihail Kalaj flicked the blue amber worry beads back and forth. Where had that passport gone? The Romanian said she had never received it and no matter what pressure he applied, her story did not change. Click click click. Back and forth went the thirty-three beads. And Boris said the little Frenchman insisted he had delivered it and Mihail Kalaj could not see why he should lie about that. So who had got it? Click click click. A mislaid passport laid a trail and that worried Mihail Kalaj. It was untidy and out of his control and he wanted the passport back. He had told Boris to do everything necessary to locate it.

Click click click. The blue amber beads caught glints of light as they flicked back and forth. Click click click. And what about that Englishman looking for him? Martin Hughes – that was his name. And his Serb friend. What were they so interested in? Some missing woman, according to Boris. Asking questions about her. Here and there and all over the place and probably gone to the police too. Another problem. Just as well he was taking steps to tidy it away before it caused any real grief. Click click click.

fifty-six

Detective Inspector Walton had a coin-sized mark on his neck which looked like a lovebite. Surely not? Not on a detective inspector. Martin couldn't take his eyes off it. 'Good of you to spare the time, Mr Hughes,' the lovebite said.

'How can I help you, Inspector?' Immediately after he qualified, when he was still taking criminal cases, Martin found it difficult to get on with the police. Older barristers, settled into the Criminal Bar, exchanged jokes with them but the officers waiting around outside the courtroom to give evidence never came over to chat and banter with him.

'Just a few questions, Mr Hughes,' the detective inspector said. 'It shouldn't take long.' He was tall with fair hair, good-looking and athletic like a footballer ending his career in the Second Division. With a lovebite. How had it found out that Martin was aiding and abetting an illegal immigrant?

Phil Matthews hovered beside the inspector. 'Can I offer you a cup of tea?' he said, meaning, 'This policeman is not a client, so what exactly is he doing here?'

'No thank you. I won't take up much of Mr Hughes's time,' Clive Walton said.

'Shall I rearrange your meeting with Linklaters?' Phil Matthews said to Martin, meaning, 'This could be trouble.'

'No, it's OK,' Martin said, meaning, 'Don't worry, Phil, it won't interfere with business.' But conniving at illegal immigration breached both paragraph 301 and Section C of the Application Form and it could seriously damage his career. How had the police found out? It could stop him getting on to the Bench. But it was not actually a crime and perhaps if he could just explain the circumstances to the policeman, it might just go away. As long as Phil Matthews disappeared now.

'Just let me know if you need anything,' Phil Matthews said, as he went out, closing the door behind him, meaning, 'I'll be keeping a close eye on this.'

Martin smiled at Inspector Walton in what he hoped was a confident way. 'How can I help you?' he said again.

And then the policeman surprised him.

'Do you know this woman, sir?' Clive Walton handed the identity card of the dead woman across the table.

Martin glanced at it. 'No,' he said quickly.

'Are you sure, sir? Would you like to take another look?'

'Of course I'm sure,' he said but as the inspector spoke, he looked again. He said he was sure because why would he know anyone who a policeman had reason to ask him about? But something seemed familiar about the face. What was it? He couldn't remember and he couldn't work out what this had got to do with Viktor.

'Take as long as you like, sir. If you're not sure, just take your time. See if you can place her.'

The face did remind Martin of someone but the photo was indistinct, eyes half closed against the camera, a set expression without life in it; the photo could have been hundreds of pretty women with dark hair tumbling to her shoulders. Martin did not recognise the language on the card either. From somewhere in Eastern Europe by the look of it. He did not know anyone from there. 'No,' he said, 'I'm sure I don't know her. Who is she?'

'As long as you're sure, sir,' Clive Walton said. 'She's been murdered and we found one of your visiting cards in her flat. Any idea why that would be, sir?'

When he was fourteen, there had been a series of thefts from the games-lockers at school and every time the headmaster had mentioned it in morning assembly, Martin had blushed so hot and red that he was sure the whole school must identify him as the culprit, although of course he wasn't and they eventually caught the boy doing it and sent him off for counselling. Now, once again, Martin's cheeks started burning.

'No,' he said, 'I don't. I give my cards out all the time to all sorts of people.' But relief came flooding in behind the blush, as he realised the policeman's visit had nothing to do with Viktor and he was not going to be interrogated about breaching paragraph 301 and Section C. Appalling as this murder was, it demonstrably had nothing to do with him and he could quickly reassure the policeman about that and then get on with his life.

'I'm sure you do, sir,' Clive Walton said. 'Do you go to prostitutes, sir?'

The rational part of his brain told Martin that this was a ploy, a predictable trick that policemen used to provoke a response, but the rest of him went straight into shock. 'What on earth do you mean, Inspector?' he said. He hoped he had managed to inject some authority into his voice.

'I meant,' Clive Walton said patiently, 'do you go to prostitutes, sir? Some men do and I just need to know for the purposes of this investigation, this murder investigation, whether you are one of them.'

The lovebite was still glaring at Martin. How would the inspector feel if Martin asked him if he had got that from a prostitute? 'No, I am not,' Martin said. 'What has this got to do with anything? I do not know this woman and I do not go to prostitutes. Now are there any other questions you wish to ask me?' Martin hoped that Phil Matthews had closed the door firmly behind him. It would be disastrous if anyone overheard this interview.

'It's just that we think the dead woman may have been working as a prostitute and that is why I'm afraid I have to ask you these questions. I'm sorry, sir, I do realise they are embarrassing but I can assure you anything you say at this stage will remain confidential, as long as it has no bearing on the case.'

Martin stared at him. The man did not believe him. He obviously thought he was lying. 'Inspector Walton,' he said, 'I can assure you I do not know this woman and I do not go to prostitutes. Is that sufficient for you?'

'If you say so, sir,' Clive Walton said. 'But I'm afraid I still have this question I need to resolve in my own mind. If you don't know her or any of her professional colleagues, why was your card found in her flat which seems to have been used as a brothel? Can you help me with that, sir?'

'No I can't.' It was anger that was now turning his face red. This policeman did not recognise boundaries. Without a shred of evidence, he was making these impudent accusations. It was intolerable. 'Have you considered the possibility that I give my card to all sorts of people all the time and one of them might have left it there? Possibly deliberately? To confuse you?'

'I try not to get confused, sir,' Clive Walton said. 'Any ideas about which of the many people to whom you give out your card might have done this?' He tried never to let personal feelings intrude into his work but he was getting irritated by this patronising lawyer.

'How do I know?' Martin said. 'All I can tell you is that this is nothing to do with me.'

'If you say so, sir.' Inspector Walton got up and put out his hand for Martin to shake. 'I hope you won't mind if I come back to you, sir, if I have any further questions.'

'Of course not.' Martin hoped this farewell was a sign that he had done enough to choke off the policeman. After all, this murder was nothing at all to do with him and the policeman had no evidence to suggest that it was. And the police clearly had no interest in Viktor, whose immigration offences were piffling compared to a murder.

And yet perhaps this rapid termination of the interview was just another ploy? Suddenly breaking off the interrogation like this could be intended to make the suspect worry and stew before returning to extract information from them. But knowing this might be a ploy did not stop Martin starting to stew and worry. What was going on here? Who had got hold of one of his visiting cards and placed it in a brothel? Was it coincidence? Or was someone doing it deliberately and if so, who and why? And what would his father say if he heard about this? Illegal immigration was one thing, murder something else.

Martin looked out at the lawns of Lincoln's Inn. What was happening? A few weeks ago, his life was settled and happy. He had met the woman he was going to marry and his career was well on course. How little he had appreciated his good fortune. Now he had lost Clare and a policeman was asking questions that could destroy his career. It was terrifying how quickly things could turn around.

fifty-seven

Rain was trickling down Viktor's neck, cold and wet against his warm skin. He yanked up his collar as he hurried down the road and yet still the rain found a way in. But Viktor didn't care because suddenly there was hope.

An hour ago, Miroslav had come into the small square room, overlooking the sullen alleyway at the back of the school, and told him there was a phone call. It was Martin who said Kalaj had just rung to arrange a meeting. Martin was, of course, sorry he could not come with Viktor as he had a conference but he wished Viktor good luck. Viktor wondered why he bothered making an excuse for something he would never have intended to do. Perhaps it was something to do with being English? But now he was going to meet Kalaj and Kalaj was the only hope he had.

He ran across the road, dodging the cars splashing on the wet road. Martin had said he should be at the Theatre Museum at twelve o'clock. It sounded odd to Viktor but if Kalaj wanted to meet him in a theatre museum then that was where they would meet. And what could happen to him in a public place like that?

Inside the museum, warmth seeped through into his bones as he waited by the entrance. A group of school-children streamed past and two old ladies talked in loud voices about Larry and dear John, whoever they were. And then a burly man in a brown suit, who seemed familiar, and a tall youth in wire-rimmed glasses and lank fair hair. No sign of Kalaj.

He moved inside. Here was a costume designed by Picasso for a Massine ballet, in 1917. He stood and looked at it. A Chinese conjurer. Some unknown dancer, mimicking a magician from China, soaring gloriously across a Parisian stage at the end of the First World War. Who had it been? This costume was all that was left of him.

'Mr Hughes?'

Now Viktor recognised the man in the brown suit standing beside him. It was Boris from the Madonna Club with Live Girls, looking different in daylight but still full of rubicund menace. And beside him was the young man in wire-rimmed glasses.

'No. I am Viktor Markov.'

'So you are not the important barrister.' His jowls trembled when he laughed.

'That was the Englishman.' And then Viktor realised the game the man was playing with him. 'And you are not Boris. You are Kalaj. Why didn't you say so at the club?'

Kalaj laughed again. 'You are a funny man, Viktor Markov.' Beside him, the young man smiled. 'Why do you want to see Mihail Kalaj?' He was still wearing the brown suit but today the shirt was blue, with a yellow tie.

The schoolchildren had come back into the room and were now busily sitting on the floor around them, sketching the Chinese conjurer costume. 'Do you want to talk here?' Viktor said.

'Why not?' Kalaj said.

The children were industriously burbling as they got down to work. Viktor was aware that Kalaj had not taken his eyes off him for a moment.

'So who are you?' Kalaj said. 'Why do you want to see Mr Kalaj?'

Beside him the young man bent down to pick up a rubber that one of the children had thrown and hit him on the leg. 'Here you are,' he said gravely, and patted the little girl on the head.

'Do you know Mila Hubchev?' Viktor said.

'No. Should I?'

Viktor thought his accent might be Albanian. 'I was told you know everything,' Viktor said.

Kalaj laughed. 'You are a funny man,' he said again and clapped Viktor on the shoulder.

'Do you know her?' he said.

Kalaj looked at the lanky youth beside him. The youth looked at Viktor. 'No,' the youth said. 'I don't know her.'

'Who are you?' Viktor said.

'I am Mihail Kalaj,' the youth said.

Viktor looked at the burly man in the brown suit.

'Yes,' the man said. 'I am Boris. Like I told you in the club. This is Mr Kalaj.'

'What do you think, Boris?' the real Mihail Kalaj said. 'Do I? Know everything?'

'Oh yes, Mr Kalaj. You do.' Boris laughed again and Viktor flinched in anticipation of another clout.

'But I don't think I know this woman,' Kalaj said. 'Why are you looking for her?'

'She's a friend.' Viktor spoke more passionately than he had intended. He saw Kalaj look at him intently, recognising the urgency in his voice.

'A special friend?' Boris said lewdly.

'What happened to her?' Kalaj said, ignoring him.

'I don't know. She disappeared,' Viktor said.

'Every good woman always does.' Boris laughed again. 'You find a good one. And then they disappear.'

'It's not funny,' Mihail Kalaj said and Boris immediately stopped laughing. 'Mila Hubchev?' Kalaj said. He looked at the costume of the Chinese conjurer ruminatively. 'I don't think so. Do you have any idea where she might have gone?'

'No. Something must have happened to her.'

The children were gathering their papers together and getting up to go. Then the room was empty and silent again.

'Where have you been looking for her?'

'Everywhere but I've found nothing.' Viktor knew he must not say anything about the passport in another name. It was potentially too important and too dangerous. And he was beginning to sense why everyone was so scared of Kalaj. 'That's why I've come to you. I was told you might be able to help.'

'I wonder why you were told that,' Kalaj said. 'I don't know this woman.' He looked away from Viktor. 'Have you tried the police?' he said carefully.

'The police?' Viktor said. He knew he had to be careful with this man.

Kalaj nodded.

'Why would they care about a foreigner?' Viktor said.

'You're right,' Kalaj said, smiling a soft gentle smile again. 'They would not care about a foreigner.' He had to be careful with this Serb. He was desperate and he was smart. Kalaj guessed he had probably already gone to the police.

'I do not know her,' Kalaj said. 'But if I hear anything I will let you know.' He had been right to take precautions. The police would be sniffing around and this man was clearly not going to stop until he found her.

'Please, Mr Kalaj,' Viktor said. 'Mila is very important to me. Very important. Please help me find her. I must find her.'

'Yes,' Mihail Kalaj said. 'I realise that.' It was just as well he had seen the problem coming.

fifty-eight

'You didn't have to go to all this trouble, Martin,' she said. 'A drink would have been fine.' A waiter took away the soup bowls as the bass player took off ambitiously on the immortal chords of 'So What'.

'I wanted it to be nice,' Martin said. And somewhere to take his mind off that policeman and his grisly questions. The saxophone came in as the waiter returned with cajun chicken and caesar salad. It was that kind of club. But the music was loud and it moved and the musicians were beginning to get off on each other and they only needed to talk between each song.

'It is nice,' she said. 'And unexpected. Nicely so.'

It had been easier than he had feared. 'Yes,' she had said when he finally managed to speak to her. 'That would be nice.' And it was. He had needed to look into those deep calm eyes and lose himself in her and jazz. Did the policeman really believe he was involved in the murder of a prostitute? How could he prove a negative? Martin took a mouthful of damp arugula. He must calm down. The inspector was only checking out all the avenues as he was bound to do. There was no reason to think Martin would ever see him again.

The pianist was now embarked on a lilting solo version of 'Epistrophy' and he reached across to squeeze her hand. 'Thank you for coming with me,' he said, looking into her eyes. She smiled at him and did not take her hand away. And at least the police had never asked him anything about Viktor. He had been panicking unnecessarily about that too. And now here he was and it all seemed to be going better than he could have hoped. He needed to get a grip and calm down.

'What about pudding?' he said.

She smiled, that lovely slow smile and shook her head. 'I've had enough,' she said. 'I'm ready to go whenever you are.'

fifty-nine

'Reverse,' Boris said. 'Reverse it, you Greek donkey.'

Stepan joggled the gear stick and then shoved it hard over to the left and towards the windscreen. 'OK,' he said and the white van inched back up the driveway.

'Wait,' Boris said. As Stepan yanked on the hand-brake, he got out and walked behind the van and opened the garage door. 'OK,' he called and Stepan reversed the van into the garage. Boris walked back out on to the driveway. He looked up and down the street. All quiet. The streetlamps glowed orange in the cold night and a thin mist hung in the air. Boris looked up at the dark sky but he could see no stars, only a dull ruddy haze. There were no stars in this city.

A man ambled past, muffled up, walking a dog. There was no-one else about. The lights in the front room of the house opposite were turned off. This was a nice neighbourhood, Boris thought, where everyone goes to bed nice and early. Somewhere in the distance there was the roar of night traffic but here everything was still and quiet.

'OK,' he called back to Stepan. 'Get them out.'

'What are you going to do?' Stepan said.

'Keep watch,' Boris said. 'Go on. Get them out. The sooner you do that the sooner we can go and get a drink.'

Boris stuck his hands in the pockets of his jacket and looked up and down the street. No-one. Silence. Behind him, he heard Stepan grunting as he lugged the cartons of cigarettes out of the van and stacked them in the garage.

The door of the house opened. Boris turned round and saw a blonde woman in a plum-coloured jumper and a slim grey skirt standing in the doorway.

'Hello,' she called into the night. 'Who's there?'

'It's all right,' Boris said. 'We are from Mr Kalaj.'

Framed against the light he couldn't see what she looked like but then as he walked back up the path towards her, he saw she was in her thirties, good-looking, with bright red lipstick.

'Hello,' he said. 'Don't worry. We're not the police.' He smiled at her.

She looked at him impassively. 'Why didn't you call?' she said.

She must be one of the matrons who looked after the girls. Boris had not realised there were any here. He had thought it was just a store house. 'Sorry,' he said cheerily. 'I didn't know there were any of you here.'

'There aren't,' she said. 'It's just me. You should have called. You frightened me.'

'Sorry,' he said. 'What about a coffee? It's cold out here.'

'What are you doing here?' she said.

'Just unloading some cigarettes. We won't be long.

We should be gone in ten minutes. Do you want some? Marlboro. Fresh off the boat.'

'I don't smoke,' she said.

'OK.' Boris looked back down the street. No-one. Nothing. The woman's breath made small clouds in the night air. 'What about that coffee?' he said. 'With some brandy in it?'

'I don't drink coffee,' she said.

'What?' he said. 'What sort of house do you keep here?'

'It's not my house,' she said. 'They just asked me to look after it for a couple of weeks.'

'Just look after it?' Boris said, moving nearer to her. 'I bet you look after it really nicely.'

'Don't,' she said.

'Come on,' he said. 'It's so cold out here.'

'Boris,' Stepan yelled from inside the garage. 'If you can talk, you can work. Come and help me.'

'Just a minute,' Boris said to the woman and he strode along the path, past the van and into the garage.

'Shut up, pig brain. Do you want the whole street to hear? What do you think Mr Kalaj would have to say about that? Just get on with it.'

'Get fucked by a blind bear.'

'Yeah, yeah. Just get on with it. How much longer will you be?'

'About five minutes.'

'OK. I'll see if I can get us a coffee off that slag in the house.' He picked up a carton of cigarettes as he left.

The woman was still standing in the doorway, peering out at the deserted street as he walked back out of the garage. 'Here you are,' he said, holding out the carton towards her. 'A present. Just because you're so pretty.'

'I don't smoke,' she said, but she took the cigarettes anyway.

'What about that coffee?' he said.

She didn't reply but continued to stare past him into the street.

She was obviously quite important to Mihail Kalaj or he would not have left her in charge of the house. So he would have to tread carefully but Boris wanted that coffee. 'Have you been here long?' he asked.

'About a week.'

'Happy?'

She said nothing.

'Where are you going next?' he said.

'How do I know? I just do what they tell me.'

'So why don't you do what I tell you?'

'You're not Mr Kalaj.'

Boris looked at her. She was a tough bitch but he was going to get that coffee. 'Much to do?'

'Too much. There were about twenty of them here. Dirty bastards. Mess everywhere. Of course, they were very careful to take all their computers with them and leave all the rubbish for me to clear up. They didn't tell me I'd have to be a maid as well.'

'What were they doing?' Boris said.

'Look,' she said. 'Enough. You're boring me. I'll make your coffee. What about your friend?'

'Yes please,' Boris said.

The woman turned back into the house and shut the door firmly behind her. Boris stamped his feet. It was getting colder. The old man walking his dog came back down the road and turned into a house three doors down and then the street was deserted again. In the distance the night-time traffic roared and rumbled along the freeway. And then Boris heard a new noise cutting through it from a few streets away. It was a motorcycle. Several motorcycles. And they were coming closer.

Boris walked down the path and looked down the street. Nothing. It was still empty, but the noise was definitely coming closer.

'Stepan,' he called. 'Get yourself down here.'

But the Harley Davidsons arrived before Stepan had time to come out from the garage. The street was suddenly full of noise as the five motorcycles roared up to the house.

Boris fumbled open his jacket to get out the Cobra but the rider on the first Harley had already dismounted and was throwing something at the house. And another one, also in black leather and a black helmet, was lashing out at him with a long chain. It caught Boris on the shoulder and he fell to his knees and yelped in pain.

And then a long black leather motorcycle boot kicked him in the chin as he fell and Boris collapsed backwards on to the lawn. He glimpsed the van exploding in a ball of fire. Apparently that first rider had been throwing a petrol bomb. And then he saw other riders throwing things at the house and then the windows shattered and flames whooshed up as the curtains caught fire. He heard the woman screaming inside.

Lights were going on in the street and then one of the riders kicked him again. And again. 'Got the message?' the rider said. 'Stop.' Then he got back on his bike and rode off into the night, over Boris's leg. And then the others followed.

And then it was silent again except for the menacing crackle of the flames as they burned up the house. The van was also burning steadily. He'd better get out. It was going to explode any moment now. But the pain in his leg was unbearable and his shoulder was beginning to ache where the chain had caught it. He was going to kill them. When he found out who they were, he would kill every one of them. Slowly. The pain was now shooting through every part of his body.

Then the door of the house opened and the woman came running out. She crouched down beside him. 'Are you all right?' she said.

'I will kill them,' he said. 'Come on, we must get out of here before the police arrive. And the van blows.' He dragged himself into an upright position. What had happened to Stepan?

'Help me up,' he said. Too bad about Stepan. If he wasn't dead, he could make his own way home. He couldn't wait around to find out what had happened to him.

'Where is the other one?' the woman said. 'We can't leave him here for the police.' She was right, of course, they couldn't leave him here. 'Kalaj will kill us,' she said. More and more lights were going on along the street. They would be ringing the police right now.

'He was in the garage. Go and see if he's dead.'

She got up and looked at the burning van. 'Hello,' she called, not moving.

'Go and get him, you stupid bitch.'

'You said it was going to explode,' she said and called again, 'Hello.'

And then Stepan came running out of the garage, skirting the burning van. He stopped when he saw Boris and the woman. 'You were meant to be on guard,' he said.

'Help me out of here,' Boris said. 'Quick. It's going to blow any second.'

The woman and Stepan each put an arm under Boris and started to lug him down the street. As they set off they heard a siren wailing in the distance. And then another one. And then the van exploded, showering burning debris into the night sky.

sixty

It had been a mistake. As he opened his eyes in the gloom of his bedroom and heard the gentle breathing beside him, Martin knew he shouldn't have done it. He turned towards her and delicately kissed the soft and downy skin above her elbow. It had been so easy and comfortable and wrong. She was lovely, lovelier than he could have imagined, but he was not ready. And now what was he going to do?

She stirred in her sleep and rolled over away from him. He lay and stared at the ceiling. A fine crack ran from the light to the door-frame. What should he say to her now? He had made the running and now he wanted to end it. He was not ready. Was it better to tell her straight away or go through a few more evenings out of courtesy, all the time edging away until it became obvious to both of them that it wasn't going to work out?

Martin disgusted himself. How could he have done this? She was a good person and she did not deserve to be treated like this. But it was no good pretending. He was not ready. He should never have done it. He had just felt so down and pressured by the policeman suddenly arriving and asking those terrible questions and he had just wanted to escape into these deep calm eyes. But that was no excuse. He should never have done it. He was not ready. No, it was even worse than that. Lying in his bed in the cold dawn, while Miranda slept beside him, Martin realised he still loved Clare.

sixty-one

Mihail Kalaj lay on the bed and wondered who had done this to him. The house was destroyed. At least Boris and Stepan and Nadia had got away but ten thousand pounds of cigarettes had gone up in smoke. And that was not funny. Someone was going to pay for this.

He got off the bed and walked over to the table where he had set out his Warhammers. He was in the middle of an Internet game with some geeks from Minnesota and São Paolo and it was looking good. He tried to think if there had been anything in the house that the police might find useful. But he was sure they had cleared everything out before Nadia moved in.

Mihail Kalaj would have written off the cigarettes as the fortunes of war except for the disturbing fact that he did not know who he was fighting. Mihail Kalaj did not like being ignorant about anything. He had thought things were going well and he was on track. The Romanian might turn out to be a problem and he would have to watch her. And that Bosnian Serb lawyer might lead to trouble but he had worked out how to deal with that. And he had sent a clear message to anyone thinking of moving in on the women. And he had moved key operations into new premises. And so he had thought he had kept everything under control since Vasili's death. But then, out of nowhere, this attack and that changed everything. It was a war and he needed to start fighting it. Which he would do as soon as he found out who to fight.

Down the corridor, Florian wondered what was going on. Boris, bruised and bad-tempered, had told him to sit in a chair before limping out of the room. Florian did not understand these people. London was not what he expected. It was grey and dirty and he spent most of his time sitting around watching television he did not understand and waiting for Boris and Stepan to return. He had been going to go on that run with the cigarettes the other night but then Boris had told him to stay behind in case Mr Kalaj needed anything. Just as well in the circumstances. Something had gone wrong, Stepan had not reappeared and Boris looked badly beaten up. He was sure he should not ask what had happened.

The door opened and Mihail Kalaj came in. 'Hello, Florian,' he said.

'Hello, Mr Kalaj,' Florian said. The young man made him uncomfortable with his staring eyes and the way Boris and Stepan were so careful around him. He never raised his voice but there was something about him that made Florian nervous.

'Happy?' Mihail said.

'Yes,' Florian said. Why shouldn't he be? What did he mean by that?

'OK,' Mihail Kalaj said and went out, shutting the door behind him.

What was that about? Then the door opened again and Stepan came into the room, squinting with a deep, congealing cut over his eye, and before Florian had time to say anything, he bound his wrists to the arms of the chair. And then Stepan left the room, shutting the door behind him. Florian felt his guts churning. What was going on here? Then the door opened again and Boris limped in with a plastic bag and a small bottle of clear liquid. He put them down on a table and then he took a Swiss Army knife out of his pocket and came over to Florian.

'What are you doing?' Florian said.

Boris did not reply but opened the knife and took the middle finger of Florian's right hand and made a small cut in it. Florian started and saw the blood beading up around the cut. But once the shock had passed, it did not hurt. What was going on here? Why did Boris do that?

'What are you doing?' he said again.

And, again, Boris did not reply. He went back to the table and picked up the plastic bag. Then he put the bag over Florian's right hand and fastened it tightly with Sellotape he took out of his pocket. Florian saw that the bag was swarming with little insects. And he felt them tickling his hand. But it did not hurt. What was Boris doing? Why was he doing this to him?

'What's going on?' he said.

Boris left the room without saying anything. Florian sat in the chair and wondered if he could get out of the straps before Boris got back. But then what would he do? Where would he go? He did not know anyone in London. And Boris and Stepan would come after him. He had no doubt about that. He knew what he would do if he were them. And they would come after him.

This was weird. These insects were just tickling him. And if Boris had wanted to hurt him then surely he would have done more than just make a tiny cut in his skin. Florian did not understand what was going on.

Then the door opened again and in came Mihail Kalaj, flanked by Boris and Stepan. 'Hello, Florian,' Mihail said. 'Comfortable?'

'Yes, Mr Kalaj,' Florian said cautiously. 'What's happening? Why are you doing this?'

'Shut up, bird prick,' Boris said.

'It's OK, Boris,' Mihail said. 'I will handle this.' He pulled up another chair and sat down beside Florian. 'We have a problem, Florian,' he said. 'Someone's attacking my business and I do not know who. Or why. And that's a problem for me. So I've been thinking about who could have done such a thing. Who knew what was going on. Now, very few people knew the cigarettes were being moved that night. Boris did. Stepan did. And you did. That's it. You, Boris and Stepan. Now Boris didn't tell anyone, did you, Boris?'

Boris shook his head and grunted.

'Look at him. Poor Boris. He wouldn't have asked anyone to do that to him, would he now? And Stepan didn't tell anyone, did you, Stepan?'

'No, Mr Kalaj.' And Stepan smiled. And it was not a nice smile. Florian's guts were now liquid.

'So that leaves you, Florian. Why did you do it?'

'What? I didn't do anything, Mr Kalaj.'

'Really, Florian?' The pale eyes stared deep into his.

'Honestly, Mr Kalaj, I didn't do anything. I just stayed here as I was told.'

'Florian, Florian.' Mihail shook his head regretfully. 'You may be wondering what is in that plastic bag that Boris has so carefully fixed on your wrist. Those little things wriggling around are the larvae of carpet beetles. Extraordinary creatures. Museums use them to clean skeletons. They can scour a bear skull in less than twenty-four hours. They love fresh meat but they don't like skin. So Boris has considerately made a little cut in your finger to help them get inside.'

Florian tried to stand up.

'It won't do any good,' Mihail said gently. 'They will still be chewing away whether you are standing up or sitting down. And Boris will be here to make sure you do not try to do anything foolish. I would not if I were you. Boris is not very happy about what your friends did to him the other night. Are you, Boris?'

Boris shook his head and grunted.

'Please, Mr Kalaj. I didn't do anything. I don't know anything. Please, Mr Kalaj. Please don't do this to me.'

He felt the little beetles tickling his hand and he tried to twist his hand away from them, but it was strapped to the chair. And then he started to whimper. 'Please, Mr Kalaj. Please.'

'Your destiny is for you to decide. It's the same for all of us. We are the masters of our fate. Aren't we, Stepan?'

'That's right, Mr Kalaj.' Stepan smiled. The same smile as before. And it was no nicer.

'You see, Florian, all you need to do is tell me who you told and why and then I will ask Boris to take that plastic bag off your hand. And we can clean the beetles out with a little bit of formaldehyde. It's a poison. And they don't like that. See that bottle over there. That one with the clear liquid in it. That's formaldehyde. So just tell me and this can all be over. Your destiny is in your own hands. As you might say.'

Boris laughed. 'Yes, Mr Kalaj. In his own hands. As you might say.'

And then Stepan finally understood and he laughed too.

'So what's it to be, Florian?'

'Please, Mr Kalaj. I don't know anything. I didn't say anything to anyone. Please.'

'All right, Florian. I can see you don't believe me. You'll have to learn the hard way. These are hungry little beetles and they love fresh meat. Remember that bear skull. Stripped clean in a day. Strap his feet, Boris.'

Florian kicked out but Boris and Stepan took a leg each and lashed them to the chair.

'Let's see how you feel in a few hours,' Mihail said. 'They should be well on their way to the bone of your middle finger by then and working their way through the rest of your hand.'

He was not sure about this one. The beetles might help dig out the truth but Florian was too stupid to be acting alone and he might even be too stupid to betray his boss, whoever that was and Mihail thought he might have to keep working at this.

'Enjoy,' Mihail Kalaj said to the beetles, and he left the room. Someone was going to pay for this.

sixty-two

'Zip.' Giles smirked at her. They sat at a table in the newspaper's coffee bar. As Charlotte knocked back an espresso, she saw Damian at the counter buying a packet of cigarettes. Choke. Please.

'What do you mean?' Charlotte said. 'Zip?' Did he know how much she had been depending on him to nail this story?

'Nothing.' Giles swigged Coca-Cola from the bottle.

'Nothing? After I paid you a thousand pounds?'

'No you haven't.'

'What do you mean I haven't?'

'Your newspaper may pay me but it has not paid me yet.' Giles leaned back in his chair and stretched out his long legs. 'To be precise.'

'Is that the problem?' Charlotte said. 'I'll get Accounts to pay you immediately. And then perhaps you'll be able to see your way clear to telling me what you've discovered.'

'No.'

'What do you mean no?'

'I mean, I have not got anything for you, whether or not you pay me today. I have nothing. Zip. Sometimes it's just like that.'

Charlotte was not sure she had ever hated anyone as much as she hated Giles Bardwell at that moment. A thousand pounds down the drain. George would go mad. And for what? Zip. How was that going to help her and Rob and Matthew get to Tarifa?

'Let me tell you something, Giles. It's not "sometimes just like that" here. And certainly not with me. If you take a thousand pounds, you deliver something for it. Conceive, achieve.'

'You are welcome to employ someone else if you don't think I'm up to it.' He smiled at her again with that loopy grin, and then got a Palm Pilot out of his pocket and started making neat little swirling motions over it with the stylus. Jab. Stroke. Swirl and point.

Charlotte looked around the coffee shop. There was no-one nearby. Damian had left to go off and get another story on the front page. 'Listen, you little monkey-spanker,' she hissed. 'You have not been paid a thousand pounds just to sit around and squeeze your spots. So don't give me this take-it-or-leave-it rubbish.'

Giles did not look up from the Palm Pilot.

'I'll make sure you never get another grand a week from anyone, you smear of piss,' Charlotte said. 'How long do you think the queue will be when we report on teenage con-men who exploit ignorance of new technologies? Featuring you. In full colour.'

Giles put the Palm Pilot back in his pocket.

'OK,' he said.

'What do you mean OK?' Charlotte said. The boy had obviously wanked himself stupid and he was ruining her life. He was meant to unlock this story so she could walk away with her self-respect. And what had he done? Zip.

'I mean: OK,' he said. 'Whatever. Do you want me to do another week or not?'

What was she going to do? Was this long streak of stale sperm ripping her off? Or was it just bad luck he had not yet come up with anything? How could she know? She was screwed either way. If she gave up now, she had wasted a thousand pounds for sure. But if she went on, how could she be certain she was not throwing good money after bad?

'Why not?' she said. 'Why not give you another thousand pounds to squeeze your spots for another week.'

'You've already made that joke,' he said equably. 'And it's not very funny.'

That was what was so unnerving about him. Nothing unsettled him. He responded to everything with the same, even reasonableness. Like a computer. A thousand-pounds-a-week computer. 'And it's not very funny that you are taking a thousand pounds a week to produce zip,' she said.

'You know,' he said, 'you're so pretty when you're angry.' He must have read that in one of his comic books.

'Out of your league,' she said. 'Stick to your classmates.'

Rob was about to leave her. She felt it. Last night he had said that she didn't seem the same any more. She had changed. He was smiling at her as he said it, over the half-finished pizza and the bottle of Pesquera, with

Matthew peacefully asleep, at last, in the bedroom. Rob probably thought it was an affectionate thing to say. It showed that they were evolving. Going somewhere. That was what he probably thought. But she knew.

'Look,' Giles said, 'Charlotte.' Oh God. 'You never know when you're going to get there. I will get it. I always do. I just never know how long it's going to take.'

'A year?'

'There's no need to take that tone.' Giles did not seem upset. 'I might get it tomorrow. It might take a few weeks. If you keep paying me, we will get there. If you decide to set a time limit, we may have got there when we reach it. Or we might not. It just depends.' He looked at her and smiled again. 'You won't find anyone better,' he said.

And then her phone rang. 'Hello, Harriet,' she said. 'Is he all right?' she said. Giles was still smirking at her across the table. 'Go away,' she said. 'No, not you, Harriet. How is he?' Giles did not move so Charlotte got up and walked away from the table as Harriet Warren explained about Matthew's tummyache.

'I'm sorry,' she said, 'I can't come to get him now. I'm at work. Have you tried Rob?'

Harriet said she had already tried Rob but he was in a meeting. Charlotte breathed in deeply, trying not to let the irritation show in her voice. Why hadn't Harriet rung the mother first? Was she that bad at it?

'Rob's always in meetings,' she said. 'Give me five minutes and I'll sort something out.' She rang Martha.

Voicemail. Alison. Busy. Her mother. Out. And finally in desperation she rang Rob. And miraculously he was back from his meeting and could go to get Matthew.

'Next time I want a private conversation about my sick son,' she said to Giles as she returned to the table, 'I'd be grateful if you could respect my wishes.'

'Of course,' he said.

'Is there anything you can do to get a result quicker?'

'Have you got anything else you can give me? Any more names? Any more details about this Mila Hubchev?'

When Rob had said she had changed, she knew it was a criticism, however nicely he was smiling when he said it. Actually, she hadn't changed. It was just that he had finally realised who she really was and it was not the sentimental fantasy he had dreamed up. Now the truth was dawning on Rob and he was going to leave her. He might not know it yet. But she did. He was going to go.

'I don't know,' she said. 'How would I know? That's what I am paying you to find out.'

'No-one can make something out of nothing.'

Where did he get all this stuff from? 'Wise, Giles,' she said. 'Very wise. What does it mean?'

'I need something more to work on. Anything that might show a pattern.'

'Like what?' she said. Of course Matthew made it more difficult. Darling sweet Matthew. What would happen to him?

'More names,' Giles said. 'Anything that might connect with something else. Addresses. I can keep trying to put it all together and the more I've got the easier it is.'

Charlotte realised Giles was trying to help but what else could she give him? Another week for a start. She could not go back to George and say she had spent a thousand pounds for nothing. Not with everything else. But what else could she give Giles to help get a result?

'Give me until tomorrow,' she said.

'OK,' he said.

'You're off the clock until tomorrow,' she said. 'The next week starts tomorrow.' Children usually stayed with the mother. But Rob had spent far more time looking after Matthew. But how could she endure seeing that darling boy only at weekends? At least now she saw him every day, even if it was only when he was asleep.

'OK,' Giles said. Nothing she said bothered him. Monkey-spanker.

'There's always a way in,' he said. 'You just have to find it.'

'There better be,' Charlotte said. Perhaps Matthew would make Rob think twice. Perhaps she was just being paranoid and he wasn't going to leave her at all.

'Don't worry,' Giles said. 'With me, WYSIWYG.'

'What?'

'What You See Is What You Get.'

'No it isn't, Giles,' she said. 'Not with you, not with anyone. You've got a week.'

sixty-three

'Is Mummy there?' Martin said.

'No,' Megan said.

'It's Martin,' he said. 'Can I speak to Mummy?'

'She's not here,' Megan said.

'She must be,' Martin said. 'You're not on your own, are you, Megan?'

'No.'

'Well, can I speak to her then?'

'She's not here.'

'Megan, please give the phone to Mummy. Tell her it's Martin.'

'She's not here.'

'Megan, please give the phone to Mummy.'

'She's not here.'

'So who's looking after you then?'

'Vicky.'

'Who's Vicky?' There was silence. 'Megan, can I speak to Vicky, please.'

'Hello,' a young girl said.

'Are you Vicky?'

'Yes. Who's this?'

'My name is Martin. Please can I speak to Clare?'

'She's not here. I'm the babysitter.'

'When will she be back?'

'I don't know. She said before midnight. I'll tell her you called.'

sixty-four

The door opened before Boris was ready. His right hand was cuddled round the Cobra and his left index finger was reaching out to ring the bell when there she was.

'Hello, young man,' she said. 'Were you looking for us?' The old lady was peering at him through the crack in the door and over the chain which fastened it to the frame. Boris opened his mouth but no words came. He had not expected the door to open like this. How had she known he was coming?

'You look nice enough,' she said and unfastened the chain. 'Would you like a nice cup of tea?'

Boris tightened his grip on the Cobra. What was going on here?

'Don't just stand there,' she said. 'I'm catching my death of cold.'

She was only an old lady so what harm could she do him? Unless, of course, she was a decoy.

'Come on in, my dear,' she said. 'I won't kill you and Gerald will make you a nice cup of tea.' She turned and shuffled back into the house, leaving the door open and calling, 'Put the kettle on, dear, we've got company.'

Boris wished he had brought back-up but Stepan's

eye was still too bad for him to come out and the peasant was busy with the beetles. He cuddled the Cobra as he stepped tentatively over the threshold and limped behind her into the house.

'Good morning.' A tall, thin old man loomed out of the gloom at the end of the hallway. His cloudy eyes stared at him out of a pale cadaverous face.

Boris slipped the safety catch off the gun and remembered that zombies had to be shot directly through the heart to kill them. Or was it that they couldn't be killed at all? This was a house of horrors and he needed to get out of here as quickly as possible.

'Come on in, dear,' Mrs Flynn said. 'We won't bite.'

A vein began to pulse in his forehead. These people were making him nervous. Perhaps it would be easier to kill them.

'I hope that's how you like it.' Mrs Flynn handed him a cup of milky tea. 'What's the matter with your hand, dear?'

Reluctantly, Boris took his hand off the Cobra and out of his jacket and placed it uneasily on the arm of the chair.

'I've come to get Mila Hubchev's passport,' he said.

'What's that, dear?'

'Mila Hubchev. She lived here.'

'I know that, dear. What's that about a passport?'

'I know it was delivered here,' Boris said. Perhaps it would be easier just to kill them. 'And it was given to him.' Boris nodded towards Mr Flynn who was mesmerised by his cup of tea and noisily blowing at it. 'Now where is it?'

'That's quite an edge you've got to your voice,' Mrs Flynn said. 'You need to relax, my dear. Enjoy your cup of tea. Gerald makes a lovely cup of tea, don't you, dear?'

'Where is it?'

'That's an interesting accent you've got, my dear,' Mrs Flynn said, ignoring him. 'Where is it you're from?'

Boris put his hand back in his pocket. Perhaps this was a ploy after all and the peasants were waiting for him, smirking in the kitchen, as the old woman played her stupid games.

'Enough,' he said. 'Where is it?'

'I don't know anything about a passport,' she said. 'Now why don't you just enjoy your cup of tea and have a nice chat. We get so few visitors. Young people are all so busy nowadays.'

Boris stood up.

'Do sit down, dear,' she said. 'I don't know anything about a passport. Do you, dear?' She looked across at Gerald who was drinking his tea.

'Yes, dear,' he said. 'I took it in from a young man the other day. In a brown envelope.'

'You didn't say anything, dear,' she said.

He took another sip of his tea and did not answer his wife.

'Are you sure?' Boris said, staring suspiciously at the old man, holding his cup under his chin with gently trembling hands.

'Oh yes. I opened it.'

'You shouldn't have done that, dear.'

Her husband did not reply.

'Where is it now?' Boris said. If he did not get it soon, he would kill them anyway. It would be an act of mercy.

'Our man took it,' he said.

'What?' Boris said.

'Which man?' Mrs Flynn said.

'The nice young man who came round the other day, dear,' Mr Flynn said. 'From Bosnia. The former Yugoslavia.'

'You shouldn't have let him do that, dear,' Mrs Flynn said. 'It wasn't his.'

'He was a big lad,' Mr Flynn said. 'He didn't think I saw him do it but I did.'

'Who was this?' Boris said.

'You'll have a heart attack, dear, if you go on like that,' Mrs Flynn said. 'Viktor Markov he said his name was.'

Got it. Maybe she wasn't as daft as she seemed. The Serb. He needed to get to him as quickly as possible and find out what had happened to it.

'You don't have to go just yet,' Mrs Flynn said, as Boris slammed the door behind him.

sixty-five

The meeting in Manchester was at eleven but Martin had come up the night before to make sure he was on time. The Wilcox papers were now spread out on the table in front of him so he could check a couple of contentious issues in the original deed.

It began to snow. Martin looked up and watched the flakes swirling past the window. The hotel was a Victorian pile that had just been refurbished and there was Internet access in the bedroom and a fluffy white robe in the marble bathroom and an Olympic swimming pool in the basement. And matching clientele for breakfast as men with pony-tails, sipping espresso, busily tapped at their laptops, and sleek young businesswomen texted over toast and cornflakes.

Martin had escaped from the Barcelona Café back to his room. It was on the top floor and he could see past new blocks of glass and steel to the warehouses and mills that had built the city. He supposed they were now lofts and studios.

He was still ashamed of himself. Miranda had smiled when he kissed her goodbye. 'That was nice,' he said and hoped that it sounded as if they had both understood it was one night only. 'At my age, you're grateful for what you get,' she said and Martin felt wretched. 'You're too good for me,' he said and she smiled again and kissed him on the cheek as she left and he felt even worse. He should never have done it. But he had felt so alone and wanted to forget the policeman's visit and he needed to prove he was over Clare. And he wasn't and he had been unforgivably selfish.

He took another file out of his squat black briefcase. A lawyer's case. Whatever else changed, business always needed lawyers. It was one of his father's favourite sayings. Whatever happens, you are safe in the law because as long as there are human beings they will argue, and as long as they argue, they will need lawyers. Outside the snow was beginning to settle on the window. Martin stood up and looked out. On the dark red buildings half a mile away he could see a dusting of white.

He felt comfortable inside this elegant hotel room, with the snow falling outside. London seemed far away with its problems, Clare and Miranda and Viktor and that offensive policeman. Martin walked over to the window. He could see the intricate crystalline structures of the flakes before they folded into the drift growing steadily round the edges of the window. He would do the meeting and then he might try the hotel spa before getting the train back down to London.

What should he do about Clare? She still hadn't returned his calls. Perhaps she was busy at work with the new exhibition? Was that why she had not been in? Or had she started going out with someone else?

He watched the snowflakes. He had studied their structure at school. Complex hexagons. There was something special about them. Was it that no two snowflakes were ever the same? Or was it that they were all the same? He remembered the old wooden chemistry benches with the sinks and Bunsen burners and the smell of gas and rubber. All knocked down now, he had heard, and replaced by a shiny new learning environment. And the harsh fluorescent lights overhead as Mr Bulstrode went on and on. And Anne Medworth, sitting at the end of the bench, with that pouting smile and those heavy-lidded eyes.

He had so fancied Anne Medworth. But she never even looked at anyone in the class, let alone him. From the age of fourteen she was going out with boys who had already left school and had jobs and cars and did drugs at the weekend. What had happened to Anne Medworth? He never heard anything about her. He had not even thought about her for years, until now.

He wondered what she would make of him now if they met up. 'I always knew you would make something of yourself, Martin,' she would say. 'You were always going to be a success.' Perhaps she was downstairs even now. One of those sleek young women on their mobile phones. Perhaps she had spotted him snuffling up his bacon and sausages. And then perhaps she thought, Oh God, there's Hughes. Keep your eyes down and hope he doesn't recognise you. He's just the same spotty dick he always was. Was that what Anne Medworth would think if she met him now? Still a geeky schoolboy?

Martin stared out of the window. It was extraordinary how a light breeze and precipitated water could turn such a grimy, muddled landscape into something beautiful. It was so white. From behind the insulated window, all was still and silent in the winter light. And then the phone rang.

'Martin?'

'Clare?' At last. 'How did you find me here? How nice to hear from you.' This was it. Why else would she be ringing? She had realised they were meant to be together.

'I rang your chambers.'

'I am so sorry, Clare,' he said.

'How do you know?' she said.

'What do you mean?' he said. 'Of course I know what you must have felt about the other night. I know what it must have looked like. But there was really nothing I could do about it.'

'What are you talking about, Martin?' she said.

'Sorry,' he said, 'I'm sorry. That's what I'm talking about. That's why I've been ringing you. To say I'm sorry and I've changed. Really.'

'I'm not ringing about that, Martin,' she said. 'I'm afraid I've got some bad news.'

He looked out of the window, at the snow drifting by and, when he thought about this moment later, he thought he had known what she was going to say just before she said it.

'Viktor is dead,' she said.

He was still staring out of the window. He knew he would always remember the snow drifting by, white against the winter sky. This was the moment his life changed.

'I'm sorry,' she said. 'I thought you would want to know.'

'How do you know?' he said.

'Steve Mimms just told me.' The head teacher. 'I'm ringing from school.'

Oh God. 'What about Suzana?'

'She doesn't know yet. She's in her classroom now. We thought it best not to tell her just yet. Not until we know more.'

'What happened?'

'I don't know. Suzana was having a sleepover with Megan and when I got to school with them, Steve Mimms told me. The police had just rung.'

Outside the window, it was still snowing. 'Where are you?' he said.

'I'm at school,' she said patiently. 'I'm ringing you on my mobile. I'm sorry, Martin. I know you had got friendly with him. I thought you should know.'

'Thank you,' he said. 'It was good of you.' She had not been ringing to get back together. And Viktor was dead. What would happen to Suzana now? Martin knew there was no reason for him to feel guilty but he did. He had been so anxious to get Viktor out of his life and now this had happened. It was nothing to do with him but his anxiety about Viktor's immigration status now seemed so petty. So selfish.

'What happened? Was it a heart attack?' He was still young and looked fit but he was always so wound up that perhaps the stress had got to him.

'I don't know,' she said. 'But from what Steve said it might be serious.'

'What do you mean?' What could be more serious than dying?

'The police said they will need to interview people at school.'

The snow was stopping now and the sky outside was a dull metallic grey. 'Nothing should necessarily be read into that,' Martin said authoritatively. 'Whenever anyone dies unexpectedly they need to tie up any loose ends. There will need to be a post-mortem to find out what happened.' He had never done much criminal law but he thought he remembered that.

'I'm not sure they need to do that, Martin,' Clare said. 'Steve said he'd been shot.'

Shot? Viktor had said he had enemies in Bosnia but could they really have followed him here? Or had he got into a fight rescuing Mila? Was it that man Kalaj they had been trying to find? Whatever had happened, he would never see that vital presence again. Martin looked out of the window and saw Viktor sitting in his office in that Balkan town, keeping the flame alive, with his pretty, principled wife and Suzana.

'Martin?' Clare said. 'Are you there?'

'Yes,' he said. 'I'm sorry. It's a shock.' Viktor Markov had been such a powerful force in his life over the last two weeks and now he had gone as suddenly as he had arrived.

'Where are you?' she said.

'I'm in Manchester for a meeting,' Martin said. 'But I'm coming back this afternoon.' What a sad end, so far from that sparkling river and the woods, and it seemed bitterly perverse when he remembered how worried Viktor had been about the risks of returning.

'Is there anything I can do?' he said. He felt another twinge of shame, as he remembered how he had wriggled away from Viktor's plea for help and how panicked he had been about paragraph 301. He had been living in his comfortable cocoon, just as Ben always accused him of doing, while Viktor had been out there, alone.

'You might be able to help with something,' Clare said.

'Yes,' he said. 'Anything.'

'Do you know if there were any relations? I can have Suzana for a few days but we need to work out what should happen after that. If we can't find a relative quickly, social services will take her and then it could be very difficult to get her settled. There'll be endless processes before they release her and she needs to get into a settled environment as quickly as possible.'

He recognised Clare had gone into her organising mode. She was the only person he knew who labelled her clothes drawers. 'He mentioned a sister,' he said. 'In Sarajevo. But I can't remember her name.' And he could never ask him now. Viktor was dead.

'It would be helpful if you could try to remember the name,' she said. 'I'll look after Suzana for a few days and I'll tell her this afternoon. But she's going to need her family around her now.'

'I'm not sure he ever told me her name,' he said. First Mila, now Viktor. What was going on? This was terrible.

'Do you know where he lived?' Clare said. Martin realised he had known very little about Viktor but he remembered the night he had taken him home.

'Yes,' he said.

'If you went round there you might be able to find an address,' Clare said. 'There might be letters or something. Would you mind going as quickly as possible? Otherwise the police will clear everything out and then we'll never get her settled before social services get hold of her. I'd go but I've got to look after the two girls.'

'Of course,' Martin said. Something was happening here. They were working on this as partners. 'I'll do it as soon as I get back this evening,' he said. And show you how I can be relied upon. It was ironic how, in life, Viktor had prised them apart on that evening they went to the Madonna Club and now, dead, he might help bring them together again.

'Thank you for letting me know,' he said. 'I'll see you later.' He put the phone down and walked over to the window. There were still a few stray flakes of snow swirling around in the breeze. Poor Viktor. He had let him down. He must not fail Suzana now. Nor Clare.

sixty-six

The child was sprawled flat on his back, little arms outstretched, gently snoring. Charlotte leaned over the bed and adored her son. Why was she leaving for work before he was awake and getting home after he had gone to sleep when she could be staying at home and playing with him? She had a choice. Why was she making it this way?

Behind her, she heard the door open and Rob came in. He put his arm around her and looked at Matthew.

'You did that,' he said.

'What do you think?' she said, standing up and leaning into him. 'Should I just chuck it in right now?'

'It's up to you.'

'I know it's up to me. But I feel trapped between what I know I love and what I feel I might still want. So I was asking you for your view. Do you have one?'

'I want you to be happy,' he said.

'That's not a view,' she said. 'That's a cop-out.'

'I'm not convinced you'd be happy if you gave up on the paper,' he said.

Matthew turned over in the bed.

'I'm not so sure,' she said. 'A year ago, you would have been right. But now I'm not so sure. I think you were on to something the other night when you said I was changing.'

'It was only a passing comment. I wasn't suggesting you gave up your job.'

'I could do something else,' she said. 'Not so demanding. I could spend more time with you and Matthew.'

'Think about it,' he said and kissed her on the lips. 'You don't have to decide right now.'

'I can't stop thinking about it,' she said. If only she could nail this story, then she would be free to start a new life, shot of Maggie, self-respect intact, armoured against her brother's condescension.

'Do you want some tea?' Rob asked.

She nodded, still looking down at Matthew asleep.

'I'll make it,' Rob said. 'Come out when you're ready.'

He pulled the door behind him as he left, shutting out the light from the hall, leaving the room shadowed by the soft glow of Matthew's night-light. She wanted to pick him up and hug him and feel him close to her but then he would wake up and she would never be able to get him back to sleep. She turned off the light and sat on his bed and listened to him breathing. One day soon, she would be reading him to sleep. Why wasn't this story working out?

'Sleep well, my darling boy,' she murmured. 'Not long now.' Children always looked so helpless when they slept. Matthew rubbed his nose in his sleep and then put his thumb in his mouth and started sucking it. Charlotte wished he wouldn't do it. It looked so needy.

And then it made her think of the little girl in the pink raincoat nestling so needfully into the man at Job Alley. Serendipity. He might be able to help. She had his card somewhere. At least, he might be able to suggest some more names for Giles. She would ring him and see where that got her.

sixty-seven

Martin could hear the bell buzzing somewhere just inside the door but nothing moved. He went back down the steps and out into the road and looked up at the house to see if there was a light on anywhere. All the windows were dark. It was a tall featureless house, just like the others ranged down the long straight street. Those Edwardian property speculators had boosted their profits by saving on architects. Every house looked like an oblong box up-ended along a line drawn against a ruler by a bored draughtsman's clerk, who, just before he had put on his coat to leave for the weekend, had hurriedly tacked on an ugly portico, approached by a steep, short flight of steps.

In coming here, Martin felt that, in some small way, he was making amends to Viktor for the way he had treated him. He was now behaving with the care and consideration he should have shown when Viktor was alive. He was going to look after Suzana. Him and Clare.

There was no-one about. The streetlight outside Viktor's house was broken and emitted a low dull hum. Behind him, Martin heard a car drive slowly down the street and then it was silent again. There were no trees and the front gardens were planted with dustbins and broken furniture. There were not even any skips with their promise of renewal. It was going to take a very long time before any property boom rippled out to this street and lifted it up. There would always be somewhere else more attractive for the young married couples with their joint salaries to take a punt on doing up a new home. This street looked as if it had always been intended to house transient migrants. And always would.

Martin went back up the steps and rang the bell again. And this time he kept his finger on it. There must be someone somewhere in this four-storey house. Another car crawled slowly down the street. He heard fireworks in the distance, cracks and a whoosh, and he saw a rocket explode over the brooding houses, red and silver into the night sky.

And then he heard someone moving inside the house, a deliberate shuffling, slowly coming closer to the door.

'Stop ringing the pissing bell, will you.' The voice was thin and angry. 'What do you want?'

'I need to talk to you.'

'And who the piss are you?'

Martin considered this question. The wrong answer might cause the voice to shuffle off again and the door would remain shut. 'Please may I have a word with you?'

'Who the piss are you?' the voice repeated.

'My name is Martin Hughes. I am Mr Markov's lawyer.'

'What the piss do you want?'

'I should like to have a quick word with you.'

'What for? He's dead.'

'Please,' Martin said. 'It will only take a minute.' There was no reply. And then he heard a shuffle, as if the landlord was preparing to move away from the door. 'I will make it worth your while,' Martin said quickly. It had worked before.

'What do you want?' But this time the voice invited a response.

'Just a minute of your time. I will make it worth your while.' This time the shuffle came nearer. And then there was a brisk clanking as a chain was fastened and then the door was cracked open. Above the chain, Martin saw a nose with a hair on the tip of it, and a pair of inquisitive eyes.

'Step into the pissing light so I can see you,' the voice said. Martin did as he was told. And then the chain was taken off the door and it opened. 'You look like a pissing lawyer,' the voice confirmed.

It belonged to one of the fattest men Martin had ever seen, wearing a shapeless unbuttoned cardigan. His belly spilled over the waistband of his trousers which had rolled back under the pressure and his greasy grey hair straggled down to his collar.

'I'm Martin Hughes,' Martin said. 'Mr Markov's lawyer.'

'I know that. I heard you. What do you want? He's dead.' The man was repulsive, in every way.

'Can I see his room?'

'What for? The pissing police have already been through it.'

'But I should still like to see it.'

'No,' the landlord said. 'It's not his room any more. He's dead.'

This did not appear to be the end of the conversation but Martin was not sure what he was expected to say next. 'Have you let it out to someone else?'

The landlord gave a sour little laugh. 'Chance would be a fine pissing thing,' he said. 'The pissing police said I couldn't let it again until they told me. Alright for them. The pissers. They're not paying the rent. That room is pissing dead space now. Dead. What am I meant to do for rent?'

Now Martin understood. 'How much is it?'

The landlord looked at Martin. A shrewd glance that went on a moment too long. 'A hundred pounds a week. In advance.'

'I'll take it for a week,' Martin said and took out his suffering wallet.

The room was larger than he had expected and looked out on a bedraggled garden. A green and red curtain partitioned it and at one end there was a sink and a hotplate. Beside it was a thin single bed and by the door a slightly longer and wider bed was covered with a batik spread. The walls were bare. He opened the cupboard in the corner. It was empty. The police must have taken everything away. There was nothing left of Viktor here.

The landlord stood in the doorway, breathing heavily. Martin got down on his knees and looked underneath the bed. Nothing. Not even any dust. There was nothing to suggest Viktor and Suzana had ever lived here, nourishing a dream of return in this drab room, while their grubby landlord wheezed up and down the stairs.

'Looking for something?' the landlord said.

Martin ignored him and stood up. There was nowhere else to look.

'It'll take longer than a week to find anything,' the landlord said.

Martin turned to look at him. What was this repulsive man talking about? He had only been here for ten minutes. What had a week got to do with anything?

'It'll take two weeks.' The landlord was leering at Martin. 'Two weeks less one week leaves one week.'

Now Martin understood. Everything was simple with this man. 'A hundred pounds?' he said.

The landlord nodded and scratched his nose. Martin still did not know what he was paying for but he had no choice. He had found nothing in the room.

'Wait here,' the landlord said. Martin heard him wheezing along the landing. He came back holding a greasy brown envelope. 'Money,' he said.

Martin opened his wallet. 'I've only got eighty left,' he said.

'Sorry,' the landlord said, grasping the envelope.

'I'm not bargaining,' Martin said. 'I really have got only eighty pounds left.'

'Let me see your wallet,' the landlord said and put out his hand for it.

'I'm telling you I've only got eighty pounds,' Martin said, holding on to it. 'Take it or leave it.'

'Sorry,' the landlord said, 'you won't find anything without another week.'

Martin stared at him for a moment and then gave him the wallet. The landlord took out the money and gave the wallet back to Martin. Then he licked his finger and counted the notes slowly and carefully before putting them in his back pocket.

'You're only getting this because the police are such pissers,' he said, giving Martin the envelope. 'How do they expect me to live, not letting the room?'

Inside the envelope were three passports and a small white card.

'Pissers,' the landlord said. 'They think they're so clever but I found what I found. And they're not getting it now.'

Martin took out the card. Charlotte Cornforth. What was Viktor doing with a card from a journalist? And from that paper? What had he been doing? Could it explain what had happened to him? Poor Viktor.

'I need to live,' the landlord said.

There were two dark blue Bosnian passports, one for Viktor and one for Suzana. And a British passport, belonging to someone called Marian Hart. There was a blurred photograph of a pretty dark-haired woman inside. She seemed somehow familiar but he could not place her. Why did Viktor have her passport?

'OK,' Martin said. 'Can I have my key?' He still hadn't found anything to help him find Viktor's sister and he might need to return.

'What do you mean? Your pissing key?' the landlord said.

'I've paid you two weeks' rent. Please may I have my key.'

'You said you would make it worth my while, you pisser.'

'I did. I have. Who else was going to pay you rent for this week?' Martin glared at the landlord and he saw him look away.

And then the fat man grunted and fished a large bunch of keys out of his pocket. He unhooked one and wiped it on his cardigan. 'Here,' he said. 'Give it back by Friday nine o'clock or it's another hundred pounds.'

'Don't worry,' Martin said. 'I'll take good care of your pissing room.'

'There's no need to talk like that,' the man said and Martin heard him muttering to himself as he shuffled off down the hall.

It was a damp misty night outside and a heavy dew was already settling on the parked cars. Martin heard the landlord locking the door behind him as he walked down the steps. Poor Viktor. What had he been doing with that passport and a visiting card for a journalist? Could Marian Hart have been a friend Viktor never mentioned? Might she know how to find his sister?

A middle-aged man with a shaven head was ambling towards him down the road, with a large smooth dog that looked as if it ought to have been banned. The dog was straining at the leash and Martin was sure he could see it slavering. He decided to wait until they had gone past him.

But they did not. They turned in to the front garden next door and walked up the steps to the front door. The man started to rummage in his pockets. Martin assumed he was trying to find his key. He heard him muttering to the dog. He was not a passing villain but a neighbour. Viktor's neighbour. 'Excuse me,' he called.

The man went on looking through his pockets.

'Excuse me,' Martin called again and this time the dog heard because he started to pull at the leash and the man turned round.

'You talking to me?' he said.

Martin took a few steps towards the neighbour's front garden. 'I'm Mr Markov's lawyer,' he said. 'Have you got a moment?'

'Who?' The man had a surprisingly soft voice.

'Viktor Markov,' Martin said. 'He lived next door.'

'Sorry. Don't know him.' The man found his key and started to put it in the lock.

'He was killed two days ago.'

The man stopped and turned round. 'Who are you?' he said.

'I'm his lawyer,' Martin said. 'Martin Hughes.'

The man was looking at him. He knew something. Martin sensed it. 'I'd be very grateful if I could talk to you for a minute.'

'Look, I'm sorry about what happened,' the man said. 'But I don't know anything.' For a man with such a fierce dog, he was surprisingly timid.

'It would only take a minute,' Martin said. He knew there was something to be learned here.

'I've told the police,' the man said. 'I know nothing.'

'But you do know what happened,' Martin said. 'You just said so. Couldn't you spare a minute? He had a six-year-old daughter. For her sake?'

The man was now looking at him, making up his mind. 'Come in,' he said eventually. 'Quickly.'

His living room had limed oak floors and French windows which looked out on a well-kept garden. There was an open fire and a large plasma screen television dominated one corner of the room. Beside it was a brushed steel rack of audio equipment with two flat panel speakers hung on the wall. A gold disc in a display frame was hung on the wall above the fireplace.

'I'll make some tea,' the man said. 'Sit yourself down.' The dog sat by the door watching Martin watching it. 'It's OK,' the man said. 'Otis won't hurt you because you came in with me. If you hadn't, he'd have ripped your throat out by now.'

Martin swallowed.

'All right, I'll take him with me,' the man said. 'Otis. Here.'

And they left Martin alone in the room. He walked over to the fireplace and looked at the gold disc. It was for 'The Hurt Inside'. One of the greatest rock ballads ever. Martin knew every word.

all the tears I cried, could never wash away, the hurt inside

He remembered the long hot summer it came out when every pore in his teenage body sweated with lust for Anne Medworth who did not know he existed. Strange how he hadn't thought about her for years and now he couldn't stop remembering her. 'The Hurt Inside'. What a great song. The only hit Chris Finlay ever had.

The man returned with two mugs of tea and no dog. 'Here you go,' he said.

'Is this you?' Martin said. 'Are you Chris Finlay?'

'Yeah,' the man said. 'That's me.'

'What a great song,' Martin said.

'Yeah,' Chris Finlay said. 'It was.' He looked at the gold disc. 'Nineteen years ago and it's still paying the mortgage. And everything else.' A diamond stud in his ear caught the light as he sat down. 'It was too good, that's the problem. No-one listens to anything else I do.'

He got up again and walked over to the audio rack. 'Listen to this, man.' And loud rock music shook the room.

'Very good,' Martin said.

'Yeah,' Chris Finlay said. 'It is. But no-one wants to hear it. All they want is "The Hurt Inside". They don't hear me, Chris Finlay, all they hear is that one fucking song. Sometimes I wish I'd never written it.'

'You shouldn't think like that,' Martin said supportively. 'It was a great song.'

'Do you want to hear some more?' Chris Finlay said. He had pleasant regular features and the faint sandy stubble and the diamond in his ear made him look like a curate in a fashionable evangelical church.

'That would be very nice,' Martin said politely. 'But I wonder if I could just ask you about Viktor Markov.'

'Just listen to this, man.' Again loud music rattled the flat.

'Very good,' Martin said as enthusiastically as he could. 'But I wonder if I could just ask you a couple of questions about Viktor Markov?'

'OK.' Chris Finlay gave a resigned shrug and got up and turned off the music. 'Just like the others. It's only "The Hurt Inside" that gets you going. If you never knew I'd done that, you'd think this was really good.'

'It is really good,' Martin said. 'Really. It's just that I need to talk about Viktor Markov. Who was murdered.' It was terrible how a man, someone who had been so powerfully alive, could just disappear, murdered, and no-one seemed to care, not his repulsive landlord, obsessed with his rent, nor his neighbour lamenting his vanished career.

'Sorry. You're right, man. Priorities,' Chris Finlay said. 'I don't always get them. Sorry.'

'Did you know anything about Viktor Markov?'

'Like what?'

'Did he ever mention his sister to you?'

Chris Finlay shook his head.

'Or someone called Marian Hart?'

Again Chris Finlay shook his head.

'Charlotte Cornforth?'

'I'm sorry, man. I didn't really know him. I just saw him from time to time in the street.'

'He never mentioned his sister?'

Chris Finlay shook his head.

'Do you know why he might have had a passport belonging to someone called Marian Hart?'

'I really don't know, man. We just chatted from time to time. He had a pretty little girl. And I think he said he worked in a language school.'

Martin remembered Viktor mentioning that. 'Do you remember what it was called?

Chris Finlay pursed his lips. 'He did say. But I can't remember. Something to do with the Queen I think. But I'm sorry. I can't remember.' He looked at Martin as if checking whether that was all.

'Do you remember any visitors?'

'No. Sorry. As I say, we only really chatted in the streets. When we saw each other. Which wasn't that often.' He was perched on the end of his chair as if he wanted Martin to go but was too polite to ask him to do so.

Martin stood up and, as Chris Finlay stood up with him, Martin suddenly remembered the look of weary resignation he had seen flit across his face when he first asked him about Viktor. He knew something he had not yet told Martin.

'Are you sure there isn't anything else?' Martin said.

Chris Finlay looked at him.

'Please,' Martin said. 'I'm a lawyer. You can trust me. Whatever you tell me, I have to keep confidential. Please.'

'Oh, man,' Chris Finlay said. 'Why are you pushing me like this?'

'Remember that little girl,' Martin said. 'We need to know what happened so we can protect her.'

Chris Finlay sighed and sat down again and stared at the floor in silence.

'Please,' Martin said. 'For the little girl.'

'Oh, man,' Chris Finlay said again and paused. 'OK,' he said eventually. 'I saw it all.'

sixty-eight

They went in through the front and the back of the small terrace house at the same time. Two large uniformed officers stood in the porch ringing the bell, with an officer from the Firearms Unit beside them, while two detectives and another armed officer went in across the scrubby grass at the back. Clive Walton never liked to call on the Firearms Unit because he felt that sort of policing did not belong in this country but the Markov murder looked like a hit and it followed the execution on the Tube and you didn't take risks with organised crime.

Clive Walton went into the house behind the inspector from Specialist Crimes because it was his case. 'What the fuck do you think you're doing?' Jeremy Phillips had said. 'You can't go in now. I've been working on this for three months and we're not ready. If we go in now, it could blow the whole thing.'

'I understand where you're coming from,' Clive Walton had said. 'I don't want to screw up your case. But I've got two murders here. And this ID card is the best lead I've got. It was found on the woman. We know it's forged. And it looks like their work. That ticks three boxes. Good enough for me.'

'Not good enough for me to blow this case,' Jeremy
Phillips had said.

But now here they were and in the downstairs living
room a sallow young man in an orange vest was
playing a computer game, watched by a pretty woman
with black hair and green eyes and a young man with
spots and long, thin brown hair.

'You are?' Jeremy Phillips said.

'What?' The man in the orange vest sounded French.

'What is your name?' Jeremy Phillips said slowly and
loudly.

'David Giraud,' the young man in the orange vest
said.

'David?' Jeremy Phillips said incredulously, rhyming
it with 'star bead'.

'Yes,' the man said. 'David.'

'What do you think the *Standard* would make of
another killing?' Clive Walton had said to Jeremy
Phillips. 'London streets set for gang war? Baby caught
in crossfire?' He had thought the other inspector, in his
tailored grey suit, would relate to that. 'And what
would they say if they found out we had known about
this and not done anything?' Clive Walton had said.
'We need to go in now.'

'Get up,' Jeremy Phillips said and then he put his
face so close to David Giraud that if anyone in the
room had been deaf they would have thought he was
going to kiss him. 'Get up now,' he said, speaking very
loudly and slowly.

Clive Walton understood why Inspector Phillips was
so upset. He would be too if he had been watching the

house in Earlsfield for weeks and then had to go in before he was ready.

'Look at this, Inspector.' One of the uniformed officers came back down the stairs carrying a large clear plastic bag. Inside was a grey box and some small bottles. 'A card-embossing machine and ultraviolet inks. Looks like he's been naughty.'

'Well, well, well,' Jeremy Phillips said. 'Looks like you've been naughty, Mr Darveed Giraud. Naughty enough for two years in jail. Credit cards was it? Or passports?'

David Giraud ignored him.

'Both? You greedy monsieur.'

'Who are you?' Clive Walton said to the other young man.

'Ferenc,' he said, after a pause. 'Ferenc Puskas.'

The young woman watched him gravely as he spoke.

'And you? What's your name?'

'Angela,' she said. 'Angela Vlas.'

'What else have you got?' Jeremy Phillips asked the uniformed policeman.

'Nothing. Yet,' he said. 'We're still looking.'

'I'm afraid you will need to come down to the station to answer some questions,' Clive Walton said to the three young people sitting on the sofa.

sixty-nine

The moment he walked into her living room Martin remembered, all over again, why he had fallen in love with Clare. It was perfect. Purple and white flowers spilled profusely over a large plain glass vase in the middle of the table and, coming from somewhere, there was an elusive scent, heady and rich. Suzana and Megan were playing with toy soldiers on the floor, silently, adorably, intense.

'Hello,' he said warily. This was the first time they had met since he stood her up and, after their phone call, he was still not sure how she would respond. 'Lovely flowers,' he said.

'A bonus from Marc,' she said.

Books covered the wall opposite and, somewhere in the background, Oistrakh and Oborin played the Spring Sonata. He had the same record. 'You don't need to stand, Martin,' she said. 'Please. Sit down.'

'Here?'

'Anywhere. Would you like a cup of tea? Or coffee?' She was wearing a soft grey pullover which came down to her knees.

'Thank you. Anything. Whichever is most convenient.'

'Both are convenient. Which would you like?'

'Actually, on second thoughts, nothing thank you,' he said. She seemed friendly. 'I've had a lot of caffeine today.' Although she also sounded a little distant. 'I am sorry about the other night,' he said. 'I really couldn't help it.'

'Not now, Martin,' she said. 'This is not the moment for that.'

'Costa Rica, Costa Rica. Her, she and me, and Costa Rica coffee,' Megan started to chant.

'Costa Rica, Costa Rica,' Suzana harmonised.

'I am so sick of that bloody commercial,' Clare said. 'They never stop singing it. And it just goes round and round in my head. So irritating. Let's go next door.'

'Have you told Suzana yet?' he said as they sat down in a small study overlooking the garden.

'No. I thought about it and then I thought it'd be better to wait to see if we could find her aunt,' Clare said. 'It might absorb the shock if she has her family around her. And, anyway, I'm not sure I've quite summoned up the courage to do it yet.'

'I'm sure it's right to wait,' he said. Partners supported each other.

'How did you get on at the flat?' she said.

'Depressingly,' he said. 'I heard a story about what happened and I've got some odds and ends, including a passport for Suzana which we'll need to get her home, but there was nothing about his sister.'

'So how are we going to find her?' she said. The plural pronoun put out its arms and hugged him.

'I've rung an agency someone in my chambers used recently. They've got a good reputation.'

'That's enterprising of you,' Clare said and Martin glowed. 'What did they say?' she said.

'They're sending someone to meet us here any moment now.'

She looked at him and he thought he saw something glint in her eye.

'Oh,' he said. 'I'm sorry. I should have asked. It's just that I thought I should get a move on after I didn't get anything at the flat and I didn't think you'd mind. But I should have asked first. I'm sorry. Is it OK? For him to come here?' Why did she make him feel so awkward?

'Of course, it's all right,' Clare said. This was not the time to have an argument about his need to control everything. 'I'm impressed. I didn't think you'd be quite so efficient.'

Why not?

'Don't look so wounded, Martin. I meant I didn't think anyone could be so efficient. Who is he?'

'He said he used to be a policeman. It's a big agency and they employ all sorts of investigators. They do a lot of insurance work but they also trace people.'

'We should get this sorted out as quickly as possible,' Clare said. 'I love having Suzana here but social services won't let me keep her. Sooner or later they'll take over and once that little girl gets into their clutches, it could take months to get her back to her family. Much better if her family can take her before she has to go through all that.'

And then the bell rang. The investigator was a neat sandy-haired man in a black woollen overcoat, with a thin black leather briefcase under his arm. As he came in, he shook hands first with Martin and then with Clare. 'Good evening, Mr Hughes, Mrs Hughes,' he said. 'Robert Wood.'

'Please sit down, Mr Wood,' Clare said. 'And it's Fletcher. Not Hughes. I kept my married name.'

Martin noticed she did not correct the investigator's impression that they were partners. His heart kicked.

'My apologies.' Robert Wood sat at the table and placed his briefcase neatly beside him.

'Would you like a cup of tea, Mr Wood?' Clare said. 'Or coffee?'

'No thank you, Ms Fletcher.' He spoke carefully. 'I'm afraid I don't have much time, today.' He took out a small notebook, bound in black leather, from his inside pocket, and a thin gold pen. And then he wrote down in his notebook what Martin told him about Viktor's sister and Suzana's aunt.

Clare watched Martin as he spoke, serious and precise, the barrister. There was something reassuring about him in this mood, earnest, capable, professional. This was his essentiality, as Marc would say.

'Thank you, Mr Hughes, Ms Fletcher,' Robert Wood said as he stood up. 'It doesn't sound as if it should be too much of a problem. I'll call you by the end of next week to give you a progress report.' He shook hands with Martin and then with Clare and then he pulled on his black leather gloves. 'Goodbye,' he said.

'You chose well,' Clare said, as she came back into the room from letting out Robert Wood.

The cold air outside had flushed her cheeks, making her look even lovelier. He really would have to be very careful not to rush it. 'Yes,' he said, 'he seemed efficient.'

'Poor little girl,' Clare said. 'I'll have to tell her soon. I just hope we find her aunt first.'

'Mummy, Mummy,' Megan screamed in the room next door and then came running out and into Clare's arms. 'Suzana's being horrible,' she cried.

Clare cuddled her. 'What happened?' she said.

'We were just playing with our toys,' Megan sobbed. 'And Suzana killed me.'

'What do you mean?' Clare said.

Martin looked up and saw Suzana standing in the doorway, mute, twisting a strand of hair in her fingers, watching expressionless as Megan sobbed in her mother's arms.

'We were racing our bikes and Suzana crashed into me and then she said a man got up and killed me.'

'It's all right,' Clare said. 'It's only a game. She didn't mean it. She was only playing.'

'No, she wasn't,' Megan wailed. 'She said it was true.'

'I'm sure she didn't, darling,' Clare said, stroking her hair. 'People don't get off bikes and kill each other.'

'Yes, they do,' Suzana said from the doorway. 'My papa told me.'

And Martin remembered what Chris Finlay had told him about what he saw when Viktor was shot and he felt sick.

'Clare,' he said, 'why don't you take Megan next door and I'll talk to Suzana.'

Clare looked at him curiously. 'OK,' she said. He was commanding in this mood. 'Come in when you're ready,' she said.

Martin went over to the doorway and took Suzana by the hand. 'Let's sit on the sofa,' he said. 'What did your papa tell you?' he said. It was too much of a coincidence. Suzana must know something. But how could she have seen it? She had been staying with Clare when Viktor had been shot by a man on a motorbike.

Suzana shook her head.

'Come on, Suzana,' Martin said, still holding her hand. 'You can tell me. I'm your friend, remember.'

'He said I must always be careful if a man drives up beside me slowly on a motorbike. He said I must run away and shout very loudly.'

Martin kept holding her hand but he felt his heart starting to hammer. How could Viktor possibly have known what was going to happen?

'Why did your papa say that?' he said.

Suzana shook her head. 'Can't remember,' she said.

'When did he say it? Yesterday?' Martin asked.

Suzana nodded. 'Yes,' she said. 'Or the day before yesterday. We were walking down the road and this man came up on a motorbike and then he said it.'

'Can you remember what happened?' Martin said gently. 'I know you've got a brilliant memory, Suzana.

I know you can remember lots and lots about what happened. Can you tell me all the things you remember about what happened?'

'Well,' she said. 'We were walking down the road where we live and this man came on a motorbike. A big, huge red motorbike, with mirrors on both sides and a black seat.'

'What did the man look like?' Martin said.

'I couldn't see,' she said.

'Why not?'

'He was wearing black everywhere and he had a helmet on his head.'

'And then what happened?' Martin said.

'He stopped the motorbike,' Suzana said. 'And he said something and we couldn't hear because he was wearing his helmet so then he took the helmet off and asked Papa where a road was and Papa said this was the road and then he put the helmet on again and went away.'

'And what did your papa do then?' Martin said.

'He said I must run away if anyone comes up like that because they can do bad things. He said where we come from bad people hurt you like that. They drive up to you and hurt you and then drive away so no-one can catch them.'

Martin stroked her hair. Viktor had been so cautious, so schooled by his life in Bosnia. He must have been worried by someone looking for his road. And still they got him. 'What did the man look like?' he said.

Suzana shrugged. 'I don't know,' she said.

'Was he young?' Martin said.

The little girl nodded.

'What colour was his hair?'

'Like mine,' she said. 'And he had a big spot by his nose.'

Now Martin realised that Suzana could give a good description of the motorcyclist who was almost certainly the man who had killed Viktor. Chris Finlay had described a motorcyclist in black leather driving up slowly on a big red motorbike to Viktor, shooting him in the head and driving off. It sounded as if the killer had been on a dry run when he met Viktor and Suzana. And now Suzana was a witness. And the killer must know that.

Martin could hear Clare next door, playing with Megan. Should he tell her what he had just found out? But to what end? It would only alarm her. But he should call the police. This could be a vital clue. Martin got up from the sofa and walked into the next room with Suzana. 'Here we are,' he said. 'Suzana's been brilliant.'

'Come on, Suzana,' Clare said. 'Come and help Megan with this painting.'

'You can have the green paint,' Megan said, her upset now forgotten.

Clare got up from the floor and came over to Martin. 'What's going on?' she said quietly.

'Nothing,' he said. 'I thought Viktor might have said something to her. But it's nothing.'

Clare looked at him but did not say anything further. She liked him in this mood. Focused, not distracted or awkward. Purposeful. If he could look after Suzana like this, perhaps he did mean what he said about her and Megan.

'I've just got a phone call to make,' Martin said, taking out his mobile. 'I'll just go next door for a minute.'

In the study, he took out his wallet and searched for the card Inspector Walton had given him. And then he stopped. Was this really the right thing to do? If he told them about this, they would question Suzana and then she would find out about Viktor before they were ready to tell her and they would have to keep her here in case she was needed as a witness, instead of going to live with her family in Sarajevo, which must be the best thing for her now. Whatever else, she was going to be in more danger here, where the killer would be looking for her, than in Sarajevo.

And what would the police think if he turned up in connection with this murder? That would be two murders in a week. No policeman would think that was coincidental. The more Martin thought about it, the more the arguments stacked up against ringing the police now. When they found Suzana's aunt and Suzana was safe in Sarajevo, then they could ring. And Clare could do it. There was no need for him to get involved. What Suzana remembered was circumstantial evidence that might help to build a case but it was hardly going to be decisive in leading the police to the killer. All things considered, Martin thought, it was best to keep this to himself for the time being while he hoped that Robert Wood found Viktor's sister quickly.

The door flew open and Suzana burst in, closely followed by Megan, laughing breathlessly. 'You're it,' she whooped.

'No, I'm not, you're it,' Suzana called back. And they ran giggling back out of the room.

But should he really just sit back passively to wait and hope others would save that little girl? There must be something he could do now. They had to rely on Robert Wood to investigate in Bosnia but surely there was something he could do here.

Clare appeared in the doorway. 'Have you made your call?' she said. 'I was just thinking if there was anything else we could do,' he said.

Clare gazed at him. This was the essence of Martin, painstakingly conscientious and caring. Would she really be taking such a risk with him? 'Was there anyone else who knew him?' she said.

And then Martin remembered. 'He taught in a language school,' he said. 'I could try there to see if anyone knows anything about his sister.'

seventy

Murdering a child? That little girl. How had his life come to this? But what choice did he have?

He looked out at the trees in the garden and re-membered just two years ago standing in another porch, watching the late summer rain beating down on the birch trees by the river as the thunder rolled and crashed over the hills in the distance. He was about to start his graduate course and the future was bright with promise. His Master's degree. And a car. America. Girls. Microsoft. More girls. How had all that so quickly turned to this?

He took a deep drag on the cigarette. At least that had not changed. The rush of nicotine still felt good.

The boss had asked him whether it had been a clean hit and he had said yes. But he had lied. He had not dared tell the truth which was that he had made a mess of it. He had been prepared, mentally ready, everything planned as he had been taught, helmet on, Ruger in his pocket, photograph of the target memorised, directions learned by heart and then someone had stolen all the street signs. At least, he could not find any. So he had stopped a pedestrian to ask the way. And the man could not hear him through the helmet. So he had taken off the helmet and as he did so, he realised, in horror, that he had stopped to ask directions from the target who was walking down the road holding the hand of a little girl in a pink raincoat and both of them had now seen his face. And he had panicked and ridden off.

Of course, he had now taken care of the man. He had returned the next day and this time it was a flawless operation. This time the man had been on his own and he had cruised up towards him so slowly on the bike, so slow and gentle, that the man had not noticed him approaching. And then he had pulled out the Ruger when he was right up beside him and it had been a clear hit, clean, one shot, and he was away, accelerating round the corner.

But that still left the other one, the little girl. She had seen him. What would she remember if the police asked her about who her father had met in the last few days? She was very little so how much would she remember about anything? And it only had been a few minutes, a chance encounter; how significant would that have been in her life?

And yet, could he afford to take the risk? He had seen how ruthless the boss was to those who failed. But then again how could he kill an innocent child? The man had brought it on himself. He had interfered and he was jeopardising the operation, as the boss had explained. But the little girl? How could he do this to her? But if he didn't, the wrath of the boss would be turned against him. And that would be the end of him.

He was trapped in a terrible choice between him and her.

seventy-one

Clive Walton was tired. He had interviewed fifteen people in the last two days, slow work where he needed to concentrate on every word, fixing it in his head, storing it away, in case it was the key that, in due course, would unlock the puzzle. He was good at his job and he knew why. He was painstaking and methodical and he could understand what made people run and what made them fight, and doing his job well like this required hours and hours and hours of grinding, exhausting work.

The woman sat meekly in front of him, hands clasped in her lap and her eyes on the floor. She was the last of the ones they had picked up in the raid which so far had yielded nothing. In the small, windowless interview room, the fluorescent light bounced off her glossy dark hair.

Not everyone recognised the importance of understanding people. Some officers thought investigations were just hard work, accumulating the evidence, more and more of it, until one day they reached the point when the case was made. And sometimes that was all that was needed. But Clive Walton knew that sometimes imagination was also needed, to get inside the head of the perpetrator. And he knew he was good at this. No-one made inspector at thirty-three unless they were good like that. But thinking, concentrating, understanding, imagining, was tiring work. And now he was feeling it.

They had not found anything much in the Earlsfield house. Just the card-embossing machine and inks. Nothing else. No forged passports or credit cards and nothing to prove that anything had been produced there. Not enough to prosecute.

It was one of those times when nothing was going as it should. They had brought them all in for questioning but so far they had got nothing. They were sure the Frenchman was producing the European identity cards and passports that were turning up all over the South-East but they had not yet found a way to nail him. Three different informants had identified him but so far they had not got enough to persuade the Crown Prosecution Service to act.

And now he had spent two hours with the little tyke who had said absolutely nothing of any use at all. David Giraud was a slight sallow man, wearing a brown suede jacket with a genuine French passport who sat there saying no to everything that Clive Walton asked him.

So, as it turned out, the risk of moving in on the house so quickly had not been worth taking. Jeremy Phillips was furious, and so was his superintendent, but there it was. Decision taken. Done. Gone. And now David Giraud, with his greasy hair, streaked with muddy blond highlights, swept back from his forehead, sat there in his rimless spectacles, excavating his nose and carefully placing what he found on the side of the desk in the interview room. Clive Walton refused to respond but patiently worked his way through the questions. And ended up with nothing.

After two hours he had let him go. Tomorrow he would turn his details over to the DST in Paris. Monsieur David Giraud would not enjoy the attentions of la Direction de la Surveillance du Territoire. It was a small compensation for the two hours he had wasted watching the greasy little forger pick his nose.

Then he had spent another hour with the other young man. He said he was Hungarian and they told him to bring his passport into the station but Clive Walton supposed it would be genuine. The young man said he was just visiting a friend he had met playing Internet games. And that was not a crime either. He was probably part of the same gang as the Frenchman but it was hard to say what he might have been doing there this afternoon. If he had been there to pick something up, they had not been able to find it.

And so now, finally, he was talking to the young woman. She seemed different from the other two, better dressed, better looking and more frightened. The two young men had sat in the interview room as if it had been a tedious necessity like queuing in a supermarket. She seemed more worried. But he guessed she was just along for the ride. Perhaps she was just the girlfriend of one of them, although she seemed too attractive to be going out with either the gangling spotty Hungarian or the sallow Frenchman who looked as if he would be happiest abusing himself. She had no papers with her and he made a note to remind himself to get them checked out.

'Who are you working for?' he asked. He had gone through the preliminaries and now he had to work his way through the main questions.

'Nobody,' she said. 'I am a self-employed computer consultant.' She would not look him in the eye but her English was fluent with a soft slurred accent. She was very pretty.

'Why were you visiting David Giraud?'

'He is a friend of my friend.'

This was going to make as much progress as the other interviews. None. He sighed deeply.

'Look,' he said. 'We are investigating two murders here. That is a serious business. If you know anything that might be relevant to our investigation, you must tell us. Or you will get yourself into trouble. Do you understand?'

'Yes,' she said. 'But why do you think this has got anything to do with me?'

'We think that David Giraud, the friend of your friend, has been forging passports and identity cards. And one of them was found on the body of the murdered woman.' He was staring her in the eye as he spoke to gauge her reaction. Nothing. He pushed further, guessing. 'And a forged passport was found in the flat of the man who was killed.' The landlord had said he had seen a passport in the name of Marian Hart in Viktor Markov's room and said it was in an envelope addressed to the woman Viktor Markov had reported missing. It was reasonable to assume the passport was forged. And that the two murders were connected in some way. 'What do you know about David Giraud?'

She shook her head. 'Nothing,' she said, looking away from him.

Then Clive Walton had one of those empathetic flashes of inspiration that he had learned to trust. 'Do you know Viktor Markov?' he asked.

'No,' she said and he saw her glance at him. 'Why?'

'He's the man who was murdered. And it was in his flat that we know there was a forged passport. Do you know Marian Hart? Or Mila Hubchev?'

'No. Why?'

There was nothing in her eyes. So much for his empathetic inspiration. It was clearly just one of those days. He had better cut his losses and go home.

'The passport was in the name of Marian Hart in an envelope addressed to Mila Hubchev,' he said.

Mila could not stop herself looking up at the tired young policeman but he was looking down at the desk and writing something down on a notepad. She realised that Viktor must have been trying to help her. He must have thought a new passport would save her. Dear Viktor. Poor Victor. How had he got hold of it?

'That's all,' the policeman said. 'Thank you for your time, Ms Vlas. You will need to report to a police station with your passport in the next seventy-two hours. Or you could be in trouble. Please do not forget. And please do not move from the address you have given us until you have checked in with your local police station.'

He stood up and offered her his hand to shake. 'And here's my card, in case you do think of anything I might need to know.'

'Thank you,' she said.

She really was very pretty. 'I'll see you out,' he said.

He looked exhausted and he was not really concentrating on her. Good. But he had been writing everything down and he would probably check it all out anyway. Mila realised she would have to move by the day after tomorrow at the latest. She had already moved her operation once to please the Albanian and now she would have to move again. This policeman didn't have a clue what was going on and he was very unlikely to come after her. But just to be safe she'd move and then she could get on with her business in peace.

seventy-two

The steam swirled up from the mug of tea and mingled with the damp fug of cigarette smoke and central heating. On the wall there were posters of Beefeaters and the Queen and Oasis and Tony Blair. Is this really the kind of country foreigners think we are, Martin wondered as he clasped his hands round the mug and felt the warmth flowing back into them and waited for the jittery director to speak.

It had taken him two days to trace the school. He remembered Viktor mentioning it but he could not remember what it was called. But Chris Finlay had thought it was something to do with the Queen and so on to the Internet he had gone and found the Windsor School. But it was not that. Then he had found the Buckingham School. Not that either. Nor the Buckingham Palace Institute, nor the Princess Diana Academy. But finally he had located the Balmoral School of English where Viktor had taught and where he hoped he might find someone who knew about Viktor's sister.

When he arrived, there were two Japanese girls in matching red leather jackets and an identical gash of red lipstick across their mouths, smoking beside the open door. 'Is this the Balmoral School?' Martin said.

They stared at him blankly.

'Is this the Balmoral School?' he said again, enunciating every syllable.

'Yes. Upstairs.' The taller one waved vaguely towards the door with the hand holding the cigarette and turned away.

At the top of the stairs there was another door and through that a small office, in which sat a large young lady with blue streaks in her hair, reading a magazine.

'Hello,' Martin said politely. 'Please can I see the head teacher?'

'No.' She did not look up from the magazine as she spoke. Martin couldn't think what to say next.

'Sorry,' he said. 'What was that?'

'No,' she said.

'I'm sorry,' Martin said. 'Why can't I see him? For all you know it could be a matter of life and death. And actually it is. So please may I now see the head teacher?'

'No.' Again she did not look up from the magazine as she spoke.

'Why not?'

'There is no head teacher here.'

'Well, who is in charge here? You?'

'There is no need to take that tone. The director.'

'Please may I see the director?'

'Take a seat. I'll see if he's available.' Reluctantly she put down her magazine and levered herself out of the chair. 'What's your name?'

'Martin Hughes. I'm a barrister.'

'OK, Mr Barrister. I'll see if he will see you.'

Martin stared at the wall. And then there was a movement outside the door but it was not the dumpy young lady returning. It was a slight, anxious, middle-aged man with receding fair hair and wire-rimmed glasses.

'Hi,' he said. 'Mr Barrister, I am Miroslav Dudek. I am the director here. How can I help you?'

'Actually, my name is Hughes. Barrister is what I do for a living.'

'Of course, of course, Mr Hughes. I am so sorry. How may I help you?' He had the careful accent of someone who had taken elocution lessons in the 1950s but never got the hang of them.

'I'm here on behalf of my client, Viktor Markov.' It was almost true. 'My late client.'

'Oh yes,' Miroslav said. 'Oh dear. What terrible news that was. What a shock.' He took Martin's right hand in his right hand and folded his left hand over it and shook it gently. 'I am so sorry,' he said. 'So sorry. Please come now into my office.'

They squeezed past the receptionist standing placidly in the corridor. As Martin passed her, his arm brushed against something fleshly. Unconcerned, she put her finger in her ear and jiggled it around.

Miroslav's office was a cubicle at the end of the corridor and they sat on two battered leather armchairs, their knees almost touching, as Miroslav tried to bite a piece of loose skin off the cuticle around his thumb.

'I am trying to trace my client's family,' Martin said. 'Do you have any names or addresses for them?'

'He was a good teacher,' Miroslav said and nodded vigorously. 'The students liked him. God rest his soul.' Kalaj had told him to be careful what he said to anyone who came round asking about Viktor Markov. All very well for him but he didn't want any trouble and yet here it was. He could tell this Englishman was going to be difficult and now worry was driving everything out of his mind. What exactly had Kalaj said? It was something specific and now it had slipped Miroslav's mind. What was it?

'Yes,' Martin said. 'God rest his soul. Did he mention anyone to you?'

'I don't think so.' What was it Kalaj had said? 'Not really.'

'What about Mr Markov's sister? Did he mention anything about her?'

Miroslav shook his head. 'I didn't know he had a sister,' he said.

'Is there anything else I should know?' Martin said. This was dispiriting. He hadn't heard from Robert Wood and this was going nowhere and they must find Viktor's sister and get Suzana to safety. Viktor had worked here for six months and this nervy man, chewing his finger, claimed to know nothing about him. It was odd. What was he concealing?

'No. Not really,' Miroslav said. Now he remembered Kalaj had said that if anyone came asking about Markov he should give them the address, as it would send a message to someone who had been causing them problems, a warning. But he had also said that he should not give it to anyone who came round. Just to certain people. Was it the police? Or anyone but the police? Miroslav could not remember.

'Are you sure?' Martin said. This man sounded as if he was concealing something.

'Let me think,' Miroslav said. He bit into the loose skin and tore it off. Why couldn't he remember what Kalaj said? The Albanian would kill him if he got it wrong.

'Any luck?' Martin said.

'Let me think. Let me think. Would you like a cup of tea?'

Martin shook his head. This man was definitely hiding something. 'If you can't remember, I could ask the police to help you.'

Miroslav looked up sharply. What was this man saying? 'No, no. Just wait. I'm thinking.' It could only be the police who were a problem. It must be OK to tell this man. This was all making him nervous and Miroslav wanted to end it. Now.

'Well?' This pleasant-looking barrister was getting testy.

'Wait. I think there was something. An address. I think I might have an address. He gave it to me once. For something. I can't remember. Wait.'

Miroslav got up and went behind his desk and opened the drawer. He knew he had written it down when Kalaj had told him. Where had he put it? In the drawer, there were tourist brochures, a boiled sweet, three pound coins and a pack of Marlboro cigarettes. And there it was. The Romanian's address.

'Yes,' he said and Martin heard the relief in his voice. 'Here it is.' He put a piece of paper on the desk and scribbled on it and handed it to Martin.

'Here you are,' he said. 'They might be able to help you.' Kalaj should be pleased. That Romanian bitch wouldn't be but he had done what Kalaj had asked. 'I hope it's helpful,' he said.

'We'll see, won't we?' Martin said. He put the address in his pocket. He'd go there tonight. If he could find Suzana's aunt, he would have done something to redeem his behaviour towards Viktor.

seventy-three

That barrister kept worrying at Clive Walton. An instinct told him that Martin Hughes might hold the key. A mistle thrush sang its lonely rattling call outside the window as he beat the milk and eggs together and then sprinkled in the vanilla and cinnamon. Under the grill, the bacon sizzled and spat. It was a dull grey dawn and he had been flattened. Jeremy Matthews and his superintendent were seriously irritated with him and he had not got anywhere with the forgers. And that had been his best lead and he had been so confident it would pay off. He dipped the bread in the batter and placed it in the pan and the rich sweet smell filled the small flat.

He did not have much else apart from the barrister. They had not established a secure identity for the dead woman and there was nothing to explain why Viktor Markov had been killed nor what connection there was between the two murders, although Clive Walton was sure they were linked in some way. He could feel it in his bones.

He carefully scooped the French toast out of the pan and placed it on a plate and then took the bacon from under the grill and added it to his breakfast and then he poured maple syrup over it all. This was how to start the day.

The only link between the two murders was Martin Hughes. His card in the woman's flat. And his relationship with Viktor Markov. Clive Walton would not have expected someone like the barrister to mix with an illegal immigrant like Viktor Markov. Pay him in cash to do a little light gardening, maybe. But mix socially with him, as his friend? Clive Walton did not think so. There was something not right about this.

He sat at the table and took a mouthful of French toast and maple syrup and bacon. Very good. Another American contribution to civilisation. He could not imagine why a barrister could have any connection with two gangland murders but there was Martin Hughes connected to both of them. It could be a coincidence but somehow it did not feel like that to Clive Walton.

He got up and made himself a cup of tea. Why might the barrister have got involved? Money probably. In Clive Walton's experience, greed lay at the heart of most investigations. Perhaps Mr Martin Hughes had some habit he needed to feed. He did not look like someone with a drugs problem but who could tell? Clive Walton had seen enough to know how easy it was to fall.

Perhaps Martin Hughes had some other vice? Was he an obsessive collector and needed the cash to keep buying the rare books? Perhaps his first steps slithering down the slippery slope had started when he was offered a unique opportunity to buy a first edition of *Waiting for Godot* in French and he had no spare cash available? Once people like that started, in Clive Walton's experience, it was very difficult for them to stop.

He took the last piece of French toast in his fingers and mopped up the maple syrup with it. Perhaps he should pay another visit to the chambers of Mr Martin Hughes.

seventy-four

'Try love.' Dori Grayson was belting it out. A classic from Dave Godin's *Deep Soul Treasures*. The man was a genius. Chris Finlay had no idea how he found these gems from the vaults. Who was Dori Grayson? Whoever she was, she had got it. Chris Finlay shuffled softly round the flat with his guitar, picking out the high notes and holding them in a thin echo of the chorus. 'Try love.'

The weak winter sun was beginning to filter into the flat and the dope had calmed him down. He had not slept much during the night, worrying about whether there were enough truly stand-out songs on the new album. He had got up while it was still dark and made himself a pot of white peony tea and rolled himself a spliff. Then he put on one of Dave Godin's masterpieces. Where did the guy find them all? Overlooked classics, every one.

He took a drag. The music business was cruel the way it chewed up talent. Look at Dori Grayson. Why had she never been a star? She should have been with that voice. It was unfair. Just like him. Year after year he had produced great songs that no-one ever bought. All anyone ever knew about him was that he had made 'The Hurt Inside'.

The THC was locking on to his nerve cells. This was a good start to the day. 'The Hurt Inside' was at least one more hit than poor Dori Grayson had ever had. According to one website, she was now working as a teacher in Louisiana. She might have died unknown to the wider world had it not been for the great Dave Godin. Thank God for Godin. Chris was feeling better now. The tea and dope were mellowing him out.

'Try love,' she sang. Yes. That was the note. He had worked it all out now. The track started again and he sat down to play along with it. Then Otis started barking. Chris tried to ignore it but the dog did not stop. 'Hush,' he called but the dog continued to bark. And then the bell rang. Chris sighed and put down the guitar.

'OK, Otis,' he said. 'This better be worth it.' As he walked into the hallway, the bell went again. He looked through the spyhole and saw two men outside. The bigger, burlier one was wearing a black leather trenchcoat. The other one was wearing a suit and Chris saw he was shivering in the cold morning air.

'Yes?' he called. 'What do you want?'

'Mr Chris Finlay?' The man in the leather coat called. He sounded foreign. 'The famous singer of "The Hurt Inside"?' It meant nothing to Boris but the fat man next door said it was important.

'Yes,' Chris Finlay called. 'What do you want?'

'We are from Russian television,' Boris said. 'We want to talk with you about television programmes. You sing all your greatest hits. Many programmes.'

'Yeah,' Chris said. 'OK.' It sounded good to him. And they sounded Russian. 'Come in.' He opened the door and the man in the leather coat pushed his way past him. The other one shut the front door behind him and stood in front of it so Chris was sandwiched between the two of them.

'OK,' Chris said. 'Come in, why don't you?' As they went down the hallway into the flat, Otis bounded up and stopped in front of the two men, growling.

'It's OK,' Chris said. He was not feeling mellow any more. There was something edgy about these men and Otis was definitely not cool with them. 'He won't hurt you. You came in with me. If you hadn't, he'd be eating your throat by now.'

'Is that so?' the shivering thin man said and kicked the flat door shut behind him with his foot and then he took a gun from inside his jacket and shot Otis in the head. The dog collapsed backwards on the floor and blood puddled around him.

Chris's legs buckled. 'Hey,' he said. 'What did you do that for?' He didn't know much about Russian television but he didn't think they shot dogs.

'Sit down, Chris Finlay,' the man in the leather coat said. 'Stay by the door, Stepan.'

'I'm Boris,' the man said as he went over to the windows and drew the curtains. 'Now, Chris Finlay, we need to talk to you.'

Chris now had a really bad feeling about this. He was not stoned any more. These men were definitely not from Russian television and he was definitely in trouble. The Dori Grayson song started to repeat and the man by the door said something in a foreign language.

'It's OK, Stepan,' Boris said in English. 'The noise will be useful.'

What did that mean? Noise? Useful for what? 'I don't know anything, man,' he said.

'Chris Finlay,' Boris said patiently. 'Please talk to us. See what happened to that dog. Think about that.'

Poor Otis. It was not fair. What had he done to deserve that? He had been a good friend. The tears welled up in his eyes. Stepan made a noise of disgust in his throat.

'It's all right, Chris Finlay,' Boris said softly. 'We don't want to hurt you. We just want to know what you know.'

Chris knew that this was not true. He was dead. He knew it was going to be a bad trip the moment they shot Otis. He was no part of whatever was going down here and he wanted nothing to do with it but it was too late. 'I don't know anything,' he said. He should have been at home indoors when the motorbike drew up alongside that bearded guy from next door. But he wasn't. Chris heard a click and turned his head to see Stepan doing something with his gun. The gun that had just killed Otis.

'Chris Finlay, Chris Finlay,' Boris said sadly. 'The fat man next door said you had a visitor. A lawyer. Now where is the fucking passport?'

Clunk, click, it all fell into place for Chris Finlay. That lawyer had said something about a passport. What was it? He couldn't quite remember but he knew he had said something. And now these dog-murderers were here talking about it. 'I don't know nothing about no passport, man,' he said.

Boris shook his head sorrowfully. 'No, no, no,' he said. 'You see, Chris Finlay, we know you know. The fat man told us about the lawyer. And the passport. And now you tell us you don't know anything. So we know you are lying. And we don't like it when people lie to us. Do we, Stepan?'

'No,' Stepan said and Chris saw that his gun was now pointing at his head. 'OK, OK,' he said. 'I saw it but I didn't see anything.'

Boris smiled at him. 'What are you talking about, Chris Finlay, you crazy man?'

Stepan was still aiming the gun at his head.

'I was just walking down the road and then I saw this guy on a bike,' he said, 'leathered up, come by, slowly, from nowhere and then pop and the bearded guy just collapsed and the other guy drove off. And that's all I saw, man, I swear it. Because then Otis started howling and I had to look after him.'

'Oh that,' Boris said and smiled again. 'Fuck that,' Boris said. 'What I want to know is where is the fucking passport?'

Relief surged through Chris Finlay. They didn't care he had seen the bearded guy getting shot. All they wanted to know about was some passport. 'Look, man, I really don't know anything. The man just came round and asked some questions. I wish I hadn't talked to him. But I did and now you've killed Otis.'

'What did you talk about?'

'He just asked if I knew these people or why the dead guy had this passport. And I just said I didn't know anything about it,' he said.

'Was that all?' Boris said. Maybe it was.

Chris Finlay nodded.

Boris looked at him, thinking about it. 'Where did he leave the passport?' he said.

'I don't know. He never even showed it to me.'

Boris turned and looked over to Stepan who was still standing by the door. It sounded as if the lawyer had still got the passport. 'What do you think, Stepan?' he said.

'I think we should kill him,' Stepan said.

'Do you?'

'Yes,' Stepan said. 'I don't like him. I didn't like his dog. And I killed his dog.'

'Please, man,' Chris Finlay said. 'Please. I don't know anything, man. I told you what I saw. That's all I know. Please. I don't want to know anything else, man. Please just let me go. I am never going to talk to anyone, ever, about anything. Please.'

Boris looked at him and then he decided. This Chris Finlay man could live today. It was the lawyer they needed to find. Boris got up and stood over Chris Finlay and put his hand on his shoulder. He felt the man trembling. 'I will believe you, Chris Finlay,' he said. 'Don't make me look stupid.'

'Please, man, I just want to make my music. I didn't see anything. I've forgotten everything.'

Stepan stepped towards him. 'Don't forget what happened to your dog.'

Chris Finlay shook his head nervously.

'Come, Stepan,' Boris said and they opened the door and left to look for the lawyer with the passport, while Chris Finlay sat in the chair shivering and staring at the blood which was still dribbling out from Otis's head.

seventy-five

'Funny how your name keeps turning up, Mr Hughes.'
Detective Inspector Walton sat comfortably in Martin's leather armchair looking steadily at him. 'Two murders, apparently unrelated, and yet your name turns up in both of them. You appear to be the missing link, Mr Hughes. Can you help me understand why that might be?'

'I'm afraid I don't know what you're talking about, Inspector,' Martin said, standing by the window, looking out at the lawns of Lincoln's Inn, crisp with frost, a familiar view which now suddenly seemed alien. Five minutes ago, he had been emerging from Viktor's nightmare. All he had needed to do was find Suzana's aunt and it would all be history, sad but past. But now he was plunged right back into it, trapped.

'I understand you knew Mr Markov. That is correct, isn't it, sir?'

Two bewigged barristers waddled by the window, alongside the barbered lawns, clutching bundles of papers, exchanging opinions. Martin nodded. What else could he say? Paragraph 301 and Section C were dancing around him, chanting, 'Illegal immigration, murder suspect, illegal immigration, murder suspect.'

'And I understand from his landlord that you went round to his flat yesterday. You must have done something to upset him, Mr Hughes, because he was not very complimentary about you. Not at all. And he said you carried out a thorough, one might almost say a forensic, examination of Mr Markov's room. Why was that, sir?'

Martin loved the view from his window, looking out on the Great Hall and the lawns. This was the community of the law, an island of logic and reason amid the chaos of life, just as Lincoln's Inn itself was a green haven in the concrete wasteland of Central London. He should not have lost his temper with the landlord. 'I was looking to see if I could find an address for his sister,' he said.

Clive Walton raised an eyebrow encouragingly.

'Someone needs to look after Suzana,' Martin said. 'Mr Markov's daughter.' In her pink raincoat.

This fellowship of the law was not bound together by blood or faith but by the pursuit of order. Into these peaceful halls came brilliant young minds from suburb and dale, village and town, from the humble and the great, generation after generation, shaped in the propagating beds of Oxford and Cambridge and brought to this cloistered calm in the great metropolis, to grow rich and powerful through the exercise of knowledge and skill.

'How well did you know Viktor Markov?' There was a new resolve in the policeman's voice.

Martin felt his face growing red and his stomach churned. How had he got tangled up in this? 'Not well.

I met him through the school his daughter goes to.' He hoped he was not going to have to explain about Megan. And Clare.

'Your children go to the same school, do they, Mr Hughes?'

Martin explained about Megan. And Clare.

Generation after generation, the Inns of Court had been home to an elite, open to the clever and industrious. How could this be happening to him?

'Would you say you were friendly?' On, and relentlessly on, went Detective Inspector Clive Walton.

'Yes,' Martin said. 'I suppose I would.' And he supposed they were. Had been.

'Can you think of anyone who might have wanted to hurt Viktor Markov? Any reason why?'

'No,' Martin said. 'I'm afraid I can't.' How could he start to explain about Mila and Kalaj and Boris? It would only make the policeman more suspicious. Better not even to start. But then he remembered that he had personally reported Mila's disappearance to the police. He must not appear to be concealing anything.

'Although,' he said, 'he did have a friend who disappeared.' And as he spoke, he felt another plank give way underneath him and he heard the turbulent water seething below.

'Would that be Ms Hubchev?'

'Yes.'

'And did you know her well, Mr Hughes?'

'No, not at all. I only met her a couple of times.' But he remembered her dark green eyes at the St Luke's fair.

'What do you think happened to her?' Clive Walton said. He was increasingly sure that this barrister was involved. He had not yet worked out how and why but as he dragged answer after answer out of him, he was more and more confident that he would find out.

'I've no idea, I'm afraid.' And Martin did not. 'That's what Mr Markov was trying to find out.'

'And did he?'

'Not as far as I know.'

'Do you think it's possible he might have upset someone when he was looking for her?'

'I suppose it's possible but I'm not aware of anything,' Martin said. Strictly that was true. Better to avoid mentioning Kalaj who sounded like a man who could get upset and kill people. Just mentioning a man like that would fuel the policeman's belief that he was somehow involved. And, in no circumstances, should he mention what he had discovered from Suzana. They needed to get her away to Sarajevo as soon as possible.

The inspector wrote everything down fast and unfussily and Martin wished he could read upside down.

'Can I offer anyone a cup of tea?' Phil Matthews put his head round the door. Today he was wearing the black suit with a fine red stripe, pink shirt and a scarlet tie that matched the stripe in the suit. 'Second time in a week that this policeman, who is not a client, has been round,' his look said. 'What exactly is going on here?'

'No, thank you,' Martin said, meaning, 'Please leave us alone, Phil. Now.'

'What about you, Inspector?' Phil Matthews said, meaning, 'I am now sure this means trouble and I want to know what it is. Nothing must interfere with the business of this chambers.' With his sculpted sideburns and hair swept raffishly behind his ears, he looked like a consultant cosmetic surgeon and talked like a sergeant major adjusting to civilian life.

'Did you know Viktor Markov was an illegal immigrant, sir?' Clive Walton said to Martin, ignoring Phil Matthews.

'Don't worry, Phil. We're all right,' Martin said and, as he spoke, he knew it was a mistake. He had just confirmed he was in trouble. Paragraph 301 pulsated and flashed and the Queen's Counsel Application Form receded with every word and he wanted Phil to get out of the room so he could recover from the clout the inspector had just given him. But now, instead of covering it up, Martin knew he had just confirmed to Phil Matthews, in so many words, that there was a problem here. So the policeman had known all along about Viktor.

'Very good, Mr Hughes,' Phil Matthews said, as he left, meaning, 'We'll talk about this later.'

'Did you know Viktor Markov was an illegal immigrant, sir?' Clive Walton repeated. The lovebite was glaring at Martin.

He should have listened to that first warning voice in his head and never got involved. What good had it done anyone? Mila disappeared and Viktor killed and now here he was, contemplating the ruin of his career. Guilty of diminishing public confidence in the administration of justice and bringing the legal profession into disrepute.

'No,' Martin said. The detective inspector must know he was lying. He wrote it down anyway. And then he looked up at Martin and smiled.

'It's all right, Mr Hughes. I don't mean to embarrass you. Don't ask, don't tell. That's how most people deal with this sort of thing. Cash in hand, no papers. How many bathrooms are refurbished in Islington on that basis? I'm not here to catch illegal immigrants. My job is to find out who killed Viktor Markov. And I just need to get as full a picture as I can.'

'And I'll do everything I can to help you,' Martin said. 'It's terrible what's happened. How could anyone have done this?' He knew that, as they spoke, Phil Matthews would be broadcasting the news about his sponsorship of illegal immigration and he needed to divert this policeman before he embarrassed him any further.

'So have you got any leads we could follow up?'

'Do you think her disappearance could be linked with what happened to Viktor?' If he asked his own questions that might divert the policeman. How could he get out of this before Phil Matthews told all Lincoln's Inn about how he was diminishing public confidence in the administration of justice?

'Might be. Might be,' Clive Walton said. 'Who can say? At this stage I need to follow up everything. Who can say what might develop?' He looked at Martin. One of those long looks that policemen give. 'So do you have any leads we can follow up, sir?'

Martin's stomach churned. There was the passport he had got from the landlord. Marian Hart's passport. And the visiting card. They might well be relevant, leads the police could follow up. But how could he mention them without implicating himself further? Why hadn't he immediately gone to the police with them? The more he thought about it, the worse it became.

'Why are you asking me?' he said. 'I hardly knew Viktor Markov. Why should I know anything about these things?' And then after the legal profession, his father would hear about it and know his dreams would never be fulfilled. He would never see his son on the Bench and it would break his heart.

'No reason, sir. I was just asking,' Inspector Walton said. 'Just in case you might be able to help. I need to follow up everything at this stage. You never know where it might lead.'

'Who do you think could have killed him?'

'Hard to say, sir. At this stage. It could have been anyone.' Inspector Walton stopped writing. 'Is there anything you can remember that might be helpful, sir?'

Martin shook his head. He was committed now. Anything he said now would only incriminate him. He could only hope it was all going to go away. The policeman appeared to be coming to the end of his remorseless questions and he had still not asked anything about the passport.

And then Martin realised he did not know anything about it. That miserable landlord was revenging himself on everyone. He had given the documents to

Martin to punish the police for preventing him from letting his room and then he had told the police about Martin's visit to repay his belligerence over the key. But that devious man had not told the police about the passport because that would have let them off their punishment. What a man.

'Quite sure?' Clive Walton said. He was giving the barrister one last chance to own up. The landlord had been quite clear he had taken the passport. 'He took it off the table before I could stop him, officer. The pisser. What could I do? My health's not good. The pisser.'

But the lawyer just shook his head again. He was involved in some way and Clive Walton was going to keep a close eye on him. For now, he would just keep him on a long rope and see where it led. And jerk it a bit, from time to time.

'You see, Mr Hughes,' he said, 'I'm still having difficulty understanding why your name keeps cropping up. Perhaps it's prostitutes. Maybe that's the link? You needn't feel embarrassed about telling me, Mr Hughes, many men use them. You should tell me if that is the link. It's not a crime. Not yet anyway. And if I knew that prostitutes were the link, it would achieve two things. First, it'd remove any other suspicions about how you might be involved in these murders. And second, you might be able to give us some useful leads. From your knowledge of the prostitutes.'

Martin flushed. This got worse and worse. 'I'm sorry, Inspector,' he said, 'I do not go to prostitutes. As I said.'

'Thank you, sir. I understand. I suppose that's all for now.' Detective Inspector Walton stood up. 'If anything else occurs to you, please give me a call. Here's my card, in case you've lost the one I gave you before.'

Martin took it. This is what came from trying to be helpful. One favour and this is where he had ended up. He had to get out of this. He would find Viktor's sister as quickly as possible to discharge his duty to Suzana. And then that would be that. Then he could get on with his life at the Bar and trying to rebuild his relationship with Clare. Martin put the card down on the desk, without looking at it.

'Don't worry, I'll see myself out,' Clive Walton said and closed the door behind him.

Martin stared at it. Had he made a mistake not being honest with the policeman? After all, he had nothing to hide. It just looked bad. It wasn't really. He had done nothing wrong. But even the appearance of wrongdoing could be damaging. As Viktor had pointed out when he blackmailed him into going to the Madonna Club. That was his problem. And how could he prove none of this had anything to do with him? How had his card been found in the murdered prostitute's flat? How had he got entangled in all this? Perhaps the police would find the perpetrators and it would, in time, be nothing more than a curious episode that passed, leaving no mark on his life.

Martin got up and walked over to the window. He hated feeling so trapped and helpless. All his life he had felt himself to be the master of his own destiny. Pass exam, move on. Get brief, win case, move up. It had all been in his own hands. But in the last two months, everything he did seemed to make his situation worse. He had tried to be a good provider for Clare and she had dumped him. He had tried to help Viktor out and now he was under suspicion of murder. He felt impotent. Even if they got Suzana safely to Sarajevo, there was still this police investigation hanging over him. Martin had the uneasy feeling that things had not yet finished going wrong.

seventy-six

'Fuck off, Fat Boy.'

Stevie crumpled the beer can in his hand and threw it at him. Joni Mitchell's sweet voice flowed from the mighty speakers.

'It's pussy music.' Fat Boy picked the can off the floor and flicked it into the bin. 'Put on Metallica.'

'Yeah,' Dean said. 'Metallica.'

Joni Mitchell sang 'Willy'.

'Metallica. Metallica,' Dean and Gary chanted together.

'Fuck off,' Stevie said. 'I want to get stoned. And this is the music I get stoned to. OK?'

'Metallica. Metallica.'

'Look, I am the fucking president. And the fucking president rules it's Joni Mitchell.'

Bernie Newman sat in the battered leather armchair and watched aghast. How could he have trusted this task to these half-wits? Joni Mitchell? 'Gentlemen,' he said. 'Could we talk business?'

'Metallica. Metallica.'

Who were these guys? Metallica?

Joni Mitchell sang 'The Silky Veils of Ardor' as Stevie deftly twisted the end of his joint.

Bernie stood up. 'Gentlemen,' he said, 'I've come a long way to get this sorted out. I came here three days ago and we agreed I'd return when I had the necessary information. Now I've got that. And I've paid you a lot of money. So can we talk?'

Dean and Fat Boy stopped chanting and Stevie looked up. 'What is it that your outfit's called again?' Dean said.

'Outlaw Poets.' Bernie saw Fat Boy smirk as he said it. What was it with these English in-breeds? 'I paid you to do a job,' he said. 'It's not finished yet.'

'You're accountants, right?' Fat Boy said.

'Some of us,' Bernie said. 'And?'

'Nothing,' Fat Boy said and started whistling along to Joni Mitchell.

'One per-centers?' Dean said.

'What the fuck is it with you guys?' Bernie said. 'I don't think we're comrades or whatever you think I think. I think you do what you do and we do what we do. And so what? And I want to pay you to do a job. And either you want the money or you don't. Choose.'

Dean scratched his neck. The Yank sounded as if he meant it. And they needed the money. The overdraft was still two grand even after the Yank's first payment. They needed the rest of it.

'I've come a long way and I don't want to hang around any longer. Now choose.' Bernie saw their slow brains clicking into gear. The moment had passed when it could have tipped into something ugly. Now the problem was how long they would take to work it all out.

Stevie struck a match. All he wanted to do was get stoned and chill out. Why did everyone want to stop him? Fat Boy burped.

Bernie glared at Stevie. 'Mr President, you did a good job last week. But it was the wrong house. My fault. Not yours. They must have moved. I now know where they live. Are you going to do them for me or not?'

'It'll be an extra two grand for another hit,' Dean said, sitting on one of the speakers and enjoying the vibrations from Joni Mitchell tickling his legs.

Bernie turned to look at him. 'You are?' he said.

'I am the fucking treasurer. And it's still another two grand.'

'Dollars.'

'English pounds. You're in England now. Yank.'

It was worth the difference to get this settled before he had to see Ken Singer again. 'Deal,' Bernie said. 'This is the address.' He passed a piece of paper over to Dean. 'Do you know where this is?' He hoped he could be certain they would deliver this time.

'We'll find it,' Dean said.

'Yeah,' Gary said.

'I'm coming with you this time,' Bernie said. 'Just to make sure.'

seventy-seven

For the third time since the policeman left, Martin was trying to get down to the Rosfield case when his mobile phone rang. 'Yes,' he said, exasperated with himself that he was finding it so hard to concentrate. He had rung Stephen Chalmers to say he was sending an opinion about how to get compensation for his wine. 'This cost how much?' Stephen Chalmers said. Martin put the phone down. How could someone as nice as Miranda ever have married someone as awful as that?

Martin opened the Rosfield file and then made himself a cup of coffee and then read two pages and then walked over to the window and then sat down again and all the time he was not thinking about the Rosfield case. He was thinking about Viktor and Detective Inspector Walton. And then his phone rang.

'Mr Hughes?' It was a brisk professional voice.

'Yes, who is this?'

'Charlotte Cornforth. You remember we met in Job Alley.'

Martin grunted in what he hoped was a noncommittal way. He did not recognise the name but she obviously knew him and she had his phone number. Should he ask who she was? But what if her name had just slipped his mind and they had met and he offended her by asking? Charlotte Cornforth? Now he thought about it, the name did seem familiar but he could not place it.

'I'd like to talk to you,' the voice said.

'What about?' he said cautiously.

'You know. What we were talking about at Job Alley.'

Where was that? And yet it did seem familiar. Or was that just because she had just mentioned it twice in the last minute? Talking to this woman was like trying to catch a fish with his bare hands. Just as he felt he was about to remember who she was and what she was talking about, it slipped away.

Charlotte felt her eyelid twitch. Why was this man being so obtuse? He had seemed keen to talk at Job Alley. And he sounded different on the phone. More English. 'Look, if you don't want to talk, that's fine. I just thought we'd agreed to keep in touch. But if you don't want to, that's fine.'

Martin thought she sounded offended. He must have met her. But he really could not remember it. This business with the policeman must be distracting him even more than he had realised. 'I'm sorry,' he said. 'My mind was somewhere else. I was just trying to remember exactly what it was we were talking about. At Job Alley.'

'Mila Hubchev. Kalaj. You know.'

Martin's heart lurched. He knew he had never mentioned those names to anyone. Why was a woman he could not remember ringing him about them now?

First his card was found on a dead woman he did not know. Then Inspector Walton tried to link him into Viktor's murder. And now this. Someone was trying to set him up.

'Who are you?' he said. Why were they doing this, whoever they were?

'Charlotte Cornforth, I told you,' the woman said.

'Who are you really?' Martin said. She knew his name and phone number and Viktor and Kalaj. This call was clearly the next stage of whatever it was that whoever it was was trying to do to him.

The woman laughed. 'I ask myself that all the time.'

There is a moment when a drowning man realises he is not just struggling to keep afloat and swallowing water. He is asphyxiating and dying and Martin had just realised that was him. What was going on here? Who was she? What were they trying to do to him?

'Look,' she said, 'do you want to talk or not?'

Martin knew he should not talk to her. He should put the phone down and call Inspector Walton and tell him everything about Viktor and Kalaj and this phone call. But what would he say? If he disclosed everything, it would only make the policeman even more suspicious. And Martin could understand why. It was suspicious that his card was found in the murdered woman's flat. It was suspicious that he had searched Viktor's flat after his death and it was suspicious that he had omitted any mention of someone who was obviously a gang boss.

Perhaps he could just tell the policeman about this phone call and his worry that he was being set up? But then he imagined Clive Walton's response. 'What makes you think that, Mr Hughes?' he would say, his face blank, his voice expressionless, writing in his little book. How would he reply? 'I don't know this woman but she knows about Viktor and Kalaj?' And then Inspector Walton would look up from his notebook. 'What is that she knows, Mr Hughes?' he would say. 'Who is Kalaj?'

'Take as long as you like,' the woman said.

'Sorry,' Martin said. 'Something's happening here.' Someone was trying to set him up and he could not go to the police about it. How had he blundered into this quagmire?

He stared out of the window. This was a police matter, no question about that, but he needed a better story to tell Inspector Walton. At the moment, his fragments of knowledge about what was going on would only damage him.

'Are you there?' Charlotte Cornforth said.

'Yes,' Martin said. 'I'm just trying to work something out here.' He was trapped unless he could find out what was going on so he could prove his innocence. Then he could go to the police and then they could sort it all out. This woman, who knew about Mila and Kalaj, was the best lead he had. No matter what her motives in contacting him, he had to meet her.

'Where do you want to do this?' he said.

'Are you free now?' she said. 'I could come to your chambers in half an hour.'

'No,' Martin said quickly. Definitely not. He could not afford any more strange people talking about any of this anywhere near Phil Matthews. 'What about a cup of tea in the Savoy?' he said. A public place like that should be safe enough.

'See you there in half an hour,' she said and rang off.

Martin decided to walk as he wanted time to think. Half a mile along the Embankment, he realised he did not know what she looked like. How was he going to find her? How would they find each other? And then he remembered that she must know what he looked like. She knew his name and his phone number after all.

In the lobby, he threaded his way through a crowd of Japanese tourists into the foyer. 'Excuse me,' he said. 'Excuse me.' As he sank back into a rococo chair, he peered around the room. She was late. No-one looked like a Charlotte Cornforth. There were three Japanese ladies drinking tea and smiling politely at each other. There were two businessmen speaking Italian very loudly, as if they were arguing. And there was a handsome blonde with a kind face in her late thirties laughing softly as she leant in towards a younger dark-haired man. She was the only possibility but she was not looking around for Martin. No-one was showing any interest in him at all.

On the other side of the foyer, Charlotte wondered where the barrister was. She sat beside a pillar, commanding a good view of the room. There were three Japanese millionaires' wives, sipping tea while their husbands were off in Birmingham, screwing another one per cent out of their hapless suppliers. Two Mafiosi bickered about a mistress. And there was a fading film-star with a toy-boy, laughing in a way that suggested they were about to disappear upstairs. And in the corner was a tall, pleasant-looking man with a thin face, in a rumpled suit, patting his hair and looking anxiously round him. No Martin Hughes. He was now half an hour late. She went up to the desk.

Martin looked at his watch. She was now half an hour late. He patted his hair down. He would give it another ten minutes and then he would have to go back to work. One of the waiters was now walking up and down, holding up a small blackboard, with a little bell attached which jingled as he walked. Tinkle, jingle. Where was she? And then he saw that the blackboard had his name written on it.

'Excuse me.' The waiter walked past him. 'Excuse me,' Martin said again but the waiter was now halfway across the room. Martin got out of his chair and caught up with him. 'Excuse me,' he said. 'Why have you got my name on the board?'

'Are you Martin Hughes, sir?' the waiter said. 'Someone is looking for you.'

'Who?'

'If you go to the desk, they will be able to help you, sir.'

There was a slim, honey-haired woman leaning by the desk as he arrived, looking past him at the foyer.

'Excuse me,' Martin said to the man behind the desk. 'I think someone is looking for me. I'm Martin Hughes.'

Beside him, the lady straightened up and looked at him. 'Are you Martin Hughes?' she asked.

'Yes,' he said. 'Who are you?'

'Charlotte Cornforth,' she said. 'And I'm meant to be meeting Martin Hughes. How weird is that? Two Martin Hugheses in the Savoy Hotel at the same time. What are the odds against that?' And her eyes moved past him back to scanning the foyer.

'No, it's me you came to meet,' he said.

'You?' Charlotte was now staring at him. 'You're not the man I met at Job Alley.'

'But I am Martin Hughes. And I don't know who you are either. But I do want to know what game you think you're playing with me and how you know Mila Hubchev and Kalaj and who killed Viktor Markov.'

'Killed?' Charlotte said, looking at him properly for the first time. 'We better have a cup of tea.'

seventy-eight

Phil Matthews had never worried about Martin Hughes until now. Bright and busily industrious, he had been a model tenant of the chambers from the moment he came, generating agreeably rising fees. Reliable was the word that came to Phil Matthews's mind when he thought about Martin Hughes. But over the last few days Phil Matthews had been growing concerned about this particular tenant of his chambers.

The clerks' offices were on the ground floor and, as senior clerk, Phil Matthews had his own small room with a window and an oblique view of the lawns. Rain streaked the glass and the room was even gloomier than usual as the senior clerk concluded that Mr Hughes was becoming a problem. Two visits from the same detective inspector in a week suggested something wrong. And even more alarming, Mr Martin Hughes did not want to talk about it. Phil had an instinct for trouble and this was it. Grief was heading for his chambers on wings of Hughes.

And if he had any doubts that it was on its way, they were now dispelled by the way this beefy bruiser was looming over his desk in a brown suit and yellow tie.

'Please sit down,' Phil said to him. 'Why do you want to see Mr Hughes?'

'When will he be back?' The thug ignored him and remained leaning over the desk.

Two minutes ago, Gary, the second junior clerk, had come into his room, so agitated that he had forgotten to knock. 'Phil, you'd better see this guy, he's causing a lot of trouble out here,' he had said and so the burly man had been brought into Phil's own office to get him out of the way but it had not calmed him down.

'If you give me your name, I'll tell him you called.' Phil stayed sitting down. It was more dignified. He was going to have a long discussion about this with Mr Martin Hughes when he returned.

'Don't jerk me,' Boris said or Phil thought it might have been 'don't joke me' but the accent was too thick for him to be sure. 'When is he coming back?'

'I don't know who you think you are,' Phil said. 'But you don't behave like this here. Sit down and be polite and then we can have a conversation.'

'I'm asking for the third time, when is he coming back?'

'And I'm telling you for the third time, you can't talk like that here. If you don't sit down and be polite, I'm going to call the police.' And Mr Hughes had better have a good explanation for this.

Boris laughed, a deep guffaw, and leaned across the desk and took Phil Matthews's tie in his hand and twisted it hard. Phil gasped as he began to choke. He was going to have to have a very serious conversation with Mr Hughes about this.

'Go on,' Boris said. 'Call the police.' And then he laughed again. 'Can't talk?' he said and let go of the tie. 'Now you can. Go on, call the police.'

Phil Matthews loosened his collar and picked up the phone.

'How long will they take to get here?' Boris said and cracked his knuckles.

Phil put the phone back. He realised he was in the presence of a professional. 'He won't be back until this afternoon,' he said. And when he did get back he had a lorry-load of explaining to do.

'I'll be back,' Boris said. 'Tell him that. And tell him I want the passport back.'

'Who shall I say called for him?' Phil said.

'Nobody,' Boris said. 'Mr Nobody,' and he laughed again.

'And when shall I say you'll call?'

'Who knows?' Boris said. 'Who knows?'

seventy-nine

'Espresso, madam. And Lapsang for sir.' The waiter bent low over the table, carefully positioning the cups and saucers.

'Is this your card?' Charlotte asked as the waiter retreated, handing it across the table to Martin.

'Where did you get this?' he said.

'Is it your card?' she said.

'Of course it is. Where did you get it?'

'I'm sorry but how do I know it's yours? How do I know you are who you say?' Charlotte said.

Martin took a deep breath. 'And who are you to ask me that?' he said.

'If you are who you say you are, then I can help you,' she said.

'And how do I know who you are?' he said. Charlotte passed him her card. Martin looked at it and then he remembered why he recognised her name. This was the card in the envelope Viktor's landlord had given him. How had Viktor got to know this woman? And how had she got his card? 'How can you help me?' he said.

'Mila Hubchev? Viktor Markov?' Charlotte said and drained her espresso cup and then looked at him.

'Yes. I know the names. But how can you help me?'

Charlotte leaned towards him. 'Don't be prissy,' she said. 'Just let me see something identifying you and then I can help you. Don't you want to find out how I got your card? Now what have you got?'

She was pushing and pushing. And, in its way, Martin found that reassuring, more irritating than threatening. That was the way journalists were. And anyway what choice did he have? He had decided to come here to find out what he could and he might as well go through with it.

'What about this?' He showed his credit cards. 'Or this?' And he pulled from his pocket a letter from the building society rescheduling his interest rate.

She looked at it and nodded approvingly. 'Nice mortgage,' she said.

'Happy?' Martin said.

'Happier with mine than yours,' she said as she handed him back the letter. 'OK,' she said. 'You are Martin Hughes. So who's handing out your visiting cards?'

'What did he look like?' Martin said.

'Tall. Well-built. Beard. Fierce eyes,' she said. 'With a little girl. In a pink raincoat.'

Viktor.

'Do you know anyone like that?' she said.

'Yes,' he said, 'I'm afraid I did.'

'And?' she said.

'It sounds as if you got my card from Viktor Markov,' Martin said. Viktor must have taken them from his flat. Why?

'The dead guy?' Charlotte said.

Martin stared at her. She had to be who she said she was. She was too ghastly to be making it up.

'The dead guy, as you put it, was my friend and the father of the little girl who is now an orphan.'

'Do you mind if I smoke?' Charlotte said. What was wrong with her? Why did doing her job nowadays make her feel so crass? How could she have said that? And now she had frightened him off.

Martin shrugged.

'I'm sorry,' she said. 'That was insensitive of me.' She put the cigarette packet back in her handbag. 'I want to get this story told,' she said. 'And you're in the middle of it. I don't know how or why but that's what I want to find out.'

And so did Martin. He wanted to know how he had ended up with someone trying to fit him up with two murders when all he had been trying to do was reassure the woman he loved that he was steady and reliable. How could that have led to this?

'So who do you think killed Viktor Markov?' she said.

'I don't know,' he said.

'You can trust me,' she said. 'You want to find out what happened to your friend. I want the story. We could work together.'

'What is your story?' Martin said.

'People-traffickers and smugglers. And I think Viktor Markov discovered something,' she guessed. 'Maybe something to do with this Mila Hubchev.'

Martin said nothing. In court he found that waiting patiently could make people say more than they should have said. Human beings could not bear very much silence.

'And I think,' Charlotte said, 'this man Kalaj is a boss.' It sounded plausible as she said it. 'Viktor Markov thought so too.' She was sure he had said something like that.

'What sort of gang?'

'Trafficking. Smuggling.'

'And Viktor thought Kalaj was responsible for Mila's disappearance?'

Got him. 'Yes.'

'What have you found out so far?' he said.

'I need to know where to find Kalaj.' She had not answered his question. Neat. And then the waiter arrived by their side. 'Another espresso,' she said. 'More tea, Martin?'

'No thank you.' Should he give her the address he had got from Miroslav? It might be better for her to investigate it. Every time he tried to do something to improve the situation, it seemed to make it worse. What could he lose? He needed to find out who was setting him up and why and quickly. And he needed help. And she had all the resources of a national newspaper behind her.

'Don't you want to know what's going on?' she said. She needed him. What else could she try if this didn't work? 'Come on. I can do things you can't.'

'I might be able to help,' he said. 'But I want your word you'll tell me what you find.'

'If you give me a good lead, I'll tell you whatever I find out as a result,' she said.

'That's not the deal. I help you. You help me. No conditions.'

Charlotte looked at him. She would have to be careful here. 'I know you're not a journalist,' she said. 'But how do I know you won't tell someone else who will blow the story? Like the police.'

'But of course I'm going to tell the police, if I find out who killed Viktor,' Martin said.

Charlotte smiled. Lift-off. 'No problem,' she said. 'Of course the police must be told. But I tell them so I can do the story with them. No problem. We can sort that out.' She sensed she was getting close now. She could taste the salt on the Tarifa breeze.

Martin was worried by Charlotte's smile. Pleasure was one thing. Triumph was another. 'But how will I know if you're telling me everything you find?' he said.

'Trust me. How do I know you're going to tell me everything you know? We have mutual interests. If you don't tell me everything you know, I won't be able to help you find out what really happened. But equally, it's in my interest to show you that you can trust me as you might still go on being useful to me, if you trust me.' Charlotte leaned across and patted him on the knee. 'Don't worry,' she said. 'We're lashed together.'

Martin could see no obvious flaw in her logic. They were going to have to trust each other. 'OK,' he said. 'I've got an address,' he said. 'I don't know who lives there. But it's something to do with Viktor. You might want to have a look at it.'

And there was one other thing that had occurred to him. Miroslav had given up the address suspiciously easily. It could be part of fitting him up. If he went there himself he might find he was just fastening the noose even more tightly round his neck. But Charlotte Cornforth wouldn't have that problem.

eighty

The boss was on his case today. He was putting in some downtime on Grand Theft Auto, moving on up to Level Five, anticipating, pleasurably, that when he completed it, he would go out into the garden for a long, slow Orient Express, when she leaned on the computer and stared at him with that look she had.

'Is there anything you want to tell me, Gabriel?' she said and although she spoke softly, he knew he was in trouble.

He shook his head. 'I was just finishing this,' he said. 'I'm just about to start on the casino business.'

'Think,' she said. 'Are you sure there isn't anything you want to tell me?'

He shook his head unhappily. 'I don't think so,' he said. He realised she was going to tell him anyway and then the grief would start but first he had to go through this.

'Nothing about the other day?' she said.

'What other day?' he said and as he spoke he saw he had made his first mistake.

'Are you really so heartless,' she said, 'you can't remember killing a man? That other day, you peasant.

All your degrees haven't made you into a human being, have they?'

She never raised her voice but he knew his response would be held against him. And she had not finished.

'Sometimes we have to remove a problem,' she said. 'And sometimes there's only one way to do it. But that doesn't mean we should ever treat it lightly. You respect them and honour their memory. What other way, indeed.' She tapped her finger on top of the computer. 'One day it could be you,' she said.

He did not doubt it.

'So, are you sure there isn't anything you want to tell me?' she said again.

'I told you what happened,' he said miserably, but he knew this would not be good enough.

She started to stroke his hair and that was when he started to get seriously worried. 'Oh dear,' she said, 'I'd like to think you're too incompetent to realise what happened but I'm getting worried that you might think you could get away with it without telling me. So, which is it?'

It didn't seem much of a choice to him.

'Well?' she said. She never complimented him when he did things well. He had done this job, hadn't he? And what about when the police picked him up with her and that greasy little French forger when they had gone to get her a new passport? He had thought on his feet and given that false Hungarian name and they hadn't got anything from him and in the end they had just let him go. Wasn't that competent? Why didn't she comment on that instead of going on about how useless he was?

'I'm sorry,' he said. 'I really don't know what you're talking about.'

Now she moved her hand on to his cheek and started gently stroking it. It felt wonderful, that soft hand gently brushing the downy hairs but he was now starting to panic. This meant real trouble.

'You were seen,' she said. 'Someone saw you do it.' Mila didn't know how Kalaj had got involved in this or how he had guessed she had arranged the hit. Perhaps he was just guessing but however he had found out and whether he was guessing or not about her involvement, he had given her some information she needed to deal with. He had told her there was a witness to Viktor's killing.

'I didn't see anyone,' he said. And even if there had been someone there, he had kept his helmet on so they would never be able to identify him. But she must not ever find out about the little girl the day before.

'No,' she said, 'you wouldn't have done.' And her quiet contempt was lacerating. She opened her little black handbag and gave him a piece of paper. 'Here's the name and address,' she said. 'It's a loose end,' she said. 'Tidy it up.'

He knew it would be fruitless to argue and point out that no-one would be able to identify him and that more killing was more risk. He knew she wouldn't believe him and she never took chances. She made certain about everything.

'And soon,' she said.

eighty-one

'I've brought you some more of those biscuits,' Martin said as he came in. His father was sitting in his chair by the window, reading the *Daily Mail*.

'How have you been?' As always, the old man did not look up from the newspaper as he spoke. 'Doing anything interesting?'

'Not really,' Martin said. 'The usual.'

'Not been doing any of these legal aid cases and making a million?' Then the old man looked up and smiled at his son. 'I read about it here.'

'You should know better, Dad,' Martin said. 'That's not typical. It's not like that for most people. You know that. Now, how have you been?'

'The usual. You've got to make your bit now,' his father said. 'To provide a cushion when you go on to the Bench. You'll need it when you start a family.' There it all was in just ten seconds. Career. Family. Duty. Guilt. The four corners of his cage.

Martin's mobile phone rang. 'Sorry, Dad,' he said as he answered it. 'I better take this.'

'Of course,' his father said. 'Clients come first.'

'You've had a visitor,' Phil Matthews said and from his tone, Martin guessed it had not been a client. It must have been that policeman again. He glanced across at his father who was reading the *Daily Mail* again.

'I'm busy at the moment, Phil,' he said. 'Let's talk when I get back.'

'It's all right, Martin,' his father said, putting down the paper. 'You can talk now. It's fine with me.'

'Who's that?' Phil Matthews said. 'That's not a client.'

'No, Phil,' Martin said. 'That's my father.'

The old man in the chair put his finger to his lips. 'Shhh,' he hissed, shaking his head. 'Unprofessional.'

'Can we talk later, Phil?' Martin said, turning away so he would not have to see his father still shaking his head.

'No,' Phil said. 'When you have visitors who are verbally and physically abusive to staff in this office, I think we need to talk now.'

'What do you mean?'

'What do I mean? This office is not some mobster's mess where you conduct whatever business you are doing on the side, Mr Hughes. I want an explanation before I go to the Head of Chambers.'

'Phil, please can we talk about this tomorrow morning? I'll be in early.'

'It's your choice, Mr Hughes. I'm going to the Head of Chambers in ten minutes. If you want me to hear your explanation before I go, then you can tell me now. If you don't, don't. It's your choice.'

'I'll just take this outside,' Martin said to his father. 'I'll call you back in thirty seconds,' he said to Phil. Outside in the corridor, he dialled his chambers. Why had that policeman come back again? What could he want to talk about now?

'Phil?'

'I am very disappointed, Mr Hughes. We had such high hopes for you.'

'What are you talking about, Phil? What's happened?'

'You're a member of these chambers. You're a member of the Bar. You're an officer of the court. How could you have done this?'

'Done what, Phil? What are you talking about?'

'Don't play games with me, Mr Hughes. We don't want your friends visiting these chambers. If you would be so kind.'

'What friends? The inspector is not a friend of mine.'

'What inspector? I am not talking about any inspector. I'm talking about your friend in a cheap brown suit and a foreign accent.'

'I don't have any friends like that.'

'Don't play games. He was round here asking for you. Threatening the staff. Not acceptable, Mr Hughes, not acceptable at all.' Phil Matthews sounded as if he was choking. It sounded as if something bad had happened.

'I'm sorry, Phil,' Martin said. 'I'm afraid I really don't know what you're talking about. Who came round asking for me? What's his name?'

'He refused to give his name.'

'Describe him then.' As Phil Matthews described Boris, Martin knew something bad had happened. This was definitely not a client. The account of the cheap brown suit and the foreign accent sounded uncomfortably familiar and Martin realised that this could be the man he had met with Viktor in the Madonna Club. And when Phil mentioned what the man had said about the passport, panic began to gurgle in his guts. They were on to him. The waters were closing over his head.

'This is unacceptable,' Phil Matthews said. 'I want an explanation, Mr Hughes.'

'I don't know what's going on,' Martin said. 'But I'll sort it out. I promise. Let's talk first thing tomorrow morning.' He had no idea what he was going to do in the meantime but now he knew, for a fact, that he was in serious trouble. Someone was setting out to destroy him.

'I'm going to see the Head of Chambers at ten o'clock,' Phil Matthews said.

'Don't worry, Phil. I'll see you first thing and I'll sort it out,' Martin said. What was he going to do now? Someone was out to get him. The planting of his visiting card. Viktor's murder. And the thug they had met looking for Kalaj who somehow knew he had the passport and was now after him. And Mila. Suddenly Martin realised where she fitted in. The dead woman about whom the inspector had come to interview him, in whose flat his card had been found, that woman must have been Mila. She had disappeared because she had been murdered. In some way he did not understand, Viktor and Mila had been living in a murky underworld and they had paid the price. And now their killers were coming after him. But why?

eighty-two

The sun rose, red and gold, through the winter trees. Soft fire. At this time of year he could see it move. The house was silent and still. No-one else had got up yet.

He turned on the coffee machine. He wondered again why the boss had decided he was the one to do these jobs. The little light started winking green. It was ready and the coffee started bubbling through into the cup, a comforting homely sound, and the rich fragrance began to fill the cold kitchen. Perhaps she had identified something he had failed to recognise in himself. An instinct for killing. He sighed and sipped the coffee. The hot bitter liquid filled his mouth. He did not like it black but they had run out of milk and he needed the caffeine.

His boots stood by the table and he sat down to pull them on over the leather trousers. A red glow now filled the room as the sun came over the trees. He picked up the Ruger from the kitchen table and felt it snug in his palm. He checked the action. All OK. This would be the second one in ten days. He put the pistol back on the table. The boss always got what the boss wanted. That was the way it was and he did not have a problem with that. But he did just wonder why it had been him who had been chosen to do it.

He took a packet of Orient Express out of his pocket and lit one of the dark cigarettes. He drew heavily on it and savoured the first hit of nicotine before exhaling. A good moment. The aromatic smoke filled the kitchen. The boss hated it so this early in the morning was the only time he could smoke inside.

And then there was still the little girl. He had not been able to find her yet. She was never around where she and the man had lived so she had obviously been moved somewhere. As soon as he done this job, he would start looking for her full-time.

He took his leather jacket off the table and put it on. Then he put the Ruger in the left-hand pocket so he could just reach across and pull it out in one movement. Just like last time.

He didn't feel any better about the little girl. But what choice did he have? He couldn't risk the boss finding out. He took another drag on the cigarette. That was good. He knew he should stop but there was nothing like that nicotine hit and the aromatic smoke reminded him of home. Orient Express were hard to find over here so he was lucky to have got this carton. The Kalaj operation could get you anything if you paid for it. He would see if he could stop when he finished the carton.

He finished the coffee and carefully took the cup over to the sink and rinsed it out. The boss insisted on it because there were too many of them in the house for anyone to be messy. According to the boss, if anyone was allowed to be untidy then it would all slip out of control and the house would become a tip.

He placed the clean cup on the draining board. There. Ready. He hoped this one would not be as complicated as the last time. The boss had not told him the target would have anyone with him. No-one had said anything about a little girl in a pink raincoat.

eighty-three

Raspberry jam dribbled down the side of the jar as Giles delicately prepared a piece of granary toast. 'I've earned my money,' he said.

'I'll be the judge of that,' Charlotte said.

Giles bit into his slice of toast and then wiped the crumbs away from his mouth with the back of his hand.

'No,' he said. 'I think you'll find that subjective judgement plays no part in this. I've got a result.'

'Well, what is it?' How hard did he have to work to be so objectionable? He had insisted she came round to his flat for breakfast if she wanted to know what he had discovered. And what sort of time was this for breakfast? But she had no choice. She was meeting George Waddington at eleven thirty and the clock was ticking more and more audibly.

'Are you sure you wouldn't like some breakfast?' Giles said, as he sipped his tea.

'No,' she said. 'Thank you.' She saw she was tapping her fingers lightly on the table. She knew she should not. It showed weakness. But she could not help it. She wanted to kill this streak of nerd.

'What about some toast? I make delicious toast.

Home-baked granary and the jam is made from or-
ganic raspberries. From Sicily. Are you sure?'

'Yes,' she said. 'Thank you.'

'There's no need to talk like that,' he said. 'I'm only
trying to be hospitable.'

'That's very nice of you, Giles. And I'm very ap-
preciative. But I have to leave very soon to go to a
meeting. About how very much money my paper has
been spending on you. And about how very much they
are going to fire me if I don't give them something in
return for the not so small fortune they have been
paying you. So if you've got something to tell me, I
really should be very grateful if you could tell me. Now.
Right fucking now.'

'I'll just put the plates in the dishwasher.'

He was unbelievable. She must not allow herself to
be wound up. That was what he wanted. To wind her
up. It was obviously some adolescent sexual game he
was playing. She would not play it. She would not be
wound up by this lanky geek.

Charlotte managed to say nothing as Giles placed
the cup and saucer and plate in the dishwasher and
then came back to the table and sat down. He
stretched his long legs out under the table and smiled
at her. 'I've done it,' he said. 'I've found the
pathways.'

Charlotte said nothing. She assumed he was about to
give up some more detailed reasons for his smugness.

'Do you want to know how?'

Charlotte could see him drawing breath to begin.
'No,' she said. 'I do not. I want you to tell me what

you've found out. Now. Before I go to my meeting. Not after they've fired me.'

Giles smirked at her. 'They're not going to fire you,' he said. 'Not after what I've discovered.'

Charlotte stared at him. It was increasingly possible that she had never hated anyone as much as this. Never. And then it got worse. He stretched across the table and took her hand.

'Charlotte,' he said. 'You're going to be so grateful to me.'

'Please remove your hand,' she said. 'And tell me or I'll have your bollocks for earrings.'

He smiled happily. 'Go on,' he said. 'More. I love it. Love it.' But he did remove his hand and leant back in his chair.

'Well,' he said. 'There's a lot going down at that address you gave me. All sorts. Credit card scams. Phishing. These are serious villains. Making shed-loads of cash.'

'What?'

'What do you mean what? This is big. Major e-crime.'

'Do not fuck with me, Giles. I mean it. Just remember. Bollocks. For earrings. So tell me. Now.'

'They're phishing,' he said.

Charlotte said nothing.

He looked at her. 'OK,' he said. 'For example. You send out an email pretending it comes from, say, a credit card company and it says for security reasons to keep your card active you need to confirm your account details. Some don't reply but you'd be amazed how many fall for it. And then bang. You're into their account and spending all their money.'

'Yes, Giles,' she sighed. 'I know what phishing is. And it's not a story.' But as she spoke she was thinking. 'How many of these phishers have they caught?' she said.

'How do I know?' he said.

'You're paid to know,' she said. ' "You really won't find anyone better." Remember?

'Of course,' he said. 'You won't. If anyone knew, I would. But no-one knows. Banks don't like to publicise these things. If someone was stealing millions of pounds from your customers, would you want to advertise it? Hardly good for business, is it?' He looked up and saw she was writing something in a little notebook. 'If you want to do this story, you'll have to get a move on. They don't work these scams very long. They tend to get caught if they run them more than a week or two. The trail I found will be cold in a few days.'

Charlotte looked ruminatively at Giles. There definitely could be something in this. 'OK,' she said and closed the little notebook. 'You can live. I'll need you for another week. We're going to do this story.'

'How do you know I'm not busy next week?'

'You are,' she said. 'Working for me. And when I say working, I mean sweating over that screen of yours until your spots pop. We're going to do this story. And fuck Damian.'

'Do I have to?' Giles said.

She stared at him. 'I've already warned you,' she said. 'Don't step out of your league. It'll give you diarrhoea.'

And then Charlotte allowed herself to smile. This was better. The barrister had delivered the address. Giles had got inside it. Now she should go and take a look at this den of electronic thieves for herself.

eighty-four

'I'm sorry,' Martin said but Phil Matthews did not reply. He was adjusting the cuffs on his shirt so they protruded half an inch further out from the cuffs of his chalk-stripe suit.

'I don't know this man,' Martin said. 'I don't know what's going on here but whatever it is, I'll sort it all out by tomorrow. I promise, Phil. You won't be bothered again.'

The clerk glanced at his reflection in the window and tightened the knot in his fuchsia tie. He hadn't heard enough yet.

'Honestly, Phil, I don't know anything about this. But I'll find out and I'll sort it.' Martin heard himself wheedling and told himself to stop it. 'Please, Phil. Just until tomorrow.'

Martin was worried sick. He had worried all yesterday evening and had woken up this morning still worrying. He had enough to worry about without Phil on his case as well.

'Please,' he begged.

Finally, the clerk stood up and relented. 'I am disappointed, Mr Hughes,' he said. 'Very disappointed. But we must look forward. I expect this to be sorted out by tomorrow. And I never want to see that man here again. Or it won't only be the Head of Chambers who I'll need to bring into this.'

'You won't need to bring anyone into this,' Martin said. 'I'll sort it.'

Back in his office, he took out his mobile phone. He didn't want Phil Matthews listening in on the landline and he was desperate.

'Ben,' he said, 'I need your help.'

'Come and join me,' Ben said. 'Do something useful for a change. Do good.'

'Please, Ben.'

'I'm serious. Come over to the light side,' Ben said. 'Dispose the disposable. Focus on the fundamental. Live the dream.'

'Please,' Martin said. 'I don't need that right now. I need your help.'

'Clare?' Ben said. 'Flowers, bespoke perfume, Mauritius and a baby.'

'Fuck off,' Martin said. 'I'm not talking about Clare.'

'Why not?' Clare said, knocking on the door as she came in. 'Who's that?'

'I've got to go, Ben. I'll call you later,' Martin said, putting the phone back in his pocket. 'What are you doing here, Clare?'

'And I'm thrilled to see you too,' she said. 'I thought you might be pleased to get a visit.' She sat down in an armchair by his desk. 'Wrong again, obviously.'

'No. You're not. I am pleased. I am,' Martin said. 'What a nice surprise.'

'Liar,' Clare said. 'I was just passing on my way to the gallery.' She had been thinking a lot about him

since his visit to the flat. She could have called but she
wanted to see him, in his chambers, in his essentiality.
If she was going to make this big decision, she needed
to see good things about him again, his seriousness, his
sense of duty.

'I am really pleased to see you,' he said. 'Really. It's
just I've got a lot on my mind right now.'

'What's changed?' She smiled. It was important to
tune out the negative and welcome the positive. 'I've
got some good news,' she said. 'From Mr Wood. He's
found Suzana's aunt and she's coming to get her
tomorrow.'

'That's wonderful,' he said. And it was. Suzana was
safe.

'I thought you'd be pleased,' Clare said. 'And I
wanted to let you know. We could go to the airport
together to say goodbye.'

Instinctively Martin reached for the diary on his desk
and then he remembered. 'I'd like that,' he said.

'Try to sound as if you mean it,' Clare said. 'I've got
one more invitation for you and you'd better sound
pleased about this one. Would you like to come to
Megan's Advent concert tonight?' she said. 'I'm sure
she'd love you to be there.'

Even in his greediest fantasies, Martin had never
imagined anything like this. Clare dropping in unexpectedly to invite him to a family evening out. And yet he
felt no pleasure. Even though Suzana was now safe, his
Balkan nightmare was still crowding everything else out
of his life. Viktor and Boris and a murdered woman,
Mila, and that policeman. And his father worrying away.

And now what a fortnight ago would have been a fantasy come true was yet another obligation.

'That would be nice,' he said.

'You don't have to,' she said. This was his last chance, she thought, and if he didn't take it, there wouldn't be another one. She'd learn the lesson finally and move on.

'No, really,' he said. 'I'll be there.' Once I've sorted out Boris and Phil Matthews and Inspector Walton and cleared myself of murder and frequenting prostitutes and conniving at illegal immigration and then been round to reassure my father that everything is going well at work and then finished off my preparation for the Rosfield case and written the opinion for Linklaters and been to Sainsbury's.

'I can see you're busy,' Clare said. 'See you at St Luke's.'

'I'll look forward to it,' he said. If I'm still alive and not in prison.

'Oh and one last thing,' she said. 'Don't forget Megan's birthday.'

At the Battle of the Kalka River in 1223, six princes of Kiev were taken prisoner by the Mongol horde and laid out under wooden boards, while the khans feasting victoriously on the platform above them pressed down and down until the hapless warriors suffocated. Martin knew how they felt.

'I'll go and get her present now,' he said.

eighty-five

Something weird was going on in the house but that had only gradually become clear. When Charlotte first arrived, nothing was happening in this quiet street of semi-detached houses. An old lady, holding a carrier bag, had hobbled down to the shops. A car had pulled up further down the street to disgorge a young woman and two squalling little children who disappeared up a path and into the house. And from time to time, a car drove down the road. Apart from that, nothing happened.

Charlotte sat in her car, watching and waiting. Sometimes she thought that was all she ever did. The old journalist's joke was that their passport entry for 'occupation' should be 'waiter'. She sat slumped in the driver's seat, parked at the corner of the street, listening to Radio 4 and observing the house in her rear-view mirror and worrying. What sort of way was this to earn a living? What did she care what her brother thought? It was boring. And it made her behave in ways that had recently begun to make her increasingly ashamed of herself. Why was she doing this when she could be spending her time with Matthew and Rob? Or finding some more worthwhile profession?

But then, as she sat, lulled gently by nice voices talking intelligently, and contemplating her life, the thought drifted into her mind that something was not quite right about the house. All the curtains were drawn and there were security grilles on all the windows. None of the other houses had such protection. She assumed that the electronic brigands were inside, phishing and pillaging the Internet but, in two hours, no-one had gone into the house or come out of it. Could they have all gone already? Giles had said they never hung around long in any one location.

Charlotte felt a familiar surge of adrenalin as she worked all this through. And then she saw the front door open and a slight young woman in a loden coat came out.

The woman turned and locked the door behind her. Three deft turns of the key and then she walked briskly down the path and on to the street. She was walking towards Charlotte's car. Charlotte watched her approach in the mirror. As she came closer, Charlotte saw she had short dark hair and enormous green eyes.

This could be an opening. She must not waste the opportunity. As soon as the young woman had passed the car, looking straight ahead, Charlotte opened the car door and got out.

'Excuse me,' she said. 'Have you got a moment?' And then as she started to say her name and the newspaper, the young woman stopped and turned towards her, with a slight smile on her face.

'Hello,' she said. 'Why do you want to talk to me?' Her voice was soft and low, with a pleasantly slurred accent, from where? Central Europe somewhere?

'I'm looking for Viktor Markov,' Charlotte said. 'And Mila Hubchev. Do you know them?'

'Why do you think I would know them?'

There was no good answer to that question. 'Do you know them?'

'Sorry. No.'

'What about a man called Kalaj? Do you know him?'

Close up, Charlotte saw the woman was not that young. There was a fine net of tiny wrinkles round her eyes but she had breathtaking cheekbones. She was beautiful.

'Sorry,' she said again. 'I do not know him.'

It was just a moment too quick. She did know him. Charlotte saw that. And she did not want to acknowledge that she knew him. The lawyer had delivered again. 'Not a problem,' Charlotte said. 'It's just that we know this address is linked to him. And we wondered what you might know about it.' The plural was good. Regiments of Charlottes round the corner.

'Who did you say you were?' Again, that gentle Central European accent.

'Here's my card.' The armies of the Fourth Estate. Again, the woman was studying the card just a moment too long. Wondering what to say.

'I'm sorry, Charlotte Cornforth, I do not know any Kalaj.'

Charlotte watched her carefully as she spoke. Something was going on in those green eyes. She seemed frightened. Perhaps Kalaj had something on her. Perhaps he had smuggled her in and she still owned him money. Perhaps he was prostituting her? But she did not look like one, Charlotte thought. A bit too old, a bit too beautiful. Still, what was it that Helen Borthwick had said to her? There's a market for every woman. Men. 'Don't be frightened,' Charlotte said. 'I want to help you.'

'How?' the woman said.

Charlotte thought she sounded curious. 'I can get you to the police and then to a safe house where these men can't find you,' she said. 'And I'll expose what's going on. And that means the government will deal with it.'

The woman looked at her, and then smiled, a slow, soft smile, but she did not say anything. Charlotte felt a momentary doubt. Perhaps she was wrong. The woman was obviously free to leave the house. If she was a sex-slave, then surely the pimps would not let her do that, would they? But perhaps they had something on her that meant she would always have to go back to them. Something on her family in, where would it be, Albania? Or perhaps they kept her passport? Or perhaps she thought they would always catch up with her, wherever she went.

'Trust me. I can help you.'

'Thank you,' the woman said. 'But I think you should leave now. It is not safe here.'

'Don't worry. I can protect you. I can make sure you're safe if you'll help me with just a few questions.'

'I can't help you. You must go now. It's not safe here.'

'Don't worry,' Charlotte said. 'This is London. You can be safe here. Somewhere these men will never find you. The paper will pay. I just need to talk to you.'

The woman looked at her, a long stare. It was strangely calm. 'Go away,' she said and then she continued walking down the street.

And then Charlotte knew what she had got to do.

eighty-six

Pearly mist hung above the lawns and the ground was still silvered with frost as Martin strode back through Lincoln's Inn, carrying the Toy Story Learning Game. He had finally devised a plan.

Every option had seemed equally disastrous. Just hoping it would all go away had not worked. But going to the police would plunge him deeper into the nightmare. Inspector Walton would become even more suspicious and stay on his case until the last shreds of Martin's professional credibility had been ripped away.

'Good morning, young Hughes.'

Martin looked up to see Ned Villiers, a portly criminal silk, waddling along the path towards him. 'Morning, Ned,' he said, looking back down on the ground, making it clear he did not want a conversation.

'*Cherchez la femme*,' Ned said and chortled at his sally.

Martin ignored him. Ned could think whatever he wanted. Martin had come to a decision. No matter what the risks, he had to ring Inspector Walton. Hoping to get out of this mess without pain had been naïve. This was not a matter of choosing between good and bad, as he had deluded himself, but striking a balance between disastrous and less disastrous. Going to the police was, just, the safe side of apocalyptic.

'Sorry.' Someone bumped into him and Martin looked up to see the irritated face of a High Court judge apologising with heavy judicial sarcasm.

'I'm sorry,' Martin said. 'I should have looked where I was going.' Surely he could convince Inspector Walton to leave him alone after he had explained everything? After all, he hadn't actually committed any crime. Martin's polished shoes slid on the frosty ground, glistening black pebbles on muslin, and he just avoided colliding with another bustling lawyer.

'Sorry,' he said. And once he had sorted things out with the police, he had decided it was time for a serious conversation with Ben. Perhaps he was right. The last few days had made him wonder if he was really happy at the Bar, doing this rarefied law with all its cloistered stress and expectations. Perhaps it was time to escape. Working with Ben would leave so much more time for Clare and Megan. He pulled out his mobile phone and rang Ben and got his voicemail.

And then he bumped into someone else. 'I'm really sorry,' he said. He hoped it wasn't another judge.

It wasn't.

'Give me the passport.' It was Boris, a burly brown presence at his shoulder, edging him forward.

Martin looked up and suddenly no-one else was near. Boris had chosen his moment well. 'I haven't got it,' Martin said. He couldn't think what else to say.

'Don't play games,' Boris said and Martin felt something poking into his side. He assumed it was a gun.

'Don't be ridiculous,' Martin said. 'You can't do that here. This is an Inn of Court. What do you think would happen to you?'

'And what do you think would happen to you?' Boris said and he laughed loudly. 'A big hole in your liver and lots of blood. Now give me the passport.'

'I don't know what you're talking about.' This was a slow-motion car crash.

'Keep walking,' Boris said. 'If you stand still, it will make people look at us and I will have to kill you.' Martin kept walking with Boris walking beside pressed up against him with the gun poking into his side. 'Now where is it?'

'I really don't know what you're talking about,' Martin said. He had to get away from this man before someone saw them. What if they bumped into someone like Ned Villiers who wanted to stop and chat?

'You're a bad liar, Englishman,' Boris said and jiggled the gun playfully in Martin's ribs. 'Your friend the pop-star told us you got it. So where is it?'

Martin was beginning to think that Boris might mean what he said about his liver. 'At home,' Martin said.

Boris laughed.

Martin couldn't recall much about that evening in the Madonna Club but he remembered that tone of jovial menace.

'Come on, Englishman,' Boris said. 'I'm a foreigner but I'm not a fool. Where is it?'

Martin stopped walking and looked at Boris. 'Honestly,' he said.

'When I hear an Englishman say that word,' Boris said, 'I want to pull the trigger.'

'It is at home,' Martin insisted. 'Why would I have it here? I don't want it. Viktor's landlord gave it to me. You can have it.'

Boris stopped smiling and stared at him, assessing what Martin had said.

'OK,' he said eventually. 'I believe you.' He took his hand out of his pocket and the pressure on Martin's ribs disappeared. Then he pinched Martin's cheek between his finger and thumb. 'Bring it to your office tomorrow morning and I'll let you live.' He pinched harder so Martin yelped and then he laughed. 'See you tomorrow,' he said and then he was off, swaggering down the path towards High Holborn.

Martin sighed deeply. His legs were trembling and he realised he had been very frightened. He put his hand to his cheek. It hurt but at least Boris had left before anyone had seen them together. What now? If he didn't hand over the passport, Boris would kill him, as presumably he had already killed Mila and Viktor. But could he hand over the passport and then throw himself on Inspector Walton's mercy? But if he didn't hand over the passport, then Boris would pursue him and he would have to trust the police to protect him. And did he believe the police could do that? Martin did not. So what should he do?

As he approached the door to his chambers, Martin realised he had to tell Inspector Walton about everything, except the passport. He had no choice. No passport for Boris meant no liver for Martin and that was even worse than failing to become a judge. And he could always hope that Inspector Walton would never find out about the passport. And why would he?

'Back so soon, Mr Hughes?' Phil Matthews said suspiciously as he came into the outer office.

'By the way,' Martin said, ignoring the knives in Phil's voice, 'I've sorted out that problem we were talking about.' Although the decision had been forced on him, it was beginning to feel right as he went down the corridor towards his room.

'I hope so, Mr Hughes,' Phil Matthews said, 'I certainly hope so.' Martin opened his door. 'By the way,' Phil called after him. 'You've got a visitor. Another visitor.'

Clive Walton was sitting in the armchair and got up as Martin came in. 'Hello again, Mr Hughes,' he said. 'Your clerk said I could wait here for you. I hope that was all right.'

'Yes, of course.' Abruptly Martin felt weary. The plan was for him to ring the inspector, not for him to turn up uninvited like this. What did he want now? 'How can I help you? Would you like some tea or coffee?'

'No thank you.' The inspector was arranging himself neatly back in the armchair. 'I find too much caffeine before lunch ruins the rest of the day.' A seagull appeared outside the window. It opened its beak and let out a long, thin cry.

'I'm afraid I've some bad news for you,' Detective Inspector Walton said. If he had had a hat, he would have now averted his eyes and run his fingers tactfully around the rim. But he did not have a hat and he was staring at Martin. 'Are you all right, Mr Hughes?'

The lovebite had gone. Perhaps it had just been a boil. 'I'm fine,' Martin said. 'I've just got a headache.'

'Lots of water, that's the trick,' Detective Inspector Walton said. 'Pints of it. Never fails. Anyway, as I was saying, I have some bad news.'

Why did this policeman, with his ominous politeness, keep coming round? He couldn't possibly have found out about the passport. Could he?

'I'm afraid that Chris Finlay was shot this morning. And killed.'

'Who?' No. Please not.

'Please, Mr Hughes. We know you knew him.'

'I'm sorry, Detective Inspector. I'm afraid I do not know anyone called Chris Finlay.' That was literally true as they had met for less than an hour.

'Mr Hughes, Mr Hughes.' The detective inspector shook his head sadly. 'We don't have time for these games. A man was murdered less than two hours ago. And we need to find who did it. And quickly. So I should be grateful if you could help us and not treat me like an idiot.'

'I'm sorry. The name sounds familiar but I just can't place it.'

'Chris Finlay lived next door to your friend, Viktor Markov. You do remember him, don't you? He also got murdered. And strangely enough it was in the same street and in much the same way. And we know you went to see Mr Finlay two nights ago.'

That poor frightened, hopeful, helpful man and his dog. And that repulsive landlord. There was clearly no point in pretending any longer. 'Oh yes. I remember now. He lived next door. How terrible. What happened?'

'He was shot. Like Mr Markov. Where were you at nine o'clock this morning, Mr Hughes?'

'You don't think I had anything to do with this, do you?'

'I try not to think anything at the moment, Mr Hughes. Not until I have some evidence on which to base my thinking. Isn't that what you barristers are trained to do? Now, where were you at nine o'clock this morning?'

'I think I must have been on my way here.'

'Think?'

'I was on my way here.'

'Quite sure, Mr Hughes?'

This policeman really did not like him. 'Yes. I am sure. Is that a problem?'

'Not at all. I'm just gathering information. As I said.' Martin noticed he was not writing anything down this morning. He was just steadily observing him as he spoke.

'Do you own a motorcycle, Mr Hughes?'

'No.'

'Do you know how to drive one?'

Martin remembered what Chris Finlay had told him and he saw where the questioning was going. How could this plod think he had perpetrated a drive-by murder? 'No. Do you think I look like a biker?'

'As I said, I try not to think anything until I have some evidence on which to base my thinking. Can you think of any reason why anyone would want to kill Viktor Markov and Chris Finlay? Any connection between them?'

'No. I'm sorry, I can't. Apart from the fact that they lived next door to each other. Why should I?' The seagull perched on the windowsill was now looking round imperiously. How had his life arrived here?

'No need for that tone, Mr Hughes. I'm just trying to tie things together at the moment. May I share with you where I have got to so far?'

Martin nodded.

'Firstly, we have two murders in the same street, within a very short period of time. That's unusual. Secondly, the murders were committed using an identical method of operation. That's also unusual.'

'What happened?' Martin recalled every word of Chris Finlay's description of how Viktor had been killed.

'It seems that a motorcycle approached the victim and the driver pulled out a gun and shot him in the head. Twice. And then drove away at high speed. In each case, the driver was dressed in black leather. It looks as if both murders were committed by a professional hitman. And despite what you might read in the newspapers, this also is unusual.'

'What's this got to do with me?'

'So far, Mr Hughes, we've only been able to find three things to link the two victims together. Firstly, they appear to have been killed in the same way, apparently by the same person. Secondly, they lived next door to each other. And thirdly, we found your card in each of their flats. And that links you with the third murder I've got on my books. And that's a lot of murders at one time. And you seem to be connected to all of them. And so, like you, I'm wondering what exactly all this has got to do with you.'

Martin looked out of the window at the seagull. His predicament was becoming horribly clear. Since he first met Viktor, every gesture of help he had made, the sort of thing anyone would do, had sucked him further into the swamp. Now Boris was threatening to kill him and Viktor and Chris Finlay had been murdered and probably Mila as well and Inspector Walton suspected him of being an accessory to all these murders. Each day was worse than the one before. At every step he could have turned back and every time he didn't, the ratchet turned another notch up.

'Well?' The policeman had still not taken his eyes off him. 'Is there anything you want to tell me, Mr Hughes?'

Martin turned his face away from the seagull to look at the detective inspector sitting in the chair and staring at him. His brain was racing and he knew he had to keep talking while he worked out what to do. Otherwise the inspector would think he was trying to hide something, although it was hard to imagine what more the policeman needed to be convinced of his guilt.

'I'm afraid I don't know anything that could possibly be of any use to you, Inspector,' he said. 'If I did, of course I would tell you.' This was now spiralling out of control and Martin knew he must not let it drift on any longer. But what could he say to the policeman now that would not make him even more convinced that Martin was implicated in three murders?

'Take your time, Mr Hughes.'

'Thank you, Inspector, but I don't need to. I have nothing to add.' If he had told the inspector everything he knew earlier, would it have saved Chris Finlay?

'Are you quite sure, Mr Hughes?'

'Why shouldn't I be, Inspector?' If he remained silent now, would more innocent people die? There was no evidence to think so and whatever he said now would only make the policeman more suspicious. What would he make of Miroslav and Kalaj and the mysterious passport? Someone was trying to set him up anyway, with that business about his business cards, and revealing all this now would only convince the inspector that he was guilty of something. And then, most alarming of all, there was that thug demanding the passport. If Martin told Inspector Walton everything, then he would not be able to give the passport to Boris and then Boris would kill him. It was an impossible situation.

'All right, Mr Hughes.' Clive Walton sighed as he got up out of the armchair. 'I'm sure we'll meet again. Don't worry, I'll see myself out.'

Martin watched the policeman's back as he closed the door behind him. Now what? He was sure the policeman was right that they would meet again. Robert Wood had found Viktor's sister and that would take care of Suzana. And maybe Boris would leave him alone once he gave him the passport. But then? Would that be the end of it? Unlikely. Martin still did not understand how it had got so bad so why should he assume there were no more unpleasant surprises? Waiting and hoping and assuming that somehow everything would work itself out had proved to be a dangerous option.

Martin watched as the seagull stretched. No-one was going to rescue him. He was going to have to do it for himself. With one lazy flap of its wings, the seagull flew away. And then Martin realised he didn't know what he was rescuing himself from. He might be able to do it if he knew but he didn't know. Who was doing the killing and why? Who was trying to frame him and why? What was Kalaj to do with this, if anything? When he knew the answers to these questions, he could work out what to do next. But what did he know? Nothing.

Martin got up and walked over to the window and looked out at the lawns of Lincoln's Inn. Nothing comes from nothing. And then he remembered the address he had given to that journalist.

eighty-seven

The swing swayed gently in the breeze that whispered in from the east. Bright green and red, around it drifted ghostly echoes of excited children shouting and laughing. The boss said it was camouflage because anyone looking over the fence or carrying out surveillance from the air would see it and think of those happy children. They would not think of a house packed with electronic criminals who never had time to play on the swing or the blue roundabout that stood forlornly beside it.

Gabriel stared at the disconsolate garden with its scrubby grass. He knew he should get back to work but he did not feel like it just yet. It had not been a good morning and he needed to stand outside a little longer in the fresh, chill air and clear his head. He took another drag on his cigarette and watched the blue smoke float away. The rich aromas of herbs and farmyard wafted past him. He looked at his watch. He had come straight back after the hit as instructed and she would have expected him to start work by now. He took one last drag and flicked the stub on to the ground and trod it under his heel.

Above him a plane murmured across the sky, a silver silhouette against the grey clouds. Gabriel slid back the

French windows and stepped through the curtains into the living room. Two shelves had been built along both of the long sides of the room and sixteen computers had been placed on each of them. At each terminal sat an operator wearing headphones, tapping and clicking. There was Rokia. And Ali. And Gerhan and Felipe and Kessie and Chen. And others whose names he did not know. A plump girl in an orange pullover and an open-faced Indonesian boy who was always smiling. All peering at the screens with their headphones on, probing and exploring through the digital gateways to find what they had been told to find.

The curtains were drawn at either end of the room and the operators worked in a pale gloom illuminated by the glow from the screens and a fluorescent strip which ran along the centre of the ceiling. Gabriel walked through it and into the hallway and up the narrow stairs with their stained floral carpet. He opened the first door on the left and went in. Ilie was sitting at one of the two computers, with his headphones on and staring at the screen. He turned as Gabriel came in.

'Hello,' he said, 'how are you?' They had agreed to speak in English to each other to show their commitment to their new country.

'OK,' Gabriel said.

'How did it go?'

'OK.' Gabriel sat down at his computer. He and Ilie shared this small room at the front of the house. The curtains were drawn here too and there was a poster of Jennifer Lopez on the wall. He turned on the computer and watched the screen as it booted up. They were on their own because they were doing a special job for the boss. Gabriel enjoyed doing the online casino. It had been a real challenge getting into it and then working out how to rig the play. But they had done it. He and Ilie were a good team and they were proud of what they had done.

The boss was pleased too. She had given them each a thousand pound bonus when they had broken through. It was generous as she paid good money anyway. Gabriel made a thousand pounds a week, in his hand. And he knew Ilie made the same and he guessed the operators downstairs were making almost as much. It was good money. Where else could a twenty-two-year-old like him make as much? He was sending home eight hundred pounds a week. His parents thought he was a millionaire and he enjoyed working with computers.

But he didn't like the other, even more secret, tasks the boss gave him to do. Gabriel knew every job involved doing some things you enjoyed less than others. And he recognised the boss had a right to ask him to help out. After all, she had paid for him to come over and he knew how lucky he had been. It had come out of the blue. He had given a paper at that university in Bucharest and the next thing he knew he was being invited to come and work in London. It was a lucky break but still he hoped the boss would not ask him too many more times to help out with these special jobs, particularly as he still had one more to do that he could not tell her about.

'Have you been smoking in here?' She had come in while he was staring at the screen and her calm beauty transformed the drab little room. Ilie took off his headphones and looked up and his eyes devoured her.

'Good morning, Mila,' he said.

'Good morning, Ilie,' she said. 'Have you, Gabriel? Been smoking?'

'No, Mila.'

'Are you sure? she said. 'I can smell it.' Her voice was as soft and mellifluous as usual but Gabriel knew he must always be careful what he said to her.

'I had a cigarette outside,' he said. 'I needed it.'

'If you must do it, please brush your teeth afterwards,' Mila said. 'It makes me feel sick.'

'Sorry, Mila.'

'How did you get on?' she said.

'Fine,' he said.

'Any problems?' she said.

'It's all done,' he said. 'Don't worry. No problems.' She would kill him if she knew about the little girl in the pink raincoat.

'Good,' she said. 'Here.' She handed him an envelope. He knew there would be twenty fifty-pound notes in it.

'Now please get to work,' Mila said. 'We've only got another four hours on the casino and we need to make the most of them. Remember we are moving this afternoon. Don't leave any unfinished business.'

And then she smiled her soft gentle smile at them and closed the door behind her. Gabriel sighed. Little as he wanted to do it, at least he now knew how to deal with the little girl.

eighty-eight

'I need your help.' They were back in the café round the corner from the refuge and a watery sun washed it with pale light.

Helen Borthwick watched Charlotte warily. 'I'm sorry,' she said. 'None of them wanted to talk to you. I told you on the phone.'

'I know,' Charlotte said. 'That's not why I wanted to see you.'

Helen Borthwick said nothing.

Charlotte sipped her tea and wondered how to break through her impassive mistrust. 'I think I've found a woman who needs your help,' she said.

'You think?'

'She was too frightened to talk to me. But she looked like she needed help to get away.' Charlotte had not been able to forget those green eyes filled with fear. It was time for her to stop waiting and watching. It was time to stop being a spectator. This demanded commitment.

'What do you want me to do?' Now Helen Borthwick was looking directly at Charlotte.

'You've got more experience in dealing with women in these situations. I thought perhaps you might be able to persuade her.'

'Excuse me,' Helen Borthwick said. 'I need another cup of coffee.'

Charlotte watched her as she walked over to the counter, a slight woman with short fair hair in a navy raincoat with the collar turned up. What was she thinking?

'Why do you think she wants to escape?' Helen Borthwick said as she sat down again.

'Who wouldn't?'

Helen Borthwick sighed. 'It's not as easy as that,' she said. 'Of course all trafficked women want to escape. But if they get caught, they get hurt. If they don't get caught, their families back home get hurt. So when they think about it, often they decide they don't want to escape that badly.'

'It can't be so hopeless,' Charlotte said. 'There must be something we can do.'

'Sometimes,' Helen said. 'When we get enough to prosecute the traffickers or when there's no family. But it takes a lot of work and I have to set priorities. I wish I didn't but this project lives from day to day. I get six months' funding from the Home Office here, three months from local authorities there. Every day I wake up wondering how we are going to get enough funding to get through to next year. There's only so much I can do. Why do you think this woman should be at the top of my list?'

'How can I know that?' Charlotte said. 'But I do know she needs help.'

'I'm sure she does but how badly? I have women so savagely raped they can't walk. Is she like that?'

Charlotte shook her head. 'There must be something we can do to help,' she said. 'She refused to talk to me but I know something's wrong. So what can I do? If I write it up it could put her in danger. So what should I do? There must be something.'

'That's what I say to myself every day,' Helen Borthwick said. 'But I'd go mad if I thought that about everyone. Every day as I fill in the forms hoping to get another three months' money to keep going, I tell myself to think about what I can do, not what I can't. Every time I have to turn someone away, I have to tell myself to look at the ones I can help, not the ones I can't.'

'How do you cope?' Charlotte said.

'Sometimes, I don't,' Helen Borthwick said. 'But if I don't keep going, who will? Every time your paper writes about asylum seekers and illegal immigrants your readers see thieves and con-men. I see people who have been abused in ways people in this country can barely imagine. And yet somehow they keep going and so must I.'

'Could I write about you?'

'What?' Helen Borthwick cocked her head to one side. 'What would you write? How much taxpayers' money is going to keep me looking after these aliens?'

'No. Something showing what you do every day. Sympathetic.'

'I don't mean to be rude but do you honestly think that even if you wrote something like that, your paper would ever print it?'

Charlotte said nothing. Helen was right but for the

wrong reason. To Maggie it would not be a scandal about taxpayers' money, it would just be boring. A story done so often there was nothing new to say about it. A story that wouldn't even make it in a slow August. It would seal her fate.

'I'm sorry,' Helen Borthwick said. 'Perhaps you do mean well but you've got to understand that every day I wake up worrying that some article in a newspaper is going to panic some politician into pulling down the shutters. There are no votes in what I do. We exist on the margins and I live on the goodwill of civil servants and the occasional minister who wants to do the right thing and hopes she won't be noticed slipping us a few thousand pounds from time to time. I've got enough to worry about without fretting how your article might turn out and the damage it will do to my work.'

Charlotte noticed how her fingers never stopped moving, tapping the side of the cup, playing with the spoon in the sugar bowl, stroking the table-mat. She did not want to be here. Talking to Charlotte was irrelevant to her clients and Charlotte thought that, in her way, Helen Borthwick was magnificent.

And that was the difference between them, Charlotte thought. Helen Borthwick knew what she was doing and took responsibility for it and Charlotte did not. It was not just that when she was at the office she was worrying about being at home and when she was with Rob and Matthew she was fidgeting about work. Comparing herself to Helen, she realised she never took responsibility for any of it herself. At work, it was down to Maggie. At home, it was down to Rob and her need to keep working to support them. For Helen Borthwick, problems were not excuses, they were demands for action.

'OK,' Charlotte said. But it wasn't. Helen Borthwick had got her priorities straight and now, in this pale café, Charlotte realised more than ever that she had got to make decisions about hers.

eighty-nine

The music was taking him away. The pure children's voices and the sweet simple melody drifted up to the rafters and washed away his sins. This was how it used to be when he was a child and his mother dragged him to church every Sunday, telling him it was bathtime for his soul.

As the angelic voices celebrated the advent of the Saviour, little children lit candles and their parents filmed every solemn step and Gabriel sat at the back of the church and thought about the complicated work-ings of fate. He thought about all the casual decisions he had made which, one by one, had brought him to work for the boss, and all the choices that Chris Finlay had made about where he was going to live and whether he was going to own a dog and what time he would take the dog for a walk and how all that had brought him fatally to cross Gabriel's path.

Across the aisle, Martin sneaked a look at the hitman and wondered what to do. At five o'clock he had suddenly remembered that Clare had told him that Megan was going to be lighting the first candle at the Advent concert. Another test. He had rushed out of Lincoln's Inn and stood gesticulating frantically in the

street for a taxi and had barely recovered his breath by
the time he arrived at the church. There was still a
small queue of parents waiting to get in and Martin
gave the taxi-driver a five pound tip in his relief at not
being late.

'Hello, Martin.' Polly had been sitting at the table
selling tickets. 'How nice to see you.' And it was nice to
see her warm smile.

'At least I'm not late,' he had said, as Polly ostentatiously looked at her watch.

'Hmm,' she had said. 'I'd take your programme and
get inside if I were you.'

He had moved away from the table and then stopped
to open the programme and look for Megan's name and,
as he did so, he had heard a man's voice behind him.

'Do you know Suzana Markov?' it had said. Martin
had stiffened, as his heart started to pound, his eyes
fixed on the text in the programme as he strained to
hear.

'Yes,' he had heard Polly say. 'She's in the choir.
Why?'

'I'm her cousin,' the man's voice had said. It had a
Central European accent.

'Oh,' Polly had said. 'I didn't know she had any
cousins in this country. I'm sure she'll be delighted to
see you. I'll tell her you're here when I go in. What's
your name?'

'Don't say anything,' the voice had said. 'I want it to
be a surprise.'

Martin had known what he would see when he
nerved himself to turn round and there in the crush

of mothers in soft coats and fathers in suits had been a fair-haired young man, in a leather jacket, holding a motorcycle helmet, making his way into the hall. Viktor had never mentioned any cousin and Martin had noticed how the young man had refused to give his name. And he had remembered what Suzana had told him about the hitman on a motorbike.

Now Gabriel listened to the choir singing with his eyes closed but when they stopped and the children filed up to light the candles, he watched them carefully, one by one. He was almost certain he would recognise the little girl as soon as he saw her and, little as he wanted to do this, he felt a comfortable satisfaction at having managed finally to find her. It had not been easy. She had never returned to the Markov flat and he had no idea where she had gone. The boss had a lot of contacts who could have asked around to find the girl but, obviously, he could not ask the boss for help.

So he had driven around the neighbouring streets a few times hoping to spot her but he had never seen anything. And then, just as he was beginning to get seriously worried, he had an inspiration. The little girl must be going to school so all he needed to do was check out all the schools in the neighbourhood. St Luke's was the third one he had tried, claiming to be a cousin, and there she was. Found. Now all he had to do was follow her home to find out where she was living and make his plans accordingly.

The man in the leather jacket tilting his head up towards the roof and listening to the choir with a seraphic expression looked harmless enough but Martin was sure he was here to kill Suzana. Who else could he be but the hitman? The man who killed Viktor and Chris Finlay had been a motorcyclist in leathers and he must know Suzana had seen him and could identify him. And what sort of cousin could he be that Viktor had never mentioned him and who didn't want Suzana to be told about him?

Gabriel looked at the teacher conducting the choir, silhouetted against the great window at the end of the church. It was dark, except for the candles and a golden light which flooded the window. The music teacher was etched against it like a Javanese shadow-puppet.

What an ideal target, Gabriel thought. He'd never done it like that before. One shot, clinical, from the back of the church, and she'd crumple in slow motion, and then there would be a shocked silence as the congregation realised something was wrong and then someone would start screaming and he would be off and away on his bike before anyone had noticed him. But, on the other hand, it would be wrong to do it in a church and, anyway, she was not the target.

Martin tried to see any suspicious bulges in the hitman's clothing that could be a gun. His hands were resting peacefully together in his lap but he could have concealed a weapon anywhere in those bulky leathers. Martin tapped his fingers anxiously on the programme. He would have to find Clare and Megan and Suzana the moment the concert ended and get them away somewhere safe.

Peace laid its hands on Gabriel. The music and the children's voices soothed him and reminded him of the magnificence of eternity and the insignificance of human life. It was vanity to attach importance to what he did. He had a job to do and that was all. Everything passes, everyone dies. It was just that some died sooner than others.

The music teacher raised her hands, signalling the grand finale, stretching up to the roof and looking as if she was about to ascend to heaven. The high voices of the choir rose and rose and the organ sounded its grand sonorous chords and the concert was over and the congregation broke out in applause.

This was a rare moment of calm for Gabriel when he had done everything he could possibly do for now. He could not do the job here in this seething throng of families. He would come back to the school tomorrow afternoon and follow her home and do it then. And then that would be that. Now he'd found her he could take care of it without the boss ever finding out and everything could go on as before.

The music teacher turned and the candles caught sweat glistening on her face before she bowed and then beckoned the choir to bow in turn to their grateful audience.

Instinctively, Martin turned to the front of the church and started clapping. And then, a moment later, he remembered that he needed to watch the hitman but when he turned round, the seat across the aisle was empty.

Martin turned right round to the back of the church but there were only parents there, those who had arrived too late to get a seat, and who were now standing and clapping enthusiastically.

Martin stood up and hurried out of the church into the street. Nothing to the left but as he turned to the right, he saw, fifty yards away, a shadowy figure swing his leg over a motorbike and start the engine. And then the bike roared off into the night.

Martin stared after it. Why had the man disappeared like that? Martin could not work out what was happening. Perhaps he had been panicking unnecessarily. If the fair-haired young man really was a hitman, why had he come to the concert and then gone off without doing anything more? But equally why would he claim to be her cousin and then not wait to see her?

Whoever the motorcyclist was, Martin knew he must find Clare immediately and warn her and then go to the police. Martin could imagine Inspector Walton's sceptical expression as he explained about the young man at the concert who had just ridden off. He would probably think he was trying to divert him. Or that he was a fantasist. But Martin knew he was not imagining what he had heard. Polly was there. She could back him up. And if Clare went with him to see the inspector, it would make it more credible. The wind whipped a crisp packet round his ankles and he realised he was still staring at where the motorbike had been. He must find Clare now. And as soon as he had spoken to her, he must call the police. He could not take any risks with Suzana's life.

Martin turned and went back into the church which was still packed with proud parents and exhilarated children. 'Excuse me,' he said as he edged back into the crowd. He could not see Clare anywhere. Nor Megan or Suzana. Three little girls were chasing each other, dodging and darting between the adults. Where was Clare?

'Polly,' he said, relieved to see someone he knew. 'Have you seen Clare anywhere?'

'She was here a moment ago,' Polly said. 'She must be somewhere nearby.'

But Martin could not find her. As he worked his way, at first apologetically and then increasingly assertively, though the crowd, he could not see her. Nor Megan or Suzana.

And then he became aware that it was getting easier to move around the church as people were going home and then there wasn't a crowd any more and then he could count the remaining stragglers and Clare and Megan and Suzana were still nowhere to be seen. They must have gone home and somehow he had missed them.

Martin was reassured that he had seen the motorcyclist disappear before they left but he still needed to warn Clare. He took out his mobile phone and rang her number and got her answerphone. They must still be on their way home.

'Clare,' he said to the voicemail. 'It's Martin. I don't want to worry you but there's something I need to talk to you about as soon as possible. I'll call again but make sure you've got all the security locked on the windows and doors.' He thought that was the right balance between a prudent warning and alarming her. And he knew that Clare, who worried about being a single woman living alone with a young daughter, had invested heavily in security grilles and alarm systems. So he was sure everything would be all right but he would call again in half an hour, when they were bound to have got home, just to be sure.

Suddenly, with that Central European voice asking for Suzana, all the complicated decisions confronting him had dissolved into one stark reality. They had to protect Suzana, even if telling the police would expose him to more embarrassment and suspicion and delay her departure to Sarajevo. She needed protection now.

And then, as he stood in the emptying church, Martin remembered what he had been going to do after the concert, before he had heard the hitman asking for Suzana. He had been going to go to that address the language school director had given him.

'Did you find her?' Polly said, coming up to him carrying two bulging plastic bags of rubbish.

'Not yet,' he said. 'But I will. Don't worry.'

'Oh Martin,' she said.

'It's fine,' he said. 'Honestly. Sorry, Polly, I've got to go.' As he was speaking, he realised that he should stick to his earlier plan and while he waited for Clare to get home, he should go to look around that house. It wasn't far away and it wouldn't take long.

'See you soon,' he said to Polly and marched out of the church before she could say anything else. However urgent the need to warn Clare, he still needed answers to the questions tormenting him. Someone had already murdered two people, probably three, and unless he could find out who and why, the police were going to continue to suspect him and it was going to be hard for anyone to keep Suzana safe in London or Sarajevo. Perhaps that address might hold some answers.

ninety

The taxi crawled out into the suburbs, cutting through dank avenues of semi-detached houses. Martin rang Clare again. Still the answerphone. Why wasn't she home by now? How had he blundered into this nightmare?

'Excuse me.' The taxi-driver broke into Clare's recorded voice. 'There's a lot of traffic ahead. Do you mind if we take the back way?'

'Whatever's quickest,' Martin said. He looked at the address in his hand. Was he being stupid just turning up? Perhaps it was where the hitman lived? But what choice did he have? It was the only lead he had. And perhaps for once something would work out. And he could get the taxi to wait as a precaution.

'If we take the back way,' the taxi-driver said, 'it's a bit longer.'

'That's fine,' Martin said and as the taxi wove its way through the suburban streets, he thought of Suzana in her pink raincoat.

'It'll be a bit more on the clock,' the driver confirmed. He clearly thought Martin looked as if he would argue about the fare.

'Yes. Fine,' Martin said. He glanced at his watch.

'Do you mind some music?' the taxi-driver said.

'That's fine,' Martin said. Was he mad to come here on his own without telling anyone? Eine Kleine Nachtmusik filled the cab. He should ring Clare and tell her where he was.

The taxi turned left. 'This is the road,' the driver said. 'What number was it?'

'Forty-one,' Martin said. The road looked like all the others they had been driving through for the last ten minutes. He rang Clare again but there was still no answer. He left a message giving the address they were looking for and said if he didn't call again in the next hour, she should call the police.

The driver stopped and peered through the window. 'Can't see any numbers,' he said.

'I'll get out here,' Martin said. 'Can you wait ten minutes?' As he walked towards the houses, he heard Vivaldi wafting through the window of the cab.

Martin walked up to the front door of the nearest house and saw discoloured brass numerals, ivy trailing round them. Sixteen. He crossed to the other side of the road and looked for a number on the house opposite. Further down the road, there was a large white van parked with its back doors open and a man was coming out of a house and carrying a computer.

Thirty-three. Martin looked down the road. It looked as if the van was parked outside forty-one. As he watched, the man handed the computer to someone inside the van and a young woman came down the path carrying another computer. What was going on? Whatever it was, it didn't look threatening.

He had been panicking unnecessarily. He hoped he hadn't sounded too hysterical on Clare's voicemail.

He walked up to the front gate. He couldn't see a number anywhere. Another young man came down the path carrying another computer, passing the young woman going back inside the house. What was this place? 'Excuse me,' Martin said. 'Do you live here?'

The man ignored him and continued walking to the van.

Perhaps this was somewhere Viktor used to live, but Martin couldn't imagine what connection Viktor might have had with these young men and women carrying computers. He walked up the path. The front door was open and he saw two computers on the floor by the open door. A young man came running down the stairs, two at a time, and picked up one of the computers.

'Excuse me,' Martin said.

The young man picked up the computer and started to walk towards the white van. It was as if Martin did not exist.

He stepped inside the hall.

'Hello,' he called. He saw into the kitchen at the end of the hallway. Someone was boiling a kettle in the kitchen but they were silhouetted against the light and Martin could see not see if it was a man or woman. He walked down the hall towards the figure. And then it spoke to him.

'Hello, Martin,' she said in the calm voice he remembered.

When he had sat in the taxi thinking of all the things he might find when he got to the house, perhaps another repulsive landlord with another manila envelope, conceivably an old address book or even one of Viktor's Bosnian friends, possibly Balkan thugs or even Boris, Martin had never thought of finding her. He had thought she was dead.

'Mila,' he said. 'Are you all right?' As he stepped towards her, he could see she was standing with her hands clasped in front of her.

'Yes, thank you,' she said.

He stepped forward again, reaching out towards her and, without thinking, took her hands in his. 'I'm so glad,' he said. 'Are you sure? What happened to you?' Her hands rested passively in his, not pulling away and yet not holding them either.

'It's a long story,' she said.

She was still beautiful and yet there was something different about her. He recognised her immediately but perhaps it was her voice that had helped him do that. There was something unfamiliar about the way she looked and he could not quite identify what it was. 'Come,' he said, pulling at her hands. 'We must get away from here. You're in danger.'

'What do you mean?' she said, not moving as he tugged at her.

Martin made himself look her in the eye. 'I have some bad news, Mila,' he said. 'Viktor is dead. He was murdered.'

'How?' She looked stunned.

In the gloom, Martin thought he saw the gleam of tears in her eyes.

'What happened?' Mila said eventually. She needed

to know what he knew. She couldn't work out how he had found her here and she needed to know.

'He was shot. The police think it was a professional hit. And they think it might be something to do with you. He was so worried when you disappeared and he looked so hard for you they think he might have found out things that upset some dangerous people. So you are in danger. And we should go now. I've got a taxi waiting outside.'

'Why do they think it was anything to do with me? How would they know my name?'

'Because when you disappeared, Viktor was so worried that we went to the police.'

She hadn't thought of that. She knew he would be upset but she had assumed he wouldn't go anywhere near the police. He would be so desperate to stay safely in London with Suzana that he wouldn't risk going anywhere near the police, she had thought. She had been wrong.

'I'm so relieved,' Martin said. 'I thought you were dead.' She stayed looking at the ground. It must have been a shock. He did not know how else to have told her.

Mila had guessed Viktor would look for her. She knew he loved her. And she had been fond of him. That was the pity of it. But the business depended on her never putting down roots and she had to make a choice. Settle down with Viktor or move on. The sort of choice couples all over the world were making every day.

She had been tempted but, in the end, she had decided to move on. And she knew that he would never have accepted a civilised parting. He was obsessive, as he had proved, and he would have kept on and on trying to change her mind, making trouble she did not need. So she had thought it would be easier if she just went. And she assumed that, eventually, he would get over it. She had thought wrong.

'Are you OK?' Martin said.

Mila nodded, still looking at the ground. She would never have thought Viktor would be so desperate and so smart. But he had kept going and going, annoying Kalaj and making so much noise around her that she knew she would have to deal with it. And she had. And the witness that Kalaj had told her about. She was sorry she had had to do it. She really had been fond of Viktor. But she had always known life was full of hard choices.

But now the police were something else. She had got away from them once, easily enough, but now they would be looking for her in connection with a murder and that was going to be far more difficult. And now this English lawyer had found her, it was all starting to unravel very fast. How had he found her?

And then there was that journalist yesterday asking about Kalaj. And now suddenly Mila understood. Kalaj was behind it all. She knew he was after something and now she knew he was after her. He was the only one who could have given her address to these people. She didn't know why but she could find that out later. Now she had to get a grip. One step at a time. She had to finish the move out of here today and then she would have to deal with Kalaj. And she knew how to do that.

But what about this Englishman now? What was she going to do about him? Gabriel was not here to deal with him and anyway there were too many witnesses around, moving out the computers. But the longer he hung around, the more he would learn. And the greater the risk. And then she realised what to do.

'This is dangerous for me,' she said. 'You being here.'

'Let's go,' he said. 'Now.'

But Mila shook her head. 'Martin,' she said, locking her eyes on to his. 'It's not so easy. These are dangerous men and I owe them a lot of money.'

'You can't enforce an illegal debt,' he said and, as he spoke, he realised how ridiculous he sounded.

'They will enforce it,' she said. 'They spent a lot of money getting me here and they want it back. That is why I must work for them.'

No. Martin squeezed her hand. Please let it not be that. Please.

'What do you mean, work for them?' he said. And he stared out through the kitchen window at the swing, swaying in the breeze. He could not bear to look at her as she answered.

'I do what they want.'

'What do you mean?'

'They do all sorts of things with computers. I help them with that.'

Computers. Thank God. Computers. 'Just come with me now,' he said. 'We'll go straight to the police and let them deal with these people. We could go out through the garden at the back here and no-one will notice. They all seem very busy.'

'Martin, Martin, you do not understand. It's not so easy,' she said and gave his hand a little gentle shake. 'They don't need to keep me here behind bars. My mother still lives in Romania and they know where she lives. That's all they need to keep me here. That's why I must do what they say.'

'There must be something we can do. They can't do this. It's slavery,' he said. 'What about getting Interpol to protect your mother? Why wouldn't that work? Then you could get away. Come on. Let's go to the police and get protection for your mother.'

He felt the power of action like a tidal wave sweeping aside the problems.

'It's not that easy, Martin,' she said.

'Yes it is,' he said. 'Why not? We can do this, Mila. We can.'

'You're a good man, Martin,' she said. 'I'm lucky to have a friend like you. But I must think what is the best way to do this.'

'I'm worried about you,' he said. 'Please come with me now.' He owed it to Viktor to make sure she was safe.

'I must think,' she said. 'I can't take risks with my mother. Come back in an hour,' she said. 'It will be quieter then and we will make our plans.'

'OK,' he said. 'But then you must let me help you.'

'Yes, Martin, I promise,' she said. 'But, Martin, you must promise me you will not say anything to anyone about me. Not even to the police. That could be very dangerous for me. And my mother. It must just be you and me.' She looked at him with her soft green eyes. 'We will do it together. Just you and me. Promise me, Martin.'

He nodded.

'Just ring the bell, any time after eight,' she said. 'I will have worked it out by then.'

ninety-one

'I Can't Stop Loving You.' It was a message from Van Morrison. 'I Can't Stop Loving You,' he sang on the BlackBerry. Joanne had made it the email alert sound and Clive Walton had not yet found time to change it. He looked at the screen. It was an email from LoveGain, not an address he recognised. It must be more spam imploring him to take advantage of bulk discounts on Viagra. He put the BlackBerry back in his pocket.

'How are you getting on, Clive?' Chief Superintendent Mark Rafter walked proprietorially into the office and sat down. 'Do you mind if I sit down for a moment?' he said.

Clive Walton smiled. 'Why not?' he said. The chief had always looked out for him but he did not think this was a casual visit.

'Any progress on the Finlay case?' his boss said.

Clive Walton nodded. 'Some,' he said. 'Still a way to go.'

'Markov?'

'Much the same,' Clive Walton said.

'And the girl on the train?'

'It takes time, Mark, you know that,' Clive Walton said. 'I'll get there.'

'I'm sure you will, Clive,' the chief superintendent said, 'but in the meantime I'm getting a lot of heat. There's media interest in all of them. Rock star, illegal immigration, it's crack cocaine for the press.'

'They'll get bored,' Clive Walton said.

'Jeremy Phillips won't,' Mark Rafter said. 'He's seriously pissed off, Clive. What happened there?'

'It was a bad call,' Clive Walton said. 'I'm sorry. It happens.'

The chief superintendent nodded ruminatively but did not say anything.

'I will get there, Mark,' Clive Walton said. 'You know me.'

'Let me know if you want to talk about it at any time,' Mark Rafter said as he got up to go and Clive Walton knew his card had been marked. And he didn't know how he was going to get it unmarked.

He knew the barrister was lying to him but he couldn't see how he could have been involved in any of the murders. He was probably just covering up some minor misdemeanours. Going to prostitutes. Using illegal immigrant labour for some building work. The rest of it was probably just coincidence. That was often the way. The Markov and Finlay murders were clearly linked, next-door neighbours and the same technique, but the connection was probably not going to produce anything. The most obvious explanation was that Chris Finlay had seen something and had been taken out as a potential witness. And where did that lead?

He was less sure that the woman on the Tube had any connection with these two murders. There was only that barrister's card linking them all together. And that was probably just a coincidence. He didn't look like he could kill anyone. And that was it, apart from the routine forensics. Nothing more. He had asked a couple of detectives to go round all the known gangs to see what they could winkle out of their informants but that had not produced anything so far. He was stuck.

'I Can't Stop Loving You,' Van Morrison called him again, reminding him he still had not read the new email. He better do it and clear it. Clive Walton kept a tidy electronic desktop. He opened his personal message from LoveGain. It was not a special offer on Viagra. It was something he really needed. For the first time in days, Clive Walton got a nice surprise.

ninety-two

The house was quiet now. The bustling activity of the afternoon had gone, the last computer had been loaded into the van and the team were now making their way to the new base. Mila sat in the living room with the lights off and the curtains drawn and her hand round the Glock in her pocket as she waited for Martin to return.

Gabriel was not answering his mobile. She was going to have to talk to him. Sometimes she worried about his commitment. In the meantime, she was going to have to do this herself. It was too dangerous to be left until tomorrow.

A car passed outside and then the house was quiet again. Somewhere in the distance a cat screeched. And then the silence returned. Gabriel's absence did not create any practical problems. It would not be difficult for her to deal with Martin herself but this was Gabriel's job and he should be answering his phone.

The house creaked. Mila had noticed that nothing in it was ever completely still or quiet. A flickering shift in temperature caused a wooden strut to contract fractionally and the sound puckered the silence. She thought of Viktor. Poor Viktor. It was such a shame.

They had been happy from the moment they met in the Clarendon where she had been trawling for workers. Sweet Viktor. So courteous and respectful, he had never even asked what she was doing there. If only he had known when to give up.

The doorbell rang. 'Come in,' Mila called gently. 'It's open.' She tightened her grip on the Glock in her pocket. She would not even need to take it out. She could do it through the fabric. She heard the front door open. Someone came in and closed the door behind them. 'In here, Martin,' she called.

Then she heard a rustling down the hallway. That didn't sound like one person. She took the Glock out of her pocket and pointed it at the door, with her finger round the trigger.

Nothing happened. She knew they must still be in the hallway, whoever they were, but everything was quiet and still. Mila sat calmly, holding the gun in her right hand, resting it on her left wrist, pointing it at the door, poised, ready.

Then the door opened and two men walked in. Bikers in helmets and black leather who stopped when they saw Mila in the chair pointing the Glock at them.

'Take your helmets off,' she said. They did not move. She fired a shot into the floor. It gave a soft whistling sigh as it hit the carpet by their feet.

'Now,' she said and they did what they were told. The tall beefy one had a round open face. The trim miniature, beside him, had brown hair curling over his pixie ears.

'You said there would just be teenage hackers here, Bernie, not some chick with a gun.'

'How would I know? That's what I was told.'

'Please be quiet,' Mila said, raising her left wrist slightly and pointing the gun between the eyes of the tall one. She was readjusting. She had been expecting Martin so who were these two? Obviously not police. 'Who are you?' she said. Whoever they were, they would be dealt with but first she needed to find out what they were doing here.

They looked at each other.

Mila twitched the gun so they would be reminded of it. 'Who are you?'

The tall one spoke eventually, in a belligerent American accent. 'Someone's been ripping us off. And we know they were doing it from here. So who are you? Are you the one stealing from us?'

'It's the person with the gun who asks the questions,' Mila said politely.

'She's right, Bernie,' the tiny man said and laughed. 'How about that, a chick with a gun?'

'Shut up, Stevie,' the beefy one said.

'Who are you?' Mila said again. 'What business are you talking about?'

'Look, miss,' Bernie said. 'I know you've got the gun but we're here on legitimate business. Someone is stealing from us and we know they're doing it from here so I think we have a right to ask who the fuck you think you are.'

'How do I know that?' Mila said, not moving. 'If you are, as you say, legitimate, why don't you get the police to come here for you?'

'She's right, Bernie,' Stevie said and laughed again. 'Why didn't you go to the police?'

'Shut up, Stevie,' the tall beefy one said. 'That's my business, miss. Now what do you know about the scam going on here? Were you involved?'

'I have the gun,' Mila said. 'I ask the questions.'

'Not if I've got a gun pointing at your head,' Dean said. 'You should always lock the back door.'

Mila felt the metal at the back of her head and then Dean reached over her shoulder and took the gun out of her hand.

ninety-three

'Yes?' The barmaid kept polishing the glass as she spoke to Martin.

'Can I have a bitter lemon please,' he said. She had spent five minutes polishing glasses, while he stood at the bar, before she spoke to him. The taxi had dropped him at the nearest pub and it was empty and smelt of stale beer but at least it was somewhere he could sit and wait until it was time to return to Mila.

The barmaid put the drink in front of him. 'One twenty,' she said and picked up another glass to polish. Martin put the coins on the bar and pulled out his phone and rang Clare. Still no answer. It couldn't take her this long to get home, could it? As he put the phone back in his pocket, he noticed his hand was shaking. Too much happening at once.

'Could I have a Jack Daniels as well?' he called to the barmaid.

She turned her back on him in a biological gesture of contempt but he saw her jiggle the optic and then push the glass across towards him. 'Two seventy,' she said.

Martin left three pound coins on the bar and took the drink over to a table by the wall and watched the barmaid. She had cropped blonde hair and dangly earrings and a green tattoo on her left arm and she was still polishing glasses with vacant dedication, ignoring him. Pick up, polish, inspect, polish, put away. One after the other.

Martin raised the glass to his mouth and jerked it so the whisky hit the back of his throat. Calling the police was the obvious thing to do. Inspector Walton's card was still in his wallet and just one phone call and it would be over. But Mila had begged him not to do that. And what would happen if the gang did get to her mother in Romania? How could he live with that? Especially after what had happened to Chris Finlay following his visit to him.

The barmaid disappeared through a door at the back of the bar and country-and-western music started playing through speakers above his head and he was alone in the pub with Garth Brooks.

Martin knew he was crossing a line again. Time after time, since he had first tried to help Viktor, he could have extricated himself by going to the police. And he should have done it. That is what he would always have expected himself to do. He was an officer of the court, after all, a buttress for the law, there to bring order to society and he should have turned for help to other professionals holding the line against anarchy and disintegration. But he hadn't. Every time he should have done it, he hadn't done it. And every time, it had made it just that bit more difficult to do it the next time.

He finished the whisky. That hadn't lasted long. He might just have time for another one but the barmaid had not reappeared.

Right at the beginning, he should have insisted
Viktor went to the police on his own. And then he
should never have gone with him to the Madonna
Club. What had he been thinking of trying to negotiate
with gangsters? And then he should have told Inspector Walton everything he knew when Viktor was killed
and he should have taken the chance to do it when
Chris Finlay was murdered. So many chances, all
spurned. And now he knew he should call the police
about Mila but how could he, after what she had said?

He took Inspector Walton's card out of his wallet
and stared at it. What if the gang were there when he
returned? One phone call. That was all it would take to
be safe. But then Mila had seemed most worried about
what they would do to her mother if she escaped and
that suggested she was not worried about any immedi-
ate threat to herself. And, after all, she had been on her
own without guards. They obviously controlled her
through fear of what they might do to her mother. That
meant there would be little risk to him if he went back.
But if he went to the police, there was a real danger the
gang would kill her mother. It seemed clear he must do
what Mila had asked.

Martin stared at his empty glass. For nearly twenty
years, the law had given him his place in the world and a
sustaining belief that virtue vanquished evil. But now
when he needed its support, it had nothing to offer him.
He had crossed its frontier and moved among the
barbarians beyond. On his own. He looked at his watch.
Time to start walking back to Mila's house. He called
Clare. 'It's me again,' he said to the voicemail.

'Martin.' Her voice cut into the beep at the end of his message. 'What on earth is the matter? This is the third time you've rung.'

'Why didn't you answer?' he said.

'I could see it was you,' she said.

'I was worried,' he said. 'I thought you'd have been home an hour ago.'

'I was,' she said. 'But I had more pressing things to do than answer my phone. It was the Advent concert tonight, as you've obviously forgotten, and I've got two over-excited little girls here. I need to settle them down and get them to go to sleep.'

'Haven't you listened to my message?' he said.

'Not yet,' she said. 'I'm sorry you couldn't make it to the concert. Megan was expecting you.'

How could he explain now? If he said that he had been there, she would only think he was lying. After this was over, he would take her out for dinner and tell her everything that had happened so she would understand. But now he had to make sure she was safe. 'Have you locked the door?' he said. 'And the windows?'

'Of course,' she said. 'Why?'

'Something's come up,' he said. 'About Suzana and all that. I think you should be very careful tonight. I'll collect you in the morning to go to the airport.'

'Fine,' she said. 'But why are you being so mysterious? What's happened?'

He heard Megan shrieking in the background.

'Sorry,' she said, 'I've got to go. Talk to you later.'

And he heard the phone click as she put it down before he could say anything more. He put his phone back in his pocket. At least he had managed to warn her. And tomorrow they would get Suzana safely off to Sarajevo. But now he had to get back to Mila.

ninety-four

Crouched in the bushes, looking down a short slope towards the basement window, Gabriel watched the woman reading to the two little girls. The security grille was locked but the curtains were open and he could smash the glass and then shoot. The front garden was well screened from the road by bushes so he would be well hidden until the moment to strike and then he would be away. The situation was not perfect but it should work.

He unzipped his jacket and loosened the Ruger in the shoulder holster. It looked as if he had made the right choice. As he had ridden away from the church, he suddenly asked himself why he was waiting. Why not just get it over with now, before anything else went wrong? He had turned round, and as luck would have it, the woman was just coming out with the two little girls. He recognised the pink raincoat immediately. And so he had followed them back to this flat and nothing could have been easier and here he was, well positioned to finish the job and clean the slate.

He would have to slither down the short slope gently to avoid alerting them, and then, as soon as he had done the job, scramble up it rapidly, and on to the bike.

He felt in his inside pocket for his mobile phone. It would be disastrous if he dropped that. It was then that he remembered he had turned it off in the church. He should check it to see if he had any messages. He turned it on and immediately it started ringing.

'Yes,' he answered in a whisper, looking anxiously through the window but they didn't seem to have heard anything.

'Why aren't you answering your phone?' The boss.

'Sorry,' he muttered. 'I turned it off.' Then he realised it was a message. 'Where are you?' her recorded voice said. He was doomed. She would insist on knowing where he was but how could he explain without damning himself? He would have to think up some plausible excuse about why he had not been answering his phone. He saw the woman get up from the floor and take one of the little girls by the hand. He would have to move now or he was going to miss this opportunity.

'Gabriel, get back here now. I need you to do a job for me. And I mean now.' There was a moment's silence. And then 'Now,' she said and the message ended.

The little girl was still sitting on the floor in the room. She was the one and it would just take a couple of minutes: carefully, carefully down the slope, up to the window, smash, one shot and away. And that would be that. Job done. Worries over.

Gabriel looked at the mobile phone in his hand. On the other hand, the boss always meant what she said. And she had said now. And she had rung twenty minutes ago. And the longer he delayed, the angrier she would be and he could not risk annoying her any more than he had already done. He better get back to base and find out what the boss wanted. He would come back for the little girl tomorrow.

ninety-five

Mihail Kalaj was hard at work. DragonLord was head to head with Vespero and Warfiend and the battle was at its height and the destiny of the Old World would shortly be decided. He would have to keep a close eye on the Romanian woman. She was greedy and he knew in his bones she was stealing his money. And now he heard the hideous wailing of the wounded on the battlefield and the stream that meandered through the meadows was running red with blood.

He would find out what she was doing and then he would deal with her. In the meantime, she was dangerous. She must have killed that Serb. It was hardly likely to have been a coincidence that the killing happened so soon after he had warned her about him. The women huddled in the cottage for comfort as the warriors smote each other mightily. Which of them would come home and which of them would have their bones strewn upon the ground?

He disliked his people freelancing. And this one was troubling. She would not have hit the Serb herself so that meant she had a team working for her. Power and greed were a poisonous cocktail and Mila was dangerous. That was why he got Miroslav to direct any enquiries to her address. If anyone did come sniffing around for the Serb, they could go sniffing round her. Let her clean up her own mess. The DragonLord tightened his grip on the jewel-encrusted handle of his huge sword and raised it high above his head. The moment of truth had arrived for Warfiend.

He had to be careful. Viktor Markov had been looking everywhere for him before he was killed. Asking questions. He could not allow anyone to link him to the killings. If anyone did come looking, they should go looking for her. And if they did catch up with her, there was little she could prove that would damage him. He had made sure of that. The firewalls were all in place. Warfiend gave a bloodcurdling yell and twisted away as the DragonLord brought down the sword. He grabbed his nail-studded club from the ground where it had fallen and he sprang to his feet. The battle was not over yet.

And then Mihail heard it. Someone was coming up the stairs. More than one person. Two people. Maybe three. Moving fast and then they were on the landing and throwing open doors, one after the other and then they were in the room with him. Two men, one tall and beefy, the other small and neat, both dressed in black leather biker jackets and trousers and wearing helmets.

'Kalaj?' the tall one said in an American accent.

The small one was pointing a gun at Mihail. 'Look at that, Bernie,' he said. 'Toy soldiers.' And he laughed. 'The great boss playing toy soldiers.'

'Who are you?' Mihail said.

'Don't fuck with us,' the tall one said. 'We know what you've been doing and we don't like it.'

'What are you talking about?' They could be talking about anything, the girls, the smuggling, the drugs. But he wasn't aware he had any problem with any Americans at the moment. He had thought everything was under control. Except for the Romanian woman but these bikers did not look as if they had anything to do with her.

'Get on with it, Bernie,' the little one said. 'Remember what happened last time when we got into questions-and-answers. Don't be a duchess.'

'Don't fuck with us,' the beefy American one said again. 'You've been ripping us off. And it's going to stop.'

'If I don't know what I'm meant to be doing, how can I stop doing it?'

'He's got a point, Bernie,' the little English one said. 'But let's do him anyway.'

'Shut up, Stevie.'

'Just tell me,' Mihail said.

There was a moment's silence. Then the American coughed. 'You've been hacking into our casino,' he said.

'What do you mean?'

'Don't fuck with us. Show him, Stevie.'

Before Mihail Kalaj realised what was happening, the Englishman had whipped the pistol across his face and kicked him in the knee so he fell to the floor. The shock hit and then the blood starting trickling from the long cut in his cheek. He stayed kneeling on the floor, his head down, trying to work out what was happening. 'Can I get up?' he said, his head still bowed down.

'If you start telling the truth.'

Mihail raised himself up and sat on a chair. His cheek stung, his knee ached and his head was throbbing. That little English bastard. 'I don't know anything about any casino. It is not what I do. Why do you think this has anything to do with me?'

'Because your pretty little sidekick told us everything.'

'Who?'

'How do I know her name? But we know all about the operation she's been running for you. She was very informative.'

It must be the Romanian. She must have been running some scam on the side and thought she could shift the blame on to him. She was dead. 'And you believed her?' Mihail Kalaj said.

'Why shouldn't we?' Bernie said.

'How did you find her?' Mihail said. Think, Mihail, think. Analyse the situation and decide. Quick. Now.

'Irrelevant,' Bernie said.

'Is it?' Mihail said. Think. Quick. Now.

'Hit him, Stevie.'

'No. Wait. Think.' Mihail held up his hand as if he was about to bless them. 'You must have found her because you discovered what was going on. I don't need to know how. You're right, that's irrelevant. But the one thing you know for certain is that she was doing whatever it was she was doing. You know that. That was how you found her.'

He saw the two men were listening. 'Put yourself in her place. If you got caught, wouldn't you try to blame someone else?'

'Shall I hit him anyway, Bernie?' the Englishman said.

'No. Wait. Not just yet. Can you prove it?'

'I can't prove it.' Mihail saw Bernie give a little nod as if to himself, as if he approved of this literal answer. 'But if you tell me what has been going on, I'll stop it. I don't want trouble with you. I don't know you. I have enough trouble with people I know already.'

Stevie laughed. 'He's got a point, Bernie.'

Bernie ignored him. 'Go on,' he said.

'I will stop it,' Mihail Kalaj said. 'And if I don't, come back. You can see, it's just me. I'm not very dangerous.'

Bernie looked at the nervy, skinny young man in front of him and his toy soldiers scattered over the floor. There was something about Kalaj that he recognised, trusted even. 'How long will it take you to stop it?' he said.

'If you tell me what it is, a day. No more than two.'

Bernie nodded again. 'OK,' he said and he explained about the casino.

'The little bitch,' Mihail said. 'I will kill her.'

'I thought you weren't very dangerous,' Stevie said and he laughed.

'Why?' Bernie said.

'She works for me but she was doing this on her own account. And no-one who works for me freelances. It only causes problems. Like this. I pay them. They work for me.'

'Right,' Stevie said.

'Never trust the staff.' Bernie said.

'Give me a day,' Mihail said. 'I will sort this out.'

'You know,' Bernie said, 'I do believe you will.'

'You won't be bothered again.'

'You know,' Bernie said, 'I do believe we won't be.'

'You should see to that bitch,' Stevie said.

And that was when Stepan chose to come into the room. And, oblivious of the bonding that was taking place, he saw the little Englishman with his gun still pointed loosely in the direction of his boss. And so he pulled out his Beretta 9000. And that was when Stevie pulled the trigger of the Glock and exploded half of Stepan's skull.

And then there was silence. 'Don't shoot,' Mihail said calmly and turned his hands palm outwards in an instinctive gesture of surrender. And then Bernie crumpled onto the floor.

'Bernie?' Stevie said, still looking at Mihail.

'I'm OK,' Bernie said. 'It's just my legs.' He tugged the helmet off his head. Then he started to breathe deeply. 'Oh no,' he said, looking down at his jacket. 'What's that?'

'Looks like bone,' Stevie said. 'And blood. That guy's blood.'

Bernie closed his eyes but the images stayed of Stepan's skull exploding and the wall spattered with fragments of bone and blood and the specks that dotted his leathers.

'Are we OK?' Mihail said carefully.

Bernie nodded. 'I'll be all right,' he said.

'No, I meant are we OK?' Mihail said.

Bernie opened his eyes and focused blearily on Mihail. 'Oh,' he said. 'I see. Yes. We're OK.'

'I'm sorry about Stepan. You won't be bothered again,' Mihail said. What a mess. That Romanian was one dead bitch.

'Come on, Stevie.' Bernie got to his feet and walked out of the room, trying to avoid stepping on any bits of Stepan. Behind him, he heard Stevie crunching over them. In the front garden, he stopped and took a deep breath of the chilly fresh air. And another one.

Dean, who had been waiting outside, stepped towards them. 'OK?' he said. 'I heard a shot.'

'No trouble,' Stevie said, blithely.

'Stevie just exploded a man's skull,' Bernie said.

Dean nodded. 'I thought it must be that,' he said.

'Are you sure you got the guarantee on the casino, Bernie?' Stevie said, putting the Glock back in his pocket.

'Fuck the casino,' Bernie said. 'I'm going back to LA.'

'It'll be another five grand,' Stevie said. 'For services rendered.'

Bernie said nothing but just stood in the front garden, breathing deeply.

'You didn't say anything about killing anyone,' Stevie said. 'And I didn't quote for saving your life.'

Bernie breathed deeply.

'Look, man, don't make me angry. Just pay me the ten grand.'

Dean stood grinning at the two of them.

'Whatever,' Bernie said. 'I am going back to LA. Now. I'll transfer it on the way to the airport.'

'I'm coming with you,' Stevie said. 'Until it's in the account. Don't make me cross.'

'Whatever,' Bernie said. Ken Singer had been right. That was the worst part of it. He was not meant to ride free. He was not born to be wild. He was an accountant and he wanted to go back to Los Angeles. Now.

ninety-six

Charlotte braked to avoid the car that had just pulled out in front of her and jammed her palm on the horn. She had to relax. She remembered the fragrance of the roses that Rob had given her for Christmas. She remembered whale songs in the Arctic. She visualised blood flowing in her veins like molasses. And she gripped the steering wheel. What was she meant to do when someone drove like that?

Breathe deep. Whale song and roses. Relax. This time she was not going to walk away. Story or not, she had to talk again to the woman with green eyes. If she stayed outside long enough, she might pass by again and this time, Charlotte would persuade her. And then she would get the police in. This was the right thing to do and she might still be able to keep the story alive.

She pulled into the road and cruised down it, looking for somewhere to park. Every day, Helen Borthwick made a difference, no matter how little or fleeting, to one or two people. And somehow, from somewhere in that grinding daily struggle, she found fulfilment. While Charlotte pursued so many abstract goals, career, the story, family, and achieved none of them. It was time to learn from Helen Borthwick. Her mobile phone rang and she pulled in three doors down from the house. It was Giles. Whale song and roses. Breathe deep. 'Yes?'

'It's me.'

'Yes.'

'It's stopped.'

'What?'

'Why are you so horrible to me, Charlotte?'

'Because you deserve it. What do you want?'

'To serve you.'

'Giles.'

'OK. OK. Don't hit me. The activity coming from that house has stopped.'

'What do you mean?'

'I'm not picking up anything any more. They've obviously shut it down. Just like that.'

Charlotte turned the engine off.

'Are you there?'

'Yes. I'm thinking.' They had gone and she had missed her opportunity. She should have gone immediately to the police.

'Can I help?'

'Yes. Shut up. How long has it been shut down?'

'Hard to say exactly. Three hours? Four. Not much longer than that.'

'Could it come back on again?'

'Could do, but I doubt it.'

'Why?'

'These people are smart. They know they've got limited time before people get on to them. People like me. The banks. The police. So usually they move on every few days. And then start up again somewhere else.'

'Will you know when they do? And where?'

'No.'

'Giles.'

'OK. I'll have to start all over again. They're not even likely to be attacking the same targets. It'll take another few weeks. And much as I love you, Charlotte, and I really think I do love you, I will have to charge you.'

'Goodbye, Giles.' Charlotte put the phone back in her pocket and looked out of the window. If she had not seen anyone go in or out in an hour, she would go and ring the bell. Nothing would happen to her on a doorstep in Southgate. And then she would know if there was still anyone there. But it was not looking good.

Charlotte turned the radio on. This was a sign. Her attempt to do the right thing had failed because she had been too slow to recognise what she should do. She must learn to move the moment she knew it was the right thing to do. And then she leant forward and peered through the windscreen. Who was that coming down the road? He looked familiar. And yes it was him. She had forgotten all about him. But here, bustling down the road, looking purposeful, came that lawyer, Martin Hughes.

ninety-seven

Mihail Kalaj was still trembling. That little English bastard. He would handcuff his arms and legs and put him in a bath of sulphuric acid and watch him burn. 'Boris,' he yelled. 'Get here now.' He heard him stomping up the stairs.

'Have you finished yet?'

'The car is outside, Mr Kalaj,' Boris said and wiped the sweat off his brow.

'Get rid of him.' Mihail Kalaj flicked his hand towards Stepan who still lay on the floor by the doorway. 'And clean up the mess.'

'Yes, Mr Kalaj.'

'And get rid of the Albanian as well.'

'Now?'

'Yes. Now.'

Mihail Kalaj heard him stomp off down the hallway and then he heard the sigh and putter of the silenced pistol. What a waste of money. He was still not certain whether Florian had betrayed him but he could not take the risk. And the beetles had finally worked their way through his right hand. So if he lived that would mean expensive operations and a long convalescence and, worst of all, intrusive questions from doctors and who knows who. Mihail Kalaj had never seen the beetles get so far into a body. It was disgusting. Usually, people owned up quicker. But the Albanian had never said anything. He was either innocent or stupid. Possibly both. Either way, it was not worth keeping him on.

Boris came back and stood in the doorway.

'Come on,' Mihail Kalaj said.

Boris put his hands under Stepan's shoulders and started to lug him out of the room.

'Hey,' Mihail Kalaj said. 'Look what you're doing.'

Boris stopped and looked at him.

'Look at the floor, kopuk.'

Boris looked at the dark red smears where he had been dragging the body. He dropped Stepan back on to the floor, without saying anything and then Mihail Kalaj heard him plodding off downstairs. He returned with a large black plastic bag and bundled Stepan into it and hauled it out of the room.

Mihail Kalaj heard it bumping down the stairs. He stood up and walked over to the window. Boris had backed the car up the driveway and opened the boot. Good Boris. No-one passing by or watching from an upstairs window across the street could have seen what was going on. As he watched, Boris appeared out of the front door. Somehow he had managed to stuff Stepan fully inside the black plastic bag. Good Boris.

And then Boris was back in the room with a cloth and a bottle of bleach. He knelt down and mopped at the blood on the carpet. Mihail Kalaj took out his wallet and counted out a thousand pounds. Twenty fifty-pound notes. 'Here,' he said.

Boris stopped mopping and looked up at him. Then he took the money, without saying anything and put it in his pocket and then went on scrubbing at the carpet. The acrid smell of bleach filled the room.

Mihail Kalaj walked over to the window. No-one was in the street. He could just see the edge of the black bag in the boot of the car. Then the noise of scrubbing stopped and when he turned round, Boris had gone. And then Mihail Kalaj heard him grunting as he lugged Florian downstairs and then he saw him putting another large black plastic bag in the boot of the car and slamming it shut.

Good Boris.

ninety-eight

Martin rang the bell. No answer. He rang it again. Still nothing. He pushed the front door and it opened.

'Martin.'

He heard her voice calling him from the kitchen down the hallway. He closed the front door behind him. On his way to the kitchen he glimpsed a man in a black leather jacket in the living room, sitting on a chair, with his back to the door, fastening a buckle on a boot. He trod more carefully as he went past the open door but the man seemed preoccupied with what he was doing.

She was standing by the window, facing him. She smiled her soft, sad smile as he came in from the hallway. Through the window, the garden was bright in the winter moonlight.

'Mila,' he said. 'Are you OK?' Refracted light cast pale shadows on her face.

'I'm fine, Martin,' she said. 'Thank you.'

'I've been thinking,' he said. 'You know what I said about alerting Interpol to look after your mother. They could protect her until you get back to Romania to take care of her. While the police here pick up this gang.' As he spoke, he felt once again the force of his logic sweeping them along. 'Come with me now,' he said. 'If we go out through the garden, we can avoid that man in the leather jacket back there.'

'It's not as easy as that,' she said gently.

'I know you're worried,' he said, 'but don't be.' He stepped towards her and took her hands in his. 'The police will know how to handle this,' he said. 'It will be all right. It will be.'

'No, Martin,' she said. 'It really isn't as easy as that.'

And then Martin heard something rustle behind him and he knew it was the man in leathers. He dropped Mila's hands and turned round. And there was the man from the church pointing a gun at his head. In the sudden clarity of that terrible moment, Martin saw the stainless-steel barrel glinting in the pale light.

'I'm sorry, Martin,' Mila said.

And as she spoke, he noticed her eyes were half closed, slurred in her face. It was the same look he had seen, blurred and indistinct, in the passport of Marian Hart. How had he not made the connection?

And then he knew she had been expecting this. She was not a victim. This was her operation. She was the boss and now there was something final in her voice.

'You can see, Martin,' she said, 'it's not so easy,' and she nodded sadly, as if she could hear him thinking.

And his brain was racing on, in this moment of revelation, careering through the tragedies of the last two weeks, and suddenly, intuitively, putting the pieces together. She had got Viktor killed. He must have discovered what she was doing. And Chris Finlay, the unforgivable witness.

And then all the tension and worry that had been simmering inside Martin gathered itself and rose unstoppably and crested in fury. As Gabriel squeezed the trigger, Martin launched himself at him, bellowing with rage. Somewhere he heard the soft crack of the gun as he landed on the leather jacket and down they went on the floor together, Martin beating him with his fists. And beating him. And beating him. Gabriel put his hands over his face and the sight of this inflamed Martin further and drove him into a new frenzy of punching and pummelling. He was shouting but he did not recognise the words that were coming from the well of anger inside him.

And then he sensed Mila scrabbling on the floor to the side of him. The gun. Where was the gun that Gabriel had dropped as Martin fell on him? He looked round. Where was it? And there it was. Under the chair. And Mila was reaching for it. Martin lunged at it and got his hand round the handle. It was ridged plastic and his finger slid round the trigger.

'I've got it,' he yelled. 'I've got the gun. Get back. Get back.' Mila stood up slowly and backed away, one, two, delicate, careful paces backwards, as if practising a dance step in slow motion.

'It's all right, Martin,' she said, calming him. 'It's all right. Be careful with the gun. Everything will be all right.'

Martin stood up slowly, breathing heavily. Pain was beginning to struggle through the shock. His hands were stinging and he had bruised his ribs in the fall, his heart was thudding against his chest and his head was throbbing in time as the blood pounded through his body.

'Don't move,' he said, pointing the gun at Mila. His hand was trembling.

Gabriel moved on the floor, as if he was trying to sit up.

'Don't move,' Martin shouted. 'I mean it. Don't move,' and he turned the gun round to point it at the man on the floor. Gabriel stopped moving.

'It's not what you think, Martin,' Mila said.

'No,' he said and pointed the gun at her again. 'Don't move.' He needed to think. He pointed the gun back at Gabriel and then at Mila. And back and forth between them, he aimed the gun. He was not sure he could stop his hands shaking. But the gun was comfortably solid and his fingers fitted snugly round the ridged plastic handle. Yet now his legs were trembling. 'You did it, didn't you?' he said. 'You killed Viktor. And Chris Finlay?'

'No, Martin, I did not.' She widened her green eyes as he spoke, looking at him with the calm intensity he remembered.

'Don't,' he said. 'Don't.' He had to force the words out. 'Don't play games with me.' How could he make the words make sense? 'You may not have killed him yourself. Not actually yourself. But you got it done. Didn't you?' He looked at Gabriel on the floor. 'He did it, didn't he?'

'It's not as simple as that, Martin,' she said. 'We all have a job to do and sometimes that means we have to do things we don't want to do.'

The humiliation of being duped must have been visible in his face because Mila said, 'Martin, Martin,' and looked at him with such warmth and love that he thought he was going mad. He could not stop his legs trembling. He looked round and sat down on the chair. And as he did so, he glimpsed Mila looking away from him and towards Gabriel, imperceptibly nodding her head at him. And as she did so, Gabriel started to get up and Martin turned and squeezed the trigger.

For the rest of his life, he lived every fraction of that second over and over again. He had never intended to fire the gun but as Gabriel was yanked into action by Mila's nod, a visceral instinct clicked back the trigger and then, as the gun fired, it kicked back, and his hand jerked, and he heard the flat breath of the bullet, and then he saw Gabriel crumple back on the floor. And that was it. Gabriel did not move again. He was dead. Martin had killed him.

'You shouldn't have done that, Martin,' Mila said, standing still, watching him. 'He meant you no harm. You've murdered him.'

'Don't move,' he said.

'You're in trouble, Martin,' she said. 'Let me help you.' She stretched out a hand towards him. 'It's a shock when someone gets killed. Now you must give me the gun before any other accidents happen. This was an accident, you know. When the police come we'll tell them it was an accident. But you mustn't be holding the gun when they arrive. You must give it to me.' She was talking rapidly, without pausing, without giving him time to think. And he needed to think.

Now she stepped towards him, one little step, with her hands outstretched. 'Please, Martin, you must let me help you.' Her tone was lulling him to relax and now his blood was slowing down. 'Just give me the gun before any more damage gets done.'

She was right. How could this have happened? How could he have done this? It had to stop now before anything else happened. Mila was right. He was not in control of himself.

She took another small careful step towards him. 'Come on, Martin. Just let me take it.'

'Stop. Let me think. Don't move, Mila, don't move.' But she kept going. Another small step and then she was stretching out to put her hand round the barrel.

'Stop,' he said.

And she paused, her hand halfway to the gun, as if she thought he meant it. Her eyes stared into his. 'Think,' she said. 'Martin, think about this. Think about Clare.'

Martin felt his eyes flicker away from her gaze. What had Clare got to do with this?

'If you calm down,' Mila said, 'there's no reason why Clare need ever get involved. I know you care about her, Martin. Just think of Clare,' and her hand reached out once again and grasped the barrel of the gun.

'Step back, Mila. Please step back.' But she kept her hand on the barrel and gave it a gentle tug. And then another one. And then he realised she was trying to take it out of his hand. And then he realised that she was going to kill him.

He knew the moment he squeezed the trigger again and heard the simultaneous quiet snick of the bullet that it was going to miss. It was going to fly between her arm and her body and hit the wall and shatter a lamp.

But it didn't.

In the same second, he saw her eyes staring at him and there was nothing in them. No fear. No surprise. They were just staring at him. And in that same second, he knew his life was going to change forever.

And then the bullet hit the window and the glass cracked and then it shattered and the crystal tears exploded over the table and the floor.

'Hello,' a voice called. 'Who's there?' Charlotte had come in from the hallway at the end of this terrifying conversation, feeling unable to interrupt, but now she felt she should alert them to her presence. 'Hello?' she said.

Mila let go of the gun and stared astonished at Martin. 'You tried to kill me,' she said. And Martin knew she was right.

'Hello?' Charlotte said again. Mila didn't look like she needed Helen Borthwick's help after all. There was a groan and Martin and Mila and Charlotte all turned to look at Gabriel who had shifted on the floor.

'Get up,' Mila said.

'My leg,' he said.

'Move,' Mila said and Charlotte and Martin watched as Gabriel obediently placed his hands on the edge of the table and pulled himself up.

'Come on,' Mila said impatiently and Gabriel limped heavily out of the room behind her.

Martin was still holding the Ruger, pointed towards the window, where Mila had been standing. They heard her running down the hall and Gabriel struggling along behind her and then the front door was slammed.

'Golly,' Charlotte said. 'You have been busy.'

They heard a motorbike start. 'I think your girl-friend's gone,' Charlotte said. 'And your victim.'

Martin realised that Mila had been planning for her and Gabriel to disappear on the motorbike parked outside as soon as they had killed him. That had been why Gabriel had been fastening the buckle on his boot when Martin arrived. Ready to go.

'Lucky you didn't kill them,' Charlotte said. 'Murder can damage a career.' This was a better story than she could ever have imagined. 'What happened?'

'She killed him.'

'Martin, wake up. They both just left.'

'She killed him.'

'I think you'll find it hard to persuade the police of that when we just saw him leave with her, alive.'

'No.' Martin finally looked up at Charlotte. 'Not him. She killed Viktor. And Chris Finlay. And then they tried to kill me.'

'You better sit down,' she said. 'You look as if you're going to faint.' And suddenly she felt fond of this ashen lawyer trembling before her.

'What happened?' she said. And, as he explained, she took notes. This barrister had just tried to kill a gangster and the woman. And he said the woman had murdered two others. Even Maggie would have to see there was a story in this.

'How could anyone be like that?' Martin said. He sat in the chair staring out into the garden. What was going to become of him? The horror of Mila. 'He was such a good man. How could anyone have done that?'

Charlotte felt in her handbag. 'Here,' she said, 'take this,' and she handed Martin a handkerchief. 'Blow your nose. You'll feel better.' He was right. How could anyone have done that? But this was bad news for the lawyer and he didn't deserve it. He had only been trying to help.

She tapped her pad with her pen as she thought. This was now her choice. If she told the police what had happened, this man could go to jail. Attempted murder. And no evidence of self-defence. He was in their house and he had fired at them and no-one seemed to have fired at him. And Mila would lie till Christmas to get him put away. He could go down for ten years or more. And for what? But if she wrote up the story, without first talking to the police, Martin Hughes could still go to jail. And for what? The story would be chip paper in twenty-four hours, and these people deserved everything they got. And this lawyer didn't deserve what would happen to him in the hands of the law.

'You need to get out of here,' she said. The time had come for her to stop being a spectator. Screw the story. The dark woman had not needed rescuing but Charlotte could still help the lawyer. Charlotte was making a choice.

'I must call the police,' Martin said.

'No, you mustn't,' Charlotte said. 'You must go.' And now she was assuming responsibility for her choice.

'I must ring the police,' he said and he put his hand inside his pocket and rummaged around for his phone.

'And if you ring them, they'll arrest you for attempted murder,' Charlotte said. 'Is that part of your plan?'

He looked at her. 'But they're gangsters,' he said. 'They tried to kill me.'

'Who says?' she said. 'You're holding the gun. And you're in their house.'

'But it's his gun,' Martin said.

'With your fingerprints all over it,' she said. Her decision was made. Up close to this tragedy, she did not care any more about the story. Or Maggie. Finally, she did not care. Now all she wanted was to do the right thing and go home. She could already taste the salt on the Tarifa breeze. They would sort the mortgage out later.

Martin put his hands over his eyes. Charlotte was right, of course. He was finished, another victim of Mila's wanton malevolence. She had done for him too.

'Come on,' Charlotte said. 'It's not that bad. Let's sort this out. First we need to get out of here. Out the front door, head down and off we go and let's hope no-one's looking out the window. Round here I doubt they will be. And anyway half the streetlights are out.'

Martin raised his head to look at her. Was she mad? What was this cheerful tone when he had narrowly avoided killing two people? And Mila had escaped, who knew where, to wreak who knew what new havoc?

'I must ring the police,' he said dully. What had she meant about involving Clare? It was obviously a threat but to do what? Had Mila meant she was going to kill her, if he hadn't done what she wanted?

'We'll wipe the door handles as we go,' Charlotte said. 'And any other forensics will be ambiguous. But you do need to get rid of the gun. Now, how should you do that?' She reflected on the problem.

'We can't do this,' Martin said. 'We must ring the police.' But, even as he spoke, he finally realised Charlotte was right. He did not regret what he had done. And, worse, he was sorry he had missed the man in leathers. He had deserved to die. And worst of all, he still wanted to kill Mila. How had he got like this?

'I know,' Charlotte said. 'Chuck it in the canal. Find somewhere a long way away. But where?'

'Stop it,' Martin said but he knew he didn't mean it.

'Yes, that's it,' Charlotte said, ignoring him. 'Go to Southall and down the towpath there. The Grand Union Canal goes all the way to Birmingham and no-one is going to trawl the whole of that. Anyway it's too far from here for anyone to think of searching there. You get yourself down there. Take the Tube and chuck it in. That should do it. Goodbye.'

Martin looked at her. Her energetic determination was infectious. Why not? After all, why not? All his life he had done the right thing and look where it had got him. Why not?

'As long as we don't leave anything obvious here, I don't think anyone's going to bother too much about those people,' Charlotte said.

Martin got up and put the gun in his pocket. From the moment he had walked through the door, the button had been pushed. There had been no choice. If he had not fired the gun, the man in leathers would have killed him. And now he knew he had no choice but to write – anonymously – to Inspector Walton about Mila. Not justice as he had known it but, in its own way, it would be done. It was turning out to be frighteningly easy to work beyond the frontier.

'Come on,' Charlotte said. 'Stop fretting. It's good riddance. Who's going to waste any time on them? Come on, I've got to go and pick up my son.'

Martin felt the gun in his pocket. Something was still troubling him. What had Mila meant about involving Clare? He could understand it if she had threatened Suzana, who was a witness. But she hadn't. And Clare wasn't a witness so why had Mila mentioned her? There could be no doubt that she was threatening her, but why? Perhaps he shouldn't get rid of the gun just yet.

ninety-nine

Mihail Kalaj packed the Warhammers neatly away in their box. Time to go. Boris had gone to dispose of Stepan and Florian after scrubbing the house down. All set to move on. They would get settled in the new house in Newham and then they would deal with that Romanian bitch and her little operation.

This had been a bad twenty-four hours. He had known she was up to something but not what and now her treachery had got Stepan killed. He had been a good worker and he had deserved better. And the little bitch was probably responsible for the trouble with Florian as well. He might have been trash but, as it turned out, he probably hadn't deserved the beetles.

Into the neat acrylic container went the Knights of Chaos and the Beastmen and WhipMaul and the Beastlord Gorthor and Warfiend and Asarnil the DragonLord. War was hell, Mihail Kalaj knew that, and there were always casualties. But why had that little Romanian bitch done this? Stepan. Florian. He would have to replace both of them. She was one dead Romanian. With beetles. Where was Boris? He should have been back by now. He fastened the lid on the box and then the bell rang.

Why was Boris ringing the bell? 'Come in,' he yelled down the stairs, 'you Greek donkey.' He heard the door open and then the steps coming rapidly up the stairs. Boris was in a hurry. And then into the room came a policeman in a kevlar vest, pointing a gun at his head, followed by a tall blond man and another policeman levelling a gun at him. And then two more armed policemen.

'Don't move,' the blond man said.

'Do I look as if I'm moving?' Mihail Kalaj said. 'Who are you?' What had happened to Boris?

'What's your name?' the tall blond man said.

'Stepan Mihailovic,' Mihail Kalaj said. 'What's yours?'

'I am Detective Inspector Walton,' the tall blond man said. 'Where is Mihail Kalaj?'

'Out.'

'All right,' Inspector Walton said to the other policemen. 'You two look round the back. And you two,' indicating them, 'stay here with me.' He sat down opposite Mihail Kalaj. 'You and I, Stepan Mihailovic, will wait here until Mr Kalaj gets back.' At least the little runt had not denied that Kalaj lived here. The email had been right about that.

The two armed policemen stood by the door and Inspector Walton sat contemplating Mihail Kalaj. 'When is he coming back?' he said. He sensed in his bones this was the breakthrough. He had not been able to trace the source of the email from LoveGain but it had given so much detail about the Kalaj operation which tied up with other sources that it must be reliable and here he was in the lair, waiting for him to return. At last. Dave Harmsworth would be sick.

'I don't know,' Mihail Kalaj said. 'He didn't say.'

Inspector Walton looked round the room. 'Have you lived here long, Mr Mihailovic?' he said.

'Not long.'

'What's that mark there?'

'What?'

'That small, dark mark on the floor.' Inspector Walton knelt down and peered down at it. 'It looks like blood.'

'Nothing to do with me.' Kalaj said. That lazy donkey must have missed some of it.

'That's as may be, sir,' Inspector Walton said. 'But I think you'll still need to come back to the station with us and answer a few questions.'

There was a noise outside. Someone else was coming up the stairs. The armed policemen tensed and one of them took his Glock out of the holster.

'All done,' Boris said as he came through the door and then stopped as he saw the policemen. He put his hands in the air. 'OK,' he said. 'It's OK.'

'And who are you?' Clive Walton said.

Boris looked at Kalaj.

'It's all right, Boris,' Kalaj said. 'These policemen are here looking for Mihail Kalaj. And I've told them he's gone out.' He hoped the peasant understood.

'So, Boris,' Clive Walton said. 'When do you think Mihail Kalaj is going to be back?'

Again Boris glanced at Mihail Kalaj. He shrugged. 'I don't know,' he said.

Kalaj nodded. He had got it. Good Boris.

'What's your other name, Boris?' Clive Walton said.
'Istogu.'

'Well, Boris Istogu, do you know anything about this?' Clive Walton pointed towards the stain on the floor. 'It looks like blood to me. What does it look like to you, Boris Istogu?'

Boris peered at it. 'I don't know,' he said.

'That's funny,' Clive Walton said. 'Here's this stain, which looks like blood to me, and you don't know anything about it. And neither does Mr Mihailovic here. Now I would have thought that someone would know something about blood on the floor and how it might have got there. Seeing as you live here and all that.'

Kalaj stared at Boris. Shut up, donkey. Do not say a word. But Boris was looking at the policeman and he started to speak.

'We don't live here,' Kalaj said quickly before Boris could say anything. 'We're just visiting. We only just came. What was it, Boris? Ten minutes ago.' He stared at him willing him to get the message. 'That's it, isn't it, Boris? Isn't it?'

'Yes, Mr Kalaj,' Boris said. He didn't like all this pressure suddenly being put upon him, just when he had thought they were on their way.

Kalaj glared at him. Fuck. Was this his reward for giving the peasant a break? He leaves blood on the floor and now the piss-addled donkey had just landed them in jail.

'OK, you two, I think you should come back to the station with us now,' Clive Walton said. 'We've got a lot to talk about. Me and you, Mr Istogu and Mr Mihailovic.'

The two armed policemen moved behind Kalaj and Boris, their hands on their guns. Kalaj felt the tension begin to seep away. They hadn't realised what Boris had just said. English policemen were as stupid as Greek donkeys and he had survived Boris's fuck-ups. His luck had turned.

Clive Walton paused in the doorway and turned round to look at Boris.

'What did you call him?' he said.

one hundred

'Clare,' Martin whispered through the door. No answer. His finger hovered over the bell. It would wake Megan and Suzana and then Clare would have to get them back to sleep. 'Clare,' he said again, more loudly. Still no reply. He tapped on the door. She must have gone to bed. He rang the bell. He had no choice. He had to talk to her and make sure she was safe and he guessed, after their last conversation, she wouldn't talk to him on the phone. Nothing stirred. He rang the bell again and now he heard a movement inside the flat.

'Who is it?' Clare called through the door.

'Me,' Martin said. 'I need to talk to you.'

'Do you know what time it is?'

'It's urgent. Please, Clare, open the door. I need to talk to you.'

'I'm asleep. Ring me tomorrow.'

'Please, Clare. It's important.'

'What you want is always important to you, Martin. But other things are important to other people. Ring me tomorrow. I'm going back to bed.'

He banged on the door. 'Don't go,' he pleaded. 'I really need to talk to you.'

'And, at this time of the night, I really do not need any lame apology from you for missing the Advent concert,' she said.

He tapped on the door again. 'Please,' he said.

'Don't bang on the door,' she said. 'You'll wake the children. I've heard your pathetic excuse about some mysterious drama already. You rang me, remember? If you really want to tell me more, do it tomorrow.'

'It's not an excuse.' Martin was stung. How could she be so obtuse? How could she have forgotten what had happened to Viktor? 'I was at the concert. And then I nearly got killed. And so did you.'

On the other side of the door, Clare laughed. 'Oh Martin,' she said. 'You must be desperate. Look, I forgive you. Let's take Suzana to the airport tomorrow and talk on the way back.'

And there it was. He was caught. Martin stared at the door. While he had been drawn deeper and deeper into Viktor's nightmare, her life had reverted to its everyday routines and concerns. He could see that, right now, the more he tried to explain what had happened, the more she would think he was constructing an elaborate fantasy as an excuse for missing the Advent concert. He needed time to explain what really happened and this was not the time. Although he thought the danger from Mila had passed, it was important Clare knew what had happened. He did not want there to be any secrets between them as they began their life together again.

'It's true,' he protested. But as he spoke, he realised that the explanation could wait till the morning. Mila and her man would presumably now be occupied in looking for ways to escape. Clare would hardly be the most pressing item on their agenda at the moment. And he needed to get this right. She had to believe him and understand so they could rebuild their life together.

'Make sure all the doors are locked,' he called. 'And don't go outside until I arrive.'

'See you tomorrow,' Clare said.

one hundred and one

'That's her.' Neat, sandy-haired Robert Wood was staring at the passengers coming out into the Arrivals Hall. He was wearing his black woollen overcoat, and, under his arm, he was still carrying a thin black leather briefcase.

'Where?' Martin couldn't see anyone who might be Viktor's sister.

'There,' Robert Wood said. 'Coming up to us now. In the green coat.'

Martin had been looking for someone around Viktor's age, expecting a proud, handsome woman, not this diminutive billowing matron in late middle age. 'Here's your auntie,' he said, bending down towards Suzana.

'Where?' she said and Martin realised that she didn't remember anything about her life in the former Yugoslavia.

'Let's go and say hello,' he said. She held Martin's hand, in the new coat he had bought her to meet her aunt. It was mauve, with a hood to keep out the Bosnian snow. The pink raincoat had been part of her terrible time in London and he didn't want her to take it back to Sarajevo.

'Hello, Mrs Vukovic,' Robert Wood said, stepping forward.

'Good morning, Mr Wood,' she said. Her voice was deep and she spoke English with a throaty accent. 'And you must be Mr Hughes,' she said, offering her hand to Martin. 'I am Sonja Vukovic.'

'Please,' Martin said, 'call me Martin.' He shook her hand.

Sonja Vukovic bent down to Suzana. 'Hello,' she said.

'Hello.' Suzana put out her hand like her aunt had just done to Martin.

And Sonja Vukovic smiled and put her arms round the little girl and hugged her and lifted her up, saying something in a language Martin couldn't understand. And as he watched, he saw tears rolling down the woman's face.

Robert Wood had only taken a week to find her. When they met at the airport, he had handed over his report to Martin and an invoice in a separate envelope. 'That was quick,' Martin said.

'It wasn't difficult,' Robert Wood said. 'It's not a big place and he was well known.' He paused. 'He was a good man,' he said and Martin guessed this quiet efficient investigator never usually went as far as this in expressing an opinion about his work.

Sonja Vukovic put Suzana down again and said something to her in the language Martin didn't understand. 'Where is Mrs Fletcher?' she said.

'She couldn't come,' Martin said. 'She said she was sorry.' And so was he. They needed to talk.

'It's me who's sorry,' Sonja Vukovic said. 'I wanted to thank her.'

'I'll tell her,' Martin said.

When he had turned up in the taxi to go to the airport, Clare was rushing to get Megan to school. 'I'm sorry,' she had said. 'I couldn't find anyone to take her. I'm sorry, you'll have to go on your own.'

'But we really need to talk,' he said. 'Why don't you both come?'

Clare shook her head. 'Martin,' she said, 'no.'

And then he realised she wanted to spare Megan a prolonged farewell at the airport. 'I'm sorry,' he said. 'I didn't think.'

'Goodbye, Suzana,' Clare had said, folding the pretty, tragic little girl in her arms.

'Goodbye, Suzana,' Megan had said.

'Go on,' Clare said. 'Give her a kiss,' and the little girl stepped forward and carefully put her arms round her friend.

'Goodbye,' Suzana had said. Nothing else.

'Can I see you after I get back from the airport?' Martin said to Clare.

'I need to be at the gallery,' she said. 'The exhibition's opening in two days.'

'Can I meet you there at six?' he had said. 'It is really important.'

'And you are really controlling,' she had said. 'We're going to Jenny's tonight. Remember? And I'll need to get ready. We can talk there.'

And so Martin had accepted defeat. This was too important for controlling to become the issue. He needed Clare to listen and not argue about who was bossing who. They would talk at Jenny's. Suzana would shortly be on her way to safety and nothing was going to happen to Clare in the next few hours. 'OK,' he had said.

'There are two hours before our flight leaves,' Sonja Vukovic said to Martin. 'Can I invite you to coffee?'

'I'll say goodbye now,' Robert Wood said.

'I'd love a coffee,' Martin said and as he walked with Suzana, solemnly holding her aunt's hand, he wondered whether he would ever see this little girl again. She had been such a part of his life for the last two months and what would happen to her now? She was safe and that was a start. But what would she ever remember about her mother? And her father and their short sad stay in London? Where would her life take her now?

'I got English money in Sarajevo,' Sonja Vukovic said, beaming proudly. 'You see I came ready to buy you coffee.'

'Thank you,' Martin said. What would Clare make of everything that had happened? Would she even believe him? Would she think he was mad?

Sonja Vukovic handed a coffee to Martin. 'Did you know my brother well?' Sonja asked.

'Not really,' Martin said.

'You were a good friend, anyway,' she said. 'Thank you.'

Martin nodded. Whatever Clare thought, he now knew he had to ask her tonight. The time had come. Somehow this tragic saga had worked its way out and he needed to get on with his life. Whether or not the inspector ever found Mila and gathered enough evidence to prosecute her, or whether she had slipped away to ply her trade in some other country, she would have more urgent matters than coming after him or Clare, whatever she had said last night.

His phone rang. 'Why haven't you called me back?' Ben said.

'Sorry,' Martin said. 'I've been a bit busy.' Sonja Vukovic watched him as he spoke.

'Slow down. Come and join me,' Ben said.

'Sorry,' Martin said.

'Don't apologise,' Ben said. 'I'm only returning your call. What did you want?'

'Nothing,' Martin said. 'The moment's passed.' And, as he spoke, he knew that it had. The idea that he would escape the Bar to work with Ben had been part of the feverish hysteria of those terrible few days, punctured by that last, horrifying evening with Mila. Now the fever had drained away, leaving him exhausted and flat and he needed all his energy now for the great change that was going to take place in his life. He had decided he was going to ask Clare to marry him. Tonight. 'I'll call you,' he said to Ben and rang off.

Suzana slurped the remnants of her milkshake up through the straw, concentrating furiously on ensuring she did not miss a drop. Sonja Vukovic watched her fondly and Martin smiled.

'Is it good, Suzana?' he asked. So much had changed. How could he ever become a judge now, knowing what he had done, not ever being certain that, one day, someone would not catch up with him? The more eminent his position, the higher his profile, the more vulnerable he would become. Could he really trust that journalist to remain silent forever? Would she really be able to resist such a good story? And how could he live with himself, dispensing justice while knowing he had broken the law he was pledged to uphold? He could never slip back into his old life as if none of this had ever happened but, as he sat with Sonja Vukovic and Suzana sipping airport coffee, he realised he did not care. His life was with Clare. That was the one sure thing.

Sonja got up. 'We will leave now. Thank you again, Mr Hughes.' She took Suzana's hand. Martin bent down to kiss her. Something was ending and, to his surprise, he realised he felt liberated. Suddenly, knowing he could never reach the goal for which he had worked so long, it was possible to imagine a new life when he did not need to clear his diary every time Phil Matthews came in with a new brief, when weekends were empty of work and full of outings with Clare and Megan. And, as he visualised it, he decided to ask Clare to marry him before he explained what had happened last night. That was the right way round. It would demonstrate his commitment to her. Then she would understand the story of Mila and Viktor in its proper context of their new life together.

'Goodbye, Suzana,' Martin said and he watched as the little girl walked off hand in hand with the portly white-haired lady, across the airport concourse, getting smaller and smaller, until he lost them in the crowds.

one hundred and two

A large fire crackled in the grate and wisps of wood smoke and scents of cinnamon and roast meat drifted through the room filled with the hospitable hum of conversation. Every year, before Christmas, Jenny and David held a buffet supper for their wider circle of friends, stretching out their generous arms to gather in all those not yet graduated to the dinner parties.

'Hello, Martin,' Polly said, giving him a swift kiss on both cheeks. 'How are you? I'm sorry we didn't get a chance to talk properly at the concert.'

'Yes,' he said. Where was Clare?

'Still looking for her?' Polly asked sympathetically. 'Here,' she said. 'Let me do this for you,' and she took his tie and tightened the knot. 'There. That's better. That's my Martin. Who can resist?'

The vein in his temple tightened. Why did women like Polly patronise him like this? Would she do it if she knew he had a neat little Ruger in his pocket? He did not dare leave it anywhere and now he was getting used to its solid weight against his thigh. 'I'm going to get a drink,' he said.

'Good luck,' she said, flashing a conspiratorial smile.

Martin nodded. It was psychedelic knowing the trigger had been pulled and no-one was coming after

him. He made his way through the crowd towards the
kitchen. He needed alcohol. And then Clare.

'Hello, Martin. All right?' David clapped his hand
on Martin's shoulder. 'Get yourself a drink. Mingle.'

'Happy Christmas, David.' Would they treat him
differently if they knew he had nearly killed two people
and had the Ruger in his pocket?

As he worked his way through the mass of people, he
heard fragments of conversation. A tall thin man was
explaining a refinancing deal. A pretty girl with red hair
was talking about a new commission from Channel 4.
An earnest man with a large nose was spelling out, with
great enthusiasm, how his life had been transformed by
his baby daughter. The usual hubbub of one of Jenny's
parties. 'Matraca Berg wrote such great songs,' he
heard a man say. 'I never understood why her solo
career didn't take off.'

By the entrance to the kitchen, there was a small
huddle of people. 'Did you hear about the terrible thing
that happened to that father at St Luke's?' one of them
said. Behind him, the crowd had reformed into a solid
mass at Martin's back. He was trapped between them
and the kitchen door.

'Who?' a man said.

'Viktor Markov. You know that tall man with a
beard. His daughter was in Lucy's class. Clare's been
looking after her,' a plump woman said. Liz, that was
her name.

'What happened?'

'He was murdered. It was like a drive-by shooting. A
hit. Professionals apparently,' Liz said. 'I'm not sur-

prised. There was always something funny about him. Violent. I bumped into his daughter at the school fair, just a little bump, it was an accident but I think he would have killed me if someone hadn't hauled him away. I was terrified.'

'Excuse me,' Martin muttered and edged his way through the conversation into the kitchen. This must be how soldiers felt returning from war, haunted by nightmares of blood and mud that civilians could never share.

'What do you want, my boy?' A stout man with a grey beard stood proprietorially behind a sparkling array of bottles.

'Something serious,' Martin said.

As he came out from the kitchen with a tumbler of Southern Suicide – 'Bourbon, Southern Comfort, orange juice and lemonade, dear boy,' the grey beard had said – he saw Marc. 'Aaron's essentiality,' he was saying, 'is ironic.'

Martin looked away to avoid catching his eye. And then he saw Clare. She was standing in a small group in the middle of the living room, smiling politely as the pretty girl with red hair was telling a story. And as he watched her as she listened, he began to feel he was coming home. Seeing her auburn hair falling to her shoulders, remembering the softness of her skin, reminded him of the good things in his life. What had happened to him was extraordinary but it was over. It did not define him. It was part of his history but everyone had histories that stayed buried.

'Hello,' he said, coming up beside Clare. 'How have you been?' He could never have imagined the twists and turns his life had taken in the last month and he could never undo or forget them. But he had escaped and they were not going to shape his future. Clare was.

'Good,' she said and took his arm. 'Come and sit with me. I need to ask you something.'

'And I need to ask you something,' he said. Around them, the party swirled and chattered as they found space on a sofa.

'Eat,' Jenny said, coming up to them and handing Martin a plate of walnut and ricotta quiche.

Martin swallowed another mouthful of Southern Suicide. 'Thank you,' he said. 'That looks delicious.'

'Leave us, Jenny,' Clare said. 'We're busy.'

'We are, are we?' Jenny said but she disappeared into the crowd.

'Shall we sit in the garden?' Martin said. 'We won't get disturbed there.'

'We'll just freeze to death,' Clare said as she followed him. Outside, clouds drifted across a cold moon and somewhere in the distance a siren wailed. Clare snuggled up to Martin. 'I've been thinking,' she said as she leaned against him. 'And I've decided I need to ask you something.' She felt for his hand and held it.

'Please let me say it first,' he said. 'I've been thinking too. And I know I haven't always shown you how much I love you and Megan. And the last few weeks have made me realise it and how much I want to spend the rest of my life with you. And I know I need to show you that. And this is the time.' He paused. 'Will you marry me?' he said.

Clare sat up. 'That wasn't what I was going to ask you,' she said and then she laughed. 'Oh don't look so hurt, Martin. I'm just surprised.' She kissed him. Suddenly she knew it was the right thing to do. He was a good man and she would find a way to keep a check on his need to control everything. They'd manage. 'I've been thinking so much about you,' she said. 'And this. And you're right. This is the time. So yes. Please. Yes, yes. Please.'

Martin cupped her face in his hand and placed his lips on hers and kissed her. 'My darling,' he said. 'Clare.' Wisps of music drifted out from the party and a cat screeched in one of the neighbouring gardens.

'What were you going to ask me?' he said. Him and Clare was how it used to be. Him steadily building his career was how it used to be. Him secure in the dignity of the law and its profession was how it used to be. Him comfortable in the company of his friends was how it used to be. And now it could all be again. Or most of it.

'I need your advice,' she said. 'It's a bit delicate.'

'Ask,' he said and kissed her again.

'I've been helping Mila,' she said. 'What's the matter? Why are you looking like that?' she said.

'What kind of help?' Martin said.

'She asked me to open a bank account for her and so I did and she's been giving me money to put in it.'

'Oh Clare,' he said. 'What have you been doing?'

'Don't sigh at me like that,' Clare said. 'She's been giving me five per cent. I needed it, Martin. You know how difficult it is for me. You know how mean Marc is. And I hated depending on you. And I really hated having to keep chasing Donald to pay up. Do you have any idea of how demeaning I've found it?'

'But, Clare, you do realise you've been laundering money, don't you?'

'No, I haven't,' she said. 'It's not money-laundering. It was to help her mother. She needed me to help her send money to her sick mother. In Romania. Everyone does it. It's just the cash economy. Everyone does it.'

'How much?' Martin said.

'A few thousand pounds,' Clare muttered.

'How few?' Martin said.

'Quite a few, actually,' Clare said. 'About twenty thousand pounds altogether.'

'And you believed her that it was for her sick mother?'

'Why shouldn't I?'

'And where do you think this money came from?' Martin said.

'I don't know,' she said. 'It's the cash economy. You know. It's just cash. You know Mila, she wouldn't do anything bad, would she?'

'Oh Clare,' he sighed.

'What? Don't get pious with me. I haven't done anything wrong.'

Martin took her hand and stroked it. It was extraordinary how Mila's poison had flowed into every part of his life. But how bad was this? Really? Mila was now gone and it was over. As Clare said it had all been cash and so no-one was likely to be able to link Mila to

Clare. The sums weren't large enough to have caught anyone's attention, particularly as they seemed to have been spread out over a period. And no-one would believe Mila if she ever said anything. And even if anyone investigated, he should be able to construct some explanation for Clare. He must not worry about it. It was something else they would have to put behind them. There was no reason why it should define their life together. It must not.

'OK,' he said. 'It's behind us now. You won't need to do that any more.' And Mila won't be back.

'It's not that,' she said. 'The last time I saw her she gave me an envelope to put in the bank for her. She said it was just for two days. And I should get it out again and give it to her. So I got it out. And she's never come to get it. So I opened it. I know I shouldn't have done. But I did. And there was a passport in it, with her photo but in the name of Marian Hart.'

The same name as the passport in Viktor's flat. Obviously a replacement when that one had gone missing. Martin felt a thousand miles from land, on a wintry green sea, ice floes drifting by on the heaving swell, as whales cried through the mist and he could not remember ever feeling so alone.

'What should I do, Martin? Do you think she'll be back for it? Or do you think someone else will come to get it?'

That is what Martin thought. Boris had never come to collect Mila's forged passport. He assumed that he had disappeared along with Mila and her hitman. But was it really safe to assume that he would not come after it and the replacement passport that Mila had left with Clare?

'Where's Megan?' he said.

'At home. Vicky's babysitting,' she said. 'Why?'

'Come on,' he said, getting up. 'We need to go and get her now.'

'Stop it, Martin,' she said. 'Please will you tell me what's going on.'

He sat down again. 'You should never have had anything to do with Mila,' he said. 'She was a crook. And very dangerous. And, yes, I do think someone could come after the passport. So you and Megan need to be with me now.'

'Isn't this rather melodramatic? It's just a passport.'

Martin took her hand. 'Mila got Viktor killed,' he said. 'And his neighbour. And she and her friends won't stop there if they want something. Last night, she nearly killed me. That's what I've been trying to tell you. And I was going to ask you what Mila might have meant when she said something to me about involving you. But I understand that now.'

Clare said nothing.

'I know it must be a shock,' he said. 'I was trying to find the best way of telling you.'

'What are we going to do?' she said. Her voice was suddenly subdued. 'Why won't they come after us anyway? Shouldn't we go to the police?'

Martin shook his head. 'Don't you understand,' he said, 'you can go to jail for five years for money-laundering.' And as he spoke, he realised he had not escaped. The past was not buried and now it was forcing him into another corner.

He knew they should go to the police but how could Clare go to jail? It would kill her. And Megan. But if he didn't tell the police about Clare, he would be acting as an accessory to the crime. And yet, how could he shop the woman he loved and to whom he had just proposed? How had it become such a mess? However he looked at it, he was still entangled in Mila's intricate snares.

'Don't worry,' he said. 'I'll work something out.' He put his arm round Clare. 'It'll be OK,' he said. 'I promise.' Clare had started to shiver and he knew he needed to sound confident. But what was he going to do? It wasn't the money-laundering. He didn't think there was any risk there. It was the passports. Whether he kept them or dumped them in the Grand Union Canal, someone, the police, or Boris, or even Mila and her hitman, was going to come after them.

And Martin did not know what to do about it. But then, as he hugged Clare and stared out into the moonlit garden, he realised that he knew someone who might.

one hundred and three

'And then she killed the Serb.' Mihail Kalaj spoke slowly so that Clive Walton could write it down in his notebook. They both knew the interview was being recorded anyway but Mihail Kalaj wanted to make quite sure that the policeman did not miss the significance of anything he was telling him.

'And why was that?' Clive Walton said.

'Because she's a vicious bitch,' Kalaj said. They stared at each other across the table in the bare interview room.

'Any other reason?' Clive Walton said, after a long pause.

'How should I know? I just did what she told me to do.'

'I see,' Clive Walton said, looking up from his notebook. 'And what was that?'

'And she killed the neighbour too,' Mihail Kalaj said, ignoring the question.

'And why was that?'

Mihail Kalaj shrugged. 'And she ran a gang of forgers,' he said.

'And what did she tell you to do for them?' Clive Walton said, still writing in his notebook.

'She did passports and credit cards. Hundreds of them.'

'Any idea where we might find them?'

Mihail Kalaj smiled thinly. 'Yes I do,' he said. He was paying off his debts. That English lawyer was mixed up in this somehow and Boris had told him that he had one of the little bitch's passports.

'You find an English lawyer called Martin Hughes. He's got one. In the name of Marian Hart.'

Clive Walton looked up from his notebook. Of course, Viktor Markov's landlord had told him and it had slipped his mind. He smiled. He had known that lawyer was mixed up in this somehow. Got him.

'Wait here,' he said as he got up from the desk and left the room. He ran up the stairs to the chief super-intendent's office. 'I told you I'd nail this, Mark,' he said. 'And I have. And it's just got better.'

Mark Rafter looked up from his desk. 'Good,' he said. 'And?'

'I've kept coming across the name of this barrister in all three murders but I couldn't quite lock him in. The Albanian's just given him up as having one of the forged passports. If I can nail him for that, it might open up some other doors.'

'Are you sure about this, Clive?' the chief super-intendent said.

'I know it,' Clive Walton said, suddenly certain. 'He's behind this. Why would a barrister get involved in small change like fencing a forged passport? No, this is bigger. If I can get him with the forged passports, we can start reeling in the whole operation. What do you think? Go for it?'

Mark Rafter nodded and smiled. 'Yes, Clive,' he said. 'Go for it. Trust your judgement. But be careful.'

Clive Walton laughed. 'I always am,' he said, and he bounded down the stairs.

'Sergeant,' he said to the policeman on the desk. 'Find out where a barrister called Martin Hughes lives and get a car to bring him in tonight.' He paused as another idea came to him. Why not? 'Actually,' he said, 'I'll go with them.'

one hundred and four

Charlotte jabbed the keyboard one last time and the computer gave a short purr as the email left. 'There,' she said to Rob. 'It's gone. Bye bye, Maggie. I'm now officially free.'

He put his arms round her where she sat facing the screen. The flat was quiet and still but somewhere in the distance a siren wailed.

'No regrets?' he said.

'None,' she said.

'What made up your mind?'

'I'll tell you in Tarifa,' she said. 'Now I'm going to bed. I've got to get up early to take Matthew to school. You should come too and see the astonishment on Ms Warren's face when the poor little boy's mother gets him to school on time.'

And then the phone rang.

'Hello?' Charlotte said and listened.

Rob looked at his watch. 'Who is it?' he mouthed at her.

'I didn't expect to hear from you again,' she said.

'I didn't know who else to ring,' Martin said. 'I need your help. I've got another problem. I don't know what to do and I couldn't think who else to ring. You've been so helpful and this is something I can't talk to anyone else about.'

'I'm not an expert,' Charlotte said carefully. 'It was just common sense, what I told you before.'

'Who is it?' Rob mouthed again.

'It's not the money,' Martin said and he explained.

'I agree,' Charlotte said. 'That shouldn't be a problem.'

'It's the passports,' Martin said and he explained.

'Yes,' Charlotte said. 'I agree that could be a problem. Let me think.'

'Just a minute,' she mouthed at Rob as she thought.

'I suppose the first thing you need to do is clear off any traces,' she said to Martin. 'Get the other passport from your flat. Then put on some gloves, get a damp cloth and carefully wipe both passports all over and on the inside pages. I've heard that gets rid of most prints.' She paused. 'And then,' she said, 'put them both in a large white envelope.'

And then she explained what Martin should do next.

'What was all that about?' Rob said.

'I'll tell you in Tarifa,' Charlotte said. 'I've just got two quick calls to make before I come to bed.'

one hundred and five

Martin looked round the living room. Had he forgotten anything? As soon as he had put the phone down, he had got into a taxi and returned to his flat, as Charlotte had said, and he thought he had now done everything she had suggested. But he could feel the tension bubbling inside him and he knew he had to stay calm and methodical and be sure that he had not forgotten anything. And so he was carrying out this final check through.

The doorbell rang. Why had Clare not waited at her flat as he had said? If he was going to be certain that he had not forgotten anything, he needed not to be interrupted.

'I'll be there in a moment,' he called. The passports were crucial. He'd got both of them, the one from Clare and now the one in his desk drawer, and put gloves on and wiped them down as Charlotte had said.

The bell rang again. Why couldn't she have done what he said? He just needed another couple of minutes. 'I said I'll be there in a moment,' he called. But it wasn't Clare.

'Police,' a deep voice shouted through the door. 'Open this door now or we'll break it down.'

Martin felt his heart stop. And start again. What were the police doing here? Now? What should he do? The voice sounded as if it meant what it said about breaking down the door. What choice did he have? He walked to the door.

'Who is it?' he said, hoping that, somehow, this reality would turn into another one.

'It's the police,' the voice said. 'And if you don't open the door immediately we'll break it down.'

'Do you have any ID?' Martin said, even though he knew it was pointless delaying. He squinted through the spyhole and someone was holding a police identity card up to it.

'Do you have a warrant?' he said, although he knew they would have.

'Open the door and we'll show it to you,' the voice said. Martin sighed and undid the locks and opened the door and there stood Inspector Walton.

'I'm sorry to trouble you so late, Mr Hughes,' he said. 'But we've got a warrant to search your flat. May we come in?'

Martin stood aside to let the inspector and three uniformed officers enter the flat. 'What are you looking for?' he said, but he knew the answer.

'I'll tell you when we find it,' Clive Walton said. 'Please could you look at the warrant, Mr Hughes, and satisfy yourself it's all in order.'

Martin glanced at it. He knew it would be. He nodded.

'Mike, you search in there,' Clive Walton said, indicating the bedroom. 'Richard, in here and John, you take the kitchen and bathroom.' He stood watching Martin. 'It shouldn't take very long, Mr Hughes,' he said.

Martin sat down. He couldn't think what else to do. As a final gesture of defiance, he did not invite the inspector to sit down.

Clive Walton looked at the invitations propped against the mantelpiece. 'It looks as if you were going to have a busy social life over the festive season, sir,' he said.

Martin said nothing. In the kitchen, he could hear the officer taking down the jars and placing them on the work surface. From the bedroom, there came an industrious rustling. Martin supposed the officer was emptying all his cupboards.

Clive Walton turned to look at Martin. 'It shouldn't take long, sir,' he repeated.

Then his phone rang. Martin watched him answer it and nod and look irritated.

'Who?' Clive Walton said and Martin then saw him nod again. Then the inspector repeated an address, which appeared to be in Docklands, and then he put the phone back in his pocket.

'Mike, Richard, John, in here,' he called. 'Find anything?' he asked the officers when they had assembled in front of him.

'Not yet, sir,' Mike said.

'Me neither,' Richard said.

'Nor me,' John said.

'It seems, Mr Hughes,' Clive Walton said heavily, 'that what we are looking for may now be somewhere else. It seems we have just had a tip-off from the highest possible level. A political level.'

He stared at Martin. 'This doesn't mean you're off the hook, sir,' he said.

Martin said nothing.

'But I'm afraid that for the time being our presence is required elsewhere. We can return later to help you tidy up, if you'd like us to do so.'

Martin assumed the elaborate courtesy was meant to be ironic. 'That won't be necessary, Inspector,' he said. 'But thank you for the offer.'

'I'm still going to be keeping a very careful eye on you,' Clive Walton said to Martin. 'I usually find who I'm looking for and then I nail them.'

Martin stared at him but said nothing. Even though he recognised it was a technique, the way this policeman spoke still made him nervous.

'A very careful eye,' Clive Walton said again as he left. 'That's how I always nail them in the end.'

one hundred and six

Maggie Fairweather was dozing on the white leather sofa when the buzzer went. Outside the large glass windows of the living room, the river flowed dark and mighty to the sea. Beyond it, lights were still dotted all over the towering blocks in the City of London, getting and spending through the night. A party boat steamed slowly by, lit up and leaving a soapy wake behind it.

Maggie stretched and went over to the intercom. 'Courier,' the voice said.

'Come up,' she said. 'Fifth floor.' The first edition was always sent over to her wherever she was. She looked at her watch. Ten minutes early. Good. She was trying to get them to work to tighter deadlines. And this edition should be good. They had two strong stories, a rising film-star arrested for cottaging, from a helpful, greedy source in the police, and some great pictures, from a freelance in Mustique, of a supermodel with flab oozing over the edge of her bikini.

'Sign here, please.' The courier stood in the doorway, respectfully holding his helmet in his hands as she scrawled her signature and took the white envelope. Not the first edition after all but the briefing she had

told her secretary to send over for the breakfast television show she was doing tomorrow morning.

'Thank you,' she said, as she closed the door behind
her. She yawned and tossed the envelope on the hall
table. She needed a cup of coffee. She'd read the
briefing after she'd gone through the first edition
and rung the night editor with her notes. She glanced
at her watch once more. Her first note for him would
be that it was late. Again.

She went into the stainless-steel kitchen and turned
on the espresso machine. And then the buzzer went.
About time.

'Yes,' she said.

'Police,' the voice said. 'May we come up?'

'What for?' she said.

'I just need to have a word with you, Ms Fairweather,' the voice said.

Maggie thought for a moment. Whatever it was, it
had better be good at this time of night but she had
never knowingly let a good story pass her by. 'Have
you got ID?' she said.

'Of course,' the man said.

Maggie pressed the buzzer. And when the doorbell rang three minutes later, she saw a tall good-
looking man, with thinning blond hair holding a
police ID card up to the spyhole. Maggie opened
the door on the chain. Behind the blond, she could
see three uniformed officers. What was this? Four
policemen. This didn't feel like they were bringing
her a story.

'Show me the ID again,' she said, searching for the

name on it. 'Inspector Walton.' She stared at him. 'What do you want?'

'I'm investigating a case and we've had some information that you might be able to help us with it.'

'What sort of case?' she said.

'I think it might be better for everyone if we didn't have this conversation in your hallway,' Clive Walton said.

Maggie looked at him as if he had interrupted her in an editorial conference but she didn't like the sound of this. 'Do you have a search warrant?' she said.

'No,' Clive Walton said. 'But I'll get one if I need to.' The only reason he had not got one was because the information, from the highest level, had said he should get to this address as quickly as possible before anything had been done to destroy the evidence. He had been told to use his ingenuity. 'My strong advice to you, Ms Fairweather, is that it would be best for everyone if we had this conversation inside your flat.'

Maggie glanced instinctively around to see if there was anyone else in the hallway. She was beginning to think the blond could be right. She sensed she would not want her neighbours to hear this.

'Come in,' she said and, when they were all standing in the lobby, she shut the door behind them. 'Do you know who I am?' she said, already drafting, in her head, the complaint to the Metropolitan Police Commissioner.

'Yes, Ms Fairweather, I do,' Clive Walton said. He had checked out the occupant when he'd been given the address and the tone of implacable authority in the editor's voice made him hope the informant was correct.

'My paper is always happy to help the police. What are you looking for?'

'I'll tell you when we find it,' Clive Walton said. 'Do you mind if we take a look around?'

'Yes, I do mind.' Maggie had had enough of this. 'Why on earth do you think anything here would be of the slightest relevance to your investigation, whatever it is?'

'As I said, Ms Fairweather, we've been given information to that effect.'

'And what makes you think any of your grubby little grasses would know anything about me?' Maggie was getting angry with this pompous, good-looking inspector.

'And what makes you think it was a grubby little grass?' Clive Walton asked. This slight, aggressive woman was beginning to irritate him. And he was starting to wonder whether her patronising manner was concealing something else. 'As it so happens, it was not a grubby little grass. It was a grubby little politician. As it so happens.' He knew he shouldn't have said that. But it was late and he was irritated. 'And that is why we are here. Instructions from the top.'

'Impossible,' Maggie said. No politician would dare do this to her.

'Inspector,' one of the uniformed officers said, as Clive Walton was about to reply. 'There's a white envelope on the table here.'

Clive Walton and Maggie Fairweather both turned to look. 'Do you mind if we cast an eye over it?' Clive Walton said.

'If you really want to read my briefing for the television show I am appearing on and if that will make you go away, then please do so,' Maggie said. She would find out who the sneaking politician was tomorrow. And this blond inspector was going to spend the rest of his career issuing parking tickets.

Clive Walton picked up the envelope and wondered if she was bluffing or if he was being set up. The phone call he had received in Martin Hughes's flat had made him uneasy. It was too convenient, coming so promptly before they had finished searching the barrister's flat. And, although he wasn't frightened by her, he knew the damage this woman could do to his career if he handled this badly.

He passed the envelope over to one of the uniformed officers. 'Open it, Mike,' he said. The room was silent and still as the officer put on a pair of latex gloves and slid his finger under the flap and ripped it open.

'Here you are sir,' he said and handed two passports over to Clive Walton. As Maggie watched him incredulously, he took a pair of latex gloves from his pocket and pulled them on before taking the passports. He inspected them carefully, turning the pages one by one, savouring the moment.

'Is there any reason,' he said eventually, 'why you should be in possession of two passports in the name of Marian Hart, Ms Fairweather?' he said. 'Forged passports?'

'I've no idea,' Maggie said. 'Let me see.'

'I'm afraid not,' Clive Walton said. 'These passports are evidence.' He was finding it hard to believe that a national newspaper editor could be engaged in forging passports. It was more likely, in his view, that she was running some investigation. But she was still likely to have committed an offence in handling the documents and that might be a handy lever in extracting useful information from her. He was going to nail this case.

'You don't honestly think I know anything about forged passports,' Maggie said angrily. 'Do you know who I am?'

'I don't think anything at the moment, Ms Fairweather, I'm just collecting evidence.' Clive Walton was beginning to enjoy himself. 'When I have all the evidence I need, then I will make an assessment of it.'

'This is nothing to do with me,' Maggie said. 'Nothing. The envelope arrived two minutes before you did.' Was someone trying to set her up?

'I'm sure you'll understand that most people claim that incriminating evidence is nothing to do with them. Some truthfully so. Others not,' Clive Walton said. 'In this case, I hope you'll agree that there are still some unanswered questions and it would be best if we went through your answers at the station. You're welcome to call your lawyer if you wish but we haven't got to that stage. Yet.'

Maggie didn't reply but picked up the phone and dialled the newspaper's courier company, furiously stabbing at the buttons. 'It's Maggie Fairweather here. Who sent me the envelope that was delivered to my home address ten minutes ago?' While she waited, she glared at Clive Walton. Then she nodded. 'Are you sure?' she said. 'Check again.' And she waited again.

And then she said, 'You'd better be sure,' and put the phone down.

'Who sent it?' Clive Walton said politely.

'They've no record of anyone sending me anything this evening,' she said. She was being set up. She would find out who was doing this and kill them. Literally.

'Shall we go down to the station now?' Clive Walton said politely. Maggie put on the green leather jacket that had been lying on an armchair. What choice did she have? She had to go through this process before she could sort out what had happened. The main thing was to get through it with no fuss. And no publicity. The proprietor hated bad publicity about his editors. No matter what the justification, he hated it when his staff became the story. Once she'd finished at the station, she'd start finding out who the politician was. The Home Office would be a good place to begin. It wouldn't take her long. Whoever it was, they were dead meat.

'Ready, Ms Fairweather?' Clive Walton had his hand on the doorknob.

She nodded. He opened the door and there was an explosion of flashguns. Behind it, she sensed at least three different photographers outside her door. Fucking paparazzi. Who'd told them? If it was this policeman, he was hamburger. God knows what she looked like. Someone was going to pay for this.

one hundred and seven

'Please fasten your seatbelt, sir.'

Martin stared at the seat in front of him and wondered how his life had turned out like this. Three weeks ago if anyone had told him he would end up here on a freezing winter night, everything he had worked for all his life thrown away and his future mortgaged, he would have laughed. He felt Clare's hand steal into his.

'It's going to be all right,' she said. 'Really. I know it is.' The engine started.

'Costa Rica, Costa Rica. Her, she and me, and Costa Rica coffee,' Megan sang. 'Costa Rica, Costa Rica.'

'Not now, darling,' Clare said.

'Costa Rica, Costa Rica.'

'I know that's where we're going, my darling, but it's a bit late to be singing. Try to sleep. It's a long flight.' Clare squeezed Martin's hand. 'This is a brilliant idea,' she said. 'Really. I'm so looking forward to ringing Marc when we arrive.'

'And I'm really not looking forward to breaking the news to Phil,' Martin said. And then he laughed. 'But then we'll get married on the beach.'

It had suddenly come to him after he had rung Charlotte, as they waited in Clare's living room for the taxi back to his flat and Megan was dancing round chanting her coffee song. Why not? Why not just leave?

Charlotte had been brilliant. Martin rarely thought of anyone as that but she was. It was Charlotte who had thought of the solution to the problem that if he simply dumped the passports in the Grand Union Canal, which had been his initial suggestion, it would not stop the police coming after him. They knew he had got one forged passport from Viktor's flat. He was the best lead they had; they would not give up on him. What was needed, Charlotte said, was to put someone else in the frame and she knew just the person.

Martin didn't think the police would seriously believe the editor of a national newspaper had been forging passports but Charlotte explained that was not the idea. The idea was that it removed the passports from him and Clare and it would send the police off in a different direction.

As Charlotte said, there could now be a running battle for months, with the police, on one side, demanding to know where Maggie Fairweather had got the passports, and the editor, on the other side, denying she knew anything about them and the police then suspecting that she was denying it because she was making an issue out of the press protecting its sources. And they wouldn't feel able to let her get away with establishing such a precedent. And so, with any luck, Charlotte said, it would end up in a high-profile court case and by the time that was all over, everyone would have forgotten that Martin Hughes had once briefly been in possession of one of the forged passports.

The aeroplane began taxiing down the runway and Martin stroked Clare's hand. Charlotte's inspiration had not ended with couriering the passports to Maggie Fairweather. When she had heard Martin's meticulously detailed account of the history of the passports, Charlotte had immediately identified the need to divert Boris as well as the police. And that was when she had the inspiration of tipping off the paparazzi. No rival newspaper would have been able to resist the temptation of putting Maggie on the front page, being led away by the police. And then her fellow editors would feel obliged to follow up with teams of their most expert investigators to find out what she had done wrong. This story was going to run and run. And Boris could not help but see it and then he would switch his attention from Martin to Maggie. Martin and Charlotte agreed that those two were welcome to each other.

As the aeroplane took off and the wheels retracted with a clunk, Martin thought how lucky he had been to meet Charlotte. The last month had been filled with bad luck but the one happy chance that had made everything else right was meeting Charlotte. She was smart. And she knew it. 'Even smarter,' she said, 'no-one's going to be able to trace this back to me.'

'Why not?' Martin said.

'I shouldn't tell you,' she said, 'because the fewer people know what I've done the better, but we're in this together and I'm off in a week and I want someone to know just how smart I've been. I met the courier in a bar and paid him in cash. So nothing there. And then I got this little Home Office minister I know to tell the police. Potentially he's the weak link. But if I'd just rung in anonymously no-one would have taken any notice. I knew if he told the police, they'd have to go straight round to Maggie's.'

Martin forgave her the self-congratulatory glee in her voice. She deserved it. This was smart.

'And anyway I think it's a safe enough risk,' she said. 'I didn't tell the little politician who lived at the address I was giving him. When he finds out it was Maggie Fairweather, he'll be petrified. He knows she'll chew him up and spit him out if she ever finds out it was him who shopped her. So I think he'll stay very quiet about this.'

As Charlotte took him through the plan, he felt more and more confident that she had covered all the angles. So why didn't he feel happier? After he put the phone down, he sat in Clare's flat, holding the cup of coffee she had made him while Megan sat playing with her dolls and chanting the Costa Rica jingle.

'What is it?' Clare said. 'What's wrong with what she said?'

'It's not Charlotte,' Martin said. 'She's brilliant. That'll all work, I think. It's not her, it's me.'

'What do you mean?' Clare stretched out her hand towards him.

Martin held it and wondered what he did mean. Why didn't he feel happier that, finally, the mysteries had been unravelled and the problems solved?

'I think I mean,' he said eventually, 'that so much has happened I'm not sure I can just turn up at chambers as if nothing had changed. Everything's different. How can I pretend it's not?'

'Some things have changed,' Clare said. 'But the important things haven't. We're together.'

'I know,' Martin said. 'You're right. But how can I carry on as if the law still meant something to me? How can it? I can't ever be a judge now and it all seems different.' These thoughts had seemed to be a liberation at the airport, saying goodbye to Suzana, but now they seemed to be closing on him, offering not escape but his old life back in different, drab colours.

'It's just a job,' Clare said softly. 'We all have to do them.'

'It used to be more than that,' Martin said.

'And it didn't make you happy,' Clare said. 'Things change. Sometimes for the better.'

'I thought of joining Ben,' Martin said. 'And then I thought I couldn't face the upheaval. Now I'm not sure I want to just carry on as if nothing had changed.'

'You'll manage,' Clare said. 'People do. It's natural you should feel a bit deflated after all you've been through. It'll pass.' She turned to look at Megan who was still happily chanting the Costa Rica coffee song. 'Hush, darling. We're talking. If you can't be quiet, you'll have to go to bed.'

'Costa Rica, Costa Rica. Her, she and me, and Costa Rica coffee,' Megan replied.

Martin looked at the little girl. Charlotte had got all that sorted out too. She was going off to Spain next week with her little son and her partner to think about what she wanted to do with her life. Lucky her. And then it struck him. Why not him too? Perhaps that was the final lesson she had to teach him about how to get out of this mess?

'But why should we have to wait for it to pass?' Martin said. 'Why don't we do something different? Why don't we go to Costa Rica? And work out what to do next from there. It's supposed to be beautiful. There's no army. And lots of coffee.'

Clare had stared at him for a moment. 'You're not serious,' she said. 'Are you?' And she looked at him. 'You are serious,' she said. 'Lovely idea but don't you think it's a little impractical?'

'Why?' he had said. 'I've got savings. Why not? Let's just go. It's what you've always said you wanted. Us spending time together. So why not?'

'What about my job?' she said and then she laughed. 'Yes, what about my job? It'll be good for Marc to do without me. It might teach him that he should have paid me better.' And then she kissed him. 'Yes,' she said. 'Why not? Let's show Megan what Costa Rica's really like.'

And so Clare packed a bag while Martin went to his flat and wrote a note to his father, explaining he was going away with Clare and he would send him a ticket to come and see them for a holiday when they got married. And then he put on a pair of gloves and wrote a note to Inspector Walton explaining how Mila had killed Viktor and Chris Finlay and signed it 'from a friend' as anonymous notes always ought to be signed.

And then, on the way to Heathrow, the taxi waited while he walked down an alleyway to the Grand Union

Canal and dropped the gun in it. And then they had walked through a deserted Heathrow and bought tickets on the next flight out.

And now here they were, Martin staring at the seat in front of him, working out how long his savings would last in Costa Rica. 'Three years,' he said.

'Watching the turtles,' Clare said.

'What do they do, Mummy?' Megan said.

'They swim under tropical stars,' Clare said. 'And come on to the sand to lay their eggs in the moonlight, as the surf breaks on the shore. And we're going to see them do it. In Costa Rica.'

'By then, I'll have worked out what to do next,' Martin said.

Clare snuggled up to him. 'And Megan might have a little sister,' she whispered in his ear.

The engines started to roar as the plane accelerated down the runway and suddenly they were flying. Out of the window, Martin saw the lights of the sleeping city winking and sparkling. Her, she and me, and Costa Rica coffee. Costa Rica, Costa Rica.